PRAISE FOR
CITY OF SAINTS & THIEVES

AN NPR BOOK CONCIERGE GREAT READS SELECTION
A *SEVENTEEN* MAGAZINE BEST YA BOOK
AN AMAZON BEST YOUNG ADULT BOOK
A CHICAGO PUBLIC LIBRARY BEST TEEN FICTION SELECTION

"This nail-biting murder mystery set in Kenya follows Tina, a Congolese refugee, as she tracks down her mother's killer in the midst of corrupt businessmen, a master thief, and a street gang." **—SEVENTEEN.COM**

"A linguistically beautiful murder mystery tale that will have you tearing through the pages, all along its twist and turns." **—BUSTLE.COM**

★ "In this fast-paced thriller . . . Anderson adeptly uses language to bring Tina's world to life as she carefully traces her heroine's history to reveal a shocking truth." **—*PUBLISHERS WEEKLY*,** starred review

★ "A wonderfully twisted puzzle of a murder mystery."
—*BOOKLIST*, starred review

★ "A solidly plotted, swiftly paced international murder mystery that's laced with just a hint of romance . . . Highly recommended for teens looking for a gritty, suspenseful, immersive read driven by a tough, smart, realistic heroine." **—*SLJ*,** starred review

★ "By setting a fast-paced crime drama with compelling characters in this fraught region, Anderson does the good service of interesting young readers in this ongoing human conflict and the tragic toll it continues to take on the people of the region." **—*BCCB***

CITY
OF
SAINTS
&
THIEVES

NATALIE C. ANDERSON

PENGUIN BOOKS

PENGUIN BOOKS
An imprint of Penguin Random House LLC, New York

First published in the United States of America by G. P. Putnam's Sons, 2017
Published by Speak, an imprint of Penguin Random House LLC, 2018
Published by Penguin Books, an imprint of Penguin Random House LLC, 2020

Visit us online at penguinrandomhouse.com

LIBRARY OF CONGRESS CATALOGING-IN-PUBLICATION DATA IS AVAILABLE.

Penguin Books ISBN 9780399547591

Printed in the United States of America

5 7 9 10 8 6

Design by Eric M. Ford
Text set in Chaparral Pro

This book is a work of fiction. Any references to historical events, real people,
or real places are used fictitiously. Other names, characters, places, and events
are products of the author's imagination, and any resemblance to actual events
or places or persons, living or dead, is entirely coincidental.

For all the girls who are more
than just refugees

SAINT CATHERINE'S PRAYER

Star of the world, Catherine,
breaker of the Wheel,
helping the chosen children,
saving each,
there at their dying.
Catherine, honored daughter,
branch of virtue,
face like an apple, breast like a swan,
a virgin not violated.
Stretch your cloak over my madness,
Son of Mary.
Beg mercy for the thief, Catherine.
Implore for me progress, that vanquishing
the enemies of my soul
I may be victorious in my last combat
and after death
be conducted by the angels.
Amen

ONE

If you're going to be a thief, the first thing you need to know is that you don't exist.

And I mean, you really have to know it. You have to own it. Bug Eye taught me that. Because if you do exist, you might snag someone's eye who will frown and wonder who you are. They'll want to know who's letting you run around. Where you'll sleep tonight. *If* you'll sleep tonight.

If you exist, you won't be able to slouch through a press of bodies, all warm arms and shoulders smelling of work and soap. You won't be able to take your time and choose: a big lady in pink and gold. You won't be able to bump into her and swivel away, her wallet stuffed down your pants. If you exist, you can't exhale and slip through the bars on a window. Your feet might creak on the floorboards. Your sweat might smell too sharp.

You might.

But I don't.

I'm the best thief in this town.

I don't exist.

I've been sitting in this mango tree for long enough to squish seven mosquitoes dead. I can feel my own warm blood between my fingers. God only knows how many bites I have. Ants are exploring my nether regions. And yet Sister Gladys, bless her, will not sleep.

Through the windows I see her bathed in the light of the common room's television. Her face shines a radiant blue, and her belly shudders with laughter. Feet propped up on a stool, her toes bend at odd angles like antelope horns. I wonder what she's watching, relaxed now that all the students are asleep. Old *Fresh Prince of Bel-Air* reruns? *Churchill Raw*? What do nuns think is funny?

I check the time on my phone and briefly consider coming back tomorrow and lifting that ancient television once and for all. Shouldn't she be praying or something?

Eight mosquitoes. My stomach growls. I clench it and it stops.

Finally, the sister's head slumps. I wait for the rhythm of her breathing to steady, then slowly lower myself over the wall that surrounds the school.

A guard dog materializes from the darkness and rushes toward me.

I put my arms up. Dirty leaps on me, slobbering all over

my face. "Shh . . ." I say to his whines. His wagging tail thumps my legs as I walk toward the washroom at the end of the dorms.

"What took you so long?" Kiki asks, pushing open a creaky window as I approach.

I wince at the noise and look around, even though I know there's no one in the tidy yard but Dirty. He leans against my thigh, panting happily as I rub the soft fur between his ears. Dirty and I are old pals.

"I think Sister Gladys has a crush on Will Smith," I say.

My sister grunts and pushes a white bun through the bars on the window meant to keep thieves like me out. It tastes sweet, store-bought. I give a bite to Dirty, who wolfs it down in one gulp, licks his lips, and whines.

"Everything okay?" I ask between bites. "The penguins aren't beating you up too bad?"

She shakes her head. "You?"

"No penguins up on my roof. Can't fly."

"You know what I mean, Tina."

"I'm fine," I say. "Hey, I brought you something." I rummage in my bag and pull out a pack of No. 2 pencils, still wrapped in cellophane. I slide them through the bars.

"Tina . . ."

"Wait, there's more," I say before she can protest, and fish out a notebook. It has a cartoon of happy kids on the front, and the words SCHOOL DAYS! in dark, emphatic capitals.

I push the goods toward her. Her eyes linger on the tattoos that cover my arms.

"The nuns will give me school supplies," she says. "You don't have to steal them."

"They'll give you the reject bits. You don't have to depend on their charity. I can get you better."

"But *you're* giving me charity."

"That's different. I'm family."

She doesn't say anything.

I step back, leaving the gifts on the windowsill. "You're welcome."

"Tina," she blurts, "you can't just live on the streets for the rest of your life."

I zip up my bag. "I don't live on the streets. I live on a roof."

Kiki's doing that thing where her brow pinches, and she looks like Mama. I see more and more of our mother in Kiki every time I come here, which hurts sometimes, but still, better Mama than *him*. He's most obvious in her lighter skin and eyes, in her loose curls. You can still see that we're sisters; I just wish it wasn't so obvious that we're half sisters. Not that I would ever call her that. I hate how it sounds. Half sister. Like half a person.

But there's no hiding that Kiki's dad, unlike mine, is white. Once she let it slip that the other girls call her "Point-Five," as in, point-five black, point-five white. I told her to tell me their names, but she just said, *They don't mean anything by it, Tina. It doesn't bother me, and besides, you can't go around beating up little kids.* But sometimes I see her looking at my dark skin, comparing it against her own, and I can tell she wonders what it would be like to fit in for once, to not be the "Point-Five" orphan.

Kiki squeezes the bars separating us, as if she could pull them apart. She's not finished. "You can come stay here with me. You know you can. Sister Eunice would let you. You're not too old. She let that other sixteen-year-old in. They've got lots of books and a piano and—"

"Shh." I put a finger to my lips. "Too loud."

She glances over her shoulder into the dark washroom. From somewhere I hear one of the other girls cough.

"Seriously, Tina," she whispers, turning back. "They could put you on scholarship, like me."

"Come on, Kiki, you know they won't. It's one per family."

"But—"

"Enough," I say sharply. Too sharply. Her shoulders sag. "Hey," I say, and reach my hand through the bars again to smooth down the curls that have escaped her braids. "Thanks for dinner. I've got to go. I have to meet Boyboy."

"Tina, don't leave yet," she starts, her face pressed up close against the metal.

"Be good, okay? Do your homework. Don't let the penguins catch you out of bed."

"You'll be back next Friday?" she asks.

"Like always."

I gently push Dirty off my leg and make sure my pack is tight on my back. Scaling the wall to get out is always harder than climbing the tree to get in, and I don't want to get caught on the barbed wire and broken shards of glass embedded in the concrete.

Kiki is still watching me. I force a grin. For a moment her face is still, and then it softens and she smiles.

For half a second, I exist.

And then I disappear in the dark.

TWO

Rule 2: Trust no one. Or if you must, trust them like you'd trust a street dog around fresh meat.

Take the Goondas, for example. Just because I am one doesn't mean I trust them. Bug Eye is okay. I probably wouldn't be alive without him. But guys like his brother, Ketchup?

No way. I learned that a long time ago.

The Goondas are everywhere in Sangui City, and they pick up refugee kids like that street dog picks up fleas. It might make my life easier if I lived at the warehouse with them, but then someone would probably wriggle in beside me in the middle of the night and next thing you know I'm like Sheika on the sidewalk with her toddlers, begging for change. Most girls don't last long with the Goondas.

I'm not most girls.

• • •

I hurry through the dark alleys, the route from Kiki's school to the Goonda warehouse so familiar that I hardly have to keep my eyes open. But I do. A girl on the streets alone after dark is prey. Generally, I try not to stand out too much. My face is usually hidden under my hoodie and my clothes are purposefully shapeless. I keep my hair cropped short. Being scrawny and flat chested helps.

I skirt mud and concrete and garbage rotting in gray pools. The pink glow of the sky over the city lights my way well enough. When I reach Biashara Avenue, I see the hawkers have gone home for the night. The only people left are night crawlers: drunks and restless prostitutes bathed in neon from the bars. The twilight girls watch me suspiciously from their side of the street. I ignore them and walk fast, until I'm at the bridge that separates Old Sangui Town, where Kiki's school is, from the industrial Go-Downs, the Goondas' home turf. The lights of the warehouses and factories shimmer in the river like a sort of magic dividing new and old.

Once I saw a body float by as I crossed over this bridge. It was the middle of the night and nobody noticed but me. I guess it floated until a crocodile got interested, or maybe it got all the way out to the mangroves and then the ocean if there was anything left. But there are no bodies tonight, just a handful of wooden dhows anchored in the current, fishermen asleep in their hulls.

By the time I reach the other side, I'm practically running. The Go-Downs are still; no bars on this side. I hear only a few far-off alarms and the growls of dogs fighting over garbage.

They don't even look up when I scurry by. I don't need my phone to tell me I'm late. I curse Sister Gladys and her TV shows. I shouldn't have gone to see Kiki. There wasn't enough time. But if I hadn't shown up like I always do on Friday nights, she would worry.

Plus, I didn't want to do what I'm about to do without seeing her first.

When I finally reach the salt-rusted warehouse door, I'm breathing hard and hungry again. I rap three times. Pause. Rap two times. Pause. Once.

A peephole opens to reveal a malevolent eye.

"It's Tiny Girl," I say.

The guard opens up for me.

Boyboy is waiting inside. "You're late," he says, skinny arms folded over his chest, petulant scowl on his face. I take in his bright pink see-through shirt and mascara.

"You were supposed to wear black," I say. As if the Goondas don't give him a hard enough time already. "Let's go."

He follows me down the hall to Bug Eye's office. I can't see them, but I hear Goondas through the walls. They're hanging out on the warehouse floor, getting high, watching football, waiting to be sent on errands. Maybe some of them are practicing in the gym, beating up old tires and lifting concrete blocks, but I wouldn't bet on it.

Another guard slouches out of the way to let us into Bug Eye's office. When I open the door, Bug Eye and Ketchup are bent over the desk, looking at blueprints and maps, their sleeves rolled up in the heat. The tattoos on their arms twitch as they jab at the paper, arguing about something. They're going over the plan one last time. Good thing too. Bug Eye got all the brains in that family. His brother, Ketchup, on the other hand, is as dull witted as two rocks in a bag. We've all worked together on break-ins before, but never one with such high stakes. I don't like it that Ketchup is in on this job. He makes stupid gay jokes about Boyboy that throw him off his game. Plus I just don't like the guy. I don't like counting on him to have my back. But it's not the sort of thing you complain about to Bug Eye. Where Bug Eye goes, his little brother goes too.

You'd never guess the two Goondas were related. Bug Eye is older, maybe twenty-five. He's muscled and broad, with a serious face and eyes that can see straight into your dirty, lying soul. People say he looks like Jay Z. Ketchup, on the other hand, is scrawny and seems way younger than his eighteen years. He has a narrow face and a laugh like a hyena. People say he looks like a starving weasel.

At their feet are two duffel bags full of gear: laptops, dark hoodies, wires, tape, potato crisps, and energy drinks. All the essentials.

I step up to look over their shoulders.

"We'll roll up here," Bug Eye says. He taps the blueprint and fixes me with his trademark unnerving stare. I nod and he turns back to the paper. "Then what, Ketchup?"

"Man, we been over this a hundred times. We drop Tiny Girl and cruise the block, try and park here." He stabs the paper with his finger.

"And what'll we do while we wait?"

Ketchup snickers and makes a dirty hand gesture. He looks at me to see if I blush. I don't.

Bug Eye smacks him on the back of the head. "*Weh*, grow up," he says, not looking up from the plans.

Ketchup rubs the back of his head and sulks, but doesn't protest. Even he knows better than to fight Bug Eye.

"Okay, Boyboy's gonna be with me in the van, doing his computer thing," Bug Eye goes on.

Boyboy keeps his arms crossed tightly over his chest, maintaining a respectful distance. He doesn't say anything. He isn't a Goonda.

"And you're lookout," Bug Eye tells his brother.

"So what's your smart ass going to be doing?" Ketchup retorts.

"Being in charge of you," he says smoothly. "Reporting back to Mr. Omoko. And that just leaves Tiny Girl. You know where you're going?"

All three are looking at me now.

I lift my chin. "Yeah."

Bug Eye jerks his head at the blueprints. It's a question, so I step forward. I reach between Ketchup's and Bug Eye's shoulders and plant my finger on the street outside the mansion. I push it past the electrified perimeter fence, through eighteen-inch-thick walls, past laser scanners, down silent carpeted hallways, and between little notes: *guards*, *camera*, *dogs*. It stops deep in the building's heart.

"There."

THREE

Rule 3: Thieves don't have friends.

Every thief has a mother, and maybe even a little sister if she's lucky, but you can't help any of that. You can have people like Boyboy's mom, who I say hi to every day on my way home. That's just keeping tabs on the neighborhood. She sells tea on the corner and tells me if cops are around, and I make sure the Goondas go easy on her boy. You can have acquaintances. But friends, people you care about, and who care about you . . .

Well, you're only going to get them into trouble.

Before you even ask, Boyboy is not my friend.

He's my business partner. Big difference. He's from Congo too, so I don't have to explain certain things to him that I'd rather not talk about, like where my family is, or why I don't really sleep, or why men in uniforms make me twitch. Sometimes he comes over to my roof and we share a smoke and watch the sun disappear into the smog that caresses the city. That's it. Boyboy has his party boys, and I have Kiki. You probably think that's sad or something, but I'm not sad.

Besides, I don't have a lot of time for making friends. I have things to do.

We use a florist's van to get there. Ketchup is driving, and Bug Eye keeps yelling at him to slow down and watch the road. It's two in the morning and cops are just as likely to shake us down for cash as care that we're running red lights, but still, better that no one remembers seeing a van full of kids dressed in black and obviously not florists. The closer we get, the more ready I am to be out and working. Ketchup's constant prattle makes me nervous. He laughs his hyena laugh and says gross stuff about the twilight girls on the street corners we pass.

In the back, Boyboy and I are quiet, getting ready. I attach my earpiece and make sure the Bluetooth is connecting to my phone.

"Let's see how the camera is feeding," Boyboy says.

I look at him, aiming the micro-camera embedded in the earpiece. His face pops up on his laptop screen. "Good." He watches himself pat his hair into place as he asks, "Mic check? Say something."

I whisper, "Boyboy got no fashion sense," and the little earpiece relays my words to my phone, and then to Boyboy's computer, where I hear myself echo.

13

He flips me off seamlessly, between the adjustments he's making to his equipment. "Can you hear me okay?"

"Yeah," I say. "You're clear."

"You have to keep your phone close to the earpiece. When you had it in your pocket on that last job, the connection was bad. Where are you putting it?"

I tuck my phone into my sports bra and wave my hands—ta-da.

"Cute."

"Secure."

"Put this one in your pocket," he says, and hands me a tiny USB adapter. "It's the key to the treasure box and I don't want it getting lost in your cleavage."

"Ha." My chest is barely larger than my eleven-year-old sister's. But I do as he asks.

Boyboy is crazy good with tech stuff. He always has been, ever since I've known him. He told me when he was little the bigger boys would beat him up and call him a fairy, so he spent a lot of time in his room, taking phones and computers apart, putting them back together. His latest trick is hacking ATMs so they spit out crisp thousand-shilling notes.

He won't join the Goondas, but he'll work with me. He does his IT genius thing when I need him, and in exchange I lift fancy gadgets for him—computers, phones, the occasional designer handbag—whatever he needs. He says he's the best hacker in East Africa, and from what I've seen, he's telling the truth.

He'd better be. He's about to break us into the most forti-fied home in the Ring.

• • •

The Ring is where you live if you can afford it. Lush, hilly, and green, it sits above Sangui City, peering down its nose at the rest of us. The houses squat on neatly clipped lawns behind fences and flame trees and barbed wire and dogs and ex-military guards with AK-47s. Fleets of Mercedes descend into the city in the mornings carrying the Big Men to work. We call these guys the WaBenzi: the tribe of the Mercedes-Benz. They come in all shapes, sizes, and colors, hail from all over the world, but speak a common language: money. When they return to their mansions in the Ring in the evening, they complain about traffic, drink imported scotch, and fall asleep early on soft cotton sheets. Their wives oversee small armies of servants and get delicate headaches when the African sun is too hot. Their kids play tennis. Their dogs have therapists.

At this time of night, the Ring is quiet except for frogs and insects. It's rained up here, and the mist is thick. The eerily familiar tree-lined streets we drive are empty. The florist van doesn't look too out of place. Maybe we have just come from a banquet. A power wedding.

I look out the window. We pass a break in the houses and trees, and I catch a glimpse of the dark Indian Ocean. Sangui: city-state on a hill, port to the world, and a fine bloody place to do business. You do the dirty work down there in town, and the Ring is where you retreat.

I should know. I've seen it all up close. I may live down in the dirt now, but once upon a time, a fortress in the Ring was my home.

• • •

Rule 4: Choose your target carefully.

Thief

Kauzi

Thegi

Voleur

Mwizi

Thief

It's a magic word. Full of power.

Just saying it out loud on the street can get somebody killed. I've seen it happen. The police are worthless, so folks are disposed to make their own swift justice. And believe me, no one feels sorry for the thief when the dust settles and blood soaks into the ground. Better be sure no one's raising a finger at you.

So listen up. Choose carefully. Choose the right target. Most of the time that means the easy target. If you're pick-pocketing, go for the drunks and people having arguments on their mobiles. If you're robbing a house, make sure it's the one where they hide the key on the doorjamb. You want to go for bank accounts? Try the old rich lady. Odds are her password is her dog's name.

There are plenty to choose from. No sense in making it hard on yourself.

But for every rule, there is an exception.

Roland Greyhill's home isn't a natural target. His gates are locked and his guard is up. The man makes his living deal-ing with warlords and armies and vast amounts of cash. He knows he's got enemies. He's spent years watching his back. He trusts no one. There is nothing easy about him.

But make no mistake: Difficult or not, tonight he is the right target.

We're getting close. I swallow the jangling feeling in my throat and roll down my window a little. The air is wet and smells like jasmine.

Boyboy is quiet beside me. I know he wants to ask how I'm feeling. Everyone else has been going over the plan all day, but I've been thinking about it for years. I'm not sure I would even know how to explain how I feel right now. Like I swallowed a hive of bees? Is that an emotion?

But Boyboy knows better than to ask me dumb questions.

When we're two houses away, Ketchup turns the lights off and rolls to a stop.

"We're here, Mr. Omoko," Bug Eye says into his phone.

The mansion takes up twice the space of any other home on the street. Over the high wall, only the red tile roof is visible. What we can't see are half a dozen dudes with AK-47s and two German shepherds prowling the grounds. But we know they're there.

Everyone looks up at the house, dead silent. Even Ketchup.

Bug Eye rubs his hands together. "You ready, Tiny Girl?"

I touch the earpiece. It's secure. I pop my shoulders and twist my back. It takes everything not to shout, I'm here. I'm doing this. This is *my* house.

"I'm ready," I say, and slip out of the van.

FOUR

Rule 5: You have to have a plan.

Have a damn good plan. It should be simple. Detail it out. Commit it to memory. You need to know it backward and forward so you don't freeze up when you're standing there with Goondas breathing down your neck, looking up at that house you're about to rob.

My plan has three parts: Dirt. Money. Blood.

It's a good plan.

Tonight we start with dirt.

I have thought long and hard about this plan, looked at all the angles. I've been careful. I've tried to think of everything.

But here's the thing you have to remember about plans: Three-quarters of the way in, it all just may blow up in your face. Equipment breaks. Maids wake up. Dogs bark. The true mark of a good thief is having the stones to keep your cool and *jua kali* that thing back together.

That's right. You've gotta be ready to improvise.

Boyboy kicks things off. As I'm slinking toward the mansion with Ketchup at my heels, he hacks into the security system. He turns off the electric perimeter fence and disables the security booth's camera feeds. Then he reroutes the feeds to his computer so he has eyes all over the Greyhills' lawn. Next he kills the first-floor window alarms. He figures that he can keep everything offline for about three minutes before security fixes things. By that time I'll be inside, and he'll have the interior cameras on a loop, so anyone who's looking will just see a nice empty house. Power outages are common enough in the rainy season. Security will probably chalk this one up to good old nature. The only thing I have to do is hurry.

Ketchup and I pull a wooden ladder out of the bushes, where a gardener on payroll who works down the street stashed it this afternoon. Then I climb right up the wall, under the shadows of the jacaranda trees that line the street. Easy peasy. At the top I listen for the hum of electricity coming through the razor wire. It's quiet, but I still touch it first with my pinky finger just in case.

"Don't you trust me?" Boyboy chides through the earpiece.

I stay quiet and concentrate on lifting myself over.

When I was a kid, I took gymnastics lessons for a couple of years until Mama said we weren't going to take charity anymore. I'm not sure if that's what did it, or if it's because I'm small or what, but doing something like climbing over razor wire on top of a fifteen-foot-high wall is just easy for me. Some people are good at computer stuff. Some are good singers. I'm good at being a thief.

I lower myself down the wall and let go, landing with a small thump in the bushes. Crouched behind dripping palm branches, I wait until I hear the van start and drive off. Bug Eye, Ketchup, and Boyboy will stay far enough away that they won't attract attention.

Boyboy's voice whispers, "Okay, the dogs are on the other side, but you got some dudes heading your way."

I hear footsteps swishing in the wet grass, and soon two guards amble by on their rounds. I sink into the dark. I level my breath, tensing to slide back into the foliage if they come near, but they walk on, oblivious. Once they've rounded the corner, I scan the yard and dart to the house. I have two minutes left for the next part.

The window over the generator is open a crack, as expected, but covered with iron bars. It's going to be tight, for sure. Good thing I had only a sweet bun for dinner.

I climb up on the generator and put my head to the bars, measuring. Ear to ear, my head just barely goes through. But it's enough. If I can get my head in, the rest of me will fit.

I don't mess around; I probably only have about ninety seconds left. I push the window the rest of the way open, get a leg in and then my hips. I breathe out and slide my chest through the cold metal bars, feel a moment of claustrophobia like always, then my head is through and I'm in.

After landing softly on the floor, I take a second to look around. I'm at the corner of the hall. Ahead I see the sitting room, and catch a hint of turquoise light from the pool outside. It's like a dream, being back here after all this time. I take a steadying breath and creep forward. No one should be here. Mr. and Mrs. Greyhill are in Dubai. The kids are away at boarding school in a cold, neutral country. The servants are asleep in their cottages at the end of the yard.

It's just me and the ghosts.

Boyboy's voice crackles through the earpiece. "Hurry, T; you've only got forty-five seconds. And that guard almost caught you with your butt hanging out the window."

I want to tell him to shut up, but resist the urge and keep moving. At the end of the hall, I glance around the corner. The sitting room is empty and still. The security control panel I'm aiming for is attached to the wall ahead. When I reach it, the panel's screen shows I have thirty-two seconds before the next round of laser scanners sweep the house. If they hit me, a silent alarm will go off immediately. It goes to the guards, who will notify an expensive but highly effective security company staffed with ex–covert ops guys from South Africa. They'll arrive within minutes. They don't turn people over to the police, who will let you go for the right price. They take you in a helicopter out over the ocean. What do they do with you? Let's just say it's a long swim back.

Thirty seconds.

I look at the screen, hoping the camera is feeding properly. "Well? Can you see it?"

"Yeah. Tilt your head up. Okay." There's a pause while I presume Boyboy is doing something productive, and it's all I can do to not shout at him to hurry. He has to disable the lasers, but he can't hack into this system; it's on a closed circuit. Instead he's going to walk me through shutting it down.

In twenty-five seconds.

"It's a TX-400. New model," Boyboy says, after what feels like an eternity. He starts rattling instructions. "Press *Alarm* on the screen. Now *Code*. Four, eight, four. *Copy*. *Program . . .*"

Boyboy leads me though the sequence, strings of numbers and buttons to push that he whispers in my ear. They sound almost like the prayers I used to fall asleep to when Mama would drag me to church. It's soothing, in a way. Still, my fingers are shaky, willing the process to go faster. Four seconds. He gives me a last series of numbers, and I punch them in. The timer stops. One second to go.

I let out my breath.

"All clear," he says.

I'm already moving. This way. Grand staircase. Up and then down the hall and to the left. I don't even have to try to be quiet. The plush carpet muffles my feet. I slink down the halls, listening hard. For a second I think there's a noise and I freeze. Through the earpiece I hear the clicking of Boyboy's fingers on his keypad. I pull it away from my ear and continue listening. After a few seconds of stillness, I put the earpiece back in and creep on.

The hallway walls are covered in photographs of the Greyhills. You can't help but notice, first of all, that he's white, she's Kenyan, and the kids between them are a perfect mix. A boy my age and a girl about Kiki's. The second thing you notice is the wealth that practically drips off them. Mrs. Greyhill comes from a family of real estate moguls, and Mr. Greyhill's mining wealth doesn't hurt. They are posed on boats in pressed coral button-downs. Smiling from Land Cruisers on luxury safaris in the Serengeti. Gold watches, pearls, diamonds on wrists and ears. They are a poster family for what the coastal city is—a mix of colors and nationalities—and what it wants to be: rich.

But I've seen it all before. I have no time for them.

I am hunting.

I turn a corner and the dark is absolute. The air is cool and dry, processed. I'm getting closer. There are no more pictures on these walls, just dark wood panels. The farther I go, the more static I can hear through the earpiece. I hope the van isn't too far away. One more turn, spiraling into the dead heart of the mansion.

And I'm there.

I stare at the heavy ebony door, my chest rising and falling. I try to slow my breath. My palms itch with sweat. I'm so close. I've been waiting for this moment practically my entire life. It feels like a thousand ants are crawling up and down my skin.

My hands tremble as I try the doorknob, which I know will be locked. No matter. I pull two bobby pins out of my hair and twist them into shape. Once I'm working, my hands stop shaking. I bite the plastic end off one pin so it makes a nice pick and bend the other into a hook. Then I slide in the hooked end and feel for tension. When it feels right, I insert my pick. I take the earpiece out again and hold it in my teeth so I can listen for the delicate sound of tumblers catching without being distracted. As expected, it takes less than a minute for the lock to yield.

I put the earpiece back on and glance down the hallway again. For a second I think I see the darkness waver and I squint.

"Get moving, Tiny," Bug Eye says, his voice slightly startling in my ear. He must be looking over Boyboy's shoulder at his computer.

I blink, but the darkness stays still. No one is there, I tell myself. Go in. You're stalling.

Once inside, I lock the door behind me. If it was dark in the hall, it's an ink pot in here. It could be high noon outside, but you'd never know. It feels like cheating, but I'm going to have to turn on a light. I double-check the door lock and flip the light switch, blinking into the sudden brightness.

The room is smaller than I remember it. A leather couch and two chairs sit in front of a fireplace. The couch is new, green instead of tan. I guess they couldn't get the bloodstains out of the old one. A buffalo head and trio of tribal masks hang over the mantel. They seem to watch me as I move. On the far side of the room a desk the size of a small rhinoceros sprawls in front of flanking bookshelves. Between them, a golden-hilted sword hangs from the wall, mounted on red silk. It looks like it came from the hip of a sheikh, and it's placed just above where Mr. G's head would be if he were sitting at the desk. As I pad forward, I realize the placement is not accidental. Cross me at your own risk, the sword says to whoever is sitting in the chair opposite.

"In the desk," Ketchup says. I can hear him, but his words cut in and out.

"I know," I say.

"In the drawer."

"Shut up," Bug Eye tells Ketchup.

The Goonda brothers and Boyboy go quiet, but I can feel their energy. I slide behind the desk and sink into the chair. It smells of leather and tobacco. Like money. For a moment, I feel the power that Mr. G must feel every day. I stare at the sofa, and for a moment, I almost see her there, watching me.

"Tiny, stop messin' around," Bug Eye growls.

I don't answer.

"What's she doing?" Ketchup asks.

I take a deep breath. Focus, Tiny Girl. Dirt, money, blood.

I slide open the top desk drawer and lift out a slim laptop. Then I reach farther and close my hand around a metal box the size of a deck of cards and pull it out.

"That's it," Boyboy says breathlessly. "That's got to be his hard drive."

Ketchup shouts, "Yeah, boy!" in my ear, and Bug Eye again tells him to shut up.

"Now what?" I ask Boyboy.

"The hard drive is probably wireless. Put it next to the computer, then plug the USB adapter I gave you into the laptop." Then he quickly adds, "But don't turn anything on yet."

I press the earpiece, trying to make sure I'm getting all of his instructions. Once I've done as he says, I hear the faint clicking of computer keys. It would be so much easier just to steal Mr. G's external hard drive, get in and get out. That was the plan I proposed to Bwana Omoko originally. But the Goonda boss didn't want to leave traces. He wanted me in and out. He thinks it's better if Mr. G doesn't know he's been robbed until we've moved on to part two of the plan, money, and it's too late.

"Is it working?" I ask, after a long pause. The USB is supposed to relay data from the computer and hard drive to my phone, and from there back to Boyboy.

"The signal is terrible," Boyboy grumbles. "I told you those thick walls were going to be a problem. Put your phone closer to the adapter."

I reluctantly pull it from my bra and set it on the desk next to the computer. "Better?"

"I think so. I've got a foot in the door, but there's a crazy *mzingo*-crypto I need to break before we're good."

We all wait in tense silence, seconds ticking by like little lifetimes until Boyboy finally says, "All right . . ." with a lot less confidence than I'd like.

26

"Did you get through?" I whisper.

"Only one way to find out. Turn it on."

If this thing works like it's supposed to, we should already be into the computer and the hard drive. If not, Boyboy will have to walk me through hacking them. It will take forever, and any mistake could trip an auto-delete switch. In Boyboy's worst-case scenario, the whole hard drive gets wiped, and a signal goes out to the black-ops guys to come and get me.

My heart is pounding as I open the screen. I press the power button. For an awful second, nothing happens and I think it hasn't worked, that I'm too far away for the transmission to come through, that silent alarms are already ringing, that guards are descending on me, but then I see a cursor blink and hear a luxurious chime.

My ears fill with excited whispers. The hard drive blinks to life.

Boyboy lets out a big breath of relief. "We're in."

Greyhill's computer has nothing on it. Boyboy already tried hacking it from afar, but it was basically empty. He was the one who bet that Mr. Greyhill kept all his business transaction data separate, offline, probably in an external hard drive like this. I have to smile at the tiny box. It doesn't seem possible it can hold so many dirty secrets.

I sit back. Now all I have to do is wait. I can hear Boyboy clicking away. I watch as the computer screen shuffles from one window to the next all by itself.

"How long's it going to take?" Bug Eye asks.

"A few minutes," Boyboy says.

I let myself enjoy a smug thrill. I did it. I got us in. Soon all of Mr. G's data will be floating out to Boyboy. Boyboy figures it will still take maybe a week for him to decrypt it all, but that's nothing. I've waited five years already; I can wait another week.

I open Mr. G's desk drawers, prowling out of habit. The first is pretty empty. I flick past a couple of pens, a paper clip, and one of those balls you squeeze for stress. I pull the next drawer open and freeze.

A handgun lies on the mahogany like a coiled snake. It is sleek and gleaming, with the words PIETRO BERETTA MADE IN ITALY NO. 11 on the side of the barrel. Is it the same one? I almost pick it up, but then close the drawer so quickly that I hear the gun thud against the wood. I take a deep breath so my voice won't shake. "How much longer?"

"Hold your horses," Boyboy says. "The signal still sucks."

The screen continues to fill with code that I don't understand, white chicken scratch on black. I have no idea what he's doing, but windows keep popping up, full of files.

I'm about to stand, feeling the need to get up and move, when one of the files catches my eye, and I have to blink to make sure I'm seeing it right. ANJU YVETTE, it's labeled. My heart starts to pound. I hesitate. I know I shouldn't mess with the computer while Boyboy's doing his thing, but my hand is moving before I can tell it not to.

When I click on her name, a photo opens.

"Hey! What are you doing?" Boyboy's typing trails into silence. "Oh my God, is that . . . ?"

I can't answer. I can't move. I recognize her face immediately, even though the photo must be twenty years old. My vision blurs.

Under normal circumstances, I like to think I would have noticed the change in the room's air pressure. I would have felt the draft, or smelled the faint odor of dirt and damp. I would have heard the door open behind me where there was no door. But instead, it takes the metallic churning of small, precise gears to get me to finally look up from the glowing screen.

I don't turn around. I know that noise.

The cold muzzle of the gun gives me goose bumps where it presses against my neck.

FIVE

I swallow, careful to not make any sudden moves.

"Get your hands up."

Everything speeds up as I take stock. It's a boy's voice, unfamiliar. Not Ketchup or Bug Eye. No one is double-crossing me. Security? The voice sounds shaky, like telling me to put my hands up is something he's only ever seen people do in movies. And young. Not security. If he were, I'd be on my way to a helicopter already. I glance at the drawer with Greyhill's gun in it, but I'll never be able to pull it open and turn on him in time. I raise my hands.

"I'm turning around," I say, trying for my best calm, in-charge voice.

The gun comes away from my head and I slowly swivel in the chair. He's breathing hard and his bright green eyes are wide. Still, he's aiming with a military stance. Even if he's never shot a living, breathing human, he's practiced. He knows how to hold the gun, how to aim it, how to keep his body loose to absorb the kickback.

He's standing before the bookcase, which has opened on hinges. It's a door that would never show up on a city council house plan. An escape route. I should have known. All snakes have one.

I turn my attention back to the boy.

Of course. Who else could it be?

"Hi, Michael," I say. "Been a while."

Rule 6 is, of course: Don't get caught.

Once when I was about nine, my mother discovered me on the Greyhills' firing range, learning from a security guard how to shoot a hole in the center of a paper man's chest. I was using a gun just like the one in Mr. Greyhill's drawer. Every time I squeezed the trigger I was in danger of being knocked onto my butt. I loved it. I felt like there was a tiny monster inside of me, and the explosions made it howl with glee.

Mama waited until I had handed the gun back to the security guard and then grabbed me by the shoulder. I could feel her hand trembling. She hauled me up to the servants' cottages, instructing the guard through clenched teeth to never let me near a gun ever again, at pain of her getting him fired. Or worse. My mother was a small woman, but her temper was legendary, her memory long. She didn't look at the boy beside me, who had, of course, instigated the shooting lesson. She may have been tough, but she was still his maid.

I waited a year until the boy was good enough to be allowed to shoot without the security guard hovering directly over him, and then had him teach me.

And he was good.

This boy who's pointing a gun at my chest.

My greeting has its intended effect.

"Ti-Tina?" he stutters.

I nod slowly, force my mouth to curve upward in a small smile. Time has made him tall like his father, thick with muscle that didn't show up in the hallway photos. I tell myself not to get distracted looking for my sister in his face, in his pale eyes or the set of his lips.

His brow furrows with confusion. The gun wavers as he unthinkingly moves it away from my chest, and at that instant I lunge. I go for the gun with one hand and jab his windpipe with my other fist. He gags but keeps his hold on the gun, so I settle for pushing his arms to the side and hooking his ankle with my foot to unbalance him. He tries to grab me, but I twist out of his reach and scramble backward over the desk, snatching my phone as I go.

It only takes him a second to recover from my hit; he's quicker than I figured he would be, and I hear him coming over the desk. I've sprinted halfway across the room when his arms wrap around me and we slam face-first into the carpet. My phone falls from my hand.

I try to squirm free, kicking and elbowing, gnashing my teeth toward his bare hand. I manage to scrape the side of my foot down his shin and hear a satisfying yelp. But then he yanks my arms up and presses his knee into the small of my back. I start to fight, but the pressure sends a streak of pain up my shoulder.

"Ow! You're hurting me!"

He hesitates but doesn't loosen his hold. "Is that really you? What are you doing here?" he croaks, lapsing into coughs.

"Let me go!"

"Tina! Stop fighting!" He keeps coughing but still doesn't release me.

"What are you doing here?" I shout.

"What?" He sounds genuinely confused. Of course he does. This is his house.

I stop thrashing but don't answer. Half my face is up against the Persian rug, and all I can see are elegant patterns winding away from my line of sight. I can feel the earpiece pressed into my chest, which I managed to shove into my bra while I ran. I'm breathing hard, and my arm is on fire, but all I can think is, how much of the data did Boyboy get? Did it transmit? Was it enough?

"You're not supposed to be here," I say through my teeth, more to myself than him. He's supposed to be tucked into bed in his Swiss boarding academy. I checked already to make sure there weren't any school holidays.

"What are you talking about?" He tightens his hold on my arms. "What am *I* doing here?"

I wipe my running nose against the carpet. "Let me up."

He doesn't move.

"Let me up. I'll explain."

I feel him hesitate, but then his weight shifts and he lets my arms go. I slowly stand and turn around to find the gun leveled at my chest. I straighten my shirt, using the few seconds to debate whether to try and take him out again. I'm close enough that I could grab the gun's muzzle, pull him off balance, and hit him again in the neck, where I've already hurt him. Probably. But he's quick, and now he's expecting it. So instead I raise an eyebrow at the gun, focusing all my energy on trying to look more in charge than I feel. "Can you put that thing down?"

He doesn't lower it. "I won't kill you," he says, after a pause. "But I will shoot you in the leg."

His face tells me he's not lying. He'll put a bullet in me. So I'm not the only one who's changed in the five years since we've seen each other. I thought it was a softy Swiss boarding school, but maybe it's a military academy his parents have got him in. That would explain the muscles. It would also make him ready for any dirty move I might throw at him. My fighting repertoire basically consists of unbalancing my opponent and going for an *N* spot: nose, neck, nuts, or knees. It's not pretty, but it's effective, and like Bug Eye said when he taught us, fighting pretty's overrated.

As we stand there, I realize Michael's looking me up and

down the same way I'm checking him out. He's taking in my face, my tattoos. I scowl and feel some of my confidence come back with his blush.

"I'm going to sit down," I say.

Without waiting for an answer, I lower myself into one of the leather chairs. I watch him, but I don't think he notices me kick my phone under the chair as I sit. I wonder if the Goondas can hear me through the earpiece. Is Boyboy still able to transfer data? How long before they have to move the van? The neighborhood security drive-by happens every hour. We must be getting close. They'll have to leave me, circle around, and come back.

"How did you even get in here?" Michael steps behind his father's desk, keeping the gun trained on my chest. He looks from the computer to me, then back, his eyes wide.

I hold my breath. Hopefully the screen doesn't show what I've been up to.

"Are you crazy?" he asks. "You've been on Dad's laptop? Do you know what he does to people who mess with his things?"

And in that wide-eyed moment, I see him, the friend I once knew. He is still the same little boy, terrified and in awe of his father, tiptoeing past his office door, watching him leave for work with a look like a dog pining after his master. That look makes me want to hit him again, and suddenly I can't stop the wash of memories that rear up and crash over me: We are seven, and Michael and I are screaming with laughter as we cannonball into the neon-blue pool. We're nine, making shadow puppets on the kitchen wall during a blackout. We are ten, making a fort in the mango tree in the backyard, discovering a nest of baby bulbuls in the process, getting chased by the mother, who flapped and pecked at our heads.

One memory after another, like they've been pent up in a cage in the back of my mind, and someone's opened the door. I was the chosen one, Michael's best friend. I knew all his secrets and fears. I was allowed free rein whenever I was with him, and shooed back to my mother's quarters when I was not.

And then all the images grind to a stop.

I'm eleven, and Michael is nowhere around. It's just me and my mother, her eyes open and staring past me, blood painted in a delicate line from the corner of her mouth to her chin. Her braids fall over the hole in her chest. By the time I saw her, her life had already poured out onto the expensive furniture in this very room.

All the anger and pain and hurt comes surging back, hot and red. For a moment it blinds me.

He must know why I'm here, why I don't care how angry his dad would be, or whether I get hurt in the process. He must. I press my hands into trembling fists and stare at them.

Michael is waiting. "So? What were you doing on his laptop?"

"Nothing."

He pulls the USB adapter out of the computer and shakes it at me. "What is this? Were you copying files?"

When I stay silent, he comes around from the desk, and then he's right up on me, hauling me to my feet and pawing over my body, searching while he keeps the gun at my temple. He is rough, and I feel flimsy under his hands, but I don't want to give him the satisfaction of seeing my fear. Instead I clench my teeth and stare past him until he finds my knife and then the earpiece. He pockets them both.

"You enjoy that? Groping me?"

For a few long seconds we don't move, just stand there, hackles up, ready to rip into each other, waiting for an opening.

"So now what?" I say finally. "Are you going to turn me in?"

The question jolts him. "*Shonde*," he curses.

"What?" I ask.

He tears his gaze from me to glance at the office door. "Security will be here any second. I hit the alarm."

I can't help it; my knees go weak and my throat dries up. I have to swallow to speak. "They'll kill me, you know."

"I *know*." He hurries to the office door. The gun stays pointed at me while he checks the peephole. I use the moment of distraction to crouch and retrieve my phone from under the chair. I slip it up my sleeve.

"Let's go," he says. When he turns, his expression has hardened into something unreadable. He grabs my arm and pushes me toward the still-open bookcase door. I resist, but then I hear something. A thumping. It's growing louder and louder: boots. Not at the door yet, but coming at us fast. Lots of them.

He gestures at the tunnel with the gun. "It's me or them; which do you want?"

I eye the dark opening in the wall, and for a second I feel like I'm looking into my grave. The footsteps halt outside the office. The doorknob rattles. This will not take long.

"I don't know," I say, but I plunge into the tunnel. Michael closes the bookcase behind us as I hear the first boot slam against the office door.

SIX

I can't believe I'm doing this," Michael says.

I don't answer. I can't believe I'm doing this either, following him into a dark wherever. I start to shuffle forward, but he grabs my arm. "Wait. There are stairs."

There's a click of a switch, and a fluorescent bulb above our heads stutters to life, like the start of a horror movie. It illuminates steps that recede steeply into the earth. The concrete walls of the tunnel are rough, with rusty water stains dripping from the ceiling like dried blood. I watch Michael press buttons on a small screen on the wall. When it turns on, we see a video feed of guards bursting through Mr. G's office door, swarming until they fill the room, guns bristling.

My breath catches. Not because of the guards but because *there is a camera in the office.*

I am frozen to the spot, watching the screen.

A camera.

Recording everything. But it must not transmit like the other CCTVs to the guard station. It, like the tunnel, doesn't show up on any of the plans or security documents Boyboy hacked. How long has it been there? Was it there five years ago? A camera. I'm practically paralyzed thinking about what it might have recorded.

Michael pushes another button on the screen and we have audio. I see a guard check behind the desk, coming in so close to the camera that his face fills the screen. I can hear him breathing. Is he going to open the door? The face recedes, blind to us. The men stand around for a little while looking confused, and then one of them says something into his radio about a false alarm and waves the crew back out.

"They won't look here?" I ask.

"No."

Michael scrolls back through the footage until he gets to the part where he first found me. He presses some buttons and I see the words ARE YOU SURE YOU WANT TO DELETE? His finger hovers for a second before he finally pushes YES, and then he quickly switches the screen off.

"Why wouldn't they look here?"

"They don't know about it." He nods down the stairs. "Walk."

With a growing feeling that the walls are pressing in on me, I start down. He hasn't tied my hands or anything; he just has the gun. I'm not sure whether I should try making a run for it or risk waiting to see what happens next. Where is he taking me? A dungeon? Some sicko Big Man torture chamber? I wouldn't put it past his dad to have one.

As my mind goes to dark places, Michael suddenly says, "Where have you been?" in such a raw voice that it startles me.

"I . . ." There's no way I'm telling him I've been living rough on a rooftop for five years. ". . . Around."

He is silent. We keep walking.

Finally he asks, "In Sangui?"

I shrug. "Where else?"

"It's been five years, Tina. Nothing. Not a word. And then, out of nowhere, here you are."

I don't answer. His tone is bitter, but what am I supposed to tell him? Sorry I didn't hang out after my mom got murdered? Also, dude has a gun stuck in my back. I don't really feel the need to be polite. "Where are you taking me?" I ask instead, but he doesn't answer either.

At the bottom of the stairs, the tunnel stretches out before us. I count four doors before we stop in front of one. It has a bolt that locks from the outside, a peephole, and a slot for passing things through. Standard torture chamber stuff. He opens it and nudges me inside with the gun barrel.

Inside the room it feels like the ceiling is pressing down on me, but I force myself to look around and take in as much as I can. It's windowless and probably soundproof, but as far as torture chambers go, I guess it could be worse. There's a cot and a table, a chair and a toilet and a sink. No tools to rip fingernails out that I can see.

Michael picks a chain up off the floor. It has handcuffs attached to the end and he ratchets me in.

"Is this really necessary?" I ask, trying to sound tough. I don't want to think about who else has been in these handcuffs. The chain is fastened to a bolt in the wall. There's a little drain in the center of the room, like you might need to hose the whole place down.

"I'm going up to talk to the guards. I'll be back."

I eye him warily. And then what? I want to ask. But Michael is already out the door. After it closes behind him, I hear the bolt sliding home, loud and final.

For a few moments it's just me and the sound of my own breath. I make for the door, but the chain yanks me back several meters short. I stand staring at the peephole, chest heaving, willing my panic to stay way down in my stomach where it belongs.

My phone buzzing in my sleeve makes me jump.

"You shouldn't have called!" I say, when I manage to get it to my ear. "He only just left me alone!"

"I can see him—cameras upstairs—" Boyboy says. "Where—at?"

I am ridiculously relieved to hear Boyboy's voice, however faintly and broken up. A camera. There's a secret camera in Mr. G's office, I want to shout to him, but I've got other problems to deal with first. "I'm in a room under the mansion."

I hear shuffling. "—not on—house plan, Tiny," Ketchup's voice whines, like it's somehow my fault.

"No shit," I say. "Torture chambers tend not to be."

"——what?"

"Nothing. What is Michael doing? Does it look like he's telling the guards about me?"

"Let me——on it."

While Boyboy's checking, Bug Eye asks, "You—cool, Tiny Girl?" Even if I don't hear exactly what he's said, I know it's not a question; it's an order.

"Yeah."

"Dammit, Tiny——gonna get caught?—Should have never—you—and—*shoga* friend—"

"Shut up, Ketchup," Bug Eye says. "—not——fault."

Ketchup continues to pout. "I——the kids were sup-posed—Switzerland or some—"

I check out my handcuffs. "They *were* supposed to be in Switzerland. I don't know why he's here."

"The guards—back—posts. I don't think—told about—" Boyboy says.

Bug Eye adds, "Looks—Michael is going—office."

"He'll be back soon." Tucking my phone between my cheek and shoulder, I reach into my hair for a bobby pin.

"Don't you say——nothin' to—, Tiny," Ketchup says.

I contort my fingers to get the bobby pin down to the handcuff's keyhole. "Think I'm stupid? You know I won't. Did you get anything off the hard drive, Boyboy?"

"What? Not sure yet——to process it."

For a moment I think they've cut out. "Hello? Hello?" The pin flips out of my hands and drops to the ground.

Then I hear Bug Eye say, "Tiny, listen, we gotta——stay strong. We——Omoko's counting on——"

"Wait," I say. I'm having trouble getting a full breath. Are the walls moving closer? Don't get excited, Tiny Girl. Breathe. "Boyboy?" My voice cracks.

I can't hear anything but static. I let myself sink to the ground and pick up the pin. The floor is damp, and the coolness of it slides into my bones. My hands are too shaky to do the handcuff lock. I clamp them together between my knees, trying to still them.

For a second the line clears. "We'll——when you're out," Bug Eye says.

I open my mouth to answer, but there's a rush of static, and they're gone.

Rule 7: It may be bad now, but you gotta remember you've been through worse and survived.

You have been left alone in the dark before. This is nothing. This is not that hole full of slick, sharp stones that bruise your bare feet. Things are not wiggling and dripping onto your shoulders.

This is not that night.

Michael takes his time coming back. When he does, it's as a disembodied voice echoing from some unseen speaker in the walls.

"You took your handcuffs off."

I look through the peephole, but it's not meant for

looking out. It's made for looking in. "They clashed with my outfit."

"Stand on the opposite side of the room."

I don't move.

"Go, Tina."

I let out the breath I've been holding, and slowly back up. The door opens.

"Stay there," Michael says. "Up against the wall."

I glower at him, but do what he says. He's brought a laptop—not Mr. Greyhill's—and the gun. He puts a plastic bottle of water on the table and invites me with a gesture. Is there any way to turn it into a weapon? No. I grab it and chug the whole bottle. Michael watches me. I watch him.

"Why are you here?" he asks.

"Did you rat me out to the guards?"

"What are you *doing* here, Tina?"

Did he turn me in? I don't think so, but I can't know for sure. Maybe security guards are waiting in the tunnel. Michael's face is a mask; it tells me nothing. At last, I shrug. "I was looking for cash, jewelry, whatever. I knew the house. It was an easy mark."

"You were just robbing us." Michael's voice drips with incredulity. "You realize this place is a fortress, right? How did you even get in?"

When I stay quiet, he says, "Jesus, Tina, our guards don't play. If you're here, it's not just 'cause you think there's loose change in Dad's desk drawers. They find you in there messing with his computer, and what are they going to think?"

"I was just looking around," I repeat, but I know how I sound.

He digs in his pocket. "Just looking around? On his computer? And his hard drive? Are there files copied onto this thing?" He holds up the USB adapter.

Ketchup is right, I think with a sinking stomach. I'm so stupid. How could I get caught?

My nonanswer tells Michael all he needs to know. He glares at me for a moment longer, then slams his fist on the table, making me start. "Why, Tina? *Why?* You take off after the funeral, then no phone calls, no letters, nothing. I thought you were dead! And now you show up out of nowhere, and you . . ." He rubs his hand over his cropped hair, hard, like he can scratch the whole situation out of his mind. "You've got all these tattoos, and . . . are you a Goonda? Is that it? Are those Goonda tattoos?"

When I still don't answer, he throws his hands up. "So you're in a gang now, and that's why you're robbing us? Why would you do that? We're . . . you're . . ." He's unable to go on, unable to put words to what he obviously sees as treason.

And I can't stand it anymore.

"You want to know *why*?" I ask, launching up.

He grabs the gun and leaps to his feet too, and then I'm up in his face, never mind that the muzzle of the pistol is now inches from my heart. I don't care. I'm beyond caring. I poke him hard in the chest to punctuate, "You. Want. To. Know. *Why?*"

Somewhere in my mind I am telling myself to stop. I

know I should. I need to listen to Bug Eye and be cool, but it's too late, it's all spilling out now. I've spent too many years being quiet, biding my time, thinking, wondering, nursing the wounded animal in my chest back from death, feeding it, training it, grooming it, until it ripples with muscle, and its claws and teeth are diamond hard and razor sharp.

Mama thought we were safe, that we were away from men in the night. Except then this boy's father showed us how *not* safe we really were. He showed us that there are men in the night everywhere. I can't stand here and listen to this spoiled Big Man's son ask me why. If he doesn't know, he's going to. I bite off and spit every brittle word:

"Because your father killed my mother."

SEVEN

After Mama's funeral, I took Kiki and walked away from the Greyhills. We were still in our Sunday clothes. I brought her to Mama's church and asked the nuns to take care of her. They tried to make me stay too, but I ran. I went to the docks and spent two weeks living in a busted-up shipping container, trying to decide whether or not to die. I would wake up with rats crawling over my legs in the middle of the night and not even care. I was so far gone that I wasn't even a person anymore. My mother had been killed. I had heard what Greyhill said to her in the garden. I couldn't stay in his home anymore. I couldn't leave Kiki there. But I couldn't take care of my sister either. I'm not proud of abandoning her. But I did it.

When Bug Eye found me, I had just stolen a mango from a street vendor. I was too weak to run away, and the vendor had caught me by the wrist. He was about to beat me silly. His fist was in the air when Bug Eye stepped in and put a bill down that would have bought fifty mangoes. Then he turned and walked away, saying over his shoulder to the man, "My little sister's a pain. Sorry, bwana. Come on, tiny girl."

And I followed. For no other reason than he still had my stolen mango in his hand. He called me something that sounded like my name, or close enough to it. And there was not one single scrap of feeling in my body telling me to do anything else.

I slept in the Goondas' warehouse that night. In the middle of a snoring pack of street kids, I lay down with no hope of anything better the next day. And maybe things would have stayed the same. I would have gone on being a useless bag of bones.

Except, early the next morning I woke to a hand creeping into my pocket.

I jerked awake like I'd been electrified, clawing at the intruder. But the weasel-faced boy slipped out of my reach, dancing backward.

"Give it back," I said, my voice rusty from disuse.

"No," he sneered. "What is it?" He squinted at the prayer card he'd pulled out of my pocket, twisting it left and right.

"Give it to me!" I rushed him, my voice growing louder. I snatched at the card, catching nothing. "It's mine!"

I was vaguely aware of the bodies stirring around us. They sniffed the air, eager for blood.

The thief was bigger than me, older. He held the card over

his head, his rag of a shirt flapping as he jumped to evade me. He could tell the card had no real value, but also that I was desperate for it.

It was currency he was interested in.

"You want it? Come and get it," he said. He waved Saint Catherine's paper face at me. I watched his fingers bend a crease across the card.

For the first time in weeks, I was alive. I was heat and fury. I threw myself at him, using my fingernails, my teeth, my toes, every ounce of raw pain I had at my disposal.

And I could hear the boys laughing, *Hey, look at the wildcat,* and then Bug Eye was pushing me away, saying, *Give it back, Ketchup,* and I saw the boy leering through the lines of blood I'd scratched down his face.

His eyes never left mine, even as he crumpled up the card and threw it at my feet.

Later, as I smoothed it, after I'd finally shed and dried my tears, I looked at Saint Catherine. Really looked at her. I looked at the wheel she rested her hand on. At the sword under her feet. At the palm branch she carried.

The prayer card had been in Mama's pocket when she died. It was all I had left of her.

I'd heard the story a hundred times from Mama—she was kind of obsessed. Saint Catherine of Alexandria was smart and beautiful, and didn't want to give it up to some king, so he put her on the breaking wheel, which is this torture device. You're laid out spread-eagle on a big wheel and people hit you with sticks until you're good and broken. Except

Catherine was holy, and the wheel broke when she touched it. So instead, the king took a sword and chopped off her head. Saint stuff is crazy violent like that. The palm branch she carries is supposed to be a symbol of triumph.

Mama would pray, *Help us to break the wheel, Catherine,* as we knelt by the bed at night. And I never got it because Catherine still got killed in the end, so what's the point? Why the palm branch? But Mama would just shush me and say, Saint Catherine may have died, but she wasn't ever *broken.* Mama would tap the palm branch with her finger like, See?

And for the first time maybe ever, I did see.

I saw that while part of me was certainly dead and gone, the whole of me wasn't going to die. I had let myself be broken, but maybe I could be remade. I could become something stronger. If I was strong, I could keep my promise to Mama. I could make sure my little sister stayed safe. Maybe she should go on living with the nuns. With them, she could have the life Mama wanted for us. She'd go to school. She'd learn about God. But not me. I would stay in the shadows and watch over her from a distance. I would never let anything hurt her.

I slept that next night with a shard of glass in my hand, and no one touched me. In the morning, when Bug Eye yelled at us all to wake the hell up, I was ready.

He wanted to see what sort of Goondas we could be, and I lined up with all the other new recruits like we were getting ready to march into battle, the most laughable little army on earth. The Ketchup boy was nowhere in sight, so I focused instead on taking stock of the other kids, deciding which ones looked weak, which ones I could beat in a fight. I was the only girl, but it didn't matter. I would be stronger than any of them.

I let my pain and exhaustion sink down and slide out of my body until I was completely empty. The day before, I had been a fragile vessel made of clay. I had been broken down to dust, but a storm had come and churned me up. Now I was a hunk of mud.

And I was ready to be put on the wheel and shaped into something else entirely.

Rule 8: Know the value of what you take.

Question: What is worth more than diamonds and gold? What is the most stable currency? What thing, when stolen, becomes most dangerous and precious of all?

Answer: a secret.

An hour of silence goes by in the torture chamber, and I feel a little calmer. I figure that if Michael were going to turn me over to the guards, he would have by now. Which means he probably doesn't know what to do with me. Which means that maybe, just maybe, I have a shot at getting out of all this.

He's frisked and handcuffed me again, this time checking my hair. My bobby pins are in his pocket. I had tried to hide the phone between the toilet and the wall, but he checked all around the room as well. Michael always was a fast learner. I try to console myself with the fact that the phone wasn't going to help me get out of here. No one is coming to rescue me.

Michael has said only one thing: "My dad didn't kill your mom."

I am not interested in what he has to say on the subject. I continue lying on the cot and staring at the ceiling, where there's a water stain that looks like an elephant with wings. Michael's sitting in front of his computer, trying to figure out if there's anything saved on the USB adapter. He doesn't seem to be having much luck getting it to do anything.

"Why are you here, anyway?" I ask. "Aren't you supposed to be in Switzerland or something?"

Michael shifts in his seat. "My school sent me home."

"Why?"

He doesn't answer.

After a while I say, "They were lovers, you know. My mom and your dad." Now I'm just being mean. It feels good. "Yep. Your dad used her, knocked her up, and when he was finished with her, he killed her."

"You're wrong. He wouldn't have killed her. He's not like that."

"I'm sorry, have you met your father? He's not exactly in line for sainthood."

"You don't know what you're talking about," Michael says. "Everyone assumes he's this terrible person because he's in mining, but it's not true. And besides . . . he told me that he didn't kill your mother."

"He *told* you."

"Yes," Michael says stubbornly, still not looking at me. "I asked him."

I watch him type. "You poor thing," I say, shaking my head. "You still worship him, don't you?"

He twitches. "Shut up."

"You still believe all the lies he's told you, about what a good provider and protector he is, how he's just working hard to feed his family. Don't you wonder what it costs? Don't you know who he really is? All the lives he's ruined so you can live like a prince? He doesn't care about little people like my mom. And he's not afraid to lie to *you* about it."

"I said shut up!" Michael says, in my face now, breathing hard, grabbing me by the shoulders like he wants to shake me. "Just shut up about him!"

I almost laugh. He's his father's son all right. I lean into his anger, relishing it, and wait for him to hit me. But he lets go, like I'm not worth the effort, and I sink back into the cot.

He swivels and paces, collecting himself. On the other side of the room, with his back to me, he takes a deep breath. "What were you doing in his office?"

I consider. "Hunting."

He eyes me over his shoulder. "For what?"

"For everything. I was hunting for everything."

"What 'everything'? Stop playing. Say what you mean."

"I mean *everything*. Bank records, proof he's working with terrorists, that he's selling them arms, buying their blood gold. Who he's working with, where. Every dirty little secret. And you know what? I got them. I got them all."

Dirt. Then money. Then blood.

Maybe it's just the light, but Michael's pale face seems to go a funny grayish color. He looks at me, then down at the USB adapter plugged into his laptop. He yanks it out, drops it to the ground, and stomps on it with his heel like it's a cockroach.

I smile at the broken pieces and lean back, my cuffed hands cradling my head. "That's not going to help. That thing was just a tool. I used it to send your dad's files to my partner. Crush it. Hit me. It's only a matter of time before every nasty, illegal thing your father's ever done is out there in the public eye."

"That's what you want to do? Drag his name through the mud?"

"Yep," I say.

That and so much more.

"Well, you're too late," Michael says bitterly. "All those lies have been paraded around in the press and he's still standing. No one has any proof. And that's because it's not true. Extracta's mines all pass their health and safety checks, every time. The miners get good wages. No one's a slave."

"I'm impressed, Mikey. You know more about Daddy's company than I would have thought. Too bad all your intel is wrong. Where did you get it? Oh, let me guess, Extracta Mining Company's head of East African operations, Mr. Roland Greyhill, aka Daddy?" I shake my head in mock sympathy. "My money's on his hard drive telling a different story.

It's true that Extracta's already under scrutiny, though. And they're going to need a scapegoat when this all comes out. Guess who that's going to be?"

"How do you know what's on his hard drive? Did you look at the files?"

"It—I just do."

"No," he says, shaking his head slowly. "You didn't have time. You weren't in there that long. You didn't see anything. He doesn't have slaves. He doesn't work with terrorists."

I suck my teeth in impatience. Does Michael live under a Swiss rock? "Don't you know how it works in Congo? Allow me to educate you. Militias and the Congolese army are fighting, and to keep fighting they need money and weapons. They use slave labor to mine gold, and your dad buys it on the cheap from them. Then he launders that gold through Extracta's mines, acting like it's all shiny and conflict free."

Michael's brow is furrowed. "No. You're crazy. Where are you getting all this?"

"I have my sources."

"It's all lies. He's bringing jobs and industry to the Congo."

He sounds like he's quoting someone, like he's memorized this speech and given it before.

"Come on, Michael." I almost feel sorry for the poor guy. "You're brainwashed. You don't get as rich as your dad is playing by the rules." I wave my handcuffed wrists around the room. "You've got me in a torture chamber, for God's sake!"

"It's not a torture chamber! It's a panic room."

I shake my handcuffs at him. "And these? Are these to keep me from panicking?" I watch him struggle to respond.

A sickish feeling has started creeping up in my stomach, and I don't like it. It's not my problem if pretty boy is in denial. Don't think about Michael, think about Mama, I tell myself. Think about all the bad things Greyhill's done. He has to pay for them. I have a plan, and I'm sticking to it. I can't be bothered with the feelings of spoiled rich boys. "It doesn't matter what you think," I say. "It's all going to be out there soon. You'll see."

Michael looks like he's fighting some sort of internal battle. Finally he asks, almost to himself, "Can you stop it? If it's even there, I mean. Can you stop this so-called proof from getting out?"

I don't answer right away. What is he asking? Is he trying to threaten me? "Listen, whatever you do, torture me, kill me, it isn't going to change things. The stuff is out of my hands now. It's going to be released."

Which, to be honest, isn't exactly true, but Michael doesn't need to know the details. Giving the dirt to Donatien is on me. I'm sure Omoko could trash Mr. Greyhill's name some other way, but I want it to be Donatien who writes all the bad stuff up and publishes it. He can get it in the big papers. He's got a stake in bringing Greyhill down and he will do it right.

Just like Boyboy will then hack Mr. Greyhill's bank accounts the right way.

And like I will do blood.

Just right.

Michael lifts his chin. "What if I can prove my dad didn't kill your mom? Would you be able to stop it?"

I frown. Normally, I feel like I'm pretty good at knowing when someone else is full of it, but Michael's got hard to read since we were kids. "What do you mean?"

He doesn't respond.

"Do you know something?"

He still doesn't move, just keeps watching me.

I'm on my feet, lunging for him. Only the cuffs and the chain stop me. "Don't play with me, Michael! Do you know something about my mother's murder?" I can't quite reach him. "Is it the video from that night? From the camera in the office? Do you have it? Do you?"

His nostrils flare. "No."

I tell myself to calm down, to let the numbness I've worked so hard to cultivate sweep me under. I do not exist. I *will* not exist, not for him. "Then you don't know anything," I say finally, backing up.

"You're going to ruin my father—ruin all of us—because you *think* he killed your mother. You don't even know for sure!"

"I do know! You know it too, or you wouldn't have asked him if he did it!"

"He said he didn't kill her, and I believe him!" Michael shouts.

Why do you care whether Michael believes it or not? I ask myself. He doesn't matter. Leave it.

But I can't. "I saw them," I say.

Michael freezes. "You saw him . . . kill her?"

"No," I say. "But I didn't need to. The night before she was killed, I saw them together in the garden. They were arguing. My mother knew his secrets, and she threatened to expose him. And do you know what he said?"

Michael doesn't move.

"He said, 'Do that, Anju, and I'll kill you.'" I pause, letting my words sink in. "She sent a message to a reporter the next day, asking him to meet her. And eight hours later, she was dead."

EIGHT

Rule 9: Thieves and refugees don't do police.

If I hadn't seen them in the garden that night, maybe my whole life would be different. Maybe I could have put her death behind me, gone to school with Kiki, convinced myself it was a robbery gone wrong, like Mr. G said. I could have tried to forget.

But I did see them.

Their angry voices pulled me out of bed. I came upon them standing under the plumeria tree. Its blossoms pulsed in the dark like attendant stars. Greyhill had his hands around Mama's throat. His threats were soft and intimate.

Seeing them, I tasted that old, familiar terror in the back of my mouth. And when I howled, Greyhill had broken away from her and slunk off.

Once he was gone, I went to Mama and she held me close. She told me to hush, that there was nothing to be afraid of. He didn't mean what he'd said. Everything was going to be fine.

I could have tried going to the police. I could have told them what I'd seen and heard, let them investigate, waited for justice to prevail.

Sure.

Right.

And Kiki and I would live happily ever after in a castle made of rainbows and gumdrops.

No, here's the thing with Sangui City (it's pretty simple; take it to heart):

The police do not give a shit.

They certainly don't if you're a thief, and especially not if you're a refugee from Congo. We are just walking ATMs to them, good for all sorts of "fees": for walking down the street; for having a mole on your chin; for wearing red shoes. What a little refugee girl had or hadn't seen in the mist was not going to interest them.

Nope. You have a problem, you deal with it yourself.

The cops came the next day to her murder scene, of course, to take photos and gawk at the famous Greyhill mansion and write up a few notes in terrible English. "Gunnshott too abnomen" was apparently the official cause of death. Says so right on the forms. I have them. Boyboy hacked the whole file out of the police server for me.

The notes explain that no one was home except for Bwana

Greyhill and a few staff, all of whom were accounted for. Mrs. Greyhill and the two children were at the beach house several hours' drive away. Mr. G heard a noise in his office. He went in, found the maid already dead. She must have startled a robber. The thief/murderer was long gone. These things happen. Open and shut.

I can just imagine how the *polisi* told it later: See, they said, Mr. Greyhill is what we call a King Midas. He brings the minerals out of the dark places in distant lands we otherwise don't like to think about. Greyhill profits and Sangui profits, and if you and I are smart, we *polisi* will profit too. After all, Mr. Greyhill's hands may not be clean, but there is gold dust mixed in with the dirt and blood.

All death is tragic. But who was this maid, anyway? Some paperless refugee from Congo, part of the refuse that washes down the mountains from the mines and ends up on the streets of our city. They bring bad morals. They steal our jobs. And really, between you and me, what was this maid doing in that office in the first place? We don't want to gossip, but it's true: Nine times out of ten, staff are behind these robberies. Good, honest maids are so hard to come by.

Heads shake sympathetically. Hands shake firmly. Cases are closed.

NINE

When I wake in the torture chamber, I figure it's morning. I have no way of knowing, what with no windows or phone. I can't believe I even fell asleep. The last thing I remember was staring at the winged-elephant stain on the ceiling after Michael left, wondering if I was going to die down here, and if so, how many Fridays it would take before Kiki realized I wasn't coming back.

I wash my face, use the toilet, then sit back down on my cot. My wrists are getting raw, and I rub them under the cuffs.

"A book would be nice," I grumble, my foot starting to tap.

Michael didn't say anything after I told him what I'd seen. He just picked up his computer and left. He didn't even respond when I yelled after him, calling him names, cursing at him. He shut the door and left me here to sit and wonder what happens next.

At first, I just wanted to kill Mr. Greyhill. If I was going to be all eye-for-an-eye about it, I would have killed someone he loved. That would have been fair. But I'm not a villain; I'm not *him*.

A few months after joining the Goondas, when I was stronger, I started going to watch Mr. G in my spare time. I would hide in an alleyway near his office, see him go in and out, in and out, day after day, like everything was fine. Like the whole world hadn't stopped making sense. I thought about getting a gun from Bug Eye and doing it right there on the street, walking up to him, letting his bodyguards have me after. I would have, if not for one thing. One small, huge thing: Kiki.

If I died like that, I realized, I couldn't keep my promise to Mama. I couldn't guarantee what would happen to her. It all played out in my mind. Maybe she could stay on scholarship, but who knows? And if they took that away, what then? Who takes care of her? All of her family would be dead. She would never survive on the streets. Never. Just the thought of her trying made me shake.

I went back to the Goondas, adrift.

I knew Mr. Greyhill had to pay, but I didn't know how. I told Bug Eye my story—what I wanted and why I couldn't have it. I shouldn't have talked, but I didn't know better then. I hadn't learned the rule about valuing secrets yet. But maybe it's like Mama used to say, that everything happens for a reason, even the bad things and mistakes.

Bug Eye told our boss, Mr. Omoko.

Ezra Omoko is a quiet, middle-aged man, Sangui City born and bred. Not very tall, graying at his temples, no tattoos. He dresses like a schoolteacher in slacks and golf shirts. But don't be fooled. Among the Goondas, he is king. He takes care of those who serve him well. He is generous with the spoils. But I've seen him eat a double-crossing Goonda's liver for breakfast. And he keeps a collection of his former enemies' eyeteeth in a bag in his pocket like an amulet.

He found me alone in the Goondas' makeshift gym a few days after I blubbered to Bug Eye. I was practicing my left hook on a shredded tire, long after all the other Goondas in training had called it a day.

"So you want to kill Roland Greyhill?" Mr. Omoko asked, standing hidden in the dark.

I turned around. I had never talked to the big boss himself before. There was no sense in asking who'd told him. That was obvious. So I just took a deep breath and said, "Yes."

"And why would you want to do a silly thing like that?" Omoko wanted to know.

I shrunk before him. Only two days before I'd heard a story that as a boy Mr. Omoko used to bite the heads off live snakes. He was immune to their poison. The punch line to the story was that if he bit you, you died.

I screwed up my courage to respond, but before I could, he continued, "Why do that, *kijana*, when you can ruin him first, and *then* kill him?"

Omoko emerged from the shadows, put a fatherly arm around me, walked me back to his office. We had a little chat.

He gave me a book, *The Count of Monte Cristo*, and told me to find him when I finished it.

It took a month and the help of a stolen dictionary, but I did it. When I came back, Mr. Omoko asked what I'd learned. "A lot of big words," I said. Then, "I'm not sure. The count got revenge, but I don't know if it made him happy."

Omoko regarded me thoughtfully. "Happy or sad isn't the point. People don't look for revenge to make them happy. They do it because they must. Do you understand?"

I thought about it. I did.

"What I'd hoped you would learn," Mr. Omoko went on, "is that if you decide to take revenge, you have to think of it as a vocation, a calling. Like a priest is called to serve. It isn't something you do once. It is something you do every day, like learning a dance. Before you can dance, you must put your time in. You must learn the rules of the dance, its rhythms, and be sure not to step too soon. If you want to master it, you must also put in your blood and your sweat. *That* is what the count learned, that his calling was revenge, but that to get it he had to have discipline. You have to want it deep in your gut like he did, more than anything.

"You have to be patient. You have to rid yourself of distraction: friends, hobbies, other ambitions. You must be able to wait for the right moment. You will have to starve yourself, to be willing to break your own bones and reshape them to make it happen. It takes sacrifice like you've never imagined possible. You practice at it every day, until there is no distinction between you and it. It is you. Do you have that in you?"

"I-I think so."

He regarded me coolly. "It won't work if you just *think* so. You have to be sure," he said. "You can kill him now. That would be the easy way. But know that if you do, people will mourn. Sure, they'll remember him as a Big Man and maybe even a businessman of, shall we say, *questionable* ethics. But around here a Big Man is as good as royalty. He'll still die revered, feared, and admired. He killed your mother, child. Is that what you want?"

"No."

Of course it wasn't.

Mr. Omoko told me to wait, and be patient. To make myself strong in the meantime, to build my own set of rules to live by, to master the practice of revenge. I was small, but I was already on the road to becoming a thief with clever hands and silent feet, and he could work with that. If I was to be a thief, though, I should be a good one.

The best.

"Why are you helping me?" I had asked.

He smiled. "I was young once, and wronged. I see myself in you. You're smart. I trust your judgment. If you say he needs your vengeance, then I believe you. I expect a cut, of course, when you take his fortunes. If you want my help, that is."

I did.

"Good."

One day there would be an opportunity for a thief like me, he told me.

That day was supposed to be today.

Hours tick by, or days. I don't know. I go through rounds of pacing, then screaming threats and obscenities at the walls and corners, and then silence, and then cycling through the whole routine again.

The master plan is simple. I made it; Omoko helped me refine it.

First I steal the dirt on Mr. Greyhill and give it to Donatien, the reporter my mother knew. Donatien knows everything there is to know about blood gold. He'll do a good job on the story, and he's got connections to get it out there into the big papers. And for this story, unlike all the others, there will be proof.

But dragging Mr. G's name through the dirt isn't the end of it. What the Goondas are interested in is the next step: money. Greyhill has his loot stashed somewhere; Omoko is sure of it. Offshore bank accounts, most likely. Boyboy thinks the treasure map is on the hard drive. We find the accounts, Boyboy hacks them, then everyone gets a cut and goes home happy.

Except me. I'm not done yet.

While the Goondas enjoy their spoils, I'll be watching Mr. Greyhill. I want to see his world slowly crumble around him. I want to see his company fire him. I want to see his debts called in. I want the banks to take his home, his cars, all his

Big Man toys. Maybe his wife will leave him. His kids will finally understand who he really is.

But it still won't be enough. He took everything from Kiki and me, and I want him to know who's taking everything back. So when the time is right, I'll step out of the shadows. I want to see the understanding dawn in his eyes. He needs to know it was me, Tiny Girl, who brought the Big Man down.

And that's when I'll kill him.

I hear the torture chamber door unlock. I've been yelling at Michael to come let me out for a good long while, but all of a sudden I'm worried it's not him behind the door.

It's actually sort of a weird relief to see his face. He's carrying the laptop like a tray with food and more water on it. He looks like he got even less sleep than me, and he doesn't have the gun anymore. Bold, Michael, I think. Or dumb. He places everything on the table and sits down in one of the chairs, waiting for me to take the other.

"Aren't you worried I'm going to beat you up and escape?"

He doesn't smile at my taunt. "I think you'll want to hear me out first."

"Still trying to bargain?" I sit down opposite him. I'm starving, but I force myself to ignore the food, even though it's making my mouth water and my stomach growl. It's been a long time since the bun I got from Kiki. Chicken stew and a creamy mound of *ugali* steam on the plate. I keep my eyes on Michael. "I already told you it's too late."

He folds his hands on the table. They look odd for some

reason, and then I realize it's because they're so smooth. There are no scars or nicks on his knuckles like everyone else I know. My eyes, as if not attached to my brain, search out the crook of his arm, looking for the one mark that I know is there, but it's hidden under his sleeve. I will not let myself think about that scar right now.

"My dad didn't kill your mom," he says.

I wait until I can manage to speak calmly. "I thought we'd cleared all that up."

"You're making assumptions. Just because he threatened her doesn't mean he killed her. Plus, I don't think he would lie to me. Not about something like that."

I want to hit him. I want to hit him so hard his pretty little eyeballs cross.

"You have to admit that you can't be sure," he continues. "Without a confession or seeing what actually happened, you'll never really know."

I shove my chair back from the table so it screams against the concrete. I want to be as far away from Michael as I can. How could we have once been friends? Played and squabbled and cried when the other one got in trouble?

He waits. He's watching me so closely. I try to keep the little muscles in my face from giving me away. Of course I know that on the surface there is room for doubt. Of course I do. How many sleepless nights have I spent staring up at the stars, wishing for some sort of proof? It's not just nightmares that keep me awake. Doubt itches like a scab. But as much as I doubt and wonder, I keep coming back to the same con-clusion: I know he was capable. He wanted to do it. He said so himself. He had, like they say in detective shows, means, motive, and opportunity. He knew no one was going to stop him, and no one was going to punish him.

Once Boyboy told me about this science theory. Somebody's razor. It says that the simplest answer is almost always the right one. Something like that. Mr. G is a bad man. He said he would kill Mama, and then she gets murdered. Who else would it be? I shouldn't need any more proof. I'm sure he did it.

I am so very ninety-nine percent sure.

But that one percent of me is who Michael is talking to now, and he knows it.

I hate that one percent.

"Look, here's my offer, take it or leave it."

"Leave it."

"Would you just listen first? *Ngai*, you have always been so stubborn."

I cross my arms over my chest.

Michael speaks slowly and carefully. "You want to find out who killed your mother."

"I know who killed my—"

"Wait," he says. "Hear me out. I want back what you took off Dad's hard drive. What I propose is this: I help you find out who killed your mom, beyond a doubt. We get proof. We figure out why. I have access to places and people you don't.

I have money. People will do things for me, talk to me. We'll find out who did it, if you promise to give me back what you took off his computer."

"First of all, who says I can even stop the data I stole from being released? I told you, it's already out of my hands."

"*Can* you stop it?"

For a long time I don't answer. I don't understand what Michael is playing at. Why not offer to buy me off? Why this? Why does he care about whether or not his father killed *this* person? Does he honestly think his dad wouldn't lie to him? That his father has some sort of code of honor? "What if it turns out your dad did it after all?"

"He didn't do it."

"Come on, Michael, it's Oaxaca's razor."

"What? You mean Occam's razor?"

"Whatever. Look, not that I'm agreeing to this—I'm not—but just for argument's sake, what if we find out your dad killed her?"

"Then you release the stuff. Do whatever you want with it."

I frown. It's infuriating that I can't read him. "You don't mean that. If I go along with you, you'll pull the rug out from under me. You'll get rid of me. Why should I trust you?"

Suddenly his eyes gleam. I can't tell whether it's hate or something else that shines from them, but there's finally some emotion in his face. "You've gone cold, Tina. We were friends once."

I laugh. "Friends? You've locked me in a cell. Your dad

killed my mother. You come from a family of high-class gang-sters. What makes you think I'm cold, and not just smart?"

He works his jaw, like he's got a bone stuck in his throat. "If you're smart, you know you want this. You want the truth, just like I do. That part of you hasn't changed, Tina."

He stands up and opens the door to leave. When he looks back at me, his eyes have lost their glow. He's got his mask on again. "And there's one more thing I can offer. That camera you saw in the tunnel? The one that would have recorded your mother's murder? The footage is gone, but I know who has it. It may take a little time, but I can get it."

There it is. The bone. I catch my breath. "Who? Who has it?"

"I'll tell you once you agree to work with me. Think about it," he says. "I'll be back in an hour."

TEN

The concrete absorbs the noise of my feet as I pace the room.

The video, the video. Everything in black and white. Is he serious? Can he really get it? How long will it take? Is he lying? The video. Proof. Who has it? Why? Where is it?

The video, the video.

Ten steps to the door, eight steps to the cot, five steps to the table. Begin again.

I talk to myself:

If he's telling the truth, if he can get it, I will know for sure. I will see him kill her.

Stick to the plan, Tiny Girl. You are so close.

Am I? Seems to me I'm stuck in a pit.

He did it. He killed her. He deserves to pay.

Her killer deserves to pay. What if it isn't him?

It is him. You know what you saw.

But what if . . .

Shut up, one percent!

But even as I fight myself, I know Michael's right. Of course I want to know everything. What if I tell him no and give up the chance of seeing what I've been wondering about all these years?

What would the count do?

Could I play along with Michael without the Goondas knowing? Boyboy says it could take up to a week to decrypt Greyhill's data. Bug Eye knows we might have to wait awhile. What if I could play both sides? For just a little while. No one has to know.

A thought stops me in the middle of my stride. What if we didn't even get all the data off Greyhill's hard drive?

That doesn't matter. You broke in once, you can do it again.

Yeah, broke in and got caught.

Back and forth, I count off the room until maybe half an hour has gone by and still I can't decide.

You have a plan. It's a good plan: dirt, money, blood. You have worked a long time getting it right.

It won't work if I don't have the dirt.

No, the data transmitted. You have the dirt. Boyboy's decrypting it. In a few days, Omoko will start asking for his money. One way or another, you're going to have to get it for him. He won't care about Mama's murderer. If it isn't Mr. G, Omoko's not going to smile and say no big deal, Tiny Girl.

Never mind. It was only millions of shillings. But we'll just forget about it.

Yeah, I know.

Michael is lying. There is no video.

But . . . what if there is?

I'm so sure Mr. Greyhill did it. I'm so sure.

I'm so ninety-nine percent sure.

Mama would have told me to pray. Maybe to Saint Ignatius, who helps us make decisions. But I don't know his prayer. I only know one prayer—Catherine's. I haven't said another in five years.

Michael will be back any minute. I'm standing in front of a blank wall. I've been staring at it so long that little spots float in front of my eyes.

What do I do?

What is the rule?

I try to push everything else aside and concentrate on what is really important: punishing Mama's killer. Her real killer.

Her real killer is Roland Greyhill.

Unless he isn't.

Can I say no to Michael, knowing that there may be some final truth out there, and maybe I could have it? Would that video show me her murderer? Would it show me Mr. Greyhill pulling the trigger? Could I finally be sure? One hundred percent sure?

I thought I was getting better at being patient. I've waited five years, making my plans, practicing my revenge, like Mr. Omoko told me to. I've put all the steps into place, like the count. Can I possibly ask myself to wait longer?

I look around at my cell. Do I have any choice?

What will Michael do to me if I say no? I don't care so much about dying, but what about Kiki? What about making Mama's killer pay? None of that is happening while I'm stuck down here.

There is a rule for this moment, but I don't want to acknowledge it. I don't like this rule. It sticks in my throat. But it tells me in a low, persistent rumble, Too bad, Tiny Girl. You may not like the rules, but you still have to play by them.

Rule 10: If the stakes are high, play a long game.

Play a long, patient game.

I learned that from watching Bug Eye.

Bug Eye is different from the other Goondas. It's what makes him Mr. Omoko's right hand. I used to watch him because long after I'd figured out what motivated all the other guys, I still couldn't put a finger on what made him tick. You have to know what Goondas want so you don't become that thing. I'd figured out what Ketchup wanted my very first day. He got off on hurting people smaller and weaker than him. Simple. I never gave him the chance to hurt me again. But figuring out his brother was harder.

Bug Eye is the chillest cat you'll ever spy. He never looked at me like the other Goondas did. He has girls when he wants, but he never *looks* at any of them. Not really. Not like he wants them. He doesn't get a hard-on for cash either, or cars or fat gold chains. It's like he sees through all of it and understands exactly what it's really worth.

He doesn't want money. He doesn't want things. But it's not that he doesn't *want*. He wants. He wants in the same way I want my revenge. He's hungry—*starving to death*—for it. And the *it*? What is it? I finally saw one day when Mr. Omoko came around.

Omoko stopped to talk to his best lieutenant, and finished the conversation by reaching out and actually patting Bug Eye on the head like you would a favorite dog. No one saw but me; no one was supposed to. Mr. Omoko wouldn't have undermined his second in command in front of the rest of us. He just wanted to make his point. He might as well have said, See? This is power. You are close to it, but do not think for a moment that you have it. What you have, I have given you, and I will smile as I take it away.

Bug Eye didn't flinch or slap his master's hand away. That is why Bug Eye is different. I saw what Mr. Omoko overlooked, something familiar. The Goonda boss was looking for insubordination and didn't find it, but he should have looked deeper. I saw it from far away, in the quick clench and release of Bug Eye's hands, in the way he watched Mr. Omoko walk away and kept watching long after he was gone.

What Bug Eye wants became obvious to me that day. He wants something of Omoko's, and only Omoko's will do. It will be best if it's taken violently. Mr. Omoko wears his crown lightly, like he doesn't really care, but Bug Eye will cherish it, hold it as carefully as the head of a newborn baby. While he waits, Bug Eye will act like a good dog: loyal, devoted.

He trains Omoko's troops to be bullies and thugs. He leads bloody raids through other gangs' streets, expanding the Goonda empire. He sends the girls out to the corners and makes sure their earnings come back to him at the end of the night. He gives me names and addresses of homes and businesses to plunder. He dishes out punishment when we step out of line. If a Goonda starts getting ideas about who's in charge, Bug Eye is the one who sets him straight: a chat usually does it, a reminder of other ankles chained to concrete blocks. Blocks dropped off the edges of piers.

Sharks love Bug Eye.

He does whatever Omoko tells him. He dirties his hands so the big boss doesn't have to. He eats the scraps off the master's table and never complains. He keeps his brother close. He knows family will have his back when the time comes.

Bug Eye is patiently waiting for exactly the right moment to bite.

So I think about the count, and Bug Eye, and Mama, and what sort of revenge I need, and what I'm willing to do to get it. And when Michael comes back, I am ready.

ELEVEN

If we do this, I want out of the torture chamber," I say. "That's first."

Michael raises an eyebrow. "You're the only girl I know who thinks she can call shots while locked up. And it's not a torture chamber."

I raise an eyebrow back at him. "It's not a five-star hotel room."

Michael opens his mouth, but I'm already speaking. "Second thing: How long will it take to get the video?"

Michael avoids my eye. "I'm not sure. A couple of weeks?"

"You have five days."

"Five! Why?"

"You asked if I can keep the data from being released. I can, but only temporarily. People are waiting for it. People you don't want to make wait. Five days is generous."

"Eight," Michael grunts.

"I can ask for a week. But no promises."

Michael takes a deep breath. "Okay, fine. But we work from here. You can't go running off."

"In the torture chamber?"

"Of course not. In the house."

I recoil. "Are you serious? With your dad there? Absolutely not."

"You're crazy if you think I'm just letting you walk out of here," Michael says. "You're staying here. You'll be my guest."

"Your 'guest.' Right. And how exactly are you going to explain me to your parents?"

"I've got an idea," Michael says. "I'll work on it. They're not back until tomorrow."

The idea of staying here, *in Mr. G's house*, without killing him seems impossible. But I see Michael's point. I wouldn't trust me to leave and keep my word either. For a second I debate suggesting I just stay in the torture chamber.

The thing is, if I didn't get all the data, I'll need to get back into Mr. G's office. What better way to get in than as a welcome guest? I shudder. Okay, *welcome* is a strong word, if I know Mrs. Greyhill, but still.

"Fine," I say, "I'll consider being your guest. But I need access to my business partner."

"Why?"

"Because I do. He's the one I have to talk to about holding back the dirt on your dad."

"Is he a Goonda?"

"You got something against Goondas?"

"Well, I did just catch one of them robbing my house."

I roll my eyes. "He's not a Goonda. He's a walking brain."

"Okay, phone calls are fine."

I shake my head. "I have to see him in person. Out there, in town."

Michael scowls, but finally jerks his chin in agreement. "But I go with you."

"We'll see about that. And, Michael?" I pause to make sure he's paying attention. "You better not be lying about being able to get this video."

"I'm not. I wouldn't lie about something like that. You know me."

I ignore this last comment. "And you realize that it's probably going to show your father murdering my mother, right? You're gambling here as much as I am. Are you sure you're ready for that kind of truth?"

Michael looks queasy but nods.

"Because when I know for sure your dad did it, I won't hesitate. I'm going to make him pay."

Michael looks at me like he's suddenly seeing me for the first time.

Good. This is me.

He sticks his hand out. The pale crescent-moon scar on the inside of his arm shines against his skin. For a brief moment I balk, unable to lift my hand. I see myself at five, standing before him just like I am now, both our wounds fresh and bare. Who have I become? Michael has no idea how far I'll go to make his father pay.

But there is no going back now. I take his hand and shake it.

When Michael finally leads me into the free world, it's night again. It feels like I've been underground forever, but Michael tells me it's only Saturday. Well, technically Sunday morning already. My Friday-night visit with Kiki seems like a distant dream. We don't go back through the office. Instead Michael takes me farther down the tunnel and unlocks a door that leads outside. I have to resist shoving him out of the way when I taste my first breath of fresh air.

The door is hidden by a thick tumble of branches. I look up and see bougainvillea and jasmine vines climbing the wall the door is cut into. "We're below the terrace balcony," I say. Suddenly I realize exactly where we are. "We've come through the *mokele-mbembe* door."

Michael looks uncomfortable. "Yeah. I finally figured out what was behind it. Not a dragon, it turns out. Dad gave me a key a couple of years ago in case there's a break-in and we have to escape through the tunnel."

He pushes past the vines and raises his hands so the patrolling guard sees it's him and doesn't shoot. The idea is to pretend that I'm some loose lady friend he's been making out with in the bushes. Michael thinks the guards will all just pretend like they didn't see anything and let him take me in the house. When he explained it, I thought it sounded like a dumb plan, until it occurred to me that Michael is one of the richest boys in Sangui City, and not bad looking in a boarding-school sort of way. Maybe this has happened before. Maybe it happens often enough to be normal.

I try not to think about getting down and dirty with Michael, and instead comb my memory for what Philippe, the old gardener, had said about the *mokele-mbembe*. As kids, Michael and I knew every inch of the Greyhills' yard. There was no way a mysterious locked door half hidden in vines was getting past us. But when we asked Philippe what was inside, he explained that when he came from Congo many years ago he brought a *mokele-mbembe* with him in his pocket.

"What's a *mokele-mbembe*?" we asked.

"Oh, just a great and terrible monster that lives in the swamps and rivers and waits for children in the shallows. I caught a baby and he became my pet."

But the little lizard had grown into a great dragon, too big to keep in his cottage. Philippe had put him behind the door in a room with a pool to splash around in and strict instructions to eat intruders. When we asked if we could see him, Philippe simply said, "Are you sure? He thinks curious children are the most delicious of all."

And then, as Michael takes my hand and leads me, grinning sheepishly, into the beam of the guard's flashlight, the smell of the night garden dredges up more memories. Memories that had been so buried and lost that I can hardly believe how crisp and clear they are now. I suddenly remember other nights in our cottage down at the end of the yard when I would wake from nightmares and find my baby sister awake and fretting, my mother's bed empty. I tamped down my fear by picking up Kiki, by rocking her back to sleep, by telling her she was being a silly baby to fuss.

Mama would always be there in the morning, and she would shush me when I asked her where she had been. "I've been nowhere," she'd say. "You're imagining things." Eventually my night terrors stopped, and Kiki stayed asleep until dawn, and I forgot about Mama's absences. Until now, when I see the *mokele-mbembe* door. Is that where she had gone? Through the door to meet up with Mr. G, night after night? The thought of her standing here where I am now, wanting to go in that door, makes me feel ill.

The guards let us pass as expected. Michael puts his arm around my shoulder and winks at them, and they grin, and it's all I can do to not grab him and flip him onto his back in the dirt. Which I can do. Bug Eye taught me.

Michael walks me to a guest room, one of many. He stands in the doorway and watches while I examine my surroundings: heavy teak furniture, intricately cut in a classic Swahili style, wide windows dressed in silk to help hide the security bars. A huge bed covered in throw pillows and hung with a gauzy mosquito net. It looks like a maharaja's palace. The knickknacks on the dresser alone would put Kiki through school for a year.

Finery or not, I want to go home to my roof so bad I can feel it in my teeth, but I ask, "When your parents get home, how are you going to explain me being here?"

"Let me worry about that."

"You're not going to rat me out to your dad, are you?"

"Why would I have taken you out of the basement if I was just going to hand you over?"

"You caught a thief. Bet he'd be proud of his little boy."

Michael doesn't rise to my needling. "If I did, would you give back the stuff you stole?"

"No."

Michael sounds like he's explaining something very simple to a child. "So why would I do that? If we're going to figure this out together, you're going to have to start trusting me."

I don't like his tone, but he's got a point. I hold my hand out. "If we're trusting each other, give me my phone back."

"What? No way."

"Hypocrite." I smirk. "How am I supposed to make arrangements to have your dad's data held without it?"

Michael eyes me. Finally he heaves a sigh and fishes in his pocket. "Fine." He slaps it into my palm. "Nothing funny, all right? We have a deal."

"I am never funny," I say.

"Yeah, I'm getting that."

I start to close the door to my room. "I'm going to make a call. In private. Nonnegotiable. I'll come and find you in a few minutes. Don't worry, I'm not calling in the cavalry."

Michael looks like he wants to argue, but finally says, "My room is down the hall, third door on the right."

"I know where your room is, Michael."

Something passes over his face, but before I can decide

what it is, he turns and walks away. I shut the door behind him, lock it, and stand there for a second, trying to hear whether he's creeping back to listen. That's what I would do. I can't hear anything, but I go to the attached bathroom, close the door, and start running water into the gleaming white sink just in case.

Boyboy picks up on the first ring. "Oh my God, Tina, is that you? Are you—"

There's a scuffle and I hear, "Tiny? Where the hell you at?"

Mavi. Not whose voice I wanted to hear. "Hey, Ketchup," I say quietly.

I can hear Ketchup swearing. "Finally."

More shuffling, and then, "Yo, Tiny Girl, what's up?" Bug Eye says. I'm on speaker. His words are easy, but his voice has that note to it. I hate that note. I can hear blood in it. "Spill, Tiny. You in lockdown or somethin'?"

I look around the bathroom. It's all white marble and gold fixtures and fluffy towels like stacks of sea foam. "Sort of. I'm only talking to you, Bug Eye," I say.

I hear Ketchup complaining, but then it's just Bug Eye's voice, close and clear in my ear. "All right. So where are you?"

I'm glad I'm not standing under Bug Eye's gaze. Stronger people than me have broken down and wet their pants under those eyes. "I'm still inside."

Bug Eye says nothing.

"But it's okay," I add quickly. "The son—Michael—he's not going to turn me over. Not to the cops, and not to Mr. G's guys."

Silence.

"I haven't said anything about you or anything else. You know I won't." Not a complete lie . . . "He had me locked up, but I played him. He let me out. He trusts me, sort of."

"This is Greyhill's kid, your little boyfriend from back in the day?"

"Um . . . yeah, my friend. I mean, it's not like that anymore; he's not—"

"Listen," Bug Eye interrupts, "Boyboy isn't sure we got everything off the hard drive."

My stomach sinks. "I can get back in. He wants me to stay here and, you know, hang out for old times' sake."

There's a long pause. "You still have the equipment you need?"

"He broke the USB thing, but I can get another one from Boyboy," I say.

"Boyboy's going to stay here with us until he figures out what we've got."

Shonde. Boyboy made me promise I wouldn't let him get sucked in this deep. He's probably freaking out right now, having to stay at the warehouse with the Goondas alone. But I know the blame for screwing up the heist lies with me, in the Goondas' eyes. I don't have a lot of room to ask for favors. As long as Bug Eye is there, I tell myself, Ketchup will behave.

"Once Boyboy's done, let him go home so he can get a new adapter for me," I say, careful to keep my voice level so it doesn't sound like I'm trying to boss Bug Eye around.

"Are you gonna have a problem getting back in the office if

we need you to?" Bug Eye asks. "That Michael kid's not going to be watching your ass?"

"I can do it. I won't mess things up this time."

There's a pause where I can hear Bug Eye breathing. Gears are turning in his mind, working through everything, letting the plan reconfigure to his satisfaction. "Okay," he finally says. "See that you don't."

TWELVE

After I get off the line with Bug Eye, I wait five minutes and then send Boyboy a text: *777*. It's our code for *call now*. I wait, tapping my foot. Michael's going to start wondering where I am soon.

I get a text back: *Paper covers rock.*

"Come on, Boyboy, I need to talk to you," I whisper. *Paper covers rock* is his code for *Not safe/No can do*. But given that he's stuck at the warehouse with a bunch of thugs, I get it.

Boyboy: *Scissors.*

Good. He'll meet in person (scissors = legs). That must mean that Bug Eye will let him walk. I want to talk to him alone.

Boyboy: *Pick up four bananas from the corner shop.*

This code is supposed to look kind of simple, like, if anyone sees it they'll think maybe it means meet him at four o'clock at a particular shop. Really, I'm going to have to consult yesterday's ferry schedule to find out exactly when to meet him. I already know where. It should be sometime tomorrow, and hopefully he'll have good news by then. Maybe he's just playing it safe, telling Bug Eye that he isn't sure all the data transferred. I'm about to go to Michael's room when I get one last text.

Boyboy: *Glad ur okay.*

I find Michael on the floor of his room, leaning against his bed, his laptop open in front of him. I close the door behind me and take in his room: the huge television; the gaming equipment; the posters of bands I've never heard of; photos of Michael on rugby teams.

I sit only as close to him as I have to in order to see what he's looking at on his computer.

"So where is the video?"

He closes the lid. "You're demanding, you know that?"

"Come on, Michael. At least tell me who has it."

Michael studies me for a beat. His lashes would make any girl envious. I find an odd heat tickling the back of my neck. Seriously, Tina? You must have a touch of Stockholm syndrome to be noticing pretty boy's eyes. I cross my arms over my chest. "So, who?"

Michael takes a deep breath. "David Mwika."

My mouth falls open. "What? I thought he was dead! You know where he is?"

Mwika was Mr. Greyhill's head of security, up until the night of my mother's murder. After that night, gone. He gave his testimony to the police and hasn't been seen since. Off the radar. Believe me, I've looked for him. Boyboy's spent hours searching for some trace of him online. He vanished.

"Wait," I say, frowning. "Mwika didn't kill my mother. You know that, right?"

"Yeah, I know. I've got the surveillance footage of him playing cards in the security booth all night. Look." He opens his computer and starts to search.

"I've seen it," I say, waving him off.

"You have? How?"

"It's in her police file."

"How do you have her police—"

I interrupt, "Why do you think Mwika has the footage?"

Michael's gaze drops. "Because that's what my dad said when I asked him about your mom's murder. He said he didn't do it, but that video showing who *did* is gone."

My excitement crashes, bursts into flame, and dies.

I open and close my mouth, twice, before I can respond. "You're an even bigger idiot than I thought you were!" I sputter, jumping to my feet. "Of course the murderer would say the proof that gets him off the hook is gone, and the one guy who mysteriously disappeared that night took it! How convenient!" I let out a quiet scream of frustration. "I was so stupid to listen to you. Mwika is dead! He's shark shit! And that footage is gone. Your dad erased it." I start for the door. "I can't believe I agreed to this. I'm out of here."

"Hey! Wait!" Michael says, getting to his feet too. "We made a deal!" He catches my arm.

"Deal's off! You're working with rotten intel." I try to shake him off. "You said you could get the footage, but you lied!"

"Stop! I didn't lie. You're letting your blindness about my dad cloud your judgment!"

"Let me go!" I try wrenching my arm from his grasp again, but he's too strong.

"Not until you listen to me!"

"I'm done listening to you," I say. "Let me go or I'll scream!"

"Tina!" Michael says. "Would you just calm down?"

I stop struggling but stay ready to bolt. "Why would Mwika even want the footage, unless it was to . . . I don't know, blackmail your dad?"

"Maybe there's something else on there he didn't want anyone to see. Maybe Mwika was involved."

"You said security didn't know about the tunnel. That means he wouldn't have known about the camera."

"They don't know *now*, but Dad fired everyone after your mom's murder. Before then, Mwika knew about it, and maybe he told the killer. Maybe he *was* the killer. Maybe that other footage of him playing cards was staged."

I let my arm go loose. It's true. Even if it wasn't Mwika who killed her, he could have been involved somehow. If any of what Michael is saying is true, that is.

Michael slowly releases me. "It's worth tracking him down, right?" he asks. "I've got money, and I have a feeling he needs it."

"Why?"

"Because of where he is."

"And where is that?"

Michael folds his arms over his chest. "Come on, Tina, how dumb do you think I am? I tell you now and you're gone."

I narrow my eyes at him. "I think you're pretty dumb. Do you really know where he is? Or did you get that info from Daddy too?"

"I know where he is," Michael says. "Don't worry. He's just . . . hard to reach. But I'll get in touch with him." He walks back over to the bed and sits on it. "Come on, you made a deal. See it through."

My brain tells me I'm an idiot if I listen to him. He could be totally lying. And if he's not lying, his father's almost certainly lied to him. Almost certainly. Stupid little one percent of doubt. It will not let my feet steer me out the door. What if Mwika really does have the video? What do I lose by staying until Michael can contact him?

Your head, if you don't get Omoko his money on time.

Your pride.

I let out an enormous sigh. "Fine."

Ridiculous. You're ridiculous, Tiny Girl. If he were anyone other than Michael, you'd be gone. But as much as I hate to admit it, other than me, Michael seems to be the only person in the world who's ever been interested in what really happened to Mama that night. Even before we made this deal, he asked his father about her murder. That took some stones. Maybe he's blind to believe him, but at least Michael bothered to wonder.

I slowly sit back down on the carpet.

"All right," Michael says carefully, like if he gets too excited I'll bolt. "Now, don't go crazy, but I have a suggestion. While I'm working on Mwika, we can still do our own investigating. If we've only got a week, then maybe we should do this properly and lay everything out logically. Maybe the video shows the murderer; maybe it doesn't. We can still go ahead and figure out who the suspects would be. Then if the video doesn't show us what we need, we might have other leads to follow."

I make a face. "You want to play detective?"

"Don't you want to know *why* your mom was murdered, not just who did it?"

I bite my tongue before I can snap that I know pretty well who did it and why. It's too late in the evening to start down that road again.

Michael picks up a folder from his bed and begins leafing through it. Despite myself, I edge closer, trying to see what he's doing. "What is that?"

He pulls out a single document and holds it to his chest so I can't see. "After I talked to the guards last night, before I came back to you, I went to make sure Dad's office was in order. His computer had frozen and I found this still up on his screen. I printed a copy before I shut it off." He finally hands it to me. "I, um, I thought you might want it."

My mouth goes dry.

It's the photo I had found just before Michael caught me. I stare at it hungrily.

"It's your mom, right?" He drops his eyes. He knows it is.

See? Can you blame me for getting distracted? My mother and another girl smile back at me radiantly. They are young, in school uniforms, with their arms twined around each other's waists. Flowers bloom behind them. I have no memory of my mother ever smiling like that. The other girl looks mischievous, like she's flirting with whoever is taking the photo. An ache wells in my throat. Other than her old refugee ID, I have no photos of Mama.

"I tried to see what else was on the hard drive, but everything was password protected." Michael waits. "Who's the girl with her?"

I finally look up. "Everything on the hard drive is encrypted," I say briskly. "My business partner is working on it." I carefully fold the paper in half and then quarters and tuck it inside my bra.

"Hey, that was for the case!"

"I'm not throwing it away, Michael. And don't call it *the case*."

"You don't know who the other girl is?"

"No."

"But—"

"I *said* I don't know." I feel the paper burning against my chest. It sounds like I'm lying, but I really don't know. A friend? A relative? "What else do you have in that folder?" I ask.

Michael hesitates, but eventually picks the papers back up. "Not enough. I was trying to find someone to bribe so I can get your mom's police file, but it sounds like you've already got it."

"Nothing useful in there."

"I still want to see it." He flips through the folder, stopping on a thick bundle. "Do you have your immigration file?"

It takes me a second to figure out what he means. "Our refugee file? You have it? How did you get that so fast?"

He avoids my eye. "I've had it."

I frown. "Why?"

"A year ago I tried looking for you and Kiki," Michael says. "I tried to find your family, where you might have gone . . ."

"How did you get our file?"

"Being a spoiled rich kid has its perks. You can buy things." He glances at me from the corner of his eye. "Couldn't find anything other than this, though. No one here, no one in your village in Congo, nothing."

"You know what village I come from?"

"It's in the file."

"What else is in there?" I demand, reaching for it.

He keeps it above his head. "Dates of birth, photos, stuff like that. And all the notes from your mother's hearing to get legal status. She had to tell them why she left Congo to prove she was a refugee."

"It's all there? Why she left?" I try not to look surprised. I don't know why, but it never occurred to me that my file at the United Nations' refugee office might have useful information. Mainly because they always seem so useless there. I've had to go and get Kiki's and my refugee documents renewed a couple of times since Mom died, but they just ask me questions about where we live and if we're in school. When we go, I comb my hair and wear clothes that cover my tattoos, and tell them Kiki goes to private boarding school on scholarship, and that I stay with a nice family and go to a public school because I'm not as clever as my little sis, but otherwise I am just fantastic. And I smile and they smile, and when they ask, I tell them no, I'm sure I'm not "engaging in survival sex" or "resorting to negative coping strategies" or doing whatever else they call *prostitution* and *selling drugs* to make them sound nicer.

Since they never have to actually do any work on my case, they like me. We get our papers stamped, and we're on our way. I wouldn't even bother with the whole thing if Kiki didn't need the documents for school. My Goonda tattoos are usually good enough ID for anyone who matters.

But I had no idea that Mama told them what happened to her. No one at the UN has ever asked me why we left Congo.

"You have the whole file?" I lean over, trying to pluck it from his hands. His arm is longer, though. I reach higher, coming closer to his chest than I'd really prefer. He is warm and smells spicy and boyish. Good boyish, not bad boyish.

Pull yourself together, Tina.

"The schools it says you go to—they're wrong, aren't they?" Michael asks. Our faces are very close.

I give up on the folder and pull back. "So? How do you know they're wrong?"

Anger finally sparks in Michael's green eyes. "Look, you're the one who left without saying anything to any of us, Tina. I've been wondering about you guys for five years."

We glare at each other. He suddenly doesn't seem cute at all.

"Where *is* Kiki?"

"She's fine," I say stiffly.

"But where is she?"

"It's not important."

"Come on, Tina, she's my sister as much as she is yours."

"She is not!" I say.

"Of course she is! Same dad, remember? Just because you took her and ran off doesn't mean she's not."

As much as I want to argue, I know he's at least technically right. But she'll never be his sister like she is mine. I finally let out a long breath. "She's in a convent school. Here in Sangui. She's safe." I pause. "Smartest kid in her class. She's on scholarship."

"Why don't you go there?"

Because I'm too busy working out how to get back at your father, I think, but instead say, "Because it's one scholarship per family."

"We would have paid for you," Michael says.

I stand up quickly. I'm starting to feel like a trapped animal. "Look, can we get back to why we're here? You and Kiki may share a father, but where she goes to school doesn't have anything to do with Mama's murder."

"Fine," he says coolly. He pulls a thick sheaf of papers out of the folder and hands it to me.

I grab it greedily and sink back onto the floor. I flip quickly through the pages, trying to take it all in at once. I pause when I get to the photos. There's one of Mama, and one of me as a six-year-old, both of us with messy hair and hollows in our cheeks. I go slower. There's a close-up photo of the burns and slashes on Mama's arms, then a page titled "Persecution History."

Michael settles down beside me, reading over my shoulder as I scan the first lines:

> Principal applicant [PA] is a single female of Nyanga ethnicity from North Kivu, Democratic Republic of Congo [DRC]. PA meets the definition of a refugee, having demonstrated that she fled her country of origin owing to a well-founded fear of being persecuted for reasons of nationality and membership in a particular social group [victim of ethnic-based violence and Congolese woman at risk] and is unable or, owing to such fear, unwilling to return to DRC. [1951 Convention Relating to the Status of Refugees, Article 1[A][2] and its 1967 Protocol.] Her fear is grounded in current objective conditions as demonstrated by recent country of origin information contained herein concerning the political and human rights situation in DRC.

I skip past more legal mumbo jumbo and read,

> She is widowed. Her husband was killed in an attack on her village —

Widowed? That's not right. I look at Michael. "This is a little personal. Do you mind?"

He squirms. "I've already read it all anyway." He shifts back to sitting on his bed and picks up his laptop.

I look back at the file. My mother never married. The only thing she ever said about my dear old papa was that I should be glad not to know him. I don't *think* she married, anyway. She definitely never said anything about a husband in front of me, and she hadn't called herself a widow.

I go on reading. Other details are off. "We're from Kasisi, not Walikale," I say under my breath. Are these mistakes or did she lie to the UN? Why would she do that? Confused, I plunge on, reading feverishly.

> Her village was attacked many times throughout her youth, both by various ethnically based groups of antigovernment militia including Mayi-Mayi and the M23 group, as well as by government soldiers. Rebels and government soldiers alike would raid her village for food and livestock to feed their troops. Often they would hurt or kill villagers in the process. Villagers were abducted and forced to join the militias or act as slaves for them . . .

So far, so normal. That's a story everybody from there knows. The unpaid government soldiers are bad, and the militia groups are just a little bit worse.

> On the material day, the applicant's village came under severe attack, whereby she was forced to flee with her small daughter. Her husband was killed in the attack.

> Together with her daughter, she fled the same day to Bukavu —

I stop, reread the paragraph, trying to see if I've missed something. "That's not right," I mutter. "They left out the whole thing about . . . Or did she not tell them . . . ?"

"What?" Michael asks.

I start when he speaks. I've almost forgotten he's here, I'm concentrating so hard on trying to match what's on the page with my few memories. I glance up at him, then go back to reading.

"You're driving me crazy, here, Tina. What are you mumbling about? Spill."

Do I tell him or not? Finally I just say, "They got our village name wrong."

"That's it?"

I look back down. "Yeah."

Why explain that what I remember and what's here are two different things? I can't trust Michael, and besides, this probably has nothing to do with Mama's murder.

Michael isn't buying it. "Tina, if you see something that might help us figure out—"

"You got kicked out of school, didn't you?"

The abrupt question surprises him, like I hoped it would. "That's why you're in Sangui, not in Switzerland, isn't it? This isn't a holiday. I checked to make sure you wouldn't be here."

"I-I didn't get kicked out. It's just a suspension."

"For what?"

He pauses, his jaw working. "Fighting." Then, "You're changing the subject."

"Beating people up, huh? Like father, like son," I say, scanning the rest of the page. There's not much more in our persecution history. Details about us coming to Sangui, but no mention of Mama finding work with Mr. G. The notes just say she was supporting herself on handouts from a church and sometimes earning money by watching other people's children and washing clothes. The interview must have been before she went to work for him. Or maybe she left that part out too.

"The other guy called me a mulatto."

I look up. The mask is off. It's obvious what Michael is thinking: He's pissed. For some reason I blush and look away, like it was me who called him a name. "Fair enough," I say.

Michael sighs and shuts the lid of his laptop. "Let's call it a night, okay? It's almost three in the morning, and my parents are supposed to be back early. They'll be here for breakfast before church."

A chill runs down my neck. I'd almost forgotten that in a few short hours I'm going to have to come face-to-face with Mr. Greyhill. Before I can suggest that I just hide in the closet and hope the maids don't come cleaning, Michael says, "Here's your story. I've got it all worked out: I'll tell my parents I ran into you at the airport on my way back."

"The airport? Why? I've never even been to the airport."

"You were on your way back from boarding school."

Now I have to laugh. "Boarding school? Michael, I didn't

make it past primary. I only know how to read because I steal books from rich people."

"You'd rather explain what you've been doing hanging around Sangui all this time?"

"I'll say I've been, I dunno, living with cousins or something?"

"This will all be easier if you're cleaned up and respectable. Nothing like a European boarding school to impress Mom." Michael looks me over. "You'll have to cover up those tattoos, though. And we're going to have to tell Dad first. He'll want you to stay, and he'll make Mom agree."

I raise an eyebrow. "Why would he want me to stay?"

Michael gives me an exasperated sigh. "Because he was worried when you left too. He cares about you and Kiki."

"Right."

Michael ignores this. "Like I was saying, we'll get Dad on our side first. Otherwise Mom'll figure out some way to get rid of you. You know how she is. She acts whiter than Dad."

I do remember. How could I forget all those looks she used to give my mother, or especially me when Michael and I were caught playing together? Mrs. Greyhill is essentially Sangui royalty. Real estate mostly, but they dabble in politics, media, shipping. She doesn't take kindly to refugee trash like me.

Not to mention that whole her-husband-having-a-kid-with-my-mother thing.

Oh yeah, this is going to be real fun.

"I'm thinking you should say you go to school in Paris," Michael muses. "They never go to Paris. You can make up whatever you want. You can say you're on scholarship, like Kiki. You speak French, right?"

"No, I was five when I left Congo."

"Well . . . it doesn't matter; my parents don't speak French either."

I slump. "But I don't know anything about boarding school. Or *Paris*. And I don't have any clothes or anything."

Michael waves my protests away. "Just stick to the basics. Parisians are rude. You're on the prelaw track. Your classes are interesting, but World History is too Eurocentric."

I stare at him. "Euro-what?"

"And Jenny's got loads of clothes. The closet in your room is full of her stuff. Just take something; she has so much, no one will notice."

I put my hands on my hips. "I'll just go home, and you can come out and meet me in secret somewhere."

The idea of pretending to be a boarding-school kid sounds bad enough, but being around Mr. G for days, maybe as long as a week? I won't be able to live under the same roof that long without murdering him.

But Michael shakes his head. "Mom's already made it clear I'm grounded because of the suspension thing. I can get away for a few hours at a time maybe, but otherwise I'm stuck here."

"I don't know . . ."

Think about the first step in your plan, Tiny. You don't know whether you got all the dirt off his hard drive. You told Bug Eye you would stay here in case you have to break back into Mr. G's office. This is your chance to get in under their noses.

"Come on," Michael says. "It's only for a few days. Until we figure this whole thing out with your mom, and then I promise you can go back to looking and smelling like a Goonda."

"Hey!" I glower at him.

He gives me a half smile. "You do kind of smell."

I bite back a retort. A proper boarding-school girl wouldn't punch someone, even if he deserved it. I just have to stay until I get the data. Then I'll reevaluate. And if I'm being honest, maybe there's even a teeny tiny part of me that finds the idea of pulling a con on the Greyhills a little thrilling. "I'll think about it," I say, standing up and walking to the door. "If I'm still here in the morning, you'll know my answer."

"Deal's a deal, Tina," Michael says. His tone is light, but I can hear the edge in his voice. "You can't leave. You want to get to Mwika and that video, you have to stay here and see this thing through with me."

I look past him at his room and think about how I'm going to take all of this away: his nice house, his toys, his fancy boarding school, his ability to make deals and promises . . . even his father. I can't tell if it's nerves churning my belly or something else. Guilt? No. I push the thought away.

"All right," I say. "Prelaw and Euro-thingy it is."

THIRTEEN

After Mama and I settled in at the Greyhills', one of the other maids explained about the strangler fig. There was one that shaded our staff cottages, and Michael and I were playing in it, climbing the twisting basket of the tree's limbs, while Mama and the other maid shelled beans.

"When it is young and slender," the maid said, "the strangler fig creeps up on a proud, strong tree that has its nose in the air and sings to it, caresses it, feeds it sweet figs, and wraps its arms around it. Over time the fig's embrace grows tighter and tighter, as it slinks up the other tree and spreads out into the light. Eventually the proud tree inside realizes it's being choked, but by then it's too late. That's why you sometimes see the hollow stranglers. The tree inside has rotted away. The strangler fig is clever, but evil," the maid concluded.

"No," my mother interjected, and snapped the apron she

had tied over her growing belly. The scraps from the beans she was shelling scattered. The chickens came running to her feet, bowing and scraping like she was a god.

"It is not evil," she said. "It is just a tree. It finds a way. It survives."

I wake with a start. For a second I can't remember where I am. I struggle out of the tangle of sheets and blankets. It's late. I've slept too long in this too-comfortable bed. The sun is coming in through the window at a firm mid-morning angle.

The smell of coffee and toast fried in butter is rich in the room. I hear voices. The Greyhills are back, I realize, and my insides twist up like worms. I curse at myself for sleeping in. That was *not* part of my plan. The plan was definitely to get up early and be ready to meet the Greyhills, not straggle down after everyone's been awake for hours with creases from the bedclothes on my face.

Michael had said his parents would probably have breakfast and head straight to church. Maybe I can avoid them until they're gone? But no, that might raise suspicion, and besides, if I'm really going to stay here, I have to face them sometime.

I tug my jeans and T-shirt on, and pat at my hair. As I walk toward the door, I pass a mirror and halt. Oh boy.

"You're not fooling anyone, Tina," I tell my reflection.

There are circles under my eyes. My short hair is clean, but flat on one side. My shapeless, black street clothes make me look exactly like the burglar I am, not anywhere close to being a boarding-school girl.

Michael said there were clothes in the closet—his sister Jenny's spillover. With a sigh, and shedding my shirt and jeans again as I walk, I head for the closet and heave the doors open.

Spillover doesn't quite cover it. More like *explosion*.

The closet is crammed with designer dresses, shirts, and jeans. Sparkles and flowers. Neon and leopard print. Gem-toned silk and virginal white cotton. A rainbow of traditional *kanga*-print dresses for social events. Shoes, dozens of them, litter the floor. Six-inch heels and strappy gold thong things. Some of them look like they've never even been worn.

Knowing full well I might never escape, I plunge in. Jenny is two years younger than me, and I remember her as a little kid with a sticky face who tagged after Michael and me and demanded to be included in our games, but this closet does not say *child*. I suppose at fourteen she's already got the body I'll never have. Swoops and curves are what these dresses require. I wrestle through the racks until I find a green blouse that will cover my tattoos and jeans that don't have glitter on them. The clothes are way tighter than anything I'm used to, and I tug at the soft fabric, uncomfortable at how much of my body is now revealed. But they seem to be the most modest things Jenny owns, which is maybe why I find them in the back of the closet.

I'm at least already clean. I ran a bath for myself last night, and I have to admit, it was a luxury I could get used to. On my roof I collect rainwater for chilly bucket baths. It's not so bad, but hot water out of the tap is a small miracle, and given what I'm about to walk into, I need a little miraculousness.

I used pretty much every bottle of smelly stuff I could find in the bathroom. Some of them twice. I realized as I soaked that this is why rich people smell different: They smell rich. Not like flowers; like *botany*. Washing and conditioning my hair was epic. The dirt under my nails turned out not to be dirt, but a stain, and I had to scrub until my fingers were raw. Only the thought of Mrs. Greyhill's nose wrinkling if she smelled the street on me kept me going. After I got out, I saw that I'd left a ring of grime around the white porcelain.

Once I'm dressed I kick my old duds under the bed, where I hope the maid neglects to clean. Then I turn to the mirror and look at the effect. Not terrible, I admit. I pull my shoulders out of a slouch and pick through my hair until it looks okay. Braids would be better, but I'll have to manage with a short 'fro. I check to make sure none of my ink is showing. I put on a perky smile.

I have manners. I gossip with my girlfriends about boys. Ask me where I want to go to university.

For a second, I despair. I can see the wild animal behind my eyes, frantic for a way out, all teeth and claws.

I pull the photo of my mother as a girl out of my pocket and stare at it. Then I look back in the mirror. I lean closer, searching for her in my reflection.

"You can do this," I whisper. "You just have to lie and smile. Smile and lie."

And with that rousing pep talk, I put the photo back in my pocket, open the door, and step out.

• • •

Hovering around the corner from the dining room, I listen to muted conversation and the refined clatter of silver on china. The voices make my heart thump.

Mrs. Greyhill is saying, "It would have been better, obviously, if Michael had asked permission *before* he brought her here, but . . ."

I hear footsteps behind me and swivel.

"You slept late," Michael says.

"What time is it?" I ask, frowning and tugging at the cuffs of my blouse.

"Almost ten. Come on," he says, forcing a smile. "They're looking forward to seeing you." He takes my elbow and without further ado steers me into the dining room. He clears his throat to announce me. And suddenly I'm standing before the Greyhills like a peasant being presented to the king and queen. For a second, no one moves.

Mr. G's coffee cup hovers just before his lips. He wears a suit and tie. He stares at me like I have two heads. Mrs. G, straightened hair in a perfect twist, pearls in her ears, looks exactly like I remember her, beautiful and severe. Maybe a bit more pinched and pulled. Her face is a portrait of polite malice. The mahogany table spreads out under their elbows like a black pool. It is so shiny that the crystal and china reflect in it like little white boats.

I suddenly feel like my feet have grown two sizes larger. My neck prickles with sweat and I'm worried that my beating heart looks like a trapped frog under my shirt.

And then Mr. G is standing up and walking toward me.

I am rooted to the spot. It seems to take forever for him to come around the table. Mrs. Greyhill watches him. He is very pale, tall and square. His shoulders, his jaw, his ears, all cut, strict angles. His eyes are deep set, sharply green, like Michael's—almost alien. They bore into me.

He extends his hand for a formal handshake. I take it in my clammy palm, trying to remember to keep breathing. I am so close to him, so close to making him pay. He's right here in front of me. My hand is touching his hand. I can smell his expensive cologne. I could pick up a knife off the table right now and plunge it into his chest. Michael tenses beside me like a stretched rubber band.

"Hello, Christina," Mr. Greyhill finally says. "We're so glad you're here."

"Thank you so much for having me," I hear myself saying.

Michael nudges me with a chair and I jump. He clears his throat, and I figure out what he's trying to do and let him scoot it under me. Is this how it's done? I feel so awkward. My eyes flicker over the dishes in front of me. Everything is edged in gold and paper-thin. Oh God, why are there so many utensils?

Mrs. G watches me and takes a tiny sip of black tea. "Clotilde," she says over the rim. "Will you serve our guest, please?"

A maid appears immediately at my elbow, and pretends like she's not sneaking glances at me as she puts food on my plate. News must have already reached her that the murdered maid's daughter is back. Clotilde arranges eggs, toast, and fruit on my plate. As she pours my tea, I see Michael very deliberately take his napkin and place it in his lap. I copy him.

"I'm . . ." Mr. Greyhill begins, then looks at his wife. "*We* are so happy to see you. It's been a very long time."

"Thank you, Mr. Greyhill," I say, and force out, "It's good to see you all too. Thank you for letting me stay."

Michael glances up nervously at his mother like he's waiting for her to burst into flames. I grip my knee below the table with my fingernails and remind myself to smile. I do and feel ridiculous, and then I don't know what to do, so I grab for my teacup and end up dribbling the first burning swallow down my shirt. I flush with embarrassment.

"Michael says you'll be staying with us for a few days?" Mrs. Greyhill asks, watching me fumble with my napkin from under smoothly arched brows.

"If that's all right with you," I say.

"Well, Michael is supposed to ask us before he invites guests—"

"Of course it is," Mr. Greyhill says quickly. His face gives no indication of whether my stay is pleasing to him or not.

"Yes, you're very welcome. *Karibu*," Mrs. Greyhill murmurs with a thin smile. "But who were you going to stay with otherwise?"

"My aunt," I blurt, at the same time Michael says, "Her cousin."

We glance at each other, and I stutter, "She's my cousin, but I call her auntie."

"I persuaded her to stay here instead," Michael says.

How does she do that? I wonder, watching Mrs. Greyhill. Smile with her mouth and send daggers with her eyes? She's hard to look away from.

"Is it a school holiday for you, dear?" she asks.

"Um, yes, madam."

"Funny. I wonder why Michael and Jenny don't have the same one."

I give her what I hope is an innocent little shrug. "I think it's a French holiday."

"Ah. I see. The French do like their holidays, don't they? Not much work ethic."

God, I wish she would stop staring at me. "Yes, madam. I mean, no." I look down at my food in great concentration like I've never seen an egg before. I rub my sweaty palms on my thighs again and try to channel my little sister. She would be just fine here. She would know how to act. The nuns are strict, and I bet they teach her proper table manners. Maybe she'd even just have it in her DNA, some natural knowledge of how to sit at breakfast with her father, which utensil to use, how to talk to the Greyhills on their level.

I should eat something. I start to pick up a fork, only to realize they're all slightly different. Is that on purpose? I sneak another glance at Michael and take the one he's taken.

Mrs. Greyhill delicately pushes her food around on her plate. "That's a lovely shirt. You know, I think Jenny has one just like it."

The fork jumps out of my grip and clatters on the plate

before I can catch it. Sweat starts to gather in the lovely shirt's armpits. "I . . ."

But Michael steps in. "The airline lost Tina's luggage, Mom. I told her to borrow something of Jenny's."

Mrs. Greyhill's eyes travel to the tea stain I've created on my chest. "Oh."

"Take whatever you need," Mr. Greyhill says, with a pointed look at his wife. "Please, Christina, make yourself at home."

"Thank you. I'm not sure when they'll deliver my bag—"

"If they find your stuff at all," Michael interjects. "I found her in baggage claim looking like a lost puppy."

A spark of anger replaces some of my nervousness. I grab on to it and give Michael a smile. "I wasn't lost, just my bags."

Mrs. Greyhill finally looks away from me to a thin gold watch on her wrist. "Christina, will you join us for services?"

Again, Michael speaks up for me. "I don't think Christina's up for church. We'll stay here."

Mrs. Greyhill blinks her long false eyelashes. "I would like for you to attend with us, Michael. Christina may borrow something of Jenny's to wear."

"No, it's fine, Sandrine," Mr. Greyhill says. "Let them stay here."

I can tell Mrs. Greyhill wants to protest, but not in front of me.

"Michael," Mr. Greyhill says. He is looking at the newspaper now.

Michael stiffens in his seat. "Yes, sir?"

"You will use today to finish your school assignments."

"I—there are a lot of—"

Mr. Greyhill shakes out his paper, looks at his son over the front page.

Michael swallows. "Yes, sir."

In the silence that follows, Mrs. Greyhill manages to press her smile back on. "So, Christina," she says. "Abroad on scholarship, Michael tells us. So fortunate for you."

"I hardly believe it myself," I agree, glancing at Michael.

"And your sister, Catherine? She's well?" Mr. G asks, putting the paper down to carefully stir his coffee.

Her name catches me off guard. I hadn't even thought about what to say about Kiki. I want to kick myself. Finally, I nod. "She's in school here in Sangui. She has a scholarship too."

"Both of you with anonymous benefactors," Mrs. Greyhill says. "You're so fortunate. Most orphans have such hard lives."

I resist climbing over the beautiful mahogany table to throttle her. "Yes, madam."

"We wondered what had happened to you," Mr. Greyhill says.

"I should have written," I say, attempting to collect myself. "But after my mother . . . I just wanted to forget." I rally everything I've got to give them my best brave-little-girl smile.

For a second, Mr. Greyhill's composure is broken and his face goes oddly slack. "Of course."

Mrs. G is motionless, but I can see the tendons in her neck straining. "Clotilde," she says, loud enough to make me start.

Clotilde pops around the door, a little too quickly. She's been eavesdropping, I realize. I'm going to have to be careful about that.

She hurries forward with the tea, but Mrs. Greyhill raises a manicured hand to stop her. "Tell the driver we're ready. I'll be in the foyer." Without another word or look at her husband or son, she stands and walks out of the room, her heels a clipped staccato.

The sound of her angry shoes sends a small, delicious thrill through me. Mr. Greyhill wipes his mouth, his shoulders sagging just a fraction. He stands too.

In a sudden moment of inspiration, I rise out of my chair as they leave, like I've seen people do in movies. Michael watches me like he's worried I might do something he'll regret.

But I just smile. After all, I'm a mannered young lady. "Have a nice time at services, Mr. Greyhill."

"Thank you, Christina," Mr. G says, before following his wife out of the dining room.

"Say a prayer for my mother," I say softly to the space that he leaves when he's gone.

FOURTEEN

Rule 11: If you want to go forward, sometimes you need to flip all the way over backward first.

Mama used to say I needed role models. I think she was talking about the saints. But if you are a thief, these are your heroes: Catwoman. Robin Hood, obviously. But not just them. There are others you should know: Phoolan Devi, vengeance-delivering "bandit queen" of India. Zheng Shi, captain of three hundred ships on the South China Sea and badass lady pirate. Not your typical heroes. Murderers, most of them. They're not winning any awards for sportsmanship. But if you think they didn't follow rules, or that they didn't know right from wrong, you're very mistaken.

What do they have in common? Well, they're good thieves, of course, or they wouldn't be famous. But the other thing that ties them all together is what made them thieves and outlaws in the first place: They all have their own little monsters caged up inside of them. Furies that urge them toward blood. Scaly, clawed things that were born in that moment when the world went so wrong that anything was possible, even the creation of monsters.

Because that's what happened. At some point, someone did them all wrong. Very wrong. Monster-making wrong. They were handed over as brides at twelve years old. Sold as prostitutes to settle fathers' debts. Pimped out, treated as property. Battered, almost completely broken.

Almost.

Look it up. You'll see.

For every action there is an equal and opposite reaction, Boyboy says. My heroes' actions aren't extreme. They are just doing what is necessary to make the universe balanced again.

Backward, to go forward.

Normally, girls don't do the whole Goonda boot-camp thing. They get sent out to the corner in a short skirt or, if they're lucky, they get to run errands. But Mr. Omoko told Bug Eye to make an exception for me, so I trained with the boys to become one of his soldiers.

I decided to set some simple goals, before moving on to how exactly I would get my revenge. For now, I would run faster, climb better, fight harder, be smarter, more of a shadow, a nothing, than any of the other Goonda boys.

I moved out of the warehouse and found a better squat:

my roof. The Goondas haven't found it yet, and I intend to keep it that way. I wanted to make sure that never again would I wake up with fingers in my pockets. But I was back every morning, the first one ready for Bug Eye's training: fighting, tactics, weapons. We were more like an army than a gang.

At first I just got pulverized like the other boys. But eventually I learned to fight dirty, and to be quick, and listen for soft footsteps creeping up behind me. I learned how to hurt people, and how to be hurt but not show it. The training wasn't pretty, but after a while I found that I liked pain better than emptiness. The little monster inside of me fed on the violence and grew strong. I imagined it as a green tiger with enormous teeth. It was quiet and prowled the cage of my ribs and licked its lips.

Part of the training was in general thuggery. We were sent out to watch how the older boys did it. They'd go to shopkeepers and ask for "chai." If a wad of money wasn't produced, fingers were broken, inventory smashed, and daughters eyed meaningfully. I went out a few times, but Bug Eye found my attempts uninspiring. More often than not, people just laughed at me, a tiny girl demanding tea.

So I looked at myself and thought about how to take advantage of being a tiny girl. I began working on my own variation on the bump and wrist flick that is a pickpocket's bread and butter. I'd be way better than Ketchup could ever dream of being. I spent hours every day forcing my body into insane postures so I'd be able to squeeze through barred windows. I decided to show Bug Eye what I could do. Maybe he could think of a better way to use me?

The first place I broke into was the home of a loan shark. My job wasn't to steal anything, but to leave him a message in black paint on his living room wall: "Hi family, tell Baba to pay up. Love, the Goondas." It worked. He paid. The very next day. Delivered the cash himself to the warehouse. I'd found my niche. There were enough Goondas who could break arms and shatter windows. I would be a scalpel. Let the other guys be clubs.

I got better and better at thievery, moving on to actually stealing cash, jewelry, electronics. And soon, when I was creeping into a dark shop or a merchant's plush home, or bumping with choreographed precision through a crowd toward a mark, I found that I was more myself than at any other time. I was a new person. A thief. Solid, strong. Unbroken.

When it came time to get tattoos, there was no question. The very first thing I asked for was a wheel on one arm, sword on the other, just like the ones on Mama's Saint Catherine prayer card. I got others later on, but those were the only two that ever really mattered.

I still had to do the exercises with the other guys. We ran, we climbed, we fought one another. Sometimes Mr. Omoko would drop by and watch us. When he did, all the boys would show off. Omoko had an elite squad of bodyguards, and they all wanted to grow up to be one. There were a million stories of all the money and cars and girls the guys in Omoko's inner circle got, but he would take only the best.

Bug Eye would make us spar in front of him. I hated it. I could hold my own against the boys, but it still made me feel like a monkey on a string being told to dance. The other Goondas thought I was crazy for not kissing up to Omoko, but I didn't care. He knew I didn't want to be his bodyguard. We'd had our chat. My destiny was shaping out in a different direction.

Mr. Omoko rarely spoke to me after that first year. But I didn't mind. His silence was approval, and that was all I needed. I was in dress rehearsal. Once I'd established what I could do, Omoko started assigning specific jobs to me. Bug Eye would relay them. Easy ones at first: breaking into an unguarded shop at night. Tailing and pickpocketing. Then harder ones: getting into homes with security, human and electronic. Cracking safes. Stealing not just things but information. When his IT guy got stumped trying to hack into a politician's email account, I said, Let me try—I know a boy who's a tech genius and owes me a favor.

I never got caught. Not once.

Not until now.

FIFTEEN

While his parents are at church, Michael and I look through everything we've got, hoping that with fresh eyes, we'll find some new detail about Mama's murder. The day is bright and sunny, but we lock ourselves in Michael's room and close the shades. It's overkill, but better than maids popping in or gardeners seeing us through the windows. I bet they think we're in here making out, especially after Michael's performance in front of the guards last night, but whatever. People thinking I'm bonking the boy of the house is the least of my problems.

I've checked the ferry schedule and know I'm supposed to meet Boyboy at three o'clock. I'm not worried about being able to get out of here, only that disappearing on my own for a few hours so soon isn't going to go over real well.

"We should set the scene," Michael says, after a while. "Like we're staging a play."

When I don't respond, he prompts, "The killer must come in through the tunnel. None of the other cameras inside show anyone but Dad and your mom in the house that night. So how does he or she get in?"

"Good question. Probably he got in through the front door because he's your dad."

"*Tina . . .*"

"Fine. I don't know how the mystery killer got in. But magically he does, then he kills my mom." I tilt my head. "Or *she* does. A jealous lover, perhaps? How many does your father have, exactly?"

Michael's eyebrows pinch. "This isn't a joke."

"Believe me, I know. Okay, jealous lover-slash-murderer does the deed. Bang. Then what?"

"He—or she—goes back out the tunnel."

"And then? Does the killer jump over the wall?"

"*You* did," Michael points out.

I have to give him that. "But I had a ladder. And someone to turn off your electric perimeter fence."

"So it can be done," Michael says, with an annoyingly smug look on his face.

"Okay, fine. But a gunshot is loud. Once the gun went off, the guards should have come running, right? How do they not catch him?"

"Well, that's what I—"

"Could be they did get him. And then your dad killed him.

Or her. Chopped the killer up into little pieces and fed him to the sharks. That's a possibility."

Michael scowls at me.

"Not that it does my mother much good, but that's better for you and your dad as far as you're concerned, right?"

"He doesn't chop people up."

"No," I say, "he just pays people to do it. Sharks gotta eat, right?"

"Maybe we should think about motives, not body disposal."

"Just trying to be helpful."

Michael sighs. "Okay, let's figure out possible suspects. Who were your mom's enemies?"

My smirk fades. "Your father."

Michael takes a deep breath but keeps his voice level. "What about in Congo?"

"Like I said, your dad."

"What are you talking about?"

I narrow my eyes at him. "They met there. She knew him from before."

Michael frowns. "Wait. So you're saying they were enemies in Congo?"

"She knew stuff about Extracta. Bad stuff. That's what she was saying she was going to go to the press with when he threatened to kill her."

"But if they were enemies, why would she come here, all the way from Congo, and ask him for a job? And why would he be like, 'Yeah, sure. Come on in'?"

"I . . ." I shake my head. "She came here because . . . Look, I don't know why we ended up here. Maybe he forced her to work for him."

"That doesn't make sense. She wouldn't have brought you here if it wasn't safe, right? And he didn't force her to . . . you know . . . Kiki . . ." Michael looks at his hands.

"He didn't force her to have sex with him? You can say it."

Michael fidgets. "I mean, I saw them together too—kissing and stuff. He didn't have a bunch of other women. They . . . liked each other."

I squeeze my hands under my armpits, practically crawling out of my skin with how much I hate discussing this.

"Anyone else?" Michael asks. He doesn't look any less uncomfortable. "Enemies," he adds quickly.

I give him a tense shrug. "I don't know. I don't think so."

"What did she do before she came to Sangui? Was she in trouble, or . . ."

"She was a *nurse*. She helped people."

"Nurses can have enemies. No ideas?"

"No. I don't know." I stand up and start to pace. How would I know if she had enemies or not? Only Donatien, the reporter, has been able to tell me about her life there. But he just knows bits and pieces. Important bits, but not enough. And Mama herself certainly never talked about Congo to me. When I think back on it, it seems like as far as she was concerned there was nothing to think or talk about.

Michael writes, *Anju Yvette's past in Congo?* on a list of

questions he's making. "Do you know anyone you could ask about her?"

I don't answer right away. "Yeah, maybe."

"Who?"

I hesitate. Would Donatien recognize Michael? Probably not. Michael is always in Switzerland, and Mrs. G is notoriously fierce about keeping her kids out of the papers. *I* barely recognized the guy. "I'll send him a text. Maybe he'll meet us."

As I'm typing, Michael asks, "What about the girl in the photo with your mom?"

I shake my head. "I told you, I don't know who she is."

My mother looked so happy in that photo. They must have been friends. But how would I even begin to find her? Would Donatien know her?

"Should we go through the police file?" Michael asks.

I make a face. "Okay. But I've looked at it a hundred times and I swear it gets less useful every time."

I use his computer to get into my online files and pull it up. I hand him the laptop, letting him scroll through.

"This is it?" Michael asks, after a few seconds.

"Astonishing, isn't it? Don't you have a whole new depth of faith in Sangui City's justice system?"

"They didn't even spell 'report' right. It has an *l* in it."

"Just wait until you see the analysis page," I say. "Completely blank."

I walk to the window to peek through the shades. I can't look at the police file. It makes me too angry. The notes from the officer's conversation with Mr. G and David Mwika barely fill a page. The forms are worse. Most are left half blank. Signatures from supervisors are missing. There are three photos: my mother's body; a close-up shot of the wound; and for some weird reason the buffalo head above the mantel in Mr. G's office.

"Maybe the buffalo did it," I say darkly.

"These two names you've highlighted here—who are they?"

I walk back to see what Michael is looking at. "The only two people besides Mr. G and staff who were at your house that day, according to Mwika and your dad. I looked them both up. Joseph Gicanda is a Rwandan army general. And Ali Abdirahman is a rich Somali dude who owns a shipping company. Extracta uses them to get minerals from Sangui City to China and Dubai."

"Any connection to your mom?" Michael asks.

"Not that I can find."

"Maybe she overheard something about one of them," Michael says. "And that person found out. We should do more digging." He writes their names on his list and taps his pen on his chin. "Who were the staff working that day?"

"You think another maid or a gardener or someone did it?"

Michael considers this. "Probably not. Dad definitely wouldn't cover for one of them. He would have turned them over to the police."

"Maybe he killed whoever it was and got rid of the body."

Michael drops his pen onto the paper. "*Ngai*, you really do think my dad's a monster, don't you?"

I don't answer. "I don't know who on staff it would have been, anyway. She didn't really have much to do with the other staff, that I remember."

"You never saw her talking to anyone? A gardener? One of the security guys?"

I shake my head. "Maybe one or two of the other maids, but not any of the men."

"You were young; maybe you just didn't notice."

I scowl at him. "*Ngai*, you really do think my mom was a slut, don't you?"

"I didn't mean—"

"Whatever."

I stand up to stalk back to the window and nudge the shades aside again. Still looks like a garden out there. Michael continues to pore through the file, but I don't bother. I've got it memorized.

On the next page he'll see the full list of all the people who were at the Greyhills that day: Mr. Greyhill; Mwika; the cook, who was about a hundred then. Two other maids, a gardener, a driver, and four security guards. Everyone else had the night off. Kiki and I are not included, even though we were there. I guess maids' illegitimate children don't count. The officer noted on the list that Mrs. Greyhill and the kids had left the day before to spend the night at their beach house up the coast. The cook confirmed it.

Then come the officer's notes. In the scantiest detail possible, he relays Mr. G's version of what happened: Mr. G heard a shot, but it took him a few minutes to make his way through the house to check on it. The officer asks why Mr. G didn't notify security first, to which Mr. G replied that he doesn't know. Even the doofus police officer must have thought that was weird, because there's a little question mark beside Mr. G's answer.

Mr. G finds my mother already dead. No mention of the tunnel. No mention of what may have happened to the killer. The murder weapon is the gun that was already in Greyhill's desk. He thinks a robber did it, but nothing was stolen and there's no footage of an intruder. Does the officer question this? Of course not.

Mwika basically says the same thing, but adds a detail. I wait for Michael to get to it.

Sure enough, his head soon pops up. "According to Mwika, the power went out a few minutes before the murder," he tells me.

I nod. "And the surveillance cameras were interrupted. But they come back on just in time to place Mwika in the guardhouse at the time your dad says he hears the gunshot."

"Very convenient for Mwika, don't you think?" Michael asks.

"You're the one keeping me from him," I say. "I'd love to ask him a couple hundred questions."

Michael scowls. "I'm working on it."

"Well, work harder."

My phone buzzes with a text. Donatien has written me back.

Meet me at Samaki Joint in an hour.

Perfect. We'll go see him, and then I can make a break and find Boyboy.

"Come on," I say, wiggling into my shoes. "We're never going to figure anything out just sitting here in the dark."

"I told you, I'm grounded," Michael says, not moving. "My parents are going to be back any minute." He glances at his watch. I wonder idly how much I could get for it at the Go-Downs.

"Do you want my help or not?" I ask. "The guy who knew my mom can meet, but we've got to go now."

Michael looks around at the papers on the floor and his laptop. There's nothing else to look at. He knows that until we get more information we're at a dead end.

"I am going to be in so much trouble," he mutters, but by then he's already following me out the door.

SIXTEEN

Where are we going?" Michael asks as we step outside the mansion. "Who are we going to see?"

"We need to get a taxi to town," I say, walking across the driveway toward the gate.

"I've got a driver."

"But do you trust him? Is he going to tell your dad where we went?"

Michael frowns, answering my question. He looks around and seems to make some sort of decision. "Okay, then. Wait here."

I check the time on my phone as he walks away. I'm not sure how I'm going to manage to shake Michael to meet Boyboy. There's no way I'm taking him with me. Maybe I can send him on an errand? Tell him I'll meet him back here? Somehow I doubt he'll go for any of that . . .

My thoughts are interrupted by a roar. I look up and my jaw drops. "You're joking, right?"

Michael rolls forward astride a motorcycle, his face hidden under a helmet. The bike is bright red, a European brand, and huge. Nothing like the little Chinese-made *piki-piki* that shuttle people and goods throughout the city.

"Your parents actually let you ride that thing?"

Michael takes the helmet off. "I won't tell if you don't. It's Dad's. He bought it in a moment of midlife crisis or something. Never uses it. He'd kill me if he knew I took it out. He doesn't even know I can ride."

"Can you?"

"Of course."

"The guards going to tell on you?" I ask.

"I bribe them."

"Of course you do. Maybe you can just bribe your driver?"

He smirks. "You scared?"

"No. Give me that," I say, and take the helmet he's offering me.

It's like wearing a cooking pot on my head. No one wears them on the *piki-piki*. Michael motions me closer and buckles something under my chin, which makes it feel more like a helmet and less like a pot, but not much. Then he flips a switch on his own helmet. I can hear his voice as clearly as though his mouth is against my ear. "It's just like a *piki-piki*. Only . . . faster."

"I'm not worried." I swing on behind him. Just like a *piki-piki*, I tell myself.

Michael nudges us forward a few inches. "Gotta hang on tight."

I scoot up until I'm right against Michael's back. I can grip a side handle with one hand, but the other has to go around Michael's waist. I am keenly aware of all the places where my body touches his. He shows me where to put my feet and then looks back. Our helmets bump.

"Ready?"

My stomach clenches. I'm afraid of what my voice will sound like, so instead I give him a firm nod.

And then we're blistering out of the gate and down the road.

I grab him around the waist with both hands. It goes so *fast*, I think stupidly.

Piki-piki have motors that sound like bumblebees and can barely outpace bicycles. This thing is like a cheetah after prey, and I don't care about anything but hanging on. We come up to our first bend in the road, and I clench my thighs, no longer caring about touching Michael.

"Lean into the curve!" Michael shouts, and I try to follow his movements. We're tilted so far over I could reach out and touch the pavement, but the last thing I would do right now is let go.

The mansions of the Ring whip past us in a blur. I scream a little when Michael rockets around a car that's going too slow. I can hear him laughing. "You okay back there?"

"Fine!" I say, my voice high. I clear my throat.

The road down from the Ring twists and winds, but it's

at least free of the potholes that cover most of Sangui City's streets. After a few minutes I start to get used to the speed and even feel my racing heart switch from fear to exhilaration. I realize I've been gripping so hard that my hands have fallen asleep. I loosen them and Michael takes a deep breath, like maybe I've been crushing his lungs.

"What do you think?" he asks.

"It's fast!"

Michael laughs. "You haven't seen anything yet!"

"No! No faster!"

Michael lets up on the gas. "Sorry. Riding just makes me feel . . . awake. Alive." He pauses, and I'm surprised to hear something like hesitation in his voice. "I thought you'd like it."

I take inventory of my senses. The air is whipping past me and the shadows and the sun ripple over my arms and legs as we rocket through the jacaranda trees that tunnel the road. Their flowers lie on the ground like purple snow. It's beautiful, and I know what he means, to have that one thing that makes you feel truly yourself and alive. It's how I felt breaking into his house two nights ago. Like no one in the world could tell me what to do; no one knew how to do my job better. Terrifying, but absolutely *right*.

"I do," I say.

SEVENTEEN

We have to slow down once we get into town, and I immediately start to sweat under the helmet. I hadn't really realized how much cooler it is up in the Ring. And down here it's a lot less fun trying to push our way through the traffic and potholes and dust. The closer we get to the harbor, the more crowded it gets. There are bicycles and chickens and children and goats, and lots of people who just stop to gape at the motorcycle, like it's a herald of the second coming.

I give directions, and Michael threads through the busy streets. We have to go practically to the other side of Sangui City, over the bridge and back into the winding, narrow streets of Old Town. We drive down Biashara Street and even pass Kiki's school. I can hear the girls shouting and laughing in the yard, and I crane my neck but don't see Kiki as we drive past the front gates. Of course, what would I say to her if I did? Hi, sis! Remember your half brother, Michael? His dad killed our mom. 'Kay, bye!

Right. She's not going to know anything about all this. Ever.

From the back of the bike, Old Town's grit fades away into the vignettes I imagine the tourists see: rambling warrens of pale limestone buildings and waving palm trees; market stalls with perfect pyramids of yellow and red mangoes, frilly bunches of greens, bananas, and peppers hung like garlands. There are serious-faced men in long white *kanzus* and women wrapped in rainbow *kanga* prints or head-to-toe *buibuis* that billow like black sails. There is clear blue sky above, and below, electric blue water. From here, it looks just like paradise.

We're almost to the fish market when Michael clears his throat. "So are you going to tell me who it is we're meeting?"

We pass the big green mosque at the center of Old Town, and the hawkers who ply their wares to tourists outside the Swahili Museum: cheap Rasta necklaces and sarongs; wooden elephants and impala that stand in military lines on Masai blankets. Michael nudges the bike around an ancient man with a donkey cart piled with charcoal. Neither the man nor the donkey seems in much hurry to get anywhere.

"Turn left up here."

Instead Michael pulls the bike over to a quiet spot overlooking the harbor and stops.

"What are you doing?" I ask.

He takes his helmet off and turns around in the seat.

"Fine," I say, pulling my helmet off too. "His name is Donatien."

"But who is he? Is he a Goonda? I don't like going in blind like this."

I almost laugh. "No, he's not a Goonda. He's just a guy who knew my mom. Come on, we're going to be late."

"*How* did he know your mom?"

I chew my lip. "You can't say anything, okay? He'll kill me if he knows I told you about him."

"Okay . . ."

"And if you do anything to him—if anything happens to him, I'll know about it."

"You think I'm going to have him fed to the sharks or something? Look, you may not believe it, but I haven't had anyone killed yet, and I promise I won't start today."

I fiddle with the helmet straps. "He's a reporter."

"A reporter?!" Michael yelps. "Are you giving him the stuff off Dad's computer?"

"No!" Not yet, anyway, I add silently. I make sure I don't break eye contact, which is a dead giveaway someone is lying. "He doesn't report on stuff like that anymore. He got . . . in trouble."

But I bet a story on Michael's dad is going to get him back in good graces.

Donatien doesn't know that I'm about to drop pay dirt in his lap, but I have no doubt that he'll leap at the chance to expose Extracta and its East African Big Man. He's been obsessed with taking them down ever since Greyhill ruined his career. But he always says he needs proof. Real proof, not just theories. Theories and speculation were what got him in trouble in the first place.

I tracked him down two years ago after I found a story he ran in Sangui's biggest newspaper right after Mama's death. He dared ask why her murder wasn't investigated, insinuating that the police covered for Mr. G, the most likely killer. It got Donatien demoted, and he's positive Greyhill, with all his connections, was behind it.

I would have gone looking for Donatien because of the article regardless, but what really made me curious was the way he wrote about Mama. He sounded angry. Almost as if he knew her.

Which it turns out he did.

I can still feel Michael's tension and try to scoot away. I think about hopping off the bike, but that might delay us even more.

"And he knows your mom how?"

"He was doing a story on Extracta in Congo," I say reluctantly. "On how they were buying gold from militias instead of digging it. She was a source."

It took me a while, but you can wear anyone down if you just sit outside their house and office and favorite bars for long enough. Donatien finally gave up and agreed to talk to me. I think maybe he was even a little lonely. Once I convinced him that I was really Mama's daughter, he opened up. He told me that he'd met Mama in Kasisi, our hometown, eleven years ago, and that she had wanted to help him with his story.

Michael's eyes narrow. "A source? What did she tell him, exactly?"

I look longingly toward our destination. "Look, once you get him started, Donatien will talk. He *loves* to talk about conflict minerals and Congo, but he's a little touchy, so just let me ask the questions, okay? Can we go now?"

Michael scans the harbor, where white-sailed dhows roll over the current. In the distance, a squat ferry is chugging toward the shore in a haze of blue diesel. Even from here you can see the rust on its hull and the throngs of people crowded at its rails. It's a struggle to not shout at Michael that we're wasting time. But finally he hefts the helmet back onto his head and starts the engine.

Open and noisy, smelling like fried chips and masala spice, the restaurant is a popular spot. It's full of fishermen at cheap white plastic tables, most of whom seem well into drinking away any profit they've made selling their catch this morning.

"Better hitch up your skirts," I say when I see Michael's face. "It's a little dirtier than what you're used to."

"I've been in places like this before. It's fine."

"Sure you have. Now, listen," I say, lowering my voice, "whatever you do, don't tell Donatien who you are, right? I don't think he'll recognize you. Better yet, don't talk."

"Great," Michael says. "So I just sit there?"

"Do what I say, okay? This is my world, and you are now *my* guest."

I lead Michael past a speaker blaring rumba. Twilight girls with short skirts and long nails cluster at one end of the bar. They flick their braids over their shoulders and watch me closely, making sure I'm not invading their turf. The smells grow denser: to the mix is added sour beer and the tang of men who sleep in fish boats.

I don't mind the noise and the stink. It's more private here, in a way, than many other dingy back rooms Donatien could have chosen to make our usual rendezvous spot. He won't meet in places like that. He says there are too many bored waiter boys whose ears are too big for their brains.

Donatien is already seated at his usual table in a shaded corner of the patio. "Who's this?" he asks, jerking a stubbled chin up at Michael before we even sit.

Donatien's the only *mzungu* in here, unless you count Michael, but even with his pasty white skin singling him out, he still looks completely at home. Empty beer bottles are starting to gather at his elbow. A pile of whole fried fish sits in front of him, several already eaten down to the glistening bone.

"He's not important," I say.

"You know I don't talk to strangers, Tiny."

"He's a friend. It's fine. He's no snitch."

"You don't *have* friends."

"Jeez, thanks a lot, Donatien. He's a new refugee. I'm showing him around."

"Looks too soft to be a refugee kid." Donatien means he's too white, but he won't say so.

"I know; that's what I keep telling him," I say.

"You're a reporter and you don't talk to strangers?" Michael asks.

I shoot him a dirty look to warn him to keep his mouth shut.

"Not ones I don't know," Donatien says. "But I'm not really a reporter. I'm on sports." He says *sports* like it's a dirty word.

"That's still reporting," Michael points out.

Donatien grunts dismissively and checks how much beer he's got left. He raises his bottle to the waiter to signal for another. "Speaking of which, I can't hang about long. I have a very important junior-league cricket match to cover in about an hour." He waves at his fish. "You want something?"

"Just soda."

Snapping his oily fingers, Donatien calls the waiter. *"Sampson, leta Tuska baridi sana. Na soda mbili."*

A man brings a fresh Tusker beer. Cold, very cold, which Donatien tests by grabbing the bottle's neck before allowing the waiter to pry the cap off. Two orange Fantas are placed in front of Michael and me. I kick Michael under the table when I see he's about to use his sleeve to wipe the mouth of the bottle.

Donatien takes a grateful swig of beer, then digs into his fish again with his fingers just like any local dude. He uses *ugali*, white corn mash, to grab up flesh and chilies. After he wolfs the whole lump down, he belches without apology. "Your loss. Best fish in town."

"Donatien is French," I tell Michael. "He's picky about his food."

"Belgian," Donatien corrects. "How many times have I got to tell you? I hate the effing French." He regards me with bloodshot eyes. "So, half-pint? What's up?"

I pull the photo out of my pocket. "Do you know who this is?" I ask, pointing at the girl beside my mother.

Donatien squints, wipes his hands, and picks up the photo for a closer look. "No idea."

I try not to let my disappointment show. "Are you sure? It was on his computer."

"What do you mean, *his* computer?"

"You know. His. Don't give me that look."

"Tina, you haven't done anything stupid, have you? If you went—"

"What, you think I broke into his house?" I scoff, ignoring Michael's twitch. "I'm good, but I'm not *that* good. Somebody hacked it for me. You sure you don't know her?"

"When was this taken?" Donatien asks, looking back at the smiling girls. "Your mother's young." He glances at Michael, still suspicious of him. "They're in school uniforms. It was taken before I met her." He pushes the photo back to me and I carefully tuck it away.

I wait until he's working on another big mouthful of fish before pressing my luck. "I keep wondering something. How did Mama know what she knew?" I go on, even though Donatien is giving me a warning look. "How does a nurse come to know someone like . . ."

"Tina . . ."

". . . like you-know-who?"

Donatien's hand creeps to the scar on his neck. "You want to talk, Christina, your new buddy has to scram."

I look at Michael and jut my chin toward the door. He scowls, but stands up and makes his way through the restaurant and out the door, leaving us alone. Donatien watches him go.

I lean in. "Donatien?"

He runs his fingers along the little hash marks on his collarbone where the flesh was sewn back together. "You trust him? You gotta be careful who you talk in front of, Tina."

"I know. You're right. Don't worry. He's just some wet-behind-the-ears 'fugee. I don't know why I let him tag along." I wait until Donatien has another swallow of beer in him and then say, "So? How did she know Mr. Greyhill?"

Donatien sets the beer down slowly. Flies cluster around the eyeball of his fish, but he doesn't seem to notice. "What are you doing, Tina? Why all the questions?"

"I just . . . Why won't you tell me how she knew what Extracta was doing?"

I've tried this tack before, with little luck. Donatien will talk all day about the rebels who sell gold dug by slaves, and shady mining companies like Extracta who sell weapons to them, but any time I ask more about Mama herself, why she was willing to talk to him, or how she found out about the deals Extracta was making with militias, he goes all tight-lipped.

"It's not my place to tell you," he says.

"So I have to wait until I'm dead to ask her?"

He winces. "It doesn't matter how she knew. She just did."

I can see a twitch in the corner of his mouth, like something wants to come out. I wait. And just as I'm about to give up, he rubs a hand over his face and says, "She should never have agreed to help me."

It's not the answer to my question, but still, it's something. I lean forward. "Because Greyhill found out and almost killed you?"

He's told me about that day back in Kasisi, right before we left. Mama was supposed to meet him at his hotel and take him to the place in the jungle where the gold-for-guns deals were made. He was going to hide and take photographs. When the knock on his door came that night, he opened it, thinking it was her. Instead, it was a couple of guys with sharpened pangas, big long knives used for hacking through brush. Or flesh. Donatien's told me multiple times how many pints of blood they had to pump into him (two) and how many stitches it took to close him up (forty-three). How he never heard from my mother again until she reached out to him the day before she was murdered, five years later.

Meanwhile, Mama and I were having our own problems.

But I don't want to think about that right now. I want to know more about Mr. Greyhill. "Why would he wait all that time to finish her off, Donatien? And why would she come here to him at all if his militia friends were the ones who chased her out of Congo?"

He studies me.

"Come on, Donatien. I'm not a kid anymore! I can handle it, whatever it is you don't want to tell me!" I lower my voice.

"You can tell me, or I can go and ask *him*. I'm tired of being in the dark. Don't think I won't."

I can tell he's running a thousand different things through his head, but in the end all he says is, "It might not have been him who ran her out."

I wait for more. But he's silent. "I don't understand. Who else would have . . ."

"Other people were involved in the deals. Greyhill didn't make the exchanges himself."

"What? But you said—"

"I said your mother had seen the exchanges, and that's how she knew that gold was being traded for money and weapons. But when I asked her if it was a white American guy making the buys, she said no. I'm the one who told her I thought Roland Greyhill was the mastermind behind it all."

Donatien won't look at me. Why is he being so cagey about this part? "So she never met him in Congo? Who exactly was making the exchanges?"

Donatien's mouth pinches into a flat line. "She didn't say. Just that the main one was a Kenyan guy."

"Did you find out who he was later?"

"No," Donatien says, and leans back. He looks past me, toward the water. "You know all this. I dropped the investigation. I didn't pick it back up until after she was murdered."

I'm suddenly overwhelmed with just how much I don't know. I mean, who was my mother, really? A nurse. That's all she told me. That's all I can tell Michael when he asks. But how did she find out so much about blood gold? How did she know when and where the exchanges were happening? They were done in some secret place, way back in the jungle, according to Donatien. My mind is churning. I can't make all the pieces fit into some solid, clear picture of her. How can I know so little about who she was and what happened back there in Congo? A question buzzes in my head like a mosquito. I bite my lip. "She wasn't in on it, was she? The gold deals?"

Donatien's attention snaps back to me. "No, nothing like that."

"How do you know?"

"She just wouldn't have been."

"But how do you know?" I demand, thumping my fist on the table. "You barely knew her! *I* barely knew her!" The words are out of my mouth before I can stop them.

He starts to reach for my arm, but then seems to think better of it. "Look, Tina, I admit it. I had the same thought. When she called me, right before she was murdered, I didn't want to talk to her. I hadn't heard from her since that day I almost got killed." He looks up at me guiltily. "I thought it was her who sent those guys to my hotel."

I don't move. "You suspected her?"

He nods and goes on, "And so when she got in touch, I asked her about it, and she . . . convinced me. Don't . . ." He puts up a hand to stop me. "Just trust me. She wasn't able to meet me and it wasn't her fault. What happened to me wasn't her fault. Men came for her that night, just like they came for me. You told me as much yourself."

It's true. In the back of my brain I see a lick of fire as high as the trees. I press my knuckles into my eyes, trying to make the image go away. I can't think about that right now. I come back to the same question. "So why would she then come here to Greyhill, if he sent the men after you and her?"

"How or why your mother eventually ended up working for Mr. Greyhill—that I don't know. She wouldn't tell me. But I'm sure whatever she did was for a good reason. She must have felt like she had to, and that it would be the best way to keep you safe. Your mother was . . . well, she was like you. Tough, but good." The corners of Donatien's eyes pinch. "Why so many questions today, Tina? Is something going on? You seem out of sorts."

I stare at him, then let my gaze stretch out to the water, thinking of my plans for the Greyhill family. "You don't know me. I'm not that good."

He opens his mouth to protest, but I cut him off. "Look," I say, swallowing down whatever emotion is trying to force its way out, "I just want to know for sure that he killed her. That's all."

Donatien heaves a deep breath. He rotates his beer on the table, leaving damp rings. He must be thinking the same thing I am, that my mother really screwed up when it came to where she thought we would be safe.

"Greyhill did it, Tina. If I'm sure of anything, it's that. She reached out to me, said she wanted to talk about him, and then she ended up dead. No one had more to lose from her talking than him."

I know all this already. But I find myself saying, "I need proof."

"And how are you going to . . ." He frowns, and then I see it in his eyes, something clicking into place. "Oh my God. That kid. I knew he looked familiar. Is that . . . ?" His eyes widen with fear.

"Don't worry about him," I say.

Donatien leans forward and grabs my arm. "Is that Michael Greyhill?" he asks in a rough whisper. "Tina, why are you with him? What are you doing?"

"I said don't worry about it."

I start to stand, but Donatien keeps a grip on me. "You can't mess around with these people, Tina," he hisses. "They go for blood. Think of your mother. Whatever you're up to with him, you have to stop, now."

I yank my arm out of his. "I appreciate everything you've done for me, Donatien," I say, "I really do. But I *am* thinking about my mother."

"Tina—"

"I have to go," I say. "I'll be in touch."

I turn and slip away before he can rise to his feet and stop me.

EIGHTEEN

When I turned seven, I went to school. Not with Michael—he went somewhere that cost a small fortune every term—but it was a decent school close to the Ring. I'm sure Mr. G paid my fees. A bus picked me up from the corner near the Greyhills' home in the morning and dropped me back every day. The teachers were smart and kind. I learned to read and count and sing the Kenyan national anthem. We colored with real crayons and played kickball in the grass. It was all very pleasant, and I was lucky.

I hated it.

I hated leaving Mama. I hated leaving Kiki. Every day I would try to fake being sick, or hide, and every day Mama would march me out into the world in my uncomfortable shoes and scratchy uniform, unmoved by the crocodile tears running down my chin. You're too big for this, she'd say with fire in her eyes. We waited on the corner for the bus, Kiki on her hip, her telling me I was fortunate to go to such a school. Did I know how many children wanted to go to school and couldn't? And my school had music class. A swimming pool. I took gymnastics in the afternoons. Gymnastics!

Kiki was only one year old and she didn't know why going to school made me pout, but her lip would quiver along with mine and this would frustrate Mama even more. Don't cry! You're going to make your sister cry and I don't have time!

Then when Kiki turned two, she was old enough to go with me. There was a nursery school attached to mine. She had to go, Mama said. There was no discussing it. But the first day Mama tried to put her on the bus with me, Kiki pitched a fit. She wailed. Screamed like she was being murdered. She didn't want to leave Mama. I got into my seat on the bus and saw the driver look at the three of us, then his watch. And Mama tried to shush Kiki and put her in an empty seat, but it wasn't working. Kiki bucked and squirmed and howled. I looked on, not knowing what to do. I mean, I didn't blame Kiki. I didn't want to go to the stupid school with their stupid songs and jump rope either. I wanted to play in the Greyhills' garden. I wanted to climb the strangler fig. I'd stay out of the way. Both of us would. I was about to open my big mouth and say so.

But then I saw Mama's face. I was too little to understand exactly what she was thinking, but somehow I knew to shut up. She looked like she was at the edge of something very high, looking down. Somehow I knew that Kiki had to go with me. I knew that if Mama went back into the Greyhills' with Kiki still clinging to her skirt, she would be in trouble. Maybe Mrs. G had put her foot down. Maybe Mama's place—and ours along with it—was in doubt. Maybe getting us out of sight, at least for a little while, was some sort of deal Mama had struck. Of course, I didn't understand any of that then; all I knew was that the look on her face made me feel ashamed. Mama needed me to stop acting like a baby.

"I'll take her," I said, and held out my arms for my sister. "Come here, Kiki, let me tell you how much fun it is at school."

And Kiki went quiet, and sniffed, and looked with her big amber eyes from me to Mama. "Schoo?"

I plastered a big smile on my face. "It's so great! The teachers are really nice, and there are swings and a slide and snack time! Come sit with me!"

"Nak time?"

She let Mama put her in the same seat with me while the other kids on the bus watched and the driver drummed his fingers on the steering wheel impatiently. She was so little that her feet stuck straight out. I buckled a single belt around us.

"You're going to make so many friends," I told her. She would. People loved Kiki, with her sunny smile and fat cheeks. Most people, anyway.

"I'll be right here when you get back," Mama said before the bus driver closed the door. She stood on the side of the road and watched us go. She was already in her maid's uniform, ready for work. Her chin was up. She stood on solid ground. She waved good-bye.

. . .

"You can drop me off here," I tell Michael.

We've come to the intersection of Dagoretti and Timau Roads, where a new shopping plaza called Paradise Island is going in. Cars and pedestrians bully and press around one another, everyone trying to get somewhere else. I've said barely a word since getting back on the bike, even though Michael has been pestering me the entire ride. I've just been running Donatien's words through my head: Greyhill did it . . . If I'm sure of anything, it's that.

But he doesn't know, does he? Not for sure. And neither do I. Mr. G is in a dirty business. He and Mama were close. Maybe it's like Michael said, and Mama heard something she shouldn't have about one of his business partners. Maybe Mr. G even told her about one of them. What if she was going to tell Donatien information that would have incriminated someone else too? How could I find out who that might be? Did we look at all the surveillance footage from the day of her murder, who went in and out? Maybe someone else besides Gicanda and Abdirahman came there, someone Mr. G and Mwika didn't mention to the police. I make a mental note to look at the footage in the police file again.

"Drop you off? Not part of the plan, Tina."

I drag myself out of my thoughts. "Stop!"

We're about five blocks from my roof, as close as I'm comfortable letting Michael get. He continues through the intersection.

"Pull over. I need to meet with my business partner."

Michael slows and turns down a quieter street. He stops the bike on the dirt shoulder of the road in front of a well-groomed apartment complex and takes his helmet off. "Our deal was that I go with you. We're supposed to be doing this investigation together."

I pull my helmet off too. "Are you still mad about being sent from the table? Because I told you I'd explain everything later—"

"The deal is that we work together. You don't get to run off."

"I have to meet my partner; he's waiting on me. It doesn't have anything to do with 'the investigation,'" I say, air quoting.

"I'm still coming with you."

I try a different approach. "Don't you want to get home? I thought you were grounded. And that you have to do home-work or something."

"I'm not going back without you."

"I'm not taking you with me."

"I'm not really asking."

As we sit there glowering at each other, I weigh jumping off and running away. I could do it, easy, and just show back up at the Greyhills' later. But then I risk Michael chasing me, and I'm seriously not in the mood. If I miss Boyboy, I'll have to wait for another cryptic message to get a date with him, and we don't have that kind of time.

But then I get an idea. "Fine," I huff. "Go that way."

I direct him through the streets, away from the bustle. We've left Old Town and are on the edge of what might one day become a suburb. For now it's just street after street of unfinished gray apartment buildings. Some are covered in scaffolding, crawling with workers like ants, but most have stagnated somewhere in between, top floors gaping open with rebar and concrete. Their owners will come back every once in a while when the money is there and build another floor, *polepole*. Slowly, slowly. My building hasn't been touched in years. It's perfect.

"Down there," I say. It's the gated entrance to the building's underground car park. I hop off and look down the street to make sure no one is around. The last thing I need is someone seeing a fancy motorcycle disappearing in here. I pull aside a sheet of metal on the rusted gate and Michael squeezes the bike through. I lead him into the dark center of the garage and tell him to park. The sudden silence after he shuts off the engine is almost deafening. I hurry us to a door signposted, HATARI! DANGER! and unlock the combination padlock keeping it closed.

There's just enough light filtering into the garage to see, but inside the maintenance room it's completely dark. I know my way by touch, but I hear Michael bang into a pile of scaffolding. I pick up the thing I need before reaching back and finding his arm, leading him by the wrist through the maze to the opposite side. I open the door and sunlight filters down on us, weak and dusty.

Michael follows me into the small concrete room and looks up. We're actually in a long shaft where a service elevator was supposed to go.

"Okay," I say, "here's the deal: Since I'm feeling generous, I'm not going to make you hang out in the dark car park."

"What are you . . ."

But he's way too slow for me. I've already ratcheted one side of the handcuffs I picked up in the maintenance room to his wrist while we were walking. Now I swiftly attach the other side to a stout pole.

Michael's eyes go wide. "You can't do that!"

"I think I just did," I say. "Don't worry, I'll be back in ten minutes. I'm not going to leave you here for hours and hours, like you left me."

"Are these from the panic room? How did you . . . ?"

"One of my practice pairs," I say. "I keep a few stashed around."

"You're just leaving me here?"

"I'm not going far. I'll be right up there." Michael starts to protest, but I say, "I'm not running away; there's nowhere for me to go."

Michael looks around. "I'm going to start yelling," he says. "This is some sort of secret hideout place, right? You didn't want anyone seeing me go in."

I narrow my eyes. "You wouldn't dare."

"Why not? You leave me here and I'm going to shout my head off. Try me. I'm tired of this, Tina." He takes a deep breath and opens his mouth.

"Wait!" I look around, knowing how his voice will echo in here. "Fine! Look, I just need a few minutes first to talk to Boyboy in private. Can you give me that?"

"Your friend's name is Boyboy?"

"Business partner."

Michael gives me an appraising look, like he's not the one in handcuffs. "Five minutes."

"Ten."

"And then you'll toss down the key to these cuffs?"

"Then I'll come down and we can get you home."

"Nope, I want to meet this Boyboy kid." He waits. "I've got a really good set of lungs, Tina. Want to hear?"

"Okay, okay! I'll throw it."

Michael looks at his watch. "Ten minutes, then I start yelling to raise the dead."

"You're such a pain in the ass," I tell him.

Michael looks like he almost wants to smile. "So how do you get up?"

The walls are damp and covered in greenish slime, but there is just enough rebar sticking out from the concrete to climb. I grab a piece above my head.

"Do I have to do everything for you? Figure it out," I say, and pull myself level with the first of ten floors.

Boyboy jumps when I pop up through the top of the elevator shaft.

"Did you get it all?" I ask before I'm even done pulling myself out.

"Good Lord, Tina, I know your mama taught you enough manners to holler *hodi*." He glares at me over his computer screen. "You trying to give me a heart attack?"

The blissfully normal sight of him sitting there makes me smile, in spite of everything that's happening. "I don't think you have to announce yourself in your own home, Boyboy. So, did you?"

Boyboy doesn't move from the safari chair he's slouched in. It's my only furniture, other than the beat-up mattress in the corner. I guess you could say I don't do a lot of entertaining. I'd taken a liking to the chair, though, and stole it off the porch of a fancy *mzungu* restaurant where they serve tourists ostrich and crocodile. I stifle my annoyance that Boyboy has claimed it, like he always does when he comes over, and pull up a cinder block.

Boyboy's fingers haven't stopped flittering over his laptop keys, even as he grumbles, "Where's pretty boy? I thought you two were supposed to be playing house."

"Downstairs. He's waiting in the pit. He, um . . . wants to meet you. Did anything transmit?"

"You brought him to the Batcave? Are you crazy?" Boyboy looks me up and down. "And what are you wearing?"

I feel heat creep into my cheeks and smooth down the green blouse automatically. I resist pointing out that Boyboy is wearing a yellow *kitenge* jumpsuit with a flying-toaster motif, platform shoes, and a head wrap. I'm sure he'd look right at home on a Lagos catwalk, but between his eye-catching outfit and the motorcycle, my secret hideout is looking less secret by the minute.

"Focus, Boyboy! What did you get off his hard drive?"

"Don't shout." Boyboy winces. "I haven't slept in thirty-six hours, and I'm running entirely on caffeine. I may go Hulk on you and toss you off the building."

I lean back to get a better look at him. "You haven't slept?"

Boyboy takes off his glasses and rubs his eyes. "Your Goonda buddies have had me working all night. I just left a couple of hours ago."

Guilt jabs at me. Boyboy is already in way deeper than he's ever been on one of my jobs. "Bug Eye was supposed to let you go home."

"Yeah, well, he did. It just took him a while," Boyboy grumbles. He drains the contents of one of the energy drinks he's got open at his side.

I don't want to ask, but I bet Boyboy's mom freaked out when he didn't come home for two days. I'll get an earful the next time I see her. Honestly, though, she treats him like he's five, not fifteen. She's not crazy about me, but on the other hand Boyboy brings home more money from our jobs than she can ever make selling tea on the corner. Five kids—that's a lot of mouths to feed, especially for a single refugee mom. Plus there's the protection being a friend of the Goondas gives them.

Boyboy puts his glasses back on. "Bug Eye wanted to see what we were able to get off Greyhill's hard drive. Which wasn't easy with Ketchup running his mouth nonstop. When he wasn't cracking on me, he was bitching about you staying at the Greyhills'. He thinks you're selling them out."

"He needs to worry about his own stupid self. I'm not double-crossing the Goondas. I don't have a death wish. They didn't follow you here, did they?"

"I don't think so. I tried to mix up my route."

"So . . . what were we able to get?"

"Only about fifteen percent of the hard-drive memory."

I curse elaborately and look over my shoulder at the elevator shaft opening. I lower my voice, even though I'm pretty sure there's no way Michael can hear us. "I'm going to have to go back in Greyhill's office and transmit again, aren't I?"

"If you want everything, yeah."

I rub my hand over my head, thinking. "Look," I say in a whisper. "Michael thinks we got it all—enough to ruin his dad, anyway. That's how I was able to make a deal with him to get out of that cell. He thinks I won't release the dirt if he can prove his dad didn't kill my mother."

Boyboy blinks at me. "What? Why would you agree to that? Greyhill killed your mom; you've always said so."

Another glance over my shoulder, and then I come in close. "I know, I know. But listen. There was a video, Boyboy. Mr. Greyhill had a camera in his office that recorded everything the night she died."

"What?" Boyboy gasps. "There was no camera on the network I hacked."

"I know. It must have been separate. Or it is now. Anyway, the footage from that night is gone. David Mwika took it when he disappeared. But Michael says he knows where Mwika is and can get it."

"And do you believe him?"

I can't look Boyboy in the face and tell him Michael got his information from his father. It sounds too ludicrous. "Yeah," I say. "I mean, we've got time, right? Even after I get the data, you need a few days to decrypt everything. Think about it, Boyboy. A video. Proof, once and for all, that Greyhill did it."

"So where is Mwika?"

I sit back. "Michael won't tell me. He thinks I'll bail." I incline my head. "He's right, of course . . ."

Boyboy puts up both hands to stop me. "Let me make sure I understand. You made a deal where Mr. Omoko may be forced to wait for his money while you play detective?"

"No. Omoko has already agreed to wait a week while you decrypt everything anyway. And he knows the bank accounts are part of what needs decrypting. I just used the time cushion we already had to make a deal with Michael—and also, you know, I thought I might need to get back into Greyhill's office. And I was right."

Boyboy lets all of this sink in. "And what if I *had* got all of it?"

I avoid his eye. "Well, you didn't, so stop complaining. I'll get everything this time. Oh, and I need a new USB thingy. Do you have one? Michael broke the other one."

Boyboy doesn't move. "But this deal you've made doesn't change anything, right? You give that reporter the dirt, I hack the bank accounts, money goes to the Goondas, you do whatever it is you're going to do to Mr. Greyhill that I do *not* want to know about. Dirt. Money. Blood."

I gnaw at my fingernail. "One, two, three. As soon as I've seen the video."

"No matter what that video shows. No matter who killed your mom, right? You with me on this?" Boyboy speaks very slowly. "Omoko is expecting his money. If he doesn't get it, those Goondas are going to kill you. And then they'll kill me. And then they'll go back and kill you again just to make sure you got the message."

"*I know.* The plan hasn't changed. The video is going to show that Mr. Greyhill killed my mom, and then I'll know for sure, one hundred percent, once and for all."

Boyboy looks ill. He opens his mouth to argue again, but he's interrupted.

"*Tina.*"

Boyboy peers over my shoulder at the elevator shaft. "Is that him?"

I go to the hole. "Shh!" I say, looking down.

Michael's bright eyes glitter in the light. "Toss me the key!"

"It hasn't been ten minutes!" I whisper.

Michael points at his watch. "It has."

I curse under my breath, but go to fish the key out of its hiding place in between the pages of one of my books. I drop it down, not even waiting to see if it hits Michael between his silly green eyes.

I hurry back to Boyboy. "Don't worry, okay? It's all going to be fine. Now, quick, before he climbs up here, is there anything worthwhile in that fifteen percent you did get?"

Boyboy still looks sick, but he sits up a little straighter. "There are a couple of juicy nuggets so far." He touches some gibberish on his screen.

I can no more understand what he's showing me than read hieroglyphics. "What exactly am I looking at?" I whisper.

"Okay, this is money going into Extracta's bank accounts from China and Dubai."

I whistle. "Those are the actual amounts? I don't know if I can even count that high."

"That's all legal. But look at this." He moves to another page. "Here's more money going out to some military contractor in South Africa for 'security advice.' But it's, like, a hundred thousand US dollars a pop for so-called consultant fees."

"So?"

"So the security advice comes in wooden crates that, according to these invoices, weigh several tons."

"He's importing something." I glance over my shoulder, but Michael hasn't appeared yet. "You think it's weapons?" I can barely keep the giddiness out of my voice.

Boyboy nods. "I'd bet my Birkin on it."

"And are there any records of these weapons going to militias? Or gold buys? Anything else about Kasisi?"

"No, not yet."

My smile fades. "Nothing?"

"This isn't nothing!" He humphs, waving at his screen.

"You're right," I say, shaking my head. "Sorry. Does Bug Eye or Ketchup know about this?"

"No, they have no idea what I'm doing. I told them I haven't been able to decrypt anything yet."

"Good. But they know we didn't get everything and I have to go back in."

"Yeah."

I start to stand to go check on Michael, but Boyboy puts

a hand on my arm. "Tina, listen, this is getting complicated. Forget the video. You know who killed your mom. Maybe we should just cut our losses. I'll find some other way to hack into Greyhill's bank accounts. You don't have to go back there."

"I— No. We need everything. This isn't enough to bring Mr. G down."

Boyboy gives me a long, searching look. "Are you starting to doubt he killed her?"

I stand up. "No. I just . . . We have time. Bug Eye's given us a week."

Boyboy still looks dubious. "I don't like it."

I cross my arms over my chest. "I-I can't force you to keep working. Do you want out? I can tell Bug Eye something."

He snorts. "And who exactly is going to decrypt Mr. G's files?"

I don't answer. He knows I don't have anyone else who can do what he does.

He sighs, digs in his bag, and pulls out a new USB adapter. "Don't lose this one. I don't have any more, and making another will take a week."

"And he has my earpiece."

"You don't need the earpiece if you're not doing acrobatics to get in. Just use your phone like normal. The USB connects directly to it."

I slip the adapter into my pocket. "Midnight tonight. I'll tell Bug Eye to drive you up. And I'll try to make sure he leaves Ketchup at home."

Boyboy looks relieved. "Good."

I shift from foot to foot. "And . . . thank you. For everything."

Boyboy just clears his throat, looking past me. "Hello, gorgeous," he says under his breath.

I turn to see Michael pushing himself up and over the lip of the elevator shaft. "Finally," I say.

He wipes his brow on his shirtsleeve. "They have these things called stairs, you know."

"Tiny doesn't like folks crawling into her nest. Makes it damn near impossible," Boyboy says. "She blocked off the stairs. Took me months before I could get up here in under a half hour."

"Wait. Nest? Do you *live* here?" Michael asks me.

I give Boyboy a dirty look.

For a second I can see my home through Michael's eyes: the rough concrete-block walls with gaping holes where windows and doors should be. Tattered plastic sheeting hung like curtains on the east side to keep the rain out. A grimy mattress, a small gas cylinder stove. My stack of stolen paperback books in one corner, fat with damp. A laundry line. Nothing on the walls. Dirt in the corners.

I shouldn't care what he thinks—it's not like he was invited. But something about the way he's looking around makes me feel naked. I can tell he doesn't see the amazing view of the city, or that I'm safe here. All he sees through his rich-boy eyes is a poor refugee girl living in a filthy, half-finished building.

"Not all of us can afford the Ring," I say.

"It *is* a penthouse," Boyboy offers. "Or it could be one day."

"No, I just mean, well . . ." Michael seems at a loss. "All by yourself?"

"Yes."

He gapes for another few seconds, then seems to come to his senses. He walks to Boyboy and sticks out his hand. If Boyboy's manner and outfit throw him, he at least has the good breeding not to say anything. "You must be, ah, Boyboy. I'm Michael Greyhill."

"I know who you are, *habibi*," Boyboy says to Michael, taking his hand briefly.

"So," Michael says, looking at Boyboy's computer, suddenly all business. "That's where all the dirt on my dad is?"

Boyboy gives me an alarmed look. Michael eyes the computer, then the open hole of a window. Boyboy, seeing where this is going, hugs his computer to his chest. "I have copies! Don't touch Priscilla!"

I step between the two of them. "Easy there, Mikey. Like you keep reminding me, we have a deal."

Michael doesn't move. His face twists. There is something dark there that makes my blood run cold. "What did you find?" he asks.

"I, ah, haven't had time to decrypt everything yet," Boyboy says, his voice squeaking.

"It takes a while." I grab Michael's arm and try to pull him. It's like trying to pull a tree. "He'll keep us informed on his progress. Come on. You've met Boyboy. Now we should go. It's getting late, and your mother is going to be livid."

Michael looks between the two of us, and for a few very uncomfortable seconds it feels like he's reading my mind. "Tina, if you're lying about actually having the data from my dad's hard drive . . ."

"Don't worry," Boyboy pipes up, "we've got it. And what I've seen so far isn't pretty. Gold laundering, arms deals. Your dad's up to his eyeballs in very dirty dirt."

Michael swallows. "Let me see."

Boyboy sucks in a breath and cringes back.

"Not yet," I say, trying not to show how nervous I suddenly am. What have I done, letting Mr. Greyhill's son up here? "That's not the deal. If you prove your dad didn't kill Mama, then you can have it all back. But until then, hands off."

Michael looks from me to Boyboy again. He's bigger and stronger than both of us, and I'm not sure I can stop him if he decides to chuck the computer—or Boyboy, for that matter—off the roof.

"What if there's something in there that can help us find your mom's killer?" Michael asks.

"Boyboy will let me know if he finds anything, won't you, Boyboy?"

I feel myself rising to my toes, ready to pounce if it looks like Michael's going to make a move. I will *not* let him take Boyboy's computer or hurt him. But then, right before my eyes, Michael's angry, calculating expression melts away until all that's left is his mask. He looks past Boyboy, out at the city. "You're right, Tina, we should go." He turns and walks to the elevator shaft.

I release my breath. "I'll see you soon," I say to Boyboy. I watch Michael lower himself in. I'm still tingling with adrenaline.

Boyboy gives me a look and mouths, *Be careful.*

I nod and follow Michael down.

NINETEEN

By the time we get back to the Greyhills', it's late afternoon. Michael tells me to go ahead upstairs while he gets a tongue-lashing from his mother. Fine by me. The less time I spend under Mrs. G's eye, the better. I'm sure she'd love to blame Michael's disappearance on my bad influence. Besides, I need to make a call.

I close myself in my bathroom again and pull out my phone. I had noticed three missed calls and five texts from Ketchup before Michael and I left my roof. Now there are six missed calls—four from Ketchup and two from Donatien. I dial Bug Eye's number with a sick feeling in my stomach.

"Heard you were in town today," Bug Eye says, low and calm in my ear, without preamble.

"You did?" I ask, trying to keep my voice from squeaking.

"Ketchup saw you on a fancy bike heading toward Old Town."

I bang my fist on my leg. "I . . . All part of the plan. I had to go get a new adapter from Boyboy." I tell myself to calm down, make my voice sound right. You didn't do anything wrong, Tina. "He told me we didn't get everything off Greyhill's hard drive. I need to go back in tonight to finish the job." I hesitate. "Can you drive him up to do the tech stuff?"

I wait for an answer that doesn't come.

"I'm sorry, Bug Eye, I couldn't get away from Michael until now to tell you what was going on."

Bug Eye is quiet. It's a game of chicken; he's trying to make sure I'm being straight with him. "Fine. I'll drive him," he finally says.

"Thank you. Um. And no Ketchup."

"Why?" Bug Eye asks, suspicious.

"Because you know how he is with Boyboy. Ketchup says stuff that makes him twitchy. We don't need our IT guy twitchy."

Bug Eye sighs. "All right. But this time you get in and get this done. No screw-ups."

"No screw-ups." I count the seconds while I wait for him to respond.

"And no more running around without permission, right, Tiny Girl? *Mdosi* Omoko's not a man used to being kept out of the loop. Get down to business. Get him what he wants."

"I will."

"Or, Tiny?"

"Yeah?"

"Don't come back."

I push the borrowed green shirt under the guest-room bed with my other clothes and find something else to wear. When I'm cleaned up, I wander listlessly back downstairs, but I can still hear Michael's mother letting him have it in the living room. I go outside and dangle my feet in the pool.

From here, on the Greyhills' patio with a distant view of the city and the ocean, you can't see the staff cottages. They're hidden by thevetia and plumeria trees. But I know our old home is there, at the end of the compound. I want to go down and look at it, but other people live there now, new servants. I can picture the narrow bed I shared with Kiki, our sagging love seat under the gaze of a tiny framed picture of Saint Catherine, the packed dirt out back where Mama and the other maids would cook and hang our laundry. I wonder if the "house" I made under the bougainvillea vines for Kiki and me to play in is still there. Maybe her rag doll, the one Kiki cried over, the one I wouldn't go back for when we left, is still rotting under the leaves.

Kiki was born in our little cottage. Other than the convent school, it's the only home she's known. If it was odd that none of the other servants were allowed to bring their children, leaving them instead with relatives back in villages or down in Sangui, no one said anything about it to me. It didn't occur to me to ask until there was no one around to ask.

I wonder what Mrs. Greyhill had to say when it became obvious that Mama was going to have another baby, just as fatherless as me. I wonder if she had already started to notice the way her husband looked at my mother. I wonder what she thought when Kiki emerged, scrubbed pink, and if Mrs. G had pulled out her own daughter's baby photos and stared at them, comparing, trying to convince herself that her husband could not possibly be that stupid, or that cruel.

I wonder about a lot of things.

Mrs. Greyhill finally lets Michael go because she and Mr. G have to leave for a dinner party. Michael doesn't tell me what she's said to him, and I don't ask.

After they're gone, we retreat upstairs but have to keep the door to Michael's room open. Maids have been tasked with checking in on us, and they pass by too frequently to allow talk about "the case," as Michael continues to call it. We try to get by whispering, but eventually it becomes so frustrating that I decide to call it a night.

I leave Michael still poring over the UN and police files, carefully adding to his notes. I've told him most of what Donatien told me—mainly focusing on the fact that he's convinced Mr. G did it. I leave out the part about Donatien warning me away from Michael.

In my room I send Boyboy a text to call me when he and Bug Eye are on their way and flop down on the bed. I pull the photo of my mother out of my pocket and stare at her face until it starts to lose shape. Her smile becomes too wide, her braids too twisty. In the background the flower vines grow thorns and start to flex and curl and slip around the girls' arms like snakes crushing prey. The other girl whispers in Mama's ear and they laugh. Tina, Mama says, come here.

I try to tell her that I can't, but my mouth is sewn shut like Donatien's scar. I want to reach for her, but my arms and legs are held tight by the vines.

Tina!

She starts to laugh, and then she throws back her head so that her mouth is a chasm, and then she begins to scream.

I come to my senses with a jolt. For a second I flounder in the dark. I hear the scream again, except it's not a scream, it's just my phone buzzing. I fumble until I find it, my arm all pins and needles. "Boyboy?"

"Finally."

"What time is it?"

"Midnight! I've been trying to call for half an hour. You too busy with Prince Charming?"

"*Mavi!* I fell asleep."

"Great. It's so nice to hear you're taking this seriously. Are you awake now? Ready to go back in?"

I flip on a light and blink into it. "Yeah," I mutter, still seeing the afterimages of my dream before my eyes. I shiver. "Give me a sec. Where's Bug Eye?"

"Driving. Pissed you didn't answer."

I slap my cheeks lightly, trying to wake up. "Can you hack

into the security cameras and make sure everyone is tucked into bed?"

"Already on it."

I hear Boyboy's fingers tapping over the line. While I'm waiting, I find dark clothes in Jenny's closet to change into. "Well?"

"Anyone ever told you patience is a virtue?"

"Only my mother, about a million times," I say, adjusting the phone as I pull a top over my head.

"Glad it sank in. Okay, Michael hasn't left his room, but the Greyhills aren't in their bedroom. It looks like maybe a car is gone."

"Perfect. They must still be at their dinner party."

"I'll try hacking into the security firm they use for their car and see where their GPS puts them. Hang on."

I turn to the mirror and only then notice that what I thought was a black top is in fact black covered in dark red kissy lips. I make a face. I can just imagine Boyboy's reaction if he could see me now.

Oh well, it's not a fashion show.

It's a robbery.

"Boyboy? Are you ready? I'm heading out."

"Wait! Don't you want to make sure they're not pulling in the driveway right now?"

I fidget while the seconds tick by. Finally Boyboy says, "Security puts them a few miles away in Miambu. Okay, I'm putting the interior cameras on a loop starting now."

"All right, here I go."

"Just a sec. Bug Eye wants to talk to you."

I hear the phone change hands, and then Bug Eye's deep voice. I wait for him to chastise me again, to warn me not to mess up, but he just says, "You got this, Tiny Girl. Soon as you're done, you can get out of that house. Get back to real life."

"Yeah," I say, not quite sure how to answer. "I'll call back once I'm in the office."

After I hang up and put my phone into my pocket, I shake my arms and legs out, getting loose. When I slip into the hall, there's no light coming from under Michael's door. Creeping back through the tomblike house, I feel my pulse quicken. The familiar surge of adrenaline brings a smile to my face. Everything suddenly feels right. This is what I know. This is who I am. A thief. A good one. This time I'm not leaving until all Mr. Greyhill's secrets are mine.

TWENTY

Two minutes later the office door lock is picked and I'm in. "Too simple," I whisper when I call Boyboy back.

His voice crackles over the line. "Just listen out for lover boy creeping up on you again."

I snort. "Lover boy?"

"Hey, girl, I just call it like I see it. That boy is sweet on you."

"You met him for, like, two minutes," I say, wondering if Bug Eye is listening in. I reach the other side of the dark room by the light of my phone and switch on the desk lamp.

"You forget that I—genius—therefore very perceptive." Boyboy's voice cuts in and out. "—too bad you're—totally mess his family up. You two would—cute couple."

"You're just saying that because you're too far away for me to punch you," I say, but I shift in Mr. G's big seat, sparks of guilt igniting in my gut. I look over at the leather couch. The thought of my mother slumping into death kindles my anger again and the moment passes.

It doesn't take long to get back into Mr. Greyhill's computer and hard drive, now that we've had practice. Soon Boyboy is shuffling screens like a card trick.

"Come to Papa," he says. After a few seconds he clucks impatiently. "The signal is still weak. I tried to boost the bandwidth, but it's slow."

He's talking more to himself than me, and I let him do his thing while I turn to inspect the bookshelf. I tuck the phone between my shoulder and my ear and run my fingers along the shelves' edges. Nothing. No hinges, no indication of a hidden door or camera. I pull books out, mess with the little wooden statues of Masai warriors that line one shelf. It doesn't move.

I look back at the computer. The screen is full of lines of code.

"Keep the phone—next—computer, Tina. I—to close the GPS tracker," Boyboy says. "It's slowing—down too much. Bug Eye will—their car pulling in."

I lay my phone next to the computer, go back to the bookshelf, and continue to poke. Where is the camera? And how did Michael get the door open? When he came through, I was too busy staring at the photo of my mother to know he was even there, much less how he got in. I don't see anything that could be a latch. Starting from the bottom, I work my way back up the shelves again. I'm at the Masai statues when I hear Boyboy's faint voice shouting my name.

I grab the phone and put it to my ear. "What?"

"Greyhills' car—pulling in right now!"

I curse, then watch as a tiny screen pops up on the computer. "What's that?" It looks like surveillance footage.

"The hallway leading to the office—keep an eye on it!"

"How much time do you need?" I ask.

"More than—got," Boyboy says. "Just—let me see what I can do."

I look around helplessly. Damn this room and its no windows. Mr. Greyhill may not come directly up to his office, but I'm not ready to stick around and find out. I've got to have enough time to get out the office door and around the corner without being seen.

"Hurry," I say.

"That's not helping," Boyboy singsongs.

I keep my eyes glued to the hallway. It's empty. For now. If Mr. G shows up on the screen it means I have about ten seconds before getting caught. Unless . . . I put the phone back next to the computer and swivel to the bookcase. There has to be a way to open it. But I've tried everything. I turn back to the desk, and grope underneath.

"It's too late," I hear Bug Eye say. I grab the phone back with one hand and keep searching with the other. "The cameras are show—coming inside. Greyhill—be there any second. Get out, Tina."

Boyboy must still be working. The computer screen continues to flash through files.

"Did he get it all?"

"You can come back later!" Bug Eye says.

I don't answer, my fingers sliding down the desk's wood paneling. There has to be a lever or a button or—"Got it!" I jab the tiny switch and turn to see the bookshelf gliding noiselessly open. A cool breath of air rushes in. "I got the secret door open!"

"Oh Lord, good thing," I hear Boyboy say in the background.

I look back at the screen.

Mr. Greyhill is coming down the hallway.

"Are you done?" I ask.

"It's almost—*mavi*."

"What?"

The computer screen flickers and then goes black.

Boyboy's curse comes through loud and clear. Suddenly a cartoon rabbit pops up on the screen and wags his finger at us. "No, no, no!" the bunny says.

"What the—?" I hear Boyboy's fingers pause, then start to tap again. More rabbits appear.

"I'm leaving," I say, and reach for the USB.

"Wait!" Boyboy shouts. "It's a fork bomb! He'll know someone's been here!"

Bunnies jump all over the screen, and choruses of "No, no, no!" grow more dense.

"We don't have time!" I look up, listening for the sound of a key scraping in the lock.

"Aaaaand, okay, now! Go!" Boyboy says.

I yank the USB out. The screen goes black, and I slap down the lid. I throw the computer and hard drive in the desk drawer, then shove myself into the space behind the book-shelf. I pull it shut just as the door to the office opens. Bracing myself on the cold damp wall, I listen, my heart hammering. I lift the phone back to my ear with a shaking hand. Through static I hear Boyboy sucking in deep asthmatic breaths, even though he's not actually in physical danger.

"Oh my God—Tina?" Boyboy gasps. "Are you okay?"

"I made it. I'm in the tunnel," I whisper.

Boyboy's breath whooshes in relief. "Now I rem—why you're the thief and I—nerd. I think I'm having—panic attack."

"Shh. Did you get it all?"

"I think—need to check."

I use my phone to find the screen next to the door and press its buttons until it comes on, bathing the tunnel in a soft gray glow.

"What are—doing in there?" I hear Bug Eye say. "Can—get out—is there—back door?"

"One second," I say. "I can see him on the camera."

I go quiet as Mr. Greyhill walks into the frame and sits down at his desk. He pulls his laptop out of the drawer and then the hard drive. I hold my breath, waiting to see if he notices anything amiss, but his tired posture doesn't change. He's poured himself a drink, which he sets beside the com-puter. I can only see the back of his head. He rubs his eyes, then loosens his tie and undoes his cuff links. I see him pull his phone from his pocket and put it to his ear.

Boyboy has stopped hyperventilating. "Is there—plug—adapter to the screen—" he whispers.

I hesitate.

"Do it," I hear Bug Eye say.

I find a place on the side of screen to insert the USB. "Did that work? Can you see?"

"Yeah," Boyboy breathes. "Turn—audio."

I press the volume button and hear Mr. G saying, "Yes, of course," into his phone. He's tapping at the computer, but his back is blocking the screen.

"Think he noticed the bunnies?" I whisper.

"No, I cleared that business up," Boyboy says. "Smart piece of screwage, that."

"Shh." I lean in closer.

"Same as before," I hear Mr. G saying in his cold, Big Man voice. "Don't let Huan-Xi give you any trouble about tariffs. He knows better than to try and pull that . . . Right. No, I'll be at the mine, so you'll have to handle it. The one in Walikale Territory, near Kasisi. No, that's the closest town, and then the mine's still ten kilometers farther into the mountains. Satellite phones only up there."

My skin prickles. Kasisi, my home village.

". . . It *is* the tin mine. That's where they bring it. I want to pick up the samples myself . . . I don't trust anyone else to do it. And I have other business there too . . . Looking into that new *comptoir* trying to get in on the action. No, I'm not worried about him. He's just proving to be harder to get rid of than the others . . . No, the rebels know better. They'll stick with us. We're reliable. No one else is going to get them the things they want at the prices we offer . . . Yeah, I tried, but this new fellow's got himself a little posse, apparently. And something about his operations just make me think he's . . . Never mind. No, it's nothing . . . Don't worry, I'll take care of it."

The way he says *take care of it* sends a chill through me. It's the same voice Bug Eye uses when he's talking about what to do about someone who's become a problem.

Mr. G goes on, ". . . Chicago certainly does *not* need to know . . . No, better you don't know either. It's just how things work out there. You'd think the militias would all be tired of fighting but . . . Sure, the offer stands, but no one seems interested in doing business that way . . . I keep telling them it would be more profitable, but . . . not in this lifetime."

I strain to hear, trying to piece together everything Mr. G is saying.

"Yeah, we work with what we've got. If I need to I'll meet with the general in Kigali before I come back to Sangui. No, that's the part you don't need to know about . . . No, the Rwandan general. I'm not dealing with those Congolese bastards. Army, militia, they can't figure out which team they're on half the time, why should I bother?"

A Rwandan general. I wonder if that's Gicanda, the guy whose name came up in Mama's police file.

". . . You just keep on greasing all the proper palms. Throw in some Johnnie Walker . . . bring a case. I should take out stock options." He makes a funny noise that it takes me a second to realize is a laugh. "Right . . . I'll let you know soon as I'm back. Mm-hm, same to you. Good night."

He hangs up and sets the phone down. Then he takes a

drink, rattling the ice cubes in his glass. For a few seconds he doesn't move. Then he opens his desk drawer and I see a flash of silver.

It's the gun.

I stare, transfixed as he picks it up and turns it over in his hands.

"What's he doing?" I hear Boyboy whisper.

"I don't know."

Greyhill holds the gun almost tenderly for a few more seconds, then replaces it in the drawer. His chair has been covering the computer screen, but then he leans back and it suddenly comes into view. When I see what he's looking at, I suck in my breath.

It's the photo of Mama and her friend.

My fist clenches, like I want to punch through the screen and snatch her away. I feel something like a growl inch up my throat.

Just then there's a knock on the office door, startling both Greyhill and me. Mr. G hits a button on the computer and Mama vanishes. "Yes?"

The office door opens a crack. "Coming to bed soon, dear?" Mrs. Greyhill asks.

"Two minutes."

She leaves and Mr. G closes the computer. He starts to follow her, but a step from the door he pauses and turns to look back in my direction. I shrink from the light of the screen, even though I know he can't see me. His deep-set eyes gleam like ice.

I hold my breath.

He looks toward my hiding spot for a moment longer, then turns and walks out of the room.

I let my breath out in a low hiss.

On the other end of the line, Boyboy and Bug Eye are quiet.

"How do I erase?" I finally ask Boyboy through a clenched jaw. He walks me through buttons on the screen until I find what I'm looking for: traces of my presence in the room. In a little while I'll creep back out in the dark. The camera won't pick me up if I don't turn on the light. There will be no sign of me left.

ARE YOU SURE YOU WANT TO DELETE? the screen asks. It is frozen on the last image of Mr. G's face.

I touch the word YES.

TWENTY-ONE

I wake at dawn to dead quiet.

It's disturbing.

Normally, mornings on my roof are full of the sound of traffic screaming through the city or the nasal chorus of ibises. But I forgot to open the window before falling into bed last night, so the air is both stale and silent. Even when I pull the curtains back and open the window I hear only the polite chirping of birds in the garden. They leave a lot of room for all the thoughts crowding my head.

I check, but there's no message from Boyboy on my phone about the files I transmitted last night, so I just send him a text that says, *?* It's probably too early to hope he's even awake, especially if he stayed up to decrypt files last night. I just hope Bug Eye let him go home.

I dress and poke my head out to see if Michael is up, but

his door is still shut. I go downstairs, and hearing Mrs. G in the kitchen giving marching orders to the servants, I head in the opposite direction, out onto the patio. The sun hasn't yet cut through the haze, and the garden has milky edges. Iridescent sunbirds shoot through the mist, flinging themselves from flower to flower. I lean against the balcony railing for a minute, looking out, feeling the damp and chill of the night rising from the ground.

Snippets of Mr. Greyhill's phone conversation float through my head. He's going to a tin mine near Kasisi and getting samples of something. Probably gold, right? And he's going to check out a *comptoir*. Donatien's used that word before. *Comptoirs* are the middlemen who buy gold from militias and smuggle it into other countries. But they're mostly small-time. Maybe this one is from a different mining company that's trying to butt in on Greyhill's deals with the militia? Greyhill is going to take him out, from the sound of it. Or maybe get a Rwandan general to do it . . . ? It *sounds* bad. It also sounds totally murky and confusing.

Will the files off his hard drive make things any clearer? The files. My shoulders tighten. What if there's nothing else on them? What if Boyboy can't decrypt them? What if there's not enough there to give Donatien? What do I do then? Move on to step two, or—

"Good morning, Christina."

I jump. Mr. Greyhill's voice sounds close in the thick air. I turn to see him walking toward me with two cups of tea in his hands. He looks ready for the office in a silk tie, his ash-colored hair combed flat to his head. He comes to stand beside me at the railing, so near that I could reach out and touch the crisp pleat on his sleeve.

"Good morning, sir."

He hands me a teacup.

"Thank you."

"It's peaceful here, isn't it?" He looks out over the yard. "I like to come here in the morning before work. Clears my head."

I follow his gaze: the roofline of my old cottage is just visible behind the trees. "Yes, sir."

He sips his tea, and I sip mine. Steam swirls around our faces. It and the birds the only things moving. I try to think of things to say, but all that goes through my mind is, Murderer. Murderer. Murderer. Does he know it was me who interrupted him the night before Mama died, when he had his hands around her throat? It was right down there, under that tree. Maybe I should just ask him what he was chatting about on the phone last night. What sort of things or people are you "taking care of" today, sir?

Finally, Mr. G says, "You know you're welcome to stay here as long as you like."

I dart a glance at his smoothly shaven face, surprised at the kindness in his tone. "Thank you, sir. But I'll have to get back to school in a few days."

"Yes, of course. Where did you say you were in school again?"

"I didn't," I say carefully. "The Alexander Academy, in Paris."

"I see. Do you like Paris?"

I try to remember what Michael said. "The people are rude."

His mouth lifts into a small smile. "Do you make it back here often? To Sangui, I mean?"

"No, sir."

"I'm sure it's quite strange being back."

You have no idea. "Yes, sir."

Mr. G keeps his eyes on the garden. "For the first few years I lived in Africa I couldn't wait to get back to the US. Every vacation, every work trip to our headquarters in Chicago, was a relief. In America, there are good roads and traffic lights, and in most places you can walk around at night without any worry."

I look at him, curious despite myself.

"But little by little, every time I went back, the place seemed more and more strange. It was too cold, too sterile. The stores were full of things that you could only buy in absurd quantities. People didn't understand why I didn't want to come home. I didn't really understand it myself. I made my trips there shorter and shorter. That was twenty years ago. Now I only go if I must, for work, and I stay no longer than I have to."

He takes a sip of tea. "Sangui City is rough around the edges. I'm sure I don't have to tell *you* that. It's a little like I imagine the American Wild West was once. There's crime and corruption, but there are also fortunes to be made if you are smart. It's old and new all at the same time—shopping malls next to centuries-old mosques. Masai herding cattle down the median on the highway. People everywhere. There's so much energy. So much *life*. I'm not sure my children understand it."

He frowns, looks down at his knuckles. "It's funny. We hardly ever get to choose where our souls find their homes."

We lapse into silence. I am so confused. Who is this man, who could speak so coldly on the phone last night about taking out his competition, and now so lovingly about his adopted city?

Mr. Greyhill turns to me. "You know, Christina, what happened here, to your mother . . ."

I tense. Out of the corner of my eye I can see his face, twisted ever so slightly in a grimace. But after a long silence, he just places a hand on my shoulder. "It was horrible. I'm so very sorry."

It takes every ounce of my will not to fling him off. His hand is heavy and warm where it sits, and my skin crawls under it. "Yes," I whisper, my eyes fixed on my old cottage. "I know."

"If there's anything I can do . . ."

He pulls his hand away, like maybe he can feel my loathing through his fingers, and when I look at him, his face is smooth again, his emotion hidden. Michael gets that from his father, I realize, the ability to put everything behind a mask.

". . . you just have to ask," Mr. Greyhill finishes.

It takes me a second, but I manage to lift the corners of my mouth into something that passes for a smile. "Thank you, sir, I will."

He turns and leaves me. Soon the mist will evaporate, and the edges of the world will become clear. But for now they fade and merge, and as hard as I try, I can't see where one thing ends and another begins.

TWENTY-TWO

I'm so sick of Michael's room I could scream. If I have to stay in this house much longer, I'll start breaking things just so it's not all so perfect. I'm desperate for word from Boyboy, but after five unanswered texts he only writes back,

LEAVE ME ALONE WOMAN ALL OK NOT DONE.

And Michael is getting tired of watching me pace a hole in his carpet, but of course he's too well mannered to say anything. Instead he taps his pen against his cheek in time with my steps, looking over his notes.

I hear him flip pages. "So according to Donatien, he and your mom were supposed to meet on April twenty-fourth, to take these photos, right? But then she doesn't show." He shuffles through the UN file. "Then you and your mom entered Kenya on May tenth." He puts the papers down. "What happened in between? What do you remember about the time right before you left?"

"Not much."

"But did something happen that would have prevented her from meeting Donatien? Something that would have made her want to leave Congo and come find my dad?"

I pause with my back to Michael. "I really don't want to talk about it."

I can practically feel him sit up at attention. "Talk about what? What happened, Tina?"

"It's . . . It doesn't have anything to do with her murder."

"How do you know? Come on, we've got nothing to work with here. Anything might help. Look at me."

I turn to face him reluctantly. His face is eager. "We got separated," I say. "Right before we left."

Michael is all ears, hunched forward, waiting for me to go on.

I pleat the edge of the borrowed shirt I'm wearing with my fingertips. "It's like the file says: Militia and soldiers used to come and attack our home, and we'd have to run and hide in the forest. Right before we left, that happened, and she sent me ahead." I can feel my throat closing up, and I take a steadying breath. "And I was there in the jungle by myself for a while."

"A while?" Michael prods.

I shrug. "I was five; I don't really remember. A few days?"

Michael's eyes go wide. "You never told me about that."

The ache in my throat turns to anger. "She didn't abandon me. She came for me eventually."

"But . . . a few days? Where was she?"

I turn my back to him again. "I don't know," I say over my shoulder. "She didn't tell me. I think she told Donatien, but he won't tell me either. And like I said, I really don't remember much about it, okay? After a while she found me in the forest and we left. End of story."

"But she never said where she had been?"

I shake my head no.

Michael is quiet while he thinks. Finally, he lets out a deep sigh. "Maybe we're looking at this the wrong way. What if something happened and she came to my dad looking for help? Maybe he was protecting her."

"Protecting her? Why would he do that?"

"Maybe she had something he wanted." He looks at me and makes a face. "No, not *that*. Something else. Gold?"

"He had plenty of gold," I say. "What would Mama have brought with her from Kasisi that he couldn't get himself? He had gold; he had power. She had nothing but me."

"Information, maybe?" Michael muses, making a note.

I tap my teeth with my fingernail. It's true that in a dirty line of work you need to know everything you can about everything. "Maybe something about the militias?" I ask. "Or someone who worked for him? You know, Donatien said your dad didn't buy the gold from the militias himself. He said there was a Kenyan guy who did it. That's who Mama had seen out there making the deals. Any idea who he would have been?"

Michael stops writing. "Wait, so you're saying she never even saw my dad in Congo?"

"I . . . I thought she had."

"You *thought* she had?" Michael says.

"Donatien never really, um, clarified that until yesterday. But it doesn't change what your dad did," I add quickly. "The Kenyan guy was there on his orders. And she knew your dad was the mastermind behind everything. Donatien told her."

"But she never actually saw him doing anything bad?"

"Don't act like he's all innocent," I snap. Suddenly I sit up straight. "Wait. Mwika! It could have been David Mwika who was doing the buys! He's Kenyan, right?"

Michael looks dubious. "Lots of people are Kenyan, Tina. And I don't know . . . He would have needed to be away a lot, right? Doing stuff in Congo? Mwika was always around, with Dad or with us."

But Mwika sounds the most likely to me. A loyal servant, doing his master's bidding. "Hey!" I say brightly. "I've got a great idea. Let's ask him!"

Michael scribbles something angrily in his notes. "I'm working on it."

My glibness evaporates. "Are you even trying?"

"Of course I am! He's not easy to get in touch with."

"Are you sure you know where he is?"

"I know, okay? I overheard Dad talking to someone on the phone about the company where he's working now."

My pulse quickens. "Which is where?"

Michael stares at me for a long time. Finally he says, "It's called First Solutions. It's a security firm working in Congo."

"First Solutions. That's great. We can find him easy!"

Michael frowns. "Did you hear me? I've been trying to get in touch, but I can't get anyone at the company to return my calls." Michael looks frustrated, but he doesn't know what magic Boyboy can do with just a smidgen of information. If anyone can find someone, it's him.

I hear my phone buzz with a text. "Finally," I say, seeing it's from Boyboy. "I've got to go." I stand up.

"What? No." Michael stands up too. "I can't leave the house. Mom basically grounded me until I'm eighty."

For a moment I just look at him, and I want to say, How strange—a mother around to ground you. It sounds like something out of a movie.

"I'm not asking your permission. I have to meet Boyboy." I put my phone in my pocket. "I'm coming back," I add, seeing the furrow between his eyebrows.

"At least let one of the drivers take you."

"So he can make sure I don't run away?"

Michael doesn't respond.

"Fine, but he's dropping me off at Saint Raphael's and I'll meet him back there. And if he follows me, I'll know and I'll slash his tires."

"Jeez, Tina. Don't be such a Goonda."

I think he means it as a halfhearted joke, but it leaves me cold.

"It's what I am, rich boy. Get used to it."

• • •

When I get to the roof, Boyboy is already there, enthroned in the safari chair again. His outfit is more demure today—a studded leather jacket and pants in a color he would probably call something like *sea foam*. His nails are painted lavender.

"You better not have forgotten anything there," Boyboy says, "because I know you are not going back. Bug Eye's orders. You stay here with me. We are done. This is it. This is everything."

"Yeah?" I say, walking over. "We got it all?"

"Yep. A few more days of decrypting, you get your muck-raking dude up and mucking, and we proceed to my personal favorite phase of Tiny Girl's Ultimate Plan for Revenge." He cracks his knuckles ostentatiously. "Liquidating bank accounts! I've already picked out the bag I'm going to buy with my cut: a Louboutin clutch in vermilion patent leather. It's the gayest thing I've ever seen, and my mother is going to have a fit and beg me not to wear it out of the house, but I will. I will wear it every day because I love it so, so, *so* much."

"Uh-huh."

He finally looks up at me. "Okay, what? Say something, Tina. You're making me nervous."

"Everything's fine," I say, and suddenly become very interested in a mosquito bite on the back of my arm. "Hey, have you ever heard of a security company called First Solutions? Michael thinks Mwika's working for them in Congo. Can you see what you can dig up?"

"You know where he is?"

"Just that. But if we can find him, maybe I don't need to wait on Michael to do it."

Boyboy gives me a long look, then sighs. "Fine. I'll add it to your tab. Come here, ingrate. I want to show you some things I found."

"Good dirt on our bad man?" I ask, perking up.

"Oh yeah. Real good bad stuff. You know that other payment I showed you yesterday and how it didn't actually incriminate him?"

"The one to the South African place for security advice?"

"Right, well, I found the key code." Boyboy points at the screen, running a lavender nail along a line. "Here's what he actually paid for: Security advice equals two tons light munitions. All of this below is the exact invoice list—a bunch of guns and stuff. Dude is one organized arms smuggler. He's going down. No question."

"Nice," I say. "Can we link it to the militias yet?"

"Working on it. I still haven't decrypted most of this stuff. I'm sure there's something here, though, if everything else is this detailed." Boyboy looks up at me. "Now is when you start doing happy backflips. Go on, let's see them."

"Sorry. Yay!" I make dazzle fingers.

Boyboy watches me for a second. "What's up with you?"

I let my smile slide. "If you see any additional payments to Mwika, will you let me know?"

"Payments?"

"Like, beyond his salary. I think Mwika might have been more than just Greyhill's head of security."

"Sure, I'll look." He pauses. "Wait. What was the name of the company he works for?"

"First Solutions. Why?"

Boyboy goes rapid fire at the keyboard. "It's in here. I know I've seen that name."

I wait, tensed on the edge of my concrete block, while he searches.

"There," he finally says. "I knew it sounded familiar. Two payments of thirty-five thousand US dollars."

I hunch in, trying to see what he's showing me. "To First Solutions?"

"Uh-huh, I think so. That's what it looks like. Both within days of each other, two years ago."

My mind races. "Are you sure?"

"Yeah. I mean, according to this."

"Does it say where the payment went? Any way to find Mwika?"

Boyboy runs his finger along the lines on the screen. "Western Union. In Walikale Town."

"That's near Kasisi," I say, my heart starting to thump.

"There's a contact phone number. Maybe it's Mwika's." Boyboy scribbles it off and hands it to me.

I stand up, staring at the little piece of paper. Mwika's phone number. He's in Walikale. Finally! Some answers! But . . . I pace toward the window. Mr. G sent him payments. Does that mean Mwika was working for him? Or was it hush money? I stop in my tracks, my stomach dropping. Maybe Mwika sold the video back to Mr. Greyhill again. In which case, I'm screwed. I've got nothing. If it showed Mr. G killing my mother, then the video is gone, obliterated.

"Did you find any video files in all that?" I ask Boyboy.

"Tina, come on. Don't you think if I found your mom's murder video I'd tell you?"

So it could be gone, or maybe Mr. G never bought it. I keep pacing.

"Hey, before you go back to being all pensive and uncommunicative, do you want to see the last thing I found?" Boyboy calls.

I circle back to look over his shoulder at the screen, my thoughts still a jumble. "The photo of my mom?"

"I checked it, after Mr. Greyhill was mooning over it last night. Just so I could mark it off the list, really. I wasn't expecting to find anything. But look." He clicks something and Mama and the girl fade, their faces replaced by what looks like a scanned sheet of notebook paper. It's covered in hand-drawn tables and figures.

I lean closer. "What is it?"

"I don't know. I mean, the photo is a stego file, obviously."

I roll my eyes. "Obviously. Meaning?"

"It has data concealed in the noisy bits."

"Noisy?"

Boyboy sighs his special sigh that means I am hopeless. "Don't hurt your fragile little brain thinking on it. It's just a way of hiding something. You'd never figure it out unless you're me."

I lean closer to study the minuscule writing. The image isn't very good; it's pixelated and hard to read. With a little electric thrill I read the heading on the paper: *Kasisi.* I trace my finger over the columns. "It looks like some sort of accounting thing. It's not another record of his secret deals?"

"I don't think so. All of Mr. Greyhill's are electronic. I can't see a guy like him using pencil and paper like this, can you?" Boyboy hands me the computer, gets up, and stretches. "Did you bring me takeaway like I asked? Tikka masala? Extra *pili-pili*?"

"I'll go out and get it in a minute. Promise," I mutter, taking his seat.

The page looks like it's been ripped out of a notebook, folded up, and smoothed back out. There are six columns. The first has words in it, odd ones: *Terminator, Ugly Twin, Slimmy, Earwax.* Maybe they're names? They sound like Goondas. Militia members? The columns next to them are filled with figures. One column of numbers is labeled MOBILE INTERESTS.

I scroll down. There's another ripped-out page just like it. And another. The last one has a dark streak across it. The pages are scanned in black and white, but the streak looks suspiciously like old blood. "Why would he hide this? What is it?"

"Two words, Tiny: *tikka masala.*"

"Okay, okay," I say, but instead I just sit there, a million thoughts pinging around in my brain. What is *Mobile Interests*? I click open a new window on Boyboy's computer and search for it. I get nothing but a bunch of cell-phone ads. I stare at the blinking cursor on the search box, then type in *Kasisi, Congo*.

It shows up as a tiny dot on the map, red dirt at a crossroads surrounded by green. So small. I zoom in. There can't be more than twenty buildings in what would be called town. I wonder which little spot was my old home; I remember our house but couldn't tell you where it was. Roads stretch from town up mountains to little bare patches that must be farms. But they don't go far. Beyond, there is nothing. Just treetops for miles and miles. The Congo rain forest. Terra incognita. There be monsters.

I stare at the green until my vision blurs. I remember looking up at the tree canopy, as tall as the roof Boyboy and I sit on today. Streams gushing cold and rocky. Flowers. Monkeys, hornbills, and shrews. Nimble-toed little antelope and bush-pigs with twitchy noses. Centipedes and butterflies as big as my hand. If I concentrate, I can smell the musk of rotting leaves.

Somewhere in all that, there are militiamen who weave narrow trails, guns slung over their shoulders, grass necklaces and amulets swinging across their chests.

I rub my eyes and look back at the hidden notebook papers. These pages don't necessarily have anything to do with my mother, I tell myself.

But I know they do. I feel it in my guts. He hid them in her photo. They're labeled with the town we lived in and fled from. There is some connection. I just can't see it yet.

I hear myself say, "I'm going there."

Boyboy blinks. He knows I'm not talking about the tikka joint. "Where?"

The idea shocks me nearly as much as it does Boyboy, but out of my mouth, it's real. There is no other way to find out what happened to my mother, who she was, and what secrets she brought out of that dark forest with her. There is nothing else here in Sangui for me to uncover. There is no one here who will tell me. Before I can keep going forward, I have to go back.

Michael is right. I have to know for sure that Mr. Greyhill killed her. If David Mwika and his video are still there, I'll find them. And if I don't, maybe whatever chased Mama out of our home and sent her to Mr. Greyhill is still there, hidden under the leaves. I'll dig it up.

I realize that I've been turning in this direction from the moment I saw my mother's face in the photo, that first night in Mr. G's office. The idea of going to the place my mother and I ran from is terrifying, but every bone in my body tells me it's what I have to do. I have to look again with new eyes. I have to know. I have to know everything.

All one hundred percent.

For myself. For her.

I jut my chin out at the map. "There. Congo. Back home."

TWENTY-THREE

Boyboy takes it pretty well.

"No way. *No way.* Are you crazy? You cannot go there." He literally stamps his foot. "I forbid it!"

"Boyboy, don't be a queen. I'm going." I stand up, start looking around to see what I should pack.

"But we just got all this dirt! Don't you want to expose him? What about your plan? What about dirt, money, and blood?"

"I'm not asking you to go with me."

"That's not the point! You think being a cat burglar in Sangui is dangerous? That place is no game! It's Mordor you'd be heading into!"

"Mordor? I'm going to Kasisi."

"No," Boyboy says, throwing up his hands, "I mean

Mordor, like *Lord of the Rings*, Eye of Sauron. You know, definition of evil?"

"I have no idea what you're talking about. Is that a nerd thing?"

"Yes, it's a . . . Never mind. Listen to me. You don't just waltz back into Congo. Why do you think our parents took us out of that hellhole in the first place?"

"Come on, you're being dramatic. I mean, lots of people still live there, right?"

"Yeah, warlords! Militias!"

I put my second-best knife in my backpack. My sweater. A plastic bottle that I fill from my rain barrel. "Not just them," I say. "Normal people too. Farmers and stuff." I look around, trying to keep my face composed, calm. No sense in letting Boyboy see that the idea of going there terrifies me too. What does one take on a trip into the eye of evil? I pick up a can of beans and add it to the pile.

Boyboy swallows, and I can tell he's trying for a rational voice. "Tina, *we* were the normal people. And bad stuff happened to us. Please don't do this."

I busy myself with arranging the stuff in my pack. "I have to, Boyboy," I say, unable to face him. "That's where Mwika is. Mr. Greyhill is going there too. Mama's murder and home—it's all tied up like a big knot. Keep working on the decryption, okay?"

Boyboy's still looking at me like I'm giving him the stomachache of his life. "What are you going to tell Bug Eye?"

I hesitate. Bug Eye told Boyboy my time was up at the Greyhills. "I'll figure something out. Maybe I can tell him I can't leave the Ring without Michael getting suspicious. I'll be back in a few days, before you're even done decrypting. He never has to know I'm gone."

Boyboy just hugs himself and shakes his head.

What I don't say is that as scary as Bug Eye is, I am sort of beyond caring what he'll do if he finds out I'm skipping town. Some things are more important than ass kickings.

It feels good to sleep in my own bed. Even the guilt I feel when the driver, and then Michael, call and text repeatedly until I turn off my phone isn't enough to bring me down. I'm just relieved to be in my own place, with my own smells, my own things, the lights of my own city stretched out like stolen diamonds on velvet.

I think about going to see Kiki, but she won't be expecting me and I'd have to knock on the dorm window. I don't want to get her in trouble. It's only Monday. I'll be back by Friday, I tell myself.

I wake up before it's even light, jittery and nervous, but excited too. I'm finally *doing* something.

It doesn't take long to get ready. I brush my teeth and tuck new bobby pins into my hair. I stuff as much of my emergency cash as I think I'll need for the trip into the seams I've ripped open in my jacket. Then I pull the concrete block up to the eastern corner of the main room and stand on it. I reach with two fingers into a crack between the bricks in the wall and pinch out a plastic bag. After I blow off the dust, I look at the prayer card, at Saint Catherine's face, her breaking wheel at her side, sword under her feet, palm branch in her hand.

Sometimes I feel like I split Saint Catherine in half. Kiki kept her name and her goodness. I kept the things that killed her.

I fold the plastic bag around the card and put it in my backpack with the photo of my mother. Maybe one day I'll add a triumphant palm branch to the tattoos of the sword and the wheel on my arms. But not yet.

The bus terminal is orchestrated chaos, as usual. Hawkers, touts, pickpockets, and travelers press past one another in the early sun. Wide-eyed men and women from up-country clutch their bags to their armpits and furtively count out bills stashed in bosoms and underwear. Steely-eyed men and women who work the buses and market stalls watch them with predatory disdain.

I nod greetings at a few of the other light-fingered crowd workers I know and give them the signal that I'm not working today. They look relieved.

And that's when I spot them.

One in a very lime-green hat and plaid capris, scanning the crowd; one trying to look like he hangs out at bus depots all the time and failing miserably because any fool can see he's a *sonko* rich boy and doesn't take the bus. It's in the way he's avoiding touching things. Also because he's half a shade whiter than anyone except the blind albino guy rattling his tin cup for coins.

"What are you doing here?" I demand, marching over.

Michael has the nerve to look relieved to see me.

"Waiting for you, of course," Boyboy says, puffing up his chest. He's going for bluster, but he shrinks under my scowl.

"How did you even find me?"

"Tapped into your phone's GPS," Boyboy says. He shoulders a travel bag.

"Why?" I ask, giving the bag a suspicious once-over. "And what is Michael doing here?"

Boyboy and Michael look at each other.

I narrow my eyes at Boyboy. "You called him? You told him?"

Boyboy puts an indignant fist to his hip. "Somebody's gotta look out for you, and I am simply not made of that sort of manly stuff."

"I can take care of myself! I don't need manly men."

"That's what you think. You're a minnow getting ready to swim with sharks. Man, woman, whoever, you need the safety of numbers."

Michael still hasn't said anything. I round on him. "And I suppose you agreed to come to make sure I keep my end of our bargain?"

His eyes glitter. "You're the one running off. Don't act all high and mighty."

I fold my arms over my chest and try to look down at him,

but it's less intimidating than I'd like, seeing as I'm a head shorter. "You seriously think you're going to tag along?"

"I don't want to just *tag along*. I want to go," Michael says. "*I* made a bargain and I'm sticking to it. I'm going to figure out who killed your mom. If that means going to Congo to find Mwika, then let's go. But yes, I also want to make sure you don't bail."

I grind my teeth. "I wasn't going to release the dirt on your dad. Yet. I haven't gone back on my word."

"The deal was to do this together."

"Aren't you grounded?"

"Don't you want to keep on not giving a shit?"

We stand glaring at each other until Boyboy rolls his eyes and says, "*Ngai*, you're like two roosters fighting over a hen. Are we done with the chest beating? Because time's wasting and we have a long way to go."

"I just don't want to be around when his father sends out a small private army to track him down!"

"You don't need to worry about my father."

"Oh really? Bet that's what my mother thought too."

Boyboy puts his sunglasses on and steps between us. "Okay! Time to go! Which bus is it?"

I take a deep breath. "So that's it, then. You're both coming?"

Michael nods.

"I'm not out here for my health, *habibi*," Boyboy says, waving off minibus fumes.

"Fine. I guess I can't stop you. But I'm not taking the bus."

"Private car?" Boyboy asks hopefully.

"No."

"All right, miss expert travel agent, what mode of transportation do you suggest, then?"

I tug the straps on my bag, cinching them down tight over my shoulders. "We'll take what all the refugees take."

Boyboy's mouth drops open when he follows my gaze. "You're kidding, right? A banana lorry?"

I smirk. "Unless you've got a private plane I don't know about."

"Michael does," Boyboy says. "His dad has an arms-smuggling helicopter."

Michael crosses his arms. "It's one thing to take my dad's motorcycle out for a ride. It's another to steal his chopper. Besides, he's using it."

He gives me a pointed look. Does he know that I know his dad is traveling?

Boyboy groans. "I detest banana lorries. I vowed never again."

"So take the bus and get stopped by border guards and bribe your way across three countries," I say. "I'm taking the lorry."

Boyboy removes his hat, gives it an apologetic look, and stows it in his bag. "I'm just putting this out there—this is the most unglamorous thing I will ever do for you, Tiny."

"I'm not forcing you!" I say, exasperated. "You're the one who wants to come. You could always stay here."

Boyboy gives me a funny look. "It's not that I *want* to come."

"Then I don't understand."

He starts to answer, then just shakes his head and walks off toward the lorry. Even Michael gives me a weird grimace, like he's embarrassed for me for some reason.

As he turns to follow Boyboy, Michael says, "For someone so smart, you sure can be an idiot."

TWENTY-FOUR

Rule 12: Always be ready to bolt.

At some point in your life, you will have to escape from something. Don't be caught unprepared. Maybe you have a fancy tunnel guarded by monsters, and cars and helicopters waiting outside to whoosh you away. Maybe you have passports and bank accounts in Europe. Maybe you have a motorcycle.

Maybe you've just got your feet. And if you're thusly unprepared, I hope for your sake a big woman with a truck takes pity on you.

But that sort of thing doesn't usually happen twice.

Mama and I got out of Congo on a banana lorry.

After we left the forest we made for Goma, on the tip of Lake Kivu. I don't remember much of that part. In Goma, though, there were too many soldiers prowling the streets and pops of gunfire at odd hours, and after sleeping a few nights on the floor at a pastor's home with a dozen other dazed and bruised bodies, the pastor told us the fighting was getting worse and we needed to leave. He managed to get us a lift with a lorry driver who had a lazy eye and a paunchy belly. He looked Mama up and down with his good eye, smiled and said he'd take us wherever we wanted. We thanked the pastor, and once he was gone, Mama found us another ride. Still a banana lorry, but driven by a huge, fierce woman named Paula Kubwa: "Big Paula."

Apparently lots of would-be refugees wanted to hitch a ride out of the country with Paula Kubwa. She was said to be the daughter of one of the militia leaders, and she took no guff from militia or police. She paid her bribes at the checkpoints like everyone else and got on her way, and if any man said boo he'd be laid out cold in the dirt, his friends just pissing themselves with laughter.

It wasn't easy to get a ride with the lady driver. Mama later told me that we included Paula Kubwa in our prayers every night because she had found us. She had rescued us. She had picked us out of the crowd of jostling refugees to act as our lady Moses, parting the sea for our escape into the promised land. I don't know if I remember her face, or if I've conjured it out of what Mama told me. In my mind she was a mountain, something marvelous and terrifying like an angel with a sword.

I'm pretty sure she didn't need my prayers.

. . .

I guess Boyboy, Michael, and I could have taken a bus and found some way to sneak across the borders, but just the idea of sitting in a cramped space for eight hours with all those bodies and all their bags and no one rolling down the windows makes me ill. Everyone eating and farting and talking too loud, little kids peeing in their pants because the bus won't stop, people sitting practically on top of you. A pirated kung fu movie on a too-small screen blasting too-loud static in the front. Contraband chickens that get loose and run squawking up and down the aisle until some poor guy grabs them and stuffs them back under his sport coat.

I like a crowd—it's great for pickpocketing—but I need to be able to escape. I'd rather pay a few shillings to sit in the back of a truck full of goods headed for the interior. It might be less comfortable, but at least you can feel the breeze.

Once, because I'm an orphan kid and no one could tell me not to, I went as far as the border checkpoint between Kenya and Uganda. My plan was to go all the way around the north side of Lake Victoria to Congo. I just jumped on a bus because I felt like it, pretending to be one of a family of ten, melting into the pack of loud, wiggly children who were being ushered on board by their overwhelmed father. I slipped under the driver's eye and slouched into a seat in the back. I didn't want to return for good, I just . . . wanted to go. To see.

But I chickened out before crossing that invisible line that turned Kenya into another country. One foot over and suddenly I'm illegal again, my refugee documents meaningless. Or so the smugglers in the lorries told me.

They call them banana lorries because the big flatbed trucks take stuff bought in Sangui—cooking oil, pots and pans, medical supplies, stuff made in China—into Congo. Then they bring produce (lots of bananas, hence the name) and timber and charcoal and people back out. Sometimes a little smuggled gold if the drivers think they can manage to get through all the checkpoints without getting caught. More often than gold, though, it's refugees, because they're easier to come by than gold, and no one wants to steal them.

The lorries go out and back, single file down the disintegrating highway. Like cows heading to pasture in the morning, returning to the barn at night. On that trip I decided to skip the bus and take a lorry back to Sangui. The man I found said I could, but if I had papers to get me across Kenya, why did I want to sit in the open? Why not sit in the nice bus? I just did. He shrugged and told me the fare—nearly as much as the bus after all—but assured me there were other ways if I didn't have the money. He gazed in unvarnished disappointment at my thighs when I pulled out my cash.

I look for a big woman among the drivers, but there are only men. We'll go a different way from my trip before, through Tanzania and Rwanda, around the south end of Lake Victoria. There are more borders to cross this way, but it's the fastest route to Goma. We want a driver with a good truck that won't break down, and one who has a wheel boy, who will switch out and drive through the night so we don't lose precious hours. First we have to talk to the touts, though, the guys who arrange the rides and take a cut. They jostle for our fare, waving and shouting and tugging our arms.

Once we've made the arrangements, we're presented to our driver. He takes one look at us, rounds on the tout, and lets him have it. Their argument is quick and loud and ends with the tout throwing up his hands and stalking off.

"How old are you?" the driver asks me.

"Eighteen."

"*Kwani?* Eighteen, my ass; come back when you're twelve." He starts to turn away.

"Fine, I'm sixteen."

He looks from me to Boyboy in his fancy trousers, to pale-faced Michael, and I can see him weighing it all out. We look like runaways. If I were him, I wouldn't want to take us either and risk getting in trouble at a police checkpoint.

"We'll pay extra," Michael says.

The driver's eyes scan around and he comes in closer. He tells Michael softly how much more he wants, a ridiculous sum.

"We'll pay half that," I interject when I can see Michael is ready to agree. I do have my pride.

The driver knows it's fair. "Be ready in twenty minutes."

The wheel boy loads up cooking oil in five-gallon jugs while the driver supervises. They're a good investment because the jugs will later be used for carrying water and the driver can get extra for them. Big aluminum cooking pots, straight from

China, go in next to boxes full of long bars of laundry soap. These will be sliced up like sticks of butter and sold off in squares. Rubber sandals, ladies' used dress shoes, football jerseys. Gum, cigarettes, plastic kazoos. It all goes in the back, the driver watching with a frown of concentration to see how badly the bottom of the truck sags. He's still got to put us back there too, after all.

While we're waiting, I move a few paces away and call up Kiki's school. I know I'll be back soon, but I feel guilty just leaving without at least checking on her.

However, "The young ladies are not allowed phone calls unless it is an emergency," a stern voice tells me. "Is this an emergency?"

"Not exactly, but—"

"No calls unless it's an emergency," the woman repeats, and before I can respond, I hear the line go dead. I grumble something uncharitable about the nun and redial the number. It rings and rings but no one answers.

I don't like the idea of leaving Sangui, much less the country, without talking to Kiki. What if I don't make it back by Friday? The idea of her sitting there in the washroom waiting on me is enough to give me a stomachache. But I'm not sure what else to do. She'll be fine, I tell myself. I try to shake off the bad feeling the call leaves, but it sticks with me the rest of the day.

We are not the only passengers. When it's time to go, I find myself in a scrum of bodies, all of them tugging overstuffed suitcases and clamoring to jump into the back of the truck at the last minute without paying the touts. Our tout fends them off, sweating and shouting and slapping at the interlopers, with his belly coming loose from under his shirt. I squeeze through the crowd toward the back of the truck, pushing Michael ahead of me, Boyboy close behind. The tout lets us climb on, but not before managing to sidle up close enough to rub his thing on my leg as I pass. He chuckles at my expression, and I can smell whatever garbage he ate for breakfast.

There are six of us in all who've secured a ride. Any more and the truck will scrape bottom. I am the only female. The three men who join us are so tall and long faced that they remind me of maize stalks. They look exhausted. One of them has bartered his way on as security and watches carefully to make sure that no one grabs the goods out of the back of the truck while we're snarled in traffic leaving the city. The others fall asleep immediately. The security man is so light and frail-looking, I can't imagine he'd be any match for someone determined to loot us. In fact, I'm afraid that if we get going fast enough, these skeleton men might fly right off the truck and blow away like empty shirts.

Michael is full of questions for the skeleton men.

He asks them one after another, and the men answer in serious, teacherish voices. And in fact, Michael soon learns that the three actually *were* schoolteachers once upon a time in Congo, but now they work as porters in Sangui's markets. The men are going to Congo to check on their farms and, on the way back to Sangui, see their wives and children who stay in a refugee camp in Rwanda. They are unwelcome in Congo, the skeleton men tell him, and when Michael learns this, he presses them for more information. Who doesn't want them there? Why? And who is fighting whom?

I cringe at Michael's earnest diction, but the skeleton men eat it up.

Skeleton Man One: "It is complicated, but the basic issue is that this country of ours is very big, and there are so many different people and languages and histories. You know, the king of Belgium once claimed the whole of Congo as his property. Imagine! Everything—the people, the trees, the minerals, the very air we breathe—this man thousands of miles away proclaimed it his own!"

Skeleton Man Two: "Our grandfathers laughed until the Belgians cut out their tongues."

Skeleton Man One: "Gaining our independence was long and bloody, and we inherited this place that now had borders, that was now a country. It cut up our ancestors' lands and cobbled together other communities into something that was supposed to be a nation. Creating one Congo like the government would like is nearly impossible, especially in the east, where we come from. The government is so far away. We know nothing of those people in the capital. Our forefathers, in fact, were kings in Rwanda long ago. That was before the borders, before the king of Belgium and the French and Americans."

Skeleton Man Three smiles: "It is a long story. We would need a week to go through all the history properly. And you asked who is fighting." He turns to his friends. "Who is it today?"

"Mayi-Mayi."

"M23."

"The army."

"Fighting one another?" Michael asks.

"Eh, depends on the day! Where are you going?"

"Walikale Territory."

The men shake their heads. "There are some bad ones there."

"FDLR."

"CNDP."

"FARDC, M23 . . ."

"And three different Mayi-Mayi."

Michael and I look at each other.

"Alphabet soup," I say. Only two of them sound familiar—Mayi-Mayi and the M23. I try to keep track when Donatien's talking about all the different groups and alliances, but it's tough. There are so many of them.

Michael starts to ask another question, but Skeleton Man Three waves his hands to stop him. "Just stay away from men with guns. They are all the same! Even the army. Even the ones with whom I share a tribe. Gangs. Bands of thirty, fifty, led by one. Sometimes by tribe, sometimes not. One day they are rebels, then the next they are government soldiers when their boss makes a deal. Then the next they are rebels again. Then they change their rebel group name. My nephew is a fighter. He told me all about it." Skeleton Man Three nods sagely.

"Your nephew? That small boy?" Skeleton Man One asks, looking distraught.

Skeleton Man Three hangs his head. "I know, I tried to talk sense to him, but these young men, they don't listen. They don't want to go to school or farm. They just want to shoot guns and drink and lie with women."

"Where would they farm?" Skeleton Man Two protests. "Where would they go to school? You can get shot just standing in your field! They round up children at school and put guns in their hands. Or, like me, you break your back to grow food for your family and the soldiers come and take everything anyway!"

The men slip into their own language, talking loudly until one seems to remember we're still listening and says, "The leaders say they are freedom fighters, but all we ever see is their lust for blood and gold. The boys who follow them are only children themselves, most of them. My poor nephew. He was such a good young man."

The men close their eyes, one by one, remembering other nephews, sons, brothers. And for a while they are too sad to speak.

TWENTY-FIVE

Boyboy told me you saved his life once," Michael says.

We've been traveling for about six hours. The skeleton men are all napping, wedged like commas around the goods in the truck. I've managed to tuck myself in between a box of individual chewing gum packets and a bag of sandals. It's not so bad. The sun is still hot, but the wind rushing over us is cool, and I like the view of the patchwork farms on the hills that rise and fall on both sides. But I can't get the skeleton men's tired voices out of my head. They made it sound like war and fighting was just the way it was, that it would go on forever. Maybe when it's been going on most of your life, that *is* what it feels like. Mama used to say that a body can get used to anything.

Michael is waiting for me to respond. He's sprawled on a

bag of sugar, looking annoyingly comfortable with his arms crossed behind his head.

I glance at Boyboy, who is swaddled in a *kanga* wrapper and is snoring with his mouth open. "Not really. I just whaled on some kids who were giving him a hard time."

"He said they were about to throw him in the river."

"He would have been fine if he could swim."

"So you *did* save his life."

I shrug. "He's being dramatic. It wasn't a big deal. I hit one of them in the face and made him bleed. They were stupid kids making noise about stuff they didn't understand, calling him names. They all took off crying at the first sight of blood."

Michael snorts a laugh. "I would have liked to see that."

I let myself chuckle. "It *was* pretty good."

We pass a man herding cattle on the side of the road, tapping their rumps with a long stick to keep them moving. The lorry barrels past, not even slowing down, and I hold my breath. A cow starts to veer off toward us, but then the man taps her in just the right spot on her flank, and she lumbers out of the way of her death.

As the man and his cows fade from view, Michael asks, "This trip isn't just about Mwika, is it? You're going to Congo because my dad's headed there."

"You know about your dad's trip?"

"He told me he was going. He has to go check on things fairly often. How did *you* know about his trip?"

"I . . . have my sources."

"And do those sources happen to hide out in secret tunnels?"

Heat rises in my cheeks. "I-I erased the footage. How do you know?"

"So you did sneak back in there."

I scowl at him. He's tricked me into incriminating myself. I wait for him to get mad, but he just says, "You think following him is going to help you figure out if he killed your mom?"

I watch him. I know what Michael is doing. He's not making a fuss about me sneaking around behind his back. He wants me to reciprocate. But I'm not used to opening up and talking like this, to *sharing*. "I don't know," I say, which is at least honest.

"Do you have a plan for when we get there?"

"Find Mwika."

He nods. "Boyboy told me my dad made payments to him a couple of years ago."

I sneak a glance up. "Do you know why?"

Michael shakes his head. I want to ask if he thinks the payment was in exchange for the video, but something in Michael's face stops me. We'll find out soon enough. For the first time I wonder if maybe all this is harder for Michael than it is for me. My mom died a long time ago, and the pain hasn't gone away, but it's dulled over the years. But how would I feel if I were discovering that she was actually a horrible person, like Michael is finding out about his dad?

Don't think like that, Tina. Don't feel sorry for him. Think about Mama. You've worked too hard for this.

Thinking of Mama reminds me of the other girl in the photo. Maybe she's still there in Kasisi and we can find her. Or maybe Mama had other friends we can talk to, or family. My family. Do I have family? Grandparents? Aunts, uncles? Mama never said a word about them, and her UN file said she was an only child, parents both dead. But if she lied about being married, maybe she lied about that too. The thought that I might find blood relatives in Kasisi sends a tingle through my body. What would they be like? What would they think of me?

I look at my tattoos, and my excitement deflates a little, imagining how they'll take my appearance. I have a feeling tats like this aren't a thing out here. And that girls wear dresses. Ugh.

I pick at a loose string on the bag of sandals. "Where did you tell your parents you were going?" I ask Michael. "Are you going to be in trouble? Are they going to send people looking for you?"

Michael is watching the hills go by. "I told them I was headed back to school, that they were letting me come back early. Got a friend to call Mom and pretend to be the principal. I had the driver drop me off at the airport and everything."

"They believed you?"

"After I got suspended, Mom was really mad. She threatened to withdraw our donations from the school. Said it wasn't fair to punish us equally for fighting if the other kid was throwing around racial slurs. I told them her threat worked."

"Did it?"

Michael sticks his arms out and looks at them. It suddenly occurs to me that they're pale by my standards, but probably not by Swiss ones.

"No."

We're quiet for a while. I tug at the hem of the *kanga* Boyboy's lent me to wrap up in. They all have sayings printed on them. This one reads *wache waseme*: "Let them talk."

Michael says, "I told them you decided to go stay with a cousin."

I didn't even think about his parents wondering where I went. I'm not really used to asking permission to go places. "Thanks."

He nods. "And since I've now covered for you, I get to ask a question."

"Okay," I say warily.

"Tell me about your tattoos."

It wasn't the question I was expecting. I had thought he'd want me to finally talk about why I ran away after Mama died. Discuss my feelings, God forbid. "Not much to tell. All Goondas get them."

"Why?"

"I don't know, it's just what you do."

"Have you always been with the Goondas? Since you left?"

"Yeah."

"Were you always a thief?" He looks at his hands. "Did you ever have to . . ."

I scowl. "Did I ever have to whore myself out? No."

"That's not what I was going to—"

"Guys always assume that. That the only way to survive on the streets or as a Goonda is to be a prostitute. 'Cause that's all girls can learn how to do, open their legs."

"Okay. Jeez, sorry. I didn't . . ."

"And even if I did, it wouldn't be any of your business."

Michael puts his hands up in surrender. "Point taken."

We sit in silence again.

"So," Michael finally ventures, "what do your tattoos mean?"

I look out at the fields, terraced rows lacing the hills all the way to the top, dotted with mud huts. I try to think how to answer. "It's how Goondas remember things," I say. "Big battles, deaths, a really good heist. It's like recording your history, just, on your skin instead of paper."

I turn around and tug my shirt down so he can see the leopard face on my shoulder blade. The spots travel around my back and arm and turn into flying birds. "I got this one after I did my first major break-in."

Michael doesn't say anything, but he leans forward attentively.

"I thought I was pretty smart. Pretty slick. Like a leopard. Did you know there are more leopards than any other big cat? You just don't see them. They can trail you like a shadow for miles and you'll never even know."

Michael looks amused.

"Yeah, I know. It's corny. But I was thirteen."

"Thirteen! And the rest of them?"

I tell him that I got my armbands of Swahili henna after I

stole a rather famous emerald from the new bride of a Kuwaiti oil sheikh. They had been on honeymoon at Sangui's most luxurious beach resort and I had admired the bride's hennaed arms. They swirl around the wheel on my left arm and the sword on my right.

"What's the wheel for?"

"That history's private."

"It's odd. It has spikes."

"Yup."

"And it sort of matches the sword on your other arm, in the same spot."

"You are very observant."

"And . . . ?"

"And it's still none of your business. Are you in the market for ink? I know a good guy named Spike . . ."

Michael smiles and rubs his arms. "I think Mom really would kill me." The thought seems to cheer him. "Maybe one day." He turns his arms over and looks at them. The pale sliver of flesh shaped like a crescent moon stands out on the inside of his left arm.

"You can still see your scar," I say.

His eyes search out my own arm, my own scar, surrounded in loops and dots, but clear. Something had made me stop Spike from tattooing over the long straight line. Michael slowly reaches over and runs his finger along it, sending goose bumps straight up my arm and a rush of blood to my throat.

Michael studies me. "Yeah. I guess my history is on my skin too."

Then he settles back down and closes his eyes.

Night. We huddle as best we can under thin blankets and tarps the driver gives us and try to sleep. Somewhere in Tanzania, I wake up and find I'm curled in between Michael and Boyboy, both of them fast asleep. The stars are so bright along the Milky Way they look like one solid mass, like a net. I think about moving, but the wind is cold and before I can make up my mind I realize it's morning again.

By midday Tanzania is behind us. Then Rwanda.

We get off before the official checkpoints and walk on well-worn paths through the bush. There are other men guarding the way here too, but it doesn't matter to them who comes and goes. They only care about getting paid. They don't haggle. If you don't want to pay what they ask, they push you to the side and take the next person in line behind you, who already has her money out and ready.

"Welcome to Congo," one of them finally says, after counting our bills. "*Bienvenue.*" He wears an AK-47 over a blue football jersey and waves us on.

When the checkpoints are out of sight, we get back in the lorry and continue down the road.

After Goma the road narrows and turns to rough, red *murram* that rattles everything and makes sleep impossible, and soon we're climbing through forests where sad-eyed monkeys dart across the path and the air is wet and cool. The towns we pass through spring up furtively where they can, like mushrooms after a rain, but then just as quickly they dissolve back into trees and tall grasses in a way that makes you wonder if maybe you just imagined them. It's as green as grasshopper dreams.

Sometimes the road threads through trees that cut out nearly all the light, and sometimes it skirts the edges of cliffs. Sometimes we see the crumpled remains of trucks far below, vines already crisscrossing them like the jungle is a sucking beast that claims everything it touches.

The skeleton men say we are almost there.

TWENTY-SIX

Kasisi," one of the men says as we finally roll to a stop on the side of the red dirt highway. I look around, eager for any sign of something familiar, but it looks no more like home than any of the other sleepy towns we've passed through. A few one-story block buildings cluster at the crossroads. Once optimistically painted white, they are now splattered red with mud. The street is full of people, goats, chickens, dogs, and trash. I can see the edge of a market ahead, men coming and going on bicycles, women balancing plastic bowls of fruit on their heads and yelling to one another in greeting. The smell of frying *mandazi* makes my stomach growl.

I jump down and join the skeleton men in stretching out the kinks nearly two days on the road has worked into us. The trip took longer than I thought it would. It's late in the afternoon on Wednesday, and now I'm worried we're not going

229

to be back in time for my Friday date with Kiki after all. But maybe we'll luck out and find Mwika quickly?

Michael goes to ask the driver about a hotel, while Boyboy hugs his designer bag to his chest and looks miserable.

"Oh, cheer up, *habibi*," I say, looking around. "Isn't it nice to be in the homeland? Maybe they've got a Prada since you've been gone."

"Don't talk to me. Hey! Shoo!"

A goat is experimentally nibbling at Boyboy's trouser cuff.

I wonder if Mr. G is here yet. Will he go straight to the mine or come through town first? Somehow I can't imagine him down here slumming it.

I hear Michael thanking the driver. When he returns he seems almost perky. "He says the best place to stay is at the guesthouse attached to the mission hospital. It's where the UN people stay when they pass through. It has electricity and everything. All the *piki-piki* know where it is. They can take us."

The hairs on the back of my neck stand up. A hospital? Is that where Mama worked as a nurse? Maybe the guesthouse is the same place Donatien stayed.

"We just need to change some money," Michael says, looking around. "The guesthouse only takes francs."

"Don't worry about it," I say. "I've got cash."

"You already changed money? That was fast."

Boyboy gives me a look.

"Yeah," I say, patting the wad of cash that I've snuggled into my waistband.

I'd got Michael's money plus interest back when the tout groped me getting into the lorry. Most of it is in wilted Congolese francs.

"And I even found out something about your mother," Michael says quietly as we walk toward the *piki-piki*, obviously pleased with himself. "A guy the driver was talking to knew your mom's name. He said that he could show us your cousin's shop in the market."

I nearly stumble. "You asked a stranger about my mother?"

Michael's smile slips. "What? I thought you'd be happy. That's part of why we're here, right? To find people who knew her and talk to them?"

"But we don't need to go announcing ourselves," I hiss. I glance around. We've already attracted stares: Boyboy in his finery, waving at us to come get on the death traps he's secured; me in my city clothes—I'm going to have to wear a skirt if I want to fit in here, and that is *not* happening—and pale, green-eyed Michael, still looking way too clean.

I slide onto the back of a motorcycle that looks like it is made of tinfoil held together with baling wire. "You are the worst detective on earth. Let's go. It's getting dark."

The caretaker for the guesthouse has to be hunted down before we can get rooms. I guess they haven't had many UN staff come through lately, because the nun we talk to wrings her hands and says something about needing to find furniture. Boyboy, Michael, and I exchange a look, but at this point anything with a roof and walls will do. We ask hopefully for blankets, which she says the caretaker can probably manage to find, and then excuses herself back to the hospital. As she hurries away, I notice a dark spot of blood on the hem of her dress.

Leaving the boys to wait, I walk off to look around the compound. It's past dusk, but there are no lights on. The shrieking of frogs and insects is nearly deafening. I thought Michael said they had electricity here, but maybe it's only for the hospital. I pass a swimming pool that is now filled in and planted with vegetables. The guest rooms curve around the pool and lawn, and what was maybe once a restaurant, though it's abandoned now, with broken tables and chairs propped up against the wall and a thatched roof that looks like it has mange. I stand looking at the tomatoes and corn that elbow for space in the kidney-shaped plot and wonder if I've seen this place before.

From somewhere beyond the garden I hear a woman cry out. I crane my neck toward the sound and see a glimmer of fluorescent light filtering through the hedge. I walk toward it and find a concrete path running between two long, low buildings, each with barred windows. The lights are coming from inside, and I walk to the open door of one. There are fifty or so hospital beds crammed in together, and there are even more bodies on pallets on the floor. No wonder the nun was worried about having extra beds. I see her across the room, flicking a needle, getting ready to give someone an injection. I hover at the edge of the darkness and hear the woman cry out again. She's somewhere out of sight off to my right, down another pathway lined with more rooms.

"*Habari ya jioni,*" a voice behind me says, and I turn. An older nun with thick glasses is watching me from the doorway of a cluttered little office.

I return the formal good evening and stand awkwardly, not sure whether to stay or go. The woman cries out again.

"Don't worry," the nun says, seeing my face. "She is just in labor. She will be all right. She is young and strong."

I nod, drinking in her accented Swahili. She sounds like my mother. I've all but lost my accent living in Sangui. Of course other refugees speak Congolese Swahili, but there is something very specifically familiar about the way the nun talks, her words sliding into each other. I swallow painfully. "I'm sorry, I didn't mean to bother anybody. I can go."

"No, it's fine, dear. Do you have a relative here?" Moths bang themselves against the lightbulb over her head like a frantic halo.

"I'm staying at the guesthouse."

She raises her eyebrows. "Oh? We don't get many visitors anymore. You look very young to be traveling. You're not alone, are you?"

I shake my head.

"Good. Girls shouldn't walk around the town alone."

"I'm pretty good at taking care of myself."

She blinks, but doesn't comment on how small and puny looking I am, like most people. Instead she says, "You are not from here, are you?"

"I am, actually, but I've been gone for a long time."

"*Karibu.* Welcome home." She smiles and the wrinkles in

her face remind me of wood grain. I decide that I like her face. "I'm Sister Dorothy," she says. "Since you're here, maybe you can help me do something?"

"Oh, uh . . ." I look toward the patients, wondering what exactly I would be able to help with.

She smiles. "Come—they won't bite. I need a strong pair of arms. What's your name, dear?" She reaches back into the office and pulls out a tall stack of itchy-looking polyester blankets.

"Christina." My name is out of my mouth before I can think to give her a fake one.

"Very pretty," she says briskly. "It gets chilly in here at night, and we have new patients who'll need these."

I take the blankets, wondering if I should steal a couple for us just in case. I follow her, after a glance over my shoulder back toward the guesthouse.

Sister Dorothy leans down to a young woman in a bed just inside the doorway. Both of the woman's hands are bandaged, and she holds them to her chest as the sister talks softly with her. Sister Dorothy takes a blanket from the top of my stack and spreads it over the young woman. The sister smoothes the wrinkles and the woman closes her eyes, never once looking at me.

We move to the next bed, an old woman with gray hair who is so withered and frail she practically disappears into the bedclothes. She's asleep, but a small child with big eyes is sitting up in bed beside her, sucking his finger. He stares at me. He looks healthy, but I wonder where his mother is.

Another blanket is delivered; I suddenly feel very guilty for thinking about stealing them. We move to the bed of the next woman, who is sitting up and has been watching us approach.

"A novice?" the woman asks Sister Dorothy, nodding at me.

"No, a guest," the sister answers.

The woman's nostrils flare. She says something in rapid French that I don't understand. But the meaning is clear enough in the way she points at my face and makes a shooing motion with her hands.

"What did she say?" I ask.

Sister Dorothy takes a blanket from me. In Swahili, she says, "That you are very pretty. She gets nervous about militia breaking in, thinks pretty girls will attract them. Now, Georgette, we've talked about this. You have to relax or you won't get better. Don't worry about this girl. She's welcome just as you are."

Sister Dorothy goes on to ask Georgette in low tones how she's feeling, while I shift awkwardly and try not to listen. Georgette shifts laboriously in the bed and speaks in French. Her pain "down there" will not go away, I gather.

Sister Dorothy nods and feels Georgette's forehead with the back of her hand. "I'll bring you some aspirin," she says, and we move on.

"It's only women here?" I ask.

"No, there are boys and men also. In the other wing, unless they are small like that one back there."

The woman in the next bed is sleeping too, and so we pull the blanket over her. There is an odd, coppery smell over her body, and something worse that reminds me of a butchery. I have to force myself not to step back from her. She has a bandage covering most of her face, and what peeks out from under it looks mangled and swollen. The sister frowns and checks the woman's pulse in her wrist. "She was just brought in today. Three of them, actually," she says, nodding down the rest of the beds against this wall.

All the women are asleep, their faces slack. White bandages on arms and faces are jarring against their dark skin. The one on the end looks barely older than me, though it's hard to tell with her bruised face.

"And one who didn't make it through surgery," Sister Dorothy adds. She tucks the woman's arm under the blanket. "They were found out at the edge of the fields, left for dead. They're medicated now, but we don't have enough to get them past the first day. Tomorrow will be hard."

"What happened to them?"

Sister Dorothy looks at me, and for a second I don't think she's going to answer. But then her eyes travel around the room, at the still bodies and blank expressions. Some of the women are looking at us, but most stare at the ceiling or the wall or they're curled into themselves like fists. Sister Dorothy says quietly, so only I can hear her, "Same thing as everyone else. The war."

My head is still full of images of broken bodies when we sit down to dinner with the nuns, after they've finished their evening prayers. I'm glad when Michael and Boyboy don't involve

me in the heated argument they're having about whether the
animal they saw run across their path on the way to the dining room was a stray cat or a civet. One is lucky and one is not,
apparently. I don't bother to ask what a civet is, though I probably should. This place could use some good luck.

We squeeze in with a dozen nuns and a priest. The electricity has been shut off throughout the compound, and everything is lit by flickering oil lanterns. The nuns tell us that since
they don't get many guests anymore, the hotel restaurant has
been disassembled and the useful parts scavenged. But the
nuns have their own kitchen, and after a blessing they dish
out steaming bowls of *dengu*, *sukuma*, and *matoke*.

"It's just beans, greens, and bananas," I tell Michael when
he doesn't seem to know what to do with his plate. "Don't be
rude."

Michael takes a tentative bite, grunts with approval,
and is soon digging in. The nuns' chatter is a warm envelope
around the table, and soon, between that and the food, I'm
feeling a little better. Exhaustion from the long ride is catching up to us. Boyboy's head nods over his plate.

"You are students?" the priest, Father Fidele, asks. "What
brings you to Kasisi?" He is young and friendly looking. His
face is still round with baby fat.

The talking subsides and there are only the sounds of
spoons clinking on plates while the nuns turn expectantly to
us for an answer. I clear my throat and wipe my mouth, real-
izing too late I've done so with the back of my hand. "Yes," I
say. "We're on, eh, an assignment."

"To talk with villagers about farming practices," Michael supplies. "We're in a conservation ecology class."

Boyboy coughs, and I smile and nod, grateful for Michael's quick save.

"That sounds like a big assignment for secondary school students. And you're traveling without chaperones?"

"We're in university," Boyboy assures them.

One of the older nuns tuts. "It's not that strange. I traveled on my own for school when I was their age."

"That was before the roads were clogged with rebels," another answers.

"There have been reports of raids over the past few days on villages to the north of here," Sister Dorothy says.

"We are very careful," I say. "We stay with pastors and priests along the way."

"You have to watch out for them too," a nun says, and the others laugh. She's given a stern look by a sister who I assume is in charge, and murmurs an apology.

"Quite all right," Father Fidele says. He's laughing too. "We'll pray for a safe journey for you."

"Um, thank you."

"Sister Dorothy says you are from here, Christina?" the priest asks.

I shift in my seat. I wish I'd thought of some other story to tell the nun, but too late now. "Yes. I left here when I was five, about eleven years ago, with my mother." I hesitate, glance at Michael and Boyboy, but they're waiting for me to go on. Can I ask about Mama? They're nuns, I think. A priest.

They take care of the villagers. Hope flashes in my chest. I could be missing my chance by not saying anything. "She was a nurse," I say carefully, watching their faces. "She may have worked here."

"Oh? What was her name?"

I take a breath. "Anju Yvette Masika."

My words are met with silence, and I look around to see spoons hovering en route to mouths, eyes widening. One of the nuns discreetly makes the sign of the cross over her chest. My stomach drops. Then, just as suddenly, the moment is over and everyone is back to eating, like nothing happened. But I see Sister Dorothy exchange a look with the older nun before returning to her food.

"Do you know her?" Michael asks, subtle as ever, when no one responds. I want to kick him under the table, but I'm afraid of hitting a nun.

A few heads shake no. No one else offers up any explanation for their reaction, and the priest clears his throat and asks for seconds. There is a flurry to accommodate him, after which the talk turns to the dwindling pharmaceutical inventory, and whether anyone should be sent to Goma for supplies, and if the malaria season will be bad this year. I glance at Boyboy, and he raises an eyebrow. Someone here knows something.

TWENTY-SEVEN

I want to catch Sister Dorothy and talk to her privately after dinner, but a young woman who works in the hospital gets to her first, tugging her arm before Sister Dorothy has even stood up from the table. The other nuns vanish in twos and threes like ghosts, and there's no opening for me to ask about my mother. We're given oil lanterns, and I'm left to trail after Boyboy and Michael, a mix of exhaustion and uneasiness settling into my bones.

The rooms we unlock are damp and feel neglected. Geckos scatter in the lamplight, barking in alarm. There are no beds, but the caretaker has found a couple of chairs and some cots that remind me of the one I slept on in the Greyhills' dungeon.

I half expect Michael to make a fuss about the conditions, but he just slings his bag onto his cot and says, "Home sweet home."

Boyboy flicks a switch on the wall experimentally in Michael's room, but nothing happens. "My laptop's not going to last long with no electricity," he says.

"I hope your brain doesn't dry up without screen time."

He makes a face. "I've got brainpower for miles, sweetie, don't you worry. It's my computer I'm worried about. I'll charge it up tomorrow. I brought a solar panel. I just won't be able to do much work until then."

"What was that all about at dinner?" Michael asks.

"I have no idea. But they obviously knew Mama." I chew my fingernail pensively.

"It's not a big town. Maybe everyone knows everyone."

"They were acting weird," Boyboy says. He pulls out his computer and turns it on.

"So what's the plan for tomorrow?" Michael asks. "Mwika was last seen in Walikale Town, which is still a few hours up the road. Are we going there or staying here for a while to look around?"

"Boyboy, can you use that contact phone number from Mr. G's files to try and track him?" I ask. "I don't want to leave here if we don't have a solid bead on him." I ignore the scowl that Michael gives me at the mention of his dad's stolen data.

"I'll try. I take it First Solutions is not the sort of outfit to have a storefront?"

Michael shakes his head. "If only it were that easy. I don't even know where they're based. They seem to just send people out to different locations. I've been trying to contact them for days but no one ever answers the phone. I've left a dozen messages. Maybe whatever contact number you have is better."

"What did you dangle?" Boyboy asks, looking over his screen.

"Dangle?"

Boyboy rolls his eyes. "Did you tell them who you are?"

"Of course not!"

Boyboy looks unimpressed. "Give me what you've got on them and I'll see what I can do to lure someone out. Someone must know where to send Mwika's pay."

Michael looks back at me. "And while he's on that, what should you and I do?"

"How far away is Extracta's mine? Can we go there and poke around?"

Michael shifts. "You want to go there? Shouldn't we stay close, in case Boyboy finds Mwika?"

"We came all this way. You want to just sit here and do nothing?"

"We're here to find Mwika, right?" Michael asks. "I mean, what else do we need?"

I stand up. "I want to find out what Mama knew about your dad that she was going to tell Donatien."

From the corner of my eye I see Michael's shoulders tense. He doesn't say anything.

"What about the hidden file thing from your mom's photo?" Boyboy asks. "Anything you two can do to make sense of it? It's got to be important somehow."

"What hidden file?" Michael asks.

I give Boyboy a pointed stare.

Boyboy blinks. "Uh. Never mind. Nothing." He ducks behind his screen.

"What file?" Michael asks again, turning on me.

"I . . . It's from your dad's data. I didn't think you needed to know. Yet. I mean, it might have nothing to do with Mama."

"Show me," Michael demands.

Boyboy looks at me and I sigh. "Go ahead."

He pulls the handwritten list of names and numbers up on his computer and shows it to Michael.

"What is this?" he asks, eyes flashing. "And when exactly were you planning on sharing it with me?"

"I'm showing it to you now, aren't I?" I say. "Besides, we don't know what it is either. It's just names and numbers."

Michael points at the screen. "Mobile Interests. Do you know what that is?"

"No," I say, crossing my arms.

He scowls. "Well, if you'd shown it to me, I could have told you."

"What is it?" I ask eagerly.

Michael just stares at me, incredulous. He opens his mouth like he's going to argue, but then just shakes his head. "It was the trucking company Extracta worked with," he says. "They transported ore to Sangui City until Dad found out they were stealing from him."

"How do you know all that?" I ask.

"It was this whole big blowup at home because Mom's family owned part of the company." His face is still clenched in anger.

I lean back. "Okay, that's good information."

"You can't keep stuff like this from me, Tina."

"Don't be a baby," I say, standing up again. "I don't have to share everything with you."

"You do if you want my help figuring out who killed your mom!"

I poke a finger in his face. "I'm still betting your dad killed my mom, so why would I want to share this with *you*?"

"Okay, children, okay," Boyboy says, coming between us. "That's enough fun for one night. I think we've all been in a banana lorry too long, and it's time to get our beauty sleep. You two can pick up where you left off tomorrow."

"Fine," I say. I grab a lantern and stalk out. I can hear Michael and Boyboy continue to talk behind me, and I slam the door to my room. Who does Michael think he is? He shouldn't even be here. I could have done this all by myself.

You still don't know where Mwika is.

Well, myself and Boyboy, then. I flop onto my cot and stare at the ceiling, feeling my anger pulse through me like a fever.

In the quiet, I realize how loud the insects and frogs are outside. Rain starts to clatter on the tin roof like thousands of tiny stones. In the dim of the lantern I pull the photo of my mother and her prayer card out of my pocket. I look at the card, then the photo, as if something in the back of my mind is telling me they're connected. But I can't see how. The photo is getting crunched up from being carried around in my pocket, but Mama's face and eyes are as sharp as ever. The face of the girl beside her pulls at some thread of recognition, but it's like trying to grab spiderwebs. She melts away under my touch. Once, she meant something to my mother. They were obviously close. I feel a tug of anger again. Shouldn't I know who this woman is? Why did Mama never say anything about her?

The hugeness of what I don't know about my mother and her life here feels like a weight on my chest, crushing me. I'm doing all this for her, but she never even bothered to tell me about *before*. Did she not think I would want to know? I mean, this is my history too, and it sort of feels like she kept it all to herself. Not just the bad, but the good stuff too. Her friends, her family. *My* family. For the first time in a long time I think about my father. Who was he? Maybe he's here too, in this very town. I could have already walked by him on the street.

I stare at Saint Catherine with her rosy cheeks and wistful gaze. She is as unflappable as ever. I take a deep breath to try to calm down, the richness of the smell of wet earth and rotting leaves outside filling my lungs. I should sleep. I turn down the lamp until the flame flutters out, and then lie back on the cot. I rest the photo and the card on my chest. I can't hear Boyboy and Michael talking anymore, only the riot of insect nightlife. The sound is oddly familiar, and I guess it should be. I must have listened to these same bugs as a little kid. Or their great-great-grandparents.

I wish Kiki could see this place. Parts of it are so different from how I think of Congo when I'm in Sangui City. It's dangerous here, I know, but it's also full of insects and frogs getting on with their business. Rain, and people worrying about making it home from the market before it starts. I think of all the herders we saw on the side of the road from the banana lorry, and women tending their fields, and kids playing in a school yard in one of the towns we passed. I guess a million little dramas happen here, just like anywhere else. The war can't stop everything. I want Kiki to see this part of who she and I are. When I started out of Sangui two days ago I didn't think I would ever tell her about this trip. But maybe I should. Otherwise, I'm just like Mama, hiding things from my family because I think I know best. But then again, Kiki's so little. If she asks why I came here, what do I tell her? That I'm here mainly to make her father pay in blood for Mama's death? My head swirls. But this trip isn't all blood and death. It's also frogs singing and kind nuns.

I realize I'm starting to doze, my thoughts flickering randomly. The rain drums like fingertips. And then I realize it's not just rain, but someone knocking gently at my door. I sit up, tucking the photo and card into my hoodie pocket.

"Who's there?" I whisper, ready to tell Michael or Boyboy that I'm in no mood to kiss and make up.

"Sister Dorothy."

I jump up and open the door. I can just barely see the outline of her face. "Wait, let me get a light."

"No. No light. Come with me."

I slip out of my room, not even bothering to put my shoes on, and follow her down the covered walkway. Rain splashes up from the edges and hits my ankles, making me shiver. I think she's leading me back to the hospital, where a few kerosene lights still burn, but instead she turns off toward a small chapel on the grounds.

The glow from the hospital doesn't reach here, and the night is thickly black. She hurries across the lawn through the rain as thunder rolls. Mud oozing between my bare toes, I follow. She doesn't go to the front door, but around to the side of the chapel, to a padlocked door. From a key on a string around her waist, she unlocks it and ushers me in.

I wipe rain from my face with my sleeves in the dark interior. There's a scratch and a burst of flame, and I finally see Sister Dorothy in the light of a candle. I glance around the empty chapel and can just make out solemn rows of pews and simple stained-glass windows speckled with rain.

"I'm sorry for all the cloak-and-dagger business," she says, and opens another door behind the altar that leads into a little room. Inside it's musty and cool like a cellar, carved out of the hill the chapel leans up against. Dusty boxes and bottles of Communion wine line the walls, but there's space for a small table and two chairs.

Sister Dorothy closes the door behind us and sits down with a tired sigh. "If I'd known who you are, I would have told you to be more careful with what you say in this town."

"Who I am?"

"Your mother."

I grip the table edge. "What about my mother? You knew her? The way everyone was acting at dinner tonight—"

"Sit," Sister Dorothy interrupts, and I lower myself into a chair across from her. She gives me a weary smile. "It's been a long time since anyone mentioned Anju." Her eyes glimmer in the light, and I wonder if she's searching for signs of Mama in my face. "You were born here. In the clinic. You didn't know that, did you?"

The words hit me like a punch. "I was?"

"You were right. Your mother worked here," Sister Dorothy says, touching the silver cross at her neck. "She did her nurse's training here. At one time she wanted to be a nun." She stops, pulls the cross absently over the chain, back and forth.

"A nun?" I ask, blinking. "Mama? What happened? Please, do you know something? I'm trying to find out who killed her." Sister Dorothy's eyes leap back to my face and I lean forward. "Did you know about that? Did you know she was murdered?"

"Yes. We get the news from Sangui. Is that why you're here? To chase her ghost?"

"I-I'm chasing her killer." I look down at my dirty nails curled in my lap. "I need to make him pay for what he's done."

Sister Dorothy doesn't act shocked or scold me, like I expect her to. Instead she studies me. "You were a child when you left. What do you remember about living here?"

"Nothing."

"Nothing at all?"

I shrug helplessly and avoid her eye. "Bits and pieces. I remember running away."

For a while she doesn't move, just looks off at the wall past my shoulder, but I know she's on the verge of telling me something. I hold my breath.

When she finally speaks again, it's as if her words are stones that she has to find and carefully push out of her mouth. "After twenty years of girls, *children*, being brought here for me to try and put back together, I cannot pretend anymore that I understand why bad things happen, or that there is some purpose to them, or that God would want . . ." She stops herself, purses her lips, then goes on. "I cannot act like there is not true evil in the world, walking among us. I am going to tell you something so that you can be vigilant." Her eyes flash to me. "Do you understand?"

I nod my head slowly. I'm not sure I do, but I don't want her to stop talking.

She nods with me. Then her eyes wander back up the wall. "Your mother was one of my favorites. We're not supposed to have favorites, but there you have it. She came here when she was eighteen to train as a nurse. She was very smart. Always curious, tremendous energy. She would have made a beautiful sister."

I see the skin around Sister Dorothy's mouth begin to quaver.

"The attack came while we were sleeping. It was the dry season, the raiding season, and the rebels had been attacking one village after another. We thought we would be safe here. The government soldiers were supposed to protect us, but none were around. None came when we called."

She takes a second to breathe deeply before going on. When she speaks again, her voice sounds odd, detached, like she is reciting something from memory. "They took five women: four nurses in training and a teacher."

My mouth goes dry.

"They were gone for three months. Two of them never returned. Of the three that did, one was the teacher, and she left immediately; I don't know what happened to her. One was a good friend of your mother's, another nurse in training." Sister Dorothy finally looks up at me. "And one was your mother. She came back barely alive, carrying you in her womb."

TWENTY-EIGHT

For a few seconds I don't move. Sister Dorothy watches me closely, but doesn't say anything, just waits. The room slips sideways.

"My father was one of them? One of the men that took her?"

"Yes."

I can barely force out my words. "Do you know who he was?"

"No. There must have been several who . . ." Sister Dorothy winces, looks away.

I start to breathe again, but I feel like I'm going to pass out. Not even an hour ago I'd been thinking about my father and now . . . but I assumed he had been a boyfriend, someone my mother just didn't want to talk about. I'd never imagined that my father was a man who had . . . had . . . I can't even think the words. I suddenly feel very hot, like I'm about to be sick. I bend and put my forehead against my fists.

For a while I just let the waves of nausea wash over me. When I lift my head, Sister Dorothy is reaching back to a shelf behind her. She pulls a bottle of Communion wine from the spiderwebs, and two little glasses. She pours for us both. It's silent as a tomb, and then a roll of thunder reaches us, and my ears stop ringing. I hear the muted rasp of rain.

"I thought nuns weren't supposed to drink," I say, numbly staring at the glass in front of me.

"All fall short of the glory of God. I think He will forgive an old woman." She brings the glass to her lips.

The thought of the wine curdles my stomach, but then I reach out and grab the glass and take it all down in one gulp. The wine is sour-sweet and thick, but it warms me. It occurs to me that this is what the Goondas do when they talk about death too. When one of them dies, they bring out a bottle and drink until no one can think about anything anymore. Goondas and nuns, drinking to the dead. A crazy giggle almost escapes my lips, but I catch it. I take a deep breath to try to steady myself.

Sister Dorothy's words echo: Two of them never returned. Of the three that did . . . I look up. "The other nurse in training they took, is she still here in Kasisi?"

"Yes," Sister Dorothy says. Her brow furrows. "Catherine is here."

The name sends a chill through me. Catherine—like Kiki, I think. Like Saint Catherine.

"Sister Dorothy," I say, pulling out the crumpled photo

from my pocket. "Is this her?" I point to the girl beside my mother, the one who looks like she has the world on a string.

The sister's eyes soften. "Yes," she says. "That's Catherine."

My heart pounds. "I want to talk to her. Do you know where she lives?"

"I don't know if that's a good idea . . ."

"Why?"

Sister Dorothy refills my glass, and then her own. "Catherine . . . struggles."

"What do you mean?"

She speaks slowly, carefully. "If a girl is taken by the militias, and then found again, it is a joyous thing. It is as if she has come back from the dead. However, the joy eventually fades, and then everyone wants the girl to forget. But it isn't possible. Some of the women have medical problems. They are in pain, or can't bear children. They are a constant reminder of how the family and the village were not strong enough to keep this sort of thing from happening. Sometimes people blame the women, or say that they have joined the rebels and have been sent back as spies. If they have children, some people say they are ghosts, or witches—that they carry evil inside them."

I go cold. That's *me*.

"Some of the women go someplace new to try and start over. And some, when they are not able to work or marry, turn to other means of survival." She hesitates. "Catherine . . . sells herself."

253

I blink. "She's a prostitute?" Sister Dorothy's face confirms the answer. "People blame her? It's not as if she asked to be taken!"

The sister suddenly looks very old. "People are complicated creatures, my dear. The ways they find of explaining the bad things that happen in the world are not always the right ones. Sometimes they are simply the easy ones. They are the ones that give them enough comfort to sleep at night, the ones that let them take the blame off themselves."

I twist my glass on the table. "That's shitty."

"Yes. I suppose it is . . . *shitty*."

"I need to talk to Catherine," I say again.

And Sister Dorothy repeats, "I don't think that is a good idea."

I look around the room as if seeing it for the first time. Windowless. Dark. Secret. "It's not that she's a prostitute, is it? You just don't want me talking to her. Why did you bring me here to this room? Why did you not want the other nuns to see us together?"

She takes a drink. "It's not the nuns. It's everyone. Talking is dangerous. The last time I saw your mother she was here, talking to a white man who was staying at the guesthouse. We later found out he was a reporter."

Donatien, I think.

"I surprised her. She didn't say anything about what they were discussing, but she seemed nervous. It was a busy time at the clinic, so I didn't give it much thought, until that man was nearly killed the next day. And then we heard that your house had been burned down, and you and your mother were missing. Days went by, and then the men came back here, looking for her. They thought we were hiding her."

"What men?"

She shakes her head. "The bad kind of men. The same kind as before. Militias. They came to the gates and started shooting in the air, asking for her by her name. The patients were all terrified. And when we told them we didn't know where she was, they started beating people and breaking things, like before."

I wait for her to take a shuddering breath before going on. "After that, people started whispering about your mother and what had happened to the reporter who was stabbed. They were afraid. The reverend mother sent the reporter back to Sangui City and forbade us from talking about Anju anymore, lest the militias come back."

"She just wanted you to forget? Act like Mama never existed?"

Sister Dorothy sighs. "These are good people who work at this clinic, Christina. We wouldn't stay here and see what horrors we do every day if we didn't care, if we didn't feel compelled by God. The nuns, the men and women who work here, they are good."

She looks past me again at the gray concrete wall. "But the awful truth of this place is that anyone who stays must choose to not ask too many questions. We cannot call the devil by his human names. You never know who is listening, who is saving up information for that moment when they need it to trade with the militias to keep their husband or children from being taken."

She looks back at me. She can see my mother in me, I can tell. "You should leave here. Take your friends and go back to Sangui City. Forget about revenge."

"I can't."

She seems to know that's what I would say. "Then I will pray for God to find you and stay with you." She drains her glass. "But sometimes I worry He gave up on this place long ago."

TWENTY-NINE

Rule 13: The good thing about bad news is that at least it's true.

And if you've spent most of your life wading around in half-truths and guesses, something real is like finding dry land in the middle of the ocean.

Not that knowing the truth helped me sleep last night.

The boy is supposed to show us the way to Catherine's house, but now he's squatting in the mud like a toad and refuses to go any farther. He points up the path and, in a mix of Swahili, some other language we don't know, and hand waving, tells us we just have to walk a bit farther. He holds his palm up. "Five minutes."

"Kid, we paid you to take us there! All the way there,"

Boyboy says, one hand on his hip, one fanning his brow. He pulls his phone out to check it again.

"Anything from the First Solutions guy?" I ask.

Boyboy spent a couple of hours digging last night, and an hour on the phone this morning, and is hopeful about this most recent lead. It's amazing how many dudes come out of the woodwork when you dangle a bit of cash in front of their noses.

I probably should have asked Boyboy to stay with his computer at the guesthouse and keep working, but after I told him the bare bones of what Sister Dorothy had told me, he insisted on coming with us to find Catherine. I just didn't have it in me to argue. I wouldn't have told Boyboy about Catherine at all if he hadn't forced it out of me. He claimed that from the way I looked when I came out for breakfast, either I'd caught some terrible intestinal parasite, or something was up. I didn't say anything to Michael, though. All he knows is that Sister Dorothy confirmed Catherine was my mom's friend and she was around. He's the only member of the party looking buoyant and rested, marching along ahead of us like a Boy Scout on patrol.

"Still no network," Boyboy grumbles, and stuffs the phone back in his pocket.

It doesn't help that the air in the forest we've been hiking through for almost an hour is warm and incredibly humid. We're all dripping. A stream rushes through a gully to our left, muddy and high with last night's rain, adding to the general feeling that we're not walking so much as swimming through the jungle.

Our first stop this morning had been to see if we could catch a rumor of Mr. Greyhill being around, but without straight up asking people on the street, it was hard to tell. We figured a rich *mzungu* coming to town would cause a bit of a stir, but no stirring seemed to be happening. Michael wondered if maybe he was staying at one of Extracta's mines in company housing. We had better luck finding out where Catherine worked. We were pointed to a bar. The cook we asked there said she wasn't around, but—after a couple of sideways looks—told us we could hire his nephew to take us to her house. Or apparently within five minutes of it.

"Come on," I cajole the kid.

The boy shakes his head adamantly. He is a good boy. Her home is a den of devils and he is going no farther.

Michael wipes sweat from his face. "It's just up there, eh? You sure?"

The boy nods, drags his finger studiously in the mud. "Five minutes," he repeats.

Five minutes can apparently mean anything from a minute of walking to an hour. His uncle had assured us that Catherine's house was only five minutes away. More like five kilometers.

"Come on," I say, taking Boyboy's elbow. "We have to be nearly there. Don't make that face. I told you not to wear those shoes."

The kid waits until we've moved up the path and then shoots away, skinny limbs flailing. I'm as skeptical as anyone else that we'll find Catherine's house as promised, but sure enough, and to everyone's relief, we soon crest a hill and come out of the forest to find a sunny field. Sheep and goats graze around a little mud-walled house in the sun.

For a second or two we just stand there, catching our breath.

"Are you sure this is it?" Boyboy whispers. "Doesn't look like a den of devils."

"I think this is the last home on the path."

The mountains and jungle rise steeply beyond the grass. The house looks like any of a dozen we've passed. The red dirt around it is swept clean, and fuchsia flowers bloom from rusted cans on either side of the doorway, which is covered by a sheet blowing in the breeze. Tiny white butterflies hover over manure in a carefully constructed cow pen a hundred feet away. In the distance I can see a girl hanging laundry on bushes that are covered in pink and orange flowers. The name of the plant pops suddenly out of some dusty corner of my memory: lantana, devil in the bushes. The scene as a whole looks postcard perfect, and I can't tell if it looks familiar, or if I just want it to.

"*Hodi*," I call, announcing us from the edge of the yard. "Hello?" My nerves are zinging. This is it. I'm finally going to meet the mystery girl from the photo.

There's no answer from the house, so I walk around toward

the back, where I can smell wood smoke. Boyboy and Michael follow. Before we can turn the corner, though, we hear a bark, and an enormous tawny dog comes bounding around the side of the house, hackles raised. He barks furiously at us.

"Whoa!" I say, putting my hands up. I hear Boyboy squealing and scrambling backward behind me.

"Hello?" Michael yells. "Is anyone back there? A little help?"

A woman follows the dog, and our hopes for rescue are quickly dashed by the AK-47 slung over her shoulder. She doesn't aim it at us, but she really doesn't need to. We all back up.

"Who are you? What are you doing here?" she asks. "*Askari!*"

At his name, the dog stops barking but hovers near his mistress, hackles still up.

I hold my breath. Her face looks familiar. She might be the girl from the photo but her expression is so different that I can't be sure.

"Uh, hello," Michael says, recovering first, but keeping his eye on the gun. "I'm Michael, and these are my friends Christina and Boyboy. We came up from town."

"Yes, and?"

"We, ah, well, we were hoping to speak with you."

The girl who was hanging laundry is now galloping over the grass toward us, another big dog at her side.

The woman looks at each of us in turn, suspicion furrowing her brow. "About?"

There's no sense in beating around the bush. I step forward. "Are you Catherine?" When I get no response, I go on, "It's about my mother, Anju. I think you knew her?"

The woman just stares at me as if I were speaking Chinese, but then her look changes, like I've thrown mud at her face. "Anju? Anju Yvette?"

The girl has reached us and stands hovering just outside of our circle, staring. She is all knees and elbows, maybe about Kiki's age. The woman holds a hand up at her, telling her to stay back.

"Yes, that's her," I say, and take a hopeful step forward. "May we come—"

"*No,*" Catherine says, and her voice is low and dangerous. The gun at her hip comes up, and she uses it to motion us back in the direction from which we've come. "I never want to hear that woman's name again as long as I live."

Then she spits on the ground.

Spits.

"Now get off my farm and don't ever come back."

We have no choice but to turn around and leave. Michael had tried to protest but was met only by a hiss, which seemed to be the signal for the dogs to attack. They started barking and leaping at us, and between that and the gun, there wasn't much more to say. We beat a quick path back down the trail.

"What the hell did your mom do to her?" Boyboy asks, in between glances over his shoulder.

"I don't know," I say, swatting at a bush that hangs over the path. "I thought they were friends."

I was *not* prepared for Catherine's response. I thought she would be glad to talk about Mama, and the shock of our violent dismissal stings. I stop, bringing the boys up short behind me.

"We can't just leave. We have to talk to her," I say.

Michael looks dubious. I know he's wondering just what exactly Catherine has to do with my mother's murder, but I'm not about to try and explain. I feel like I *need* to talk to her. She might be the only person in the world who can tell me what happened to her and Mama that led to my birth. She was my mother's friend and they must have suffered through it together. My urge to talk to her goes beyond figuring out who killed Mama. It's deeper than that, personal.

So why will she not talk to me?

Boyboy puts his hands on his hips. "I'm not going back up there. Lady's got a Rambo complex. Who has guns like that unless they're part of a militia?" Just then Boyboy's phone buzzes. He pulls it out of his pocket and grunts at what he sees. "Voice mail. Finally."

"What did you have to pay this guy at First Solutions to talk to you?" Michael asks.

"Nothing." Boyboy puts the phone up to his ear. "But you paid him plenty. Well, technically your trust fund did, but it was for a good cause."

"What? How did you—"

"What's he say?" I ask Boyboy, shushing Michael.

Boyboy frowns, concentrating on the message. He puts a finger up to tell us to wait.

While he's busy, I turn back to Michael. "We have to talk to Catherine. She was Mama's friend. She knows . . . stuff."

Michael is still giving Boyboy a disgruntled look, but sighs and says, "Maybe we can get Sister Dorothy to talk to her." He frowns. "What is it?" he asks Boyboy.

When I turn around, I don't like the expression on Boyboy's face. He takes the phone away from his ear. "Bad news," he says. "Mwika's dead."

Boyboy's contact didn't leave a lot of details, just that Mwika got knifed in a bar fight about two years ago near a diamond mine in Katanga where he was working.

"But he left me Mwika's email address. I'll hack it," Boyboy says, putting a hand on my arm. "There may be something there."

Michael nods. "We shouldn't give up yet."

"How could you not have known he was dead?" I ask Michael. Two years ago was when Mr. Greyhill made payments to Mwika. There's got to be some connection to his death. "*Did* you know?"

"No!" Michael says, stepping toward me. "Of course not!"

I lurch back from him, trying to read the truth in his face. He looks as genuinely shocked as Boyboy, but if I know anything, it's that the Greyhills are good liars. "I can't believe I trusted you," I say. Without waiting for him to respond, I turn around and start walking down the path.

No video.

This whole deal with Michael was to get to Mwika and his supposed video, and now we find out he's been dead for *two years*. Did Michael know? Was he just leading me on?

Between Mwika and Catherine, the trip so far has been a disaster. The only thing I've learned by coming here is that my mother went through some horrible, unspeakable shit and that I'm the war baby she never wanted. A baby that ruined her life and probably reminded her every single day of what had happened to her. I suddenly want very badly to see my sister. Not to tell her what's happening, just to see her, to have her tilt her head at me and ask me what's wrong like she sometimes does. I never tell her, but I like it when she asks. I could really use that about now.

When we get back to the guesthouse I go to my room, lock the door behind me, and stand there. I have no idea what to do next. Do not cry, Tiny Girl. Maybe Boyboy will still find something in Mwika's emails.

Outside my window I can hear Boyboy telling Michael not to knock on my door, that I just need some time. I listen to the sounds of Boyboy getting set up outside, checking his solar panel, turning on his computer.

Now what? Should we just go home? I want to talk to Catherine, but how? Sitting in here pouting isn't going to help. I take a deep breath and dig for my phone in my bag. Maybe I can help out and call Boyboy's contact back myself, get more information. Maybe Mwika had a house, a place where he stashed stuff. I start to go outside, but stop when

I see that I've missed a dozen calls from Ketchup, three calls from numbers I don't recognize, and most worrying, one from Bug Eye. A single text from him: *where you at call now.*

Knots begin to twist in my stomach, one after another. As I'm staring at my phone, trying to decide whether to call Bug Eye back and pretend like everything is cool and I'm still in Sangui, it starts to vibrate with an incoming call. I curse, sure it's him or Ketchup, but the number isn't one of theirs. I know I probably shouldn't answer it—it's most likely one of them calling from a different line, trying to get me to answer—but some weird urge kicks in. "Hello?"

"Tina? Is that you?"

My knees go wobbly and I almost lose my footing. "Kiki? Are you okay?"

"I've been trying to get you for days!"

"What is it? What's wrong?"

I hear her whisper something to someone nearby. "What? No, nothing's wrong. Where are you?"

I can hear girls talking in the background. My heartbeat starts to slow, and I wipe my mouth with a trembling hand. I take a deep breath and try to sound normal. "I left the city."

"You did what? Why? Where are you? I can barely hear you."

"I-I had to do some stuff. I'll only be gone a couple of days."

"Oh. But you'll be back by Friday night?"

"I'm going to try. But if I'm not, don't worry, okay?"

"One of the other girls overheard someone telephoning for me. It was you, right?"

"Yeah, the nun wouldn't let me talk to you."

"That was Sister Agnes. She is *so* strict. No phone calls, no phones. She thinks we'll call our boyfriends or order take-away food or something. But my friend Simone has a mobile that she hides in her mattress. She let me use it to call." My sister speaks in a breathless stream. "This guy said you had skipped town. I was worried; that's why I asked Simone to use her phone."

"What guy?"

"Um. I don't know his name, but he came to the school while I was outside at recess yesterday. He said he was a friend of yours. He said I should call you." She goes quiet. "Tina, who was he? Why did you leave Sangui? Are you okay?"

"I'm fine," I say, working hard to keep my voice level. "What did he look like?"

"Like, kind of tough. Tattoos and stuff all up and down his arms, like yours. The other girls thought he was cute, but I thought he looked like a meerkat."

I lick my lips. "You remember any of the tattoos?"

"Not really. He had a bunch. Um, okay, there was a big tomato on the back of his hand. I remember that."

My vision tunnels.

Ketchup.

At Kiki's school. Talking to Kiki.

I will kill him.

"He told me that if I hear from you, to tell you to call him. Or if you came by, to give you a note."

"A note? What does it say?"

"Hang on. It's in my pocket." I can hear shuffling, and then,

"Okay, it says, 'Tiny, Your wasting time. Tell your sister hi.' What does that mean?" She pauses. "He spelled *you're* wrong."

I have to hold my hand over the mouthpiece so Kiki doesn't hear my breathing go ragged. Ketchup tried to call me. And when I didn't respond, he did what he knew would get my attention. He wanted me to know he'd seen Kiki in person. That he knows where she is, how to get to her. How did he even find her? I've been so careful.

"Tina? I have to go. Simone says I'm using up all her airtime."

"Yeah, okay," I manage. "Listen, if that guy comes back to the school, don't talk to him, okay?"

"I won't." Suddenly her voice falters. "But you're okay, right? He's not, like, hurting you or anything?"

I shake myself. "No, nothing like that. C'mon, don't worry so much, okay? I'll see you soon."

"Friday?"

"Friday. I'll be there for sure."

"Okay, good. Bye!"

I have a sudden urge to tell her I love her, but I wait too long, and the words get stuck in my throat. And then the line clicks off and she's gone.

THIRTY

Rule 14: Bad luck comes in multiples of so many more than three.

By mid-afternoon both Boyboy and Michael are tired of my jittery energy, and Boyboy pleads with me to go do something productive somewhere else while he works. But I don't know what that would be. This trip was a stupid idea, and now my sister might be in trouble.

We've got to leave super early in the morning if I'm going to make it back in time to meet Kiki. I keep picking my phone up to dial Bug Eye and then stopping, reconsidering. Do I call and try to convince him I'm still at the Greyhills'? Ketchup told my sister that I had skipped town. But how would he know? If I call, could Bug Eye somehow hack my GPS and find out where I really am? Boyboy traced me to the bus station, after all. It's possible Bug Eye could find someone to trace me all the way here. And then how much trouble would I be in? How much trouble would Kiki be in?

"Let's go back to town," Michael says, pulling me out of my thoughts. "We can go to your cousin's shop that the lorry driver's friend was talking about. And maybe my dad's around by now."

I put my phone in my pocket and follow Michael out of the guesthouse, still not sure whether or not to call. I'll think about it while we're on our way. There's nothing to do at the guesthouse anyway except drive Boyboy crazy. Sister Dorothy is too busy to talk and Mwika's email is proving harder to crack than Boyboy would have thought. A call to the First Solutions guy hadn't given us any more to go on.

Getting to town at least gives me a sense of purpose, but I still haven't decided what to do by the time we arrive. Kiki's safer at school than most places, I tell myself, but I know it's not true. If the Goondas know where she is, they can get to her. I wish there were someone I could call to go and keep an eye on her, but the only person I trust is back at the guesthouse, trying to hack David Mwika's email. And what could he do anyway, to protect my sister from Goondas?

As we walk toward the market, I check my phone to make sure Boyboy hasn't tried getting in touch while we were on *piki-piki*, but the only call is from Ketchup. Again.

"Look," Michael says, "you have to believe me. I didn't

know Mwika was dead. I wouldn't have come all the way out here with you. I wouldn't have let you go, period."

He must think I'm being weird because I'm still mad at him. I scowl down the street, not responding. Should I tell him what's going on with Kiki? No. She's my sister and I'll handle it. He would remind me that technically we're both related to her the same way, but whatever. It's *not* the same. I'll call Bug Eye when we get back to the guesthouse, I decide. I can go find a quiet corner to talk where no one will hear me. I'll convince him everything's going according to plan.

I have to.

When we get there, my cousin's shop is closed.

Of course it is.

And no one we pass in the busy market seems to be gossiping about the arrival of a rich, white stranger in their tiny town.

Of course they're not.

I give the locked door of the overambitiously named Grace of Jesus MegaSuperMart a good kick. It scares away a bony cat that's been sleeping in the tin shack's shade, but nothing else moves.

Michael doesn't even try to make me feel better, which is good, because I'm ready to kick him too. We just turn in silence and walk back the way we came, through women presiding over produce, young men hacking sugarcane into pieces for children to suck on, chickens in wire cages, pots and pans, sweet-smelling straw baskets, bold sides of meat hung for shoppers' inspection.

Michael absently picks up a mango from a fruit seller's stall, tosses it gently in his palm. "I'm as frustrated as you are that we didn't find Mwika."

I snort.

"How am I supposed to prove my dad didn't kill your mother without his video?" he asks.

The mango seller eyes Michael over her piles of fruit. "Buy that or quit squeezing, *kijana*."

"Sorry," Michael says, and quickly replaces the mango.

As we walk away, I give him a sideways glance. "You really didn't know he was dead? You didn't just make this whole crazy bargain to distract me or something?"

Michael stops and reaches for my arm to stop me too. He comes around to face me. "No. I didn't know he was dead. I promise. Why would I go to all this trouble? Basically running away to Congo? I could have taken Boyboy's computer a long time ago. Or had you both fed to sharks." He waits, trying for a smile.

My shoulders slump. I'm so tired. I feel a corner of my mouth lift without my permission. "All right," I finally concede, "I believe you. Mostly."

Michael returns my smile. "Come on."

We've only gone a few meters when I feel it. My smile fades as I get that weird prickly sensation like someone's watching me, and when I look up, I swear I see Ketchup duck into an alley. My heart pounding, I race to the gap between the buildings, but no one is there except a woman washing pots behind a restaurant.

"What?" Michael asks, catching up with me.

"Nothing," I mutter. "Thought I saw someone."

"Who?"

"No one. It wasn't him."

Ketchup is not here, I tell myself. You've just got him on the brain. I wish he were here. At least that way I wouldn't have to worry about how close he is to Kiki.

The breeze has picked up and whorls of dust go flinging through the narrow lanes between the goods. Clouds are gathering, the clear skies of the morning a distant memory. Shoppers and hawkers start to take note of the change in weather. Women adjust their wrappers and fuss with their wares. They eye the sky, not wanting to pull plastic over their stacks until the last minute.

Suddenly Michael grabs my hand and lurches into a stall with blue tarpaulin walls.

"What are you doing?"

He pulls me past disemboweled electronics on the vendor's tables and through to the other side. The vendor stares at us as we peer back around the corner.

"I—nothing."

"Look, I didn't see anyone back there," I say. "Don't worry."

He continues to scan the shoppers. "Yeah, I know. It's just that, right before you said you saw someone, I was trying to figure out if a couple of guys were following us." He looks down and notices he's still holding my hand. "Sorry," he says, and drops it quickly, which for some stupid reason makes me blush and wish I'd pulled my hand away first.

I look around too, avoiding his eyes. "Do you see them now?"

"No."

"There are plenty of people around. Nothing's going to happen to us here."

Michael gives me a look. "You say that like you're expecting something to happen."

I don't respond. "Come on, let's get back before the storm starts."

We hurry, following the crowds toward the street. The purple sky looks like it's about to explode. In the distance I see sheets of gray where rain is already coming down.

We aim for the spot we found *piki-piki* the day before. A drop plops down on my face, and I see the ground ahead freckle with rain. I look back at Michael, who's still checking over his shoulder. "It's nothing," he says.

We start to jog. I can see the *piki-piki* in the distance, but they're quickly disbanding, either taking on riders or going to seek shelter. I curse under my breath.

"Aren't you supposed to be a hard-core street kid or something? Can't take a little rain?" Michael asks. His tone is light, but I can hear the worry underneath.

"The guy in the blue shirt and his buddy in the hat?" I ask.

"Yeah, how did you—?"

"Stop looking. They'll know we're on to them."

"Pickpockets maybe?"

We pick up our pace, and I'm holding out hope for the

last motorcycle, which is idling and ready, but then a plump woman bustles over and scoots on sidesaddle. The *piki-piki* driver buzzes off.

"Same guys you saw in the market?" I ask. The rain is starting in earnest now. Tap, tap on my skull.

"Yeah."

"Then probably not pickpockets. They would have got you there."

"Me? Why me?"

"You're obviously the one with cash." Before he can protest, I add, "Next street corner, turn fast to the right and follow me. Don't speed up until then. Act normal. *Don't* look back," I add as he starts to turn his head. "Okay, one, two, three, *now*."

We pop sideways, sliding a little on the mud, and Michael follows my lead when I take off in a sprint. I swerve around a corner, and we're suddenly in a maze of tin-shack homes. The sky opens. The rain comes too hard to hear footsteps, but I'm pretty sure I hear a shout behind us.

I duck between two shacks and send a flock of wet chickens scattering. An old man protests toothlessly from a doorway. I'm totally drenched now, and little rivers of mud are starting to fill the pathways. I glance behind and can't see anyone, but hear another yell. Michael is right at my heels. We dodge between wet laundry flapping on lines, leap over a pushcart, wrench a turn, and come suddenly to a dead end.

"Here!" Michael says, and webs his hands for me to step into and launch over the rickety wall.

"What about you?"

"I'll be fine! Go!"

He pushes me up and over the fence and I land on the other side, splattering mud. I can hear him scrambling behind me. At the same time I hear someone yell, "There he is!"

Michael drops down beside me with a hiss. It looks like he's sliced his hand, but there's no time to check; we take off. We slide around a corner and Michael goes down, holding his hand to his chest. I catch a flash of dripping red as I grab him up by the elbow and we keep on, trying to listen for the splash of running feet behind us. Then without warning the shacks end and we're at the edge of a half-finished apartment block, something that looks like it was way too ambitious for this place. Someone obviously didn't anticipate the rainy season making this area a swamp, and water fills the bottom floor. Algae and duckweed and floating trash clump in the gaping spaces where doors would be. Michael starts down the path that leads back into the shacks, but I grab him—"This way!"—and we slip into the water, moving toward the abandoned building's door.

We slosh through, and in the half-light I see there's a man already inside the building, perched on a rickety-looking platform raised on concrete blocks, up out of the water. He stands, skinny, jaundice-eyed, ready to shoo us out. On the platform I see the minimal trappings of a squatter.

"Get your wallet," I whisper at Michael.

"What?"

"Do it!"

Michael retrieves it, and the man watches hungrily as I

yank out a handful of bills. "You didn't see us," I tell him, waving the money toward his nose. I make sure he's paying attention, wad the cash in my hand, and pull Michael along with me, through the swamp and down a hallway, toward other rooms that I hope to God have an exit. We slosh through water up to our knees and turn a corner into a room with a stairwell.

I nod at it, and Michael follows me. We can hear more shouting now, and I can only hope the other guys won't offer the squatter man cash too. We slide up the moss-slicked stairs and into a room with a window that looks back out the way we came. We crouch on either side of it, the spray of rain catching us, and it's only then that I realize how crazily my heart is pounding.

"Who are they?" Michael mouths, breathing hard.

I shake my head and risk a peek out the window. I quickly pull back. "They're right outside," I breathe.

Michael sneaks a glance too, while I scan the room for something, anything, to use as a weapon, but the best we've got is an old beer bottle.

The men are stopped at the edge of the water, arguing over whether to keep going down the path or look in the building. I hear one of them whistle and shout, "*Mzee!* You seen a couple of kids? They stole my phone!"

I hold my breath and squeeze my eyes shut, hoping.

Below I hear a splash, which must be the old man climbing down from his perch and coming to the doorway. "They go that way," he yells, and I pray his gnarled finger is pointing toward the path. "Girl and boy? You catch them! Beat them for me too!"

I hear feet running, wait a second, then take another quick look. The guys are sprinting away from us, down the path through the rain.

"Sweet Jesus." I collapse against the wall. Michael does the same, and we just sit there for a few seconds, catching our breath.

A head pops up from the stairs. "Money!" the man says, sticking his bony hand out.

"Okay, okay," I say, lumbering to my feet. "You earned it."

"Give it all to him," Michael says. "I'd kiss him, but I'm a mess."

I'm shocked to find myself grinning like an idiot as I hand the money to the old man, who clutches it to his chest with a high little cackle. "Two minute," he says, holding out his fingers. I don't know where the old man comes from, but Swahili isn't his forte. "Two minute, you go!"

"Sure, *mzee*, we will," I say.

He disappears down the stairs and I collapse next to Michael, waiting for my legs to stop trembling.

Michael looks at his hand, peeling back a fistful of his T-shirt that he's been using to stanch the blood. There's a jagged cut through his palm. "What was that all about? Who were those guys?"

"I don't know. Let me see that." I take his hand and inspect it. "This needs to be cleaned out. We'll get one of the nurses to patch you up when we get back to the guesthouse."

Michael is quiet. I rip off the bit from his shirt that he's already bloodied. My fingertips tingle as they brush against his chest in the process. I wrap the fabric around his wound.

"Are you sure you don't know?"

I glance up at him. "What do you mean?"

"I mean, you're keeping stuff from me about your mom. That hidden file behind her photo . . . Catherine—don't think I didn't notice you being weird . . . and who did you think you saw back in that alley?"

I don't answer.

"Look," Michael says, pulling his hand back, "we can't figure out who killed your mom if we're not sharing information."

"The deal was that *you* find out. I'm still not convinced it wasn't your dad." I'm going for anger, but I'm surprised to hear uncertainty behind my words.

"Come on, Tina! Someone sent those guys. Probably someone who's heard we're asking about your mom and doesn't like it. Why would my dad do that? He wouldn't have them chase *me* around."

"How do you know they wouldn't have left you alone and only taken me?" I say stubbornly.

Michael starts to answer, but just then I feel a buzzing in my pocket. I pull out my phone. "Hello? Boyboy?"

Boyboy's voice is crackly on the line. "You better get back here. I found something in Mwika's email that both of you need to see."

"What?"

"It's a video. Hurry."

THIRTY-ONE

We can't find a *piki-piki*, so getting back to the guest-house takes forever. Plus we're slowed down by ducking into the bush on the side of the road anytime someone goes by. I can't tell if it's because Michael is angry, or his hand is hurting, or he's just anxious about finally seeing the video, but we don't talk.

By the time we get in, it's dusk. We rush to our rooms, where Boyboy is waiting.

"You should have that taken care of," I say, gesturing to Michael's hand.

"Not until we see this," he says firmly. I should make him go—that hand needs stitches—but I don't. I can't imagine waiting a second longer than we have to.

As we're waiting for Boyboy's computer to boot up, I see that someone has brought plates of *matoke* and beans to our rooms. It's only then that I realize I haven't eaten since break-fast and I pick up a plate. It's still warm and I take a few bites, but I must be too nervous because everything seems to have a bitter taste. I quickly give up.

"The video was in Mwika's email?" Michael asks.

"Mwika sent it to someone and said he wanted half a million."

"Sent it to who? Mr. Greyhill?" I ask.

Boyboy purses his lips. "I haven't been able to find out yet. It's a dummy email and I didn't want to use up my computer battery tracing who it belongs to. I wasn't able to charge for very long, and I've only got enough power left to watch the video. Maybe not even that. And the hospital hasn't had electricity all day. Apparently there's no fuel in this godforsaken town to run the generators."

But I'm barely listening. My eyes are glued to the grainy image that he's opened on his screen. "Is that it?"

"Yeah," he says, but pauses before clicking PLAY. "But it's not . . . you shouldn't . . ."

"Just show us!" I say, and reach over him to start the video.

The scene jerks to life. At first there's only static and a time stamp: five years earlier, the day my mother was murdered. The time: 1:13 a.m. My breath quickens as a light comes on, illuminating a room in black and white.

I lean forward. "That's it. That's Greyhill's office." My heart thrums. It's the same view from the camera mounted on the bookcase door.

The camera pans to the side. The bookcase door is opening, I realize. It closes, showing the office again.

And standing there like a magic trick is my mother.

My vision blurs. I blink rapidly to see through the water springing to my eyes. She's come through the tunnel. I was right. She *had* been disappearing in the night, meeting Mr. G in his office.

The dour, black maid uniform she wears utterly fails to mask her beauty. Coming around the desk, she kicks off her shoes. She is so much smaller than I remember her, fragile looking as a sapling tree. As she makes her way slowly toward the sofa, she pulls her braids from a knot at her neck and shakes her head. She rubs her scalp with her fingertips. She takes off her earrings. Puts them in her pocket.

I am having trouble breathing. She looks completely at home. Comfortable.

I can't watch. I have to watch. I can't watch. I can't look away.

The scene swivels again, and Mama is lost from view. I rise to my knees. "What's—" Then it swings back, showing the room again.

And there he is.

He has followed her out of the tunnel.

Her murderer.

My face is inches from the laptop. Michael's shoulder presses up to mine, trying to see too. All that's visible of the man is his back. I barely have time to register that his hair and skin are dark—black skin, not Mr. Greyhill—before a gun floats up in his hand.

My mother turns to him.

"No," I whisper. "No. Get out . . ."

The look on her face when she sees the gun is strange, like she's not even surprised. Like she'd been waiting for this. She stares at him for a long moment, before her expression hardens into something else. Something almost . . . defiant.

"No," I moan, shaking my head.

"Turn it off! Don't watch, Tina," Michael says, like he's suddenly understanding what's about to happen, but I furiously slap his hands away from the keypad.

"Tina," he pleads.

Wordlessly, Mama starts forward toward her killer, and just like that . . .

Bam.

She stumbles back.

I feel an animal noise rip from my throat, and my hands fly to my face. Beside me I hear Boyboy choke. But I can't look away. A glossy sheen hovers near her heart. Blood on her black uniform. She keeps stepping back. Her knees buckle; the sofa catches her.

She lets her head sink into the cushions, like she's just going to rest for a second.

And for a while nothing happens. For nearly a minute it's just her, sitting there, and you can see her chest heaving, like she's exhausted, like she's run a race. The killer places the gun in the exact middle of Mr. Greyhill's desk. He continues to watch Mama, never turning to show his face to the camera.

I'm making some noise, over and over again.

Then the screen whips away again and back.

"He just left through the tunnel," Michael rasps. "I didn't see his face. Did you see his face? Was it Mwika?"

I can't answer. I'm starting to tilt sideways. I feel Boyboy holding me up.

My mother is dying as I watch. Someone help her. Please. And just then, behind her, the door to the office flies open and there's a blur and the next thing I see is Mr. Greyhill on his knees before her, pressing at her chest.

"What's he doing?" I gasp. Black flows between his fingers.

It's too much. My vision is going. I can't breathe anymore. Water is running down my face and neck. My heart feels like it's being pressed through a sieve. For one moment an impossible hope flutters in my chest. He'll save her. He'll get her to a hospital and she'll be okay.

And that's when I see her head rise and her eyes open. She's still conscious. For a moment I think she's going to try to push Mr. Greyhill away. But she just looks at him, reaches her hand to the side of his face. He presses into it, his whole body shaking. Then her hand falls. Her head rolls back.

And my mother dies.

Her spirit peels away from her body and she is gone.

And I cannot breathe.

I hear something. My name. I feel hands on my arms, on my back. I can't move.

The world is spiraling into one bright and terrible point, sparking at the edges.

THIRTY-TWO

I don't remember standing up, or walking out of the room. I find myself in the grass outside, taking in gulps of wet air. The world pulses and blurs. I see the reflection of the lamp catching beads of falling rain in the dark like a million little needles. I can't keep myself upright, and I fold, holding on to my knees, rain on my back.

Bent over double, I hear footsteps behind me. They stop. I know without turning around that it's Michael. He stands there for so long, watching my hunched shoulders without speaking, that I can't stand it anymore and finally round on him, my fists curled. "What?" I gasp. "What do you want me to say? You were right! Your dad didn't do it! He didn't kill her!"

"Tina." He reaches out.

I reel back, for a second thinking I'm going to fall. "Don't touch me!"

He doesn't. He steps forward slowly. I stand there, rain pounding all over me. My whole body is shaking and hot like I have a fever.

"I'm so sorry, Tina," he says. "You shouldn't have had to see—"

"Stop! Just stop!"

"This doesn't change anything," he tries, moving toward me again. "Maybe that was Mwika. We'll still find out who killed her. I'll help you."

"I don't want your help! I don't care about you, or your dad, or Mwika or Omoko!"

Michael looks confused, and I realize he doesn't know who Mr. Omoko is. I'm screaming like a crazy person. I don't care.

"Come back inside, Tina. The rain . . ." He takes my wrist.

"Don't." I try to yank my hand away, but he holds it tight. "Don't," I repeat. I can't look at his face. I am drowning. I need to sit. If I don't sit I'm going to fall.

"Tina." He moves closer. "Look at me. I'm so sorry . . ."

"No," I whisper, but I'm stuck, unable to go forward or back. The light and the dark are swirling in and out. The rain feels like blisters on my skin. I still can't breathe.

"It's going to be okay," he says so quietly that I almost don't hear him. His face swims in front of me. I feel his arms under my palms like the branches of a tree, sturdy and hard. "We're not going to stop. We'll figure out who killed her."

He is so close that I can feel the heat coming off him through the rain. His eyes are luminous. I can't see anything but his face, soft and familiar. I am so dizzy. My body stops fighting. My lids start to droop. There's a strange, chalky taste in my mouth.

Wait, a small voice in my mind says. Something's not right.

My eyes snap open. "No," I choke out, and push clumsily out of Michael's embrace. "No."

"Tina, wait . . ."

But I just stagger backward, turn, and run into the night.

THIRTY-THREE

Rule 15: A rule from my mother: run.

"Don't come back. Don't you dare even look back. Run like you do when you're racing and you beat all the boys. Go in the forest and wait for me at our place. You remember? You will find it? Good. Go now. Run."

And then she shoved me out the window.

Sprinting through the forest at night isn't easy like they make it look in the movies. There are holes in the ground and trees fallen over and vines with thorns and invisible things that sting and claw. And if it's dark and you're just a little kid, it's almost impossible. Unless there is the smell of gasoline and smoke behind you, and the only light is a faint glimmer of flame on the underbellies of leaves in the limbs above, coming from the direction of your home. Then light does not comfort you, and you run farther. You search out the dark and the thorns and the crevices in the earth, because they are better than what you've left burning.

I'm standing in the stupid rain, like a stupid stray dog.

I am dully aware of the stitch in my side and a stinging in my foot. The only reason I've stopped is because I am at the edge of a gully. I can't see below the shine of the black water's surface, but it moves in an angry boil, like eels. My toes curl in the soft mud at the edge, my legs toying with the idea of leaping in, not wanting to be stilled.

I'm in the forest, but I don't remember getting here. I have been running. My lungs burn. There is nothing but this creek and dripping leaves and the shrill of insects. There is supposed to be a bridge here. My thoughts come slowly, like the mud that is breaking below my weight and splashing into the creek. How long have I been standing here? I step back. I am hot, dripping sweat, and now my feet are singing with pain and I remember a stony path. My head feels like a melon on a stick, pulling me sideways. There's a clearing ahead, beyond the creek. A sweep of pale grass. The dark hut, barely visible. Nothing to see by other than a distant pulse of lightning.

There is movement in the bush behind me. Probably the *mokele-mbembe*, come out of the water on his scaly legs, swinging his dragon tail, licking his dragon teeth and ready to slurp me up. Let him.

At the same time my knees hit the ground, I feel a strong hand gripping my elbow. There is a too-bright light in my face.

"Mama," I say.

Stumbling through short grass. It tickles my ankles.

A face in a window, surrounded by orange light. The *mokele-mbembe*? It has horns. No. Not horns, ears. A dog.

Water, very cold, splashing my legs and arms.

My mother says my name—"Christina"—like I'm in trouble, and I want to answer her—Yes, I'm here—but my mouth won't move.

A smell I haven't known in years: blankets dried in the sun on lantana bushes.

And then nothing.

I wake up alone in a sagging bed that creaks when I move. When I try to sit up, my head pounds, and for a few seconds my vision fades. I'm able to turn my head and blink, and when my sight comes back, I see walls made of saplings, covered in mud. The ground is laid with a tightly woven grass mat. There is the smell of wood smoke and dry earth.

The signs of a woman and a girl are in the things I can see around me—dresses hung on pegs and Sunday shoes arranged neatly beside the door. School books and a Bible, a calendar from four years ago showing white children ice-skating that hangs next to a photograph of a serious-looking elderly couple. An AK-47 sits above the couple's heads, out of the reach of a child, on the ledge between the wall and the roof.

Sunlight comes in under the shutters and the door in crisp lines. Close by are birds, and farther away the sound of goats bleating and shaking their bells. I get up slowly. I'm still in my slightly damp clothes. Other than my aching head and very tender feet I seem to be okay. It takes me a while, but I stagger to the door. My mouth is bone-dry. I feel like a human balloon that's been filled with sand.

I push the door open a crack and blink into the brightness. A red dirt yard, hatch marks showing it's been freshly swept with a twig broom, and grass and the forest beyond. I step outside and the sun is immediate and hot on my skin.

I know where I am.

"Catherine?" I croak. I clear my throat and try again. Running up the path to her home last night comes back to me suddenly, like a fever dream. *She* picked me up off the ground, not my mother. My memory is hazy, full of gaps. I feel a sudden and intense wave of hot and cold, and rush to the edge of the yard, where I throw up.

"You were drinking last night?"

I finish heaving, wipe my mouth with my sleeve, then turn toward the voice.

Catherine has come around the side of the house. She's drying a metal pot. "Or are you pregnant?"

"No," I say quickly. "Neither."

She snorts. "You came here sick. Talking crazy about your mama."

I try to think. What had happened? Had I been drugged? The only thing I'd eaten yesterday had been food from the nuns. "I wasn't drinking. Maybe something bit me."

"Spider, maybe," she says, but not like she believes it.

"Where did you find me?"

She jerks her chin, motioning up the hill. I see a dark place on the edge of the forest where it looks like the path turns in, toward the creek.

"You were trying to get to your farm?"

"My farm . . ." Slowly it dawns on me, why her home looked familiar before. I look from her to the path. "We lived there."

I start to walk, struggling against the heat and my stiff limbs and the hill. Behind me Catherine says nothing. She's probably laughing at me, and I resolve not to look back. Once I reach the path I'm in the shade again, but I have to pause to catch my breath and let my heart stop pounding in my ears. "Spiders," I pant. "Or a snake."

"Or somebody poison you," a small high voice says. I look up to see the long-limbed girl. Either she is very quiet, or I am still groggy, because both she and her yellow dog have come up on me without my hearing. She walks forward and hands me a stick to lean on, and waits for me to go first. It isn't far to where the path dips into the creek, which has gone down in the night. I see well-placed stepping stones now, leading across.

I look to the other bank and try to find memories that match this place. The mud plaster is crumbling off the walls of the hut, and what is left of the roof is caved in and black from fire. The shed is gone, burned to nothing. Weeds reach the windowsills. Where is my climbing tree? Where was the garden? We had rabbits once, and chickens. They are long gone now, but maybe I'll see a wild descendant in the field. I step across the creek. The dog splashes through the water and races past me as I climb the bank.

"You are coming to claim this place?"

I turn to see Catherine stepping nimbly over the rocks behind her daughter.

"No." I reach out a hand to help her, but she ignores it.

"I told you not to come back here."

"I know."

She breathes out her nose, walks past me toward the hut. At the edge of the yard, she stands with her hands on her hips. Her daughter goes on, down an invisible path through the weeds. There is an avocado tree back there, I remember now.

"Why are you here, then?" Catherine asks.

It's not an answer, but it's all I can say: "My mother is dead."

Catherine doesn't move.

"Someone killed her. Five years ago." Still nothing, and I find myself relieved at the silence, the utter lack of sympathy. I keep talking. "I thought I knew who killed her, but last night I found out for sure I was wrong. Maybe I went a little crazy." I try to smile, but it doesn't quite stick.

Five years I've lost hating Mr. G. Hating him. Plotting my revenge. Letting that hate drive me. Dirt. Money. Blood. It was so easy. And now . . . it's like suddenly losing a limb. I keep trying to walk, forgetting I've lost my leg.

"You know the weird thing?" I say, talking basically to myself now. "I think I already knew he didn't do it." I swallow and nod. Catherine is still quiet, and I'm grateful.

Can't I just keep on hating Mr. Greyhill? That would be so much easier. Turning my anger at David Mwika feels like asking the earth to start spinning in the opposite direction. David Mwika? He's dead. I can never ask him why he did it. Was it even him in the video? I have nothing to go on now.

"Who killed her?" Catherine finally asks. Her face is still hard, but the softness of her voice, unexpected, pierces through me, and I sink to the ground. The world seems too bright; there's too much of it.

"I don't know. I think maybe a security guard she worked with? But I-I don't know why."

I should go home. Coming back here to Congo was a stupid idea. I don't know what I'm doing. I should go home to Kiki and . . . and what? Beg forgiveness from Bug Eye? Give Mr. Omoko Mr. Greyhill's money like I promised? I've opened this door and now I don't know how to shut it. If I keep going, his whole family will be ruined. Michael, his sister, mother, everyone. That was the whole point. But I can't do that now. Can I? No. Yes. I have to. Mr. Omoko is waiting. Goondas who disobey orders get chained to cinder blocks and tossed off piers. I may get killed anyway, just for running off like an idiot.

I push my fingers into my temples, trying to press my thoughts and the pounding away.

With a grunt Catherine lowers herself to the ground beside me. She tucks her legs in under her and watches the yard, where the dog pounces on something in the grass and the girl runs over to investigate. "You don't remember me, do you?"

"No," I say. "I don't. But you knew my mother. Probably better than me."

Catherine shifts and pulls a piece of paper from her apron. Her hands are dark and rough, used to work. She unfolds the paper and I realize she's taken the photo of her and my mother out of my pocket while I slept. She looks at it for a long time, then slowly hands it back to me. "She was my best friend," she says. Her mouth pinches.

I look at Catherine's younger face. Plumper, eyes brighter. The Catherine sitting next to me is still attractive, but her eyes are a thousand years older.

"Anju was my cousin, but just like a sister to me. We grew up together. When she had you, I helped her."

I stare at Catherine. She and her daughter are family. The only family I know, other than Kiki. And suddenly, sitting here with the smell of grass and the coolness rising from the creek, a memory comes to me: the sound of my mother and another woman laughing at something I had said. It was her, Catherine. My voice breaks as I ask, "So why do you hate her now?"

Catherine sighs. "I don't think I hate her anymore."

"But yesterday . . ."

"I hated her yesterday. I loved her and she left me and I've hated her for it. But now that I see you . . ." She looks from me to her daughter. "Now I think I understand."

"Please, Catherine, understand what? I don't understand anything."

She smiles a little. "Nobody calls me Catherine anymore, just the nuns. It's Cathi."

I look down. "Catherine's my sister's name. No one calls her that either. She's Kiki."

"Sister?" Cathi looks surprised. Her voice falters. "Named Catherine? Your mother got married?"

I hesitate. "No."

She looks at her daughter again, who has found a long stick and is poking at the avocados. Cathi puts two fingers to her mouth, but doesn't say anything. An avocado falls from the tree and the girl retrieves it, adds it to the others she's carrying in her skirt. She looks to be about the same age as Kiki, maybe a bit older.

"They took you too, didn't they?" I blurt. "When they took my mother? When she got pregnant with me?"

Cathi starts to stand. I've pushed too hard, said something wrong. "Wait," I say, lowering my voice, reaching for her arm. "Please. I came here to find out who killed my mother, but every time I think I'm getting closer it just gets more confusing. Help me. I have to understand."

Her arm is stiff under my hand, tense. I let go.

She takes a couple of long, deep breaths. "I haven't seen Anju since before this sister of yours was born. I don't know who killed her."

"But you knew her better than anyone! Help me understand what happened to her here. Because I think somehow, everything has something to do with this place. With her—your—capture and what she saw and knew. She ran from here, and maybe someone followed her. I don't know why they killed her, but . . . please. I don't know her anymore. I think maybe I never knew her. Just tell me what you can. Anything."

"You are too young," Cathi says after a long moment, but in that same tone, like she doesn't really believe it. She bends forward. "My Anju . . . my poor Anju . . . I forgive you, of course I do . . ." Staring at the dirt between her feet, she begins a shallow rocking, back and forth.

I reach out to touch her again, afraid I will lose her to whatever blackness is hovering nearby, ready to sweep her up. "Please, Cathi. I have to go back to Sangui, but I can't leave knowing less than when I got here."

Cathi looks up suddenly, her eyes bright. "And what will you do, eh? What will you do with my story? I don't have answers! I don't know who killed your mother! I don't know who my Ruth's father is! I can tell you what was done to us, but why? What does telling do? Those days brought me nothing but evil! No one gets punished; those men are all still there, just up the mountain," she says, waving her hand toward the jungle. "There is no justice that comes from telling! Do you know what I do now to get my daily bread? About the men who come to me at the bars because no one will let me sell my vegetables in the market? No. It is not a story for telling. It is nothing but pain."

"You think I'm not in pain now?" I cry.

She resumes her rocking. "You know nothing of pain. You are a child. You have no idea." She clamps her mouth shut.

We sit there, with insects buzzing around our heads, looking back at my broken and burnt old home.

For just a moment I can squint and see the way it might look, if we hadn't had to run away: Curtains in the window. Two flowerpots framing the door like at Cathi's house. My mother hanging laundry. I look beyond, in the direction Cathi says the militiamen still are, into the forest.

I take a deep breath. "I may not remember you. But I remember that night."

Cathi inclines her head just slightly toward me, watches me from the corner of her eye.

"I was five years old. I remember loud noises, and seeing fire through the window. There was yelling. Screaming." I put my hands together and squeeze them between my knees. "Mama pulled me from bed, pushed me out the back window, and told me to run."

I swallow, looking at the yard, trying to see which way I would have gone. "I'm a good runner. I ran for a long time, to a place near a stream where she used to take me. Maybe you know it. There was a little cave there. I went inside and waited. For . . . I don't know how long. Days. I ate plants and fruits that made me sick, and drank dirty water from the cave floor. I was afraid of the animals. I was afraid someone would come and find me. I was afraid no one would come and find me.

"I could hear the men passing all around me through the jungle. I was supposed to stay in the cave, but one of those days I had to come out and relieve myself. I was doing my business when I heard the men coming and didn't have time to get back. I was just squatting there and I had to bury myself in leaves, right on my stink, and hope they didn't step on me or smell me. One man came so close I could have reached out and untied his boot. I saw his eyes." I finally look back at Cathi. "He would have killed me as easily as breathing."

We sit. The clouds are rolling across the sky. Cicadas drone in the heat. My head is starting to feel a little more clear.

"Now," I say, "I didn't spend those days in a hole, lying in my own filth, for nothing. My mother didn't say anything about where she had been when she finally came and pulled me out. She never spoke of that time, or any time before. One day I might have asked her, but she was murdered before I could, and I am going to find out why. I'm not asking you. I am telling you. Help me understand."

Cathi's daughter returns to us with a smile like sunlight on water, her dress full of fruit. Cathi watches her and says nothing for a long time. Ruth shows her mother what she's gathered, sneaking glances at me. I can see the woman in this girl, hovering like a shadow.

"Go and take these to *Nyanya* Florence," Cathi says. "Her old teeth will like them. Take the dog."

The girl nods and runs off, a child again, and we watch her until she is across the creek and out of sight. The silence grows thick and green around us. Then Cathi takes a deep breath and begins.

THIRTY-FOUR

A Story of Two Girls:

Once upon a time, there were two girls who lived in a lush land far, far away.

One of the girls was loud and giggly, while the other one was quiet and stern. One liked boys and the other preferred books. One was plump like a mango and the other was skinny like a pencil. One girl was pretty, but the other was as beautiful as the moon.

As different as they were, they loved each other fiercely, and one was never found without the other. They grew from girls to young women, and after they finished secondary school, not wanting to be separated, both went to the hospital in town to be trained as nurses. The girls worked hard and became strong women and clever healers.

One year into the training, the loud one's sweetheart gave

her father five cows and asked for her hand in marriage. The quiet one was happy for her best friend, but had decided long ago to give her hand to God. Each was pleased for the other, though secretly, deep in their hearts, they both wished they would never have to be apart.

Midway through their second year of training, a whisper reached the hospital that gold had been found in the mountains. And the nuns made the sign of the cross on their chests and said, "Brace yourselves, because we've seen this before, and war is coming."

At first it was just a rumbling in the distance, disappearances, a scarcity of medicine and food. It was hardly war, and more like a howling of wild dogs somewhere far off. An unseen shivery sound that you would close the window against and try to forget.

And so despite the nuns' warning, the girls weren't prepared when the war came through the front gates of the hospital, ripping and slashing. It moved fast. They weren't ready for the way it spilled blood and flung bedpans and laughed at the nuns praying to God. It shot a priest. It took whatever caught its fancy: morphine and tinned puddings. And before it left, it placed its hands on five young women, including the two young women who would not be separated, and said, These are mine. And it stole them away into the night.

It was a dark night. A very, very dark and long night. A night that lasted for months, though it was hard to say how many, as the girls used their monthly bleeding to count the days, and when the bleeding stopped, counting became difficult.

The warlords brought the women they had stolen into the mountains, to their kingdom, where trees covered the sky. In that place the women realized some of the men were in fact little boys with red eyes and slack faces. When the men and boys went out to fight, they wore leaves and flowers in their hair because it made them invisible to bullets. There were other women in the warlords' kingdom, but they spoke a different language, when they spoke at all, and moved like ghosts.

The men had chosen this place because their god lived there, deep in a hole in the mountain. Every day, the five women were sent with the other captives into the hole to pick away at the flanks of the god of gold and bring out his shiny scabs.

And at night? Every night was hell embodied as a man or a boy, five or six times over. The loud one didn't know them; she just closed her eyes and let her soul drift far away while she waited for it to be over.

But the war saw the quiet one's beauty, and she was held back and given like a gift to a man they called Number Two, who came and went from the kingdom on a powerful white man's bidding. He would fly in on a helicopter, bringing guns and money. When he came, he always asked for her. No one was allowed to touch the quiet one but him.

They said he came from a city named for blood, Sangui.

• • •

Of the five women:

One ran, and the boys laughed and put a bullet in her back.

One woman began to drink the poisoned water in the god's hole, even when the others begged her to stop, and she died raving in a fever.

One woman had been the two girls' teacher, a nun, and when she could, she diverted the hell from her students. But most of the time she couldn't.

And the two girls survived, but only because neither wanted to die and leave the other one alone in the terrible kingdom.

One day the men were ambushed by other men that looked exactly like the first men, and there was fighting and gunfire and explosions that shook the earth and chaos, and the teacher said run, and the girls and the teacher ran and ran and ran, until they came back to their town, and stumbled into the hospital and were finally, finally safe.

The two friends expected things to get better after their escape, and for a while they did.

But soon after they healed and could get up and walk around again, they noticed something strange: a smell. People around them would cringe and move away. The three women sniffed the wind and tried to figure out where it came from. It was rotten like outhouses and the medical garbage pile, and it grew stronger whenever the three were together. Eventually, they realized that it wasn't being borne in on the wind; it was coming from them, out of their pores, caught in their hair, redolent on their breath.

The women scrubbed and scrubbed, and drank sweet teas, but no matter what they did, the hell they had passed through lingered over them, clearing rooms with its stink. It was pungent, embarrassing, pervasive, and impossible to get rid of.

A smell that was not a smell.

Then one day the loud woman's sweetheart took his cows back. They later heard he had waited a week, and then given them to another girl's father.

The quiet woman's stomach grew round and large and the reverend mother called her to her office and explained that, while the quiet one could still be a nurse, the cloistered life was no longer appropriate. Not for a mother.

The teacher who had escaped with them left for the city called Sangui, saying she couldn't remember what God's face looked like anymore. She asked the two girls if they wanted to go with her. The quiet girl might have gone, except by then she was too big to travel. The loud girl would not leave her friend.

There was ripping and screaming and a baby was born. They named her Christina.

The two women moved back to their parents' neighboring farms. The loud one's mother and father died within a year of her return, one after the other. The quiet one's father had died while she was away in the terrible kingdom. Her mother grew small.

The quiet one still worked as a nurse at the hospital, but the loud one's hands would shake with every new broken woman brought in. She tried to sell vegetables instead, but grew tired of the other sellers' stares and wrinkled noses.

So she found a new occupation. She no longer liked boys, but for the work she did, she didn't have to like them. She just had to close her eyes and let her soul drift far away.

Though the women still loved each other, they knew something had fractured between them that could not be entirely mended. They both focused on the baby, who grew quickly. The quiet one sometimes caught herself staring at her daughter's face. And sometimes she could not look at her child at all, and when that happened the loud one would pick up the little girl and walk away, kissing the salt off her baby cheeks until she laughed.

Years passed. War lingered around the edges, coming and going, like the seasons. Sometimes it would steal cattle and goats. Sometimes they would see it hanging around in the bars in town, laughing and drinking. Sometimes they would hear it coming and run and hide in the forest in a secret place, and pretend for the sake of the child they were on a great adventure.

One of those times, the quiet one's mother, who had grown smaller and frailer, refused to leave and hide, even though her daughter begged and pleaded. When they came back, they found her mother still in bed, as if perhaps only sleeping. There was little blood, and the girls washed her body in the creek and wrapped her in her best Sunday *kitenge*. They buried her on the hill, next to the quiet girl's father.

Something about the death of the quiet one's mother changed her. She was still quiet, but there was a look in her eyes that worried the loud one. The quiet one started leaving the child with the loud one, and walking off into the forest alone. She would come back with filthy feet, sticks in her hair, and a look in her eyes like an animal gone wild.

Five years after the birth of the child, a white man came to town and started asking questions.

He wasn't the first white man to come through. The war had brought pilots and journalists and blue helmets of all colors who followed the fighting like spectators. Lord knows that business was good for the loud one when she worked the bars closest to the hotels. The war brought do-gooders and missionaries who looked bewildered and thrilled all at once, and mining men who acted like the kind of dogs that never bark, that only bite.

But this man was different. He asked too many questions. Said the names out loud that everyone else knew to whisper.

When the loud woman found out that the quiet one had spoken to him, she was terrified. She told the quiet one to stop, but the quiet one said she was tired of being silent.

• • •

The war came back, like the loud one knew it would. It came the very night after the quiet one talked to the white man. This time it didn't come for goats or cattle. It came for the two girls, now women. It chased them into the forest. It put its hands on them, and said, These are still mine. And it took them back to the terrible kingdom.

Only the child escaped.

There was no digging this time. Only hell. The two women were separated, and the loud one could hear the screaming of the quiet one, and she screamed herself, and thought about letting her soul drift away and not come back. But she knew she couldn't because that would mean leaving the quiet one alone.

But then, four days later, the quiet one was gone.

The men came in screaming for her, "Where did she go? Where did she go?" They beat the loud one, who was not so loud anymore. They put their knives in the fire and laid them sizzling on her legs. But it didn't matter. The not-so-loud woman didn't know how her friend had escaped, or where she had gone. All she knew was that the quiet one, who had become not-so-quiet, had left her.

She was alone in the terrible kingdom.

They beat her almost to death. But as they really only cared about the once-quiet woman, eventually they lost interest. They packed up their camp and left the once-loud woman there, alone on the forest floor. And when the once-loud woman realized she wasn't going to die, there was nothing to do but go home.

And there she was still alone, except for the seed in her belly. A strange thing, because it should not have survived. But it did, which was lucky, or awful. Or both, because it was the only thing that clung to her soul and kept it from flying away for good.

THIRTY-FIVE

When Cathi is done she gets up and brushes the dirt from her dress. She walks to the edge of the forest and stands looking into it, like she's waiting for someone to appear.

It's late in the afternoon when we speak again, and we only do because Ruth comes back full of chatter. She's had her hair braided by Nyanya Florence's granddaughter and wants us both to compliment her. It's enough to ease us both back into the real world.

"Very pretty," I tell her, and she beams. She doesn't look like Kiki, but I can't help thinking again of my sister. I feel an ache in my chest, an urge to protect this girl I've only just met. It must make Cathi crazy, thinking the same thing that happened to her could someday happen to her daughter. They are so far from town, just on the edge of the jungle, and Cathi knows the men are still out there. Suddenly the AK-47 and two giant dogs seem very reasonable.

"Will you stay for dinner, Christina?" Ruth asks.

"I should go back to the hospital," I say.

"Are you still sick?"

"No, I'm better now," I say. "We're staying at the guest-house there."

Cathi frowns. "It will be dark very soon. Maybe you should stay the night again."

"My friends will be wondering where I am," I say reluctantly. And there's still Kiki to think about. I need to get back to call Bug Eye and head off any more visits from Ketchup. Running away like a madwoman in the rain left me not only shoeless but phoneless. Not that I would have had service up here, I bet. I've stayed too long already. But it's hard to leave. Cathi has started dinner out back and the smell of onions and garlic and chilies is making my stomach growl. It's familiar, this place. Even if I can't really remember it, the sense of home is here.

"I thought those boys would come looking for you," Cathi says, "and you could walk back to town with them."

"I'll be fine," I say. "I don't need an escort."

"I will go up the hill and call Father Fidele on my mobile. He can meet you halfway, at least. No one will bother you if you are with him."

"Oh, don't do that," I say. "I'm sure he's busy."

But Cathi ignores me and takes her phone out to the field

and walks up the hill. I hear her talking and feel a surge of fondness for Father Fidele, even though I've barely met him. He must know what Cathi does to survive, and yet she's still able to call on him for help.

"He's coming," Cathi says when she returns. "If you stay on the main path you'll meet him."

I stand up, ready to go. "Bye, Ruth."

"Good-bye, Christina."

I take the photo of Cathi and my mother out of my pocket and hold it out to her. "Keep it," I say.

Catherine takes it from me like it's as fragile as a butterfly wing. She tucks it in between the pages of her Bible.

"Thank you, Cathi," I say, swallowing hard to keep from crying.

She places her hand on Ruth's shoulder. They watch me with the same bright eyes. "We will pray for Anju. And you."

"Will you come back someday?" Ruth asks softly.

"I hope so."

"You are welcome," Cathi says. "You are family."

I want to go fast, so Father Fidele won't have to walk too far to meet me, but the path is full of stones and my feet are still bruised. I should have taken the sandals Cathi offered, but I could tell they were her only pair. Instead I pick my way through the rocks as best I can. There is no one on the path, and the only noise is the stream rushing past and birds calling above. The late-afternoon sun sends gold spears through the branches. As I walk, the tangled, painful web of what

Cathi has revealed about my mother begins to unwind, and the strands reweave themselves, joining with what I already knew. They form the start of a picture.

I organize everything into a sort of timeline of what I know and what I still don't:

> Mama and Cathi were captured by militia and taken to work in a mine.
>
> Mama was singled out by Number Two. This psycho is probably my father. He was sent here by a white guy, who must be Mr. Greyhill.
>
> Mama and Cathi escaped from the militia. I was born. Time passed.
>
> Donatien came around asking questions, and Mama agreed to show him where the deals happened.
>
> Before she could, militia came again to our home and captured her and Cathi again. She pushed me out the window and I escaped. The same day, someone tried to kill Donatien.
>
> Mama somehow escaped again from the militia, found me, and we left Congo. Mama took us to Sangui City.
>
> Mama went to work for the Greyhills, even though Donatien told her that Mr. Greyhill was bad guy Number One, Number Two's employer. Why? Why did she go there, and why did he agree to employ her?
>
> Mama had Kiki; Mr. G is her father.

Mama threatened to expose Mr. G; he threatened to kill her.

Mama was murdered in Mr. G's house, but not by Mr. G. David Mwika, head of security, takes the video of the murder and then later tries to blackmail someone with it. Who?

David Mwika could be the murderer, but what's his motive? And if not him, who? And why? The killer didn't take anything; he wasn't a robber. He was deliberate about killing Mama. Was it someone who wanted to stop her from doing something? Or get revenge for something she had already done? Or was it some other reason entirely?

I slow to a stop and stand looking at the creek. Because I realize that while I have a million questions, what I really need to know first is fairly simple. It's the same question I keep coming back around to: Why did Mama search out Mr. Greyhill? Why ask for a job? And why did he agree to let her work there, let me stay there—essentially sheltering us? What did he gain? If I knew that, I think I'd know a lot more about who might want to kill her.

That's what I need to find out.

And it won't be easy, but I know who I have to ask. I need to get back to Boyboy and Michael and a phone. I swivel from the creek back to the path, determined.

And there, standing right in my way, is Father Fidele.

He startles me, and I take a step back. His approaching footsteps had been muffled by the rushing water. I feel the creek bank crumbling underfoot and he grabs my hand to keep me from falling back. "Careful!"

I start to thank him, but something in his eyes stops me. I don't have time to scream before he's pulling me close with the hand that is gripping my wrist. With his other hand he presses a cloth over my face. I start to fight, but stinging vapors hit my lungs, and everything goes bright and swirls and fades to nothing.

THIRTY-SIX

"G ood, now bring the cloth around on both sides so we can tie it in the middle," Mama said.

We were outside our cottage, standing at the edge of the grass, Mama, Kiki, and me. It was warm and sunny, and all over the Greyhills' yard I heard the familiar sounds of the staff at work. Maids chatting, the chop of the gardener's panga cutting back weeds. A thump and the occasional sneeze as dust was beaten out of a carpet. They were preparing for a party.

Mama was needed in the house, so I had a job too. I was bent over at the waist, baby Kiki a squirmy warm mass on my back. Mama's sure hands guided mine as we gathered the ends of the *kanga* cloth—one over my shoulder, one around my middle—and made Kiki snug against me. Today I would wear Kiki and take her with me wherever I went. Mama told me it was a big responsibility, but I was six and a half years old and ready for it.

"Can you make the knot?" she asked me.

I could. I made it too tight at first, but Mama helped me loosen it. Kiki made happy little baby noises to herself.

"Now stand slowly; make sure she isn't going to slip." Mama stepped back to observe.

I looked up at her, waiting for judgment. Those eyes saw everything. Every loose corner of the fabric, every stray hair come out of my braids, the scabs on both my knees from playing with Michael, my secondhand skirt already getting too short. She would find something wrong; she always managed to.

So I was surprised when she crouched at my level and kissed my forehead. "You are my good girl," she said, and her smile was something rare and brilliant that I wanted to capture, to hold tight in my fist and reexamine later when I was alone. "Take care of your sister," she said.

"I will," I said.

And I did. Not just that day, but every day after.

A hand smacks me across the face. My head bobs back and forth. The sting is enough to draw me out of the darkness, but for a few seconds I still don't know what's going on. Someone is yelling at me, I realize.

"Tiny. Tiny Girl. Wake up."

My eyes feel glued together. At first, when I get them open, I think there are several people before me, but then I understand I'm seeing double. I lift my head at the exact same moment freezing water hits my face, as sudden as a slap. I sputter and cough.

But it does the trick; I'm awake. I blink and look up. The figure steadies. He's holding a bucket and grinning at me like a hyena.

Ketchup.

I try to get to my feet, but I'm held fast. My hands are bound behind me, and I realize, after a second or two of fuzzy thinking, that I'm tied to a chair. Once that's cleared up, the pain in my wrists and ankles emerges where the bindings are. I'm in some sort of room with cloth walls. A tent. I hear birds singing; I think it's morning. There's another chair and a slept-in cot, but otherwise, except for the Goonda and me, the tent is empty. The ground underneath my feet is bare dirt covered in dead leaves.

Ketchup laughs. "You look like a chicken left out in the rain."

I test my wrists. The ties are metal, maybe. From the feel of it, they've cut my skin already. "Where am I?" I mumble. My face is numb.

"Uh-uh, Tiny Girl," Ketchup says, and comes close enough to grab my jaw and lift my face to his. "We're asking the questions now."

I can smell cheap home brew on his breath. His eyes are red and slightly unfocused.

I try to shake my head out of his grip, but the best I can do is give him a dirty look. Ketchup? Here? So I really hadn't imagined him in the marketplace. I work up some saliva and spit it on his hand.

He calls me a name and slaps the spit onto my cheek. He pulls back to hit me harder, but just then the tent flap opens and a man walks in.

At first I don't recognize him. But that's just because he looks so out of place here. It's been a long time since I've seen him in the flesh. He seems a little older, his round face starting to sag, the hair above his ears going gray. He's wearing a short-sleeved polo shirt and chinos, everything neatly pressed and spotless. More than anything, he looks like he just stepped off the golf course.

Ketchup hesitates, then lowers his hand. "Mr. Omoko. I was just coming for you, sir."

"She's awake," the Goonda boss says. He's talking to Ketchup, but looking at me.

"Yeah, I just got her up," Ketchup says. He backs out of the way so Mr. Omoko can approach me.

"I can see that," he says, frowning.

Where is Bug Eye? I wonder. Mr. Omoko wouldn't bring Ketchup and leave him behind.

The Goonda boss sits down in the chair across from me. "Wait for us outside, Mr. Ketchup."

Ketchup glowers at his back. Mr. Omoko has somehow managed to make his name sound even more ridiculous than it already is. But Ketchup retreats silently.

Mr. Omoko pulls a handkerchief out of his pocket and uses it to wipe my face. I don't have much choice but to let him. After he puts it away, he says, "You skipped town. We were worried."

Nothing about his composure looks worried.

The cold water has soaked my shirt, and I start to shiver. "I didn't think Bug Eye would allow me to go. So I didn't ask."

"No. He wouldn't. That's because I wouldn't have." Mr. Omoko tilts his head quizzically. "What are you doing here, girl? Why leave, when you were so close to getting everything you wanted? I thought we had a plan. Dirt, money, blood."

"I was going to be back by the time the data was decrypted and we were ready to go for the bank accounts," I say, growing more and more tense under Mr. Omoko's unwavering gaze. I'm starting to see something glittering in his eyes like the edge of a knife.

"Oh, but that wasn't the deal, was it? Your instructions were to leave the Greyhills' home as soon as you knew you had the data."

I shift in my seat. Where is Michael? And Boyboy? Surely they're looking for me by now.

"I don't like being left in the dark, Tiny Girl," Omoko says. And suddenly he's right up in my face, so close that I have no choice but to turn to the side. For a second I feel the frantic need to get away, as if he's about to bite me. But he just asks, "Why are you here? Don't you know this place is dangerous?"

"I . . ."

He leans back and I let out a shaky breath. "Thankfully, you were not hard to track down," he says.

"Look, Mr. Omoko, the data we took from Mr. Greyhill—"

Omoko interrupts me. "I have it. Or, I have your friend's computer, anyway. I can take it from here. He's not the only person in town who can hack bank accounts." He studies his fingernails, a fat gold ring on his hand glinting in the low light. "But maybe I won't even have to go to the trouble."

"You have Boyboy's computer?" I wait, feeling cold sweat prickle under my hair. "I don't understand. Is Boyboy here? Is Michael?"

Mr. Omoko smiles indulgently. "You're not one for playing by the rules, Tina, are you? Most of the time I like that about you. I ask for Greyhill's treasures, and that's what you bring me. Just not exactly how I'd expected."

"What do you mean? The accounts—"

"Michael."

Blood thrums in my ears. "What about Michael?" I ask slowly.

"With him, there's no need to do all that work."

I swallow, look around, as if I could see through the canvas. "Michael and Boyboy are both here?"

"Yes, exactly. The priest was supposed to round you all up together, but apparently he missed you. You do like to run off."

"You drugged us," I say.

"No, not me. I have people who do that sort of thing for me—that's the benefit of being the boss. The priest helped me. When he told me you were in Kasisi I almost didn't believe him. My Tiny Girl? In Congo? He was supposed to make sure you all stayed put until I got here. It took him a few tries, but he managed at last. He was lucky that whore called him up and told him where you were."

"You paid Father Fidele?"

"We have an arrangement. I give his hospital a little breathing room from the militias; he keeps me informed. I'm sure he's very conflicted about the whole thing, but that's between him and God." Omoko rubs his chin. "So. Plans. They're a little off, but salvageable. I'm thinking you'll have to forget the whole dirt part. That was never the highlight, anyway. No one cares about those sorts of news stories; they've heard it all before. One more white colonial type profiting off Africa. It'll be back-page fodder at best. Let's go straight to money, shall we? With a twist."

His eyes gleam. "Instead of anonymously draining Greyhill's bank accounts, we should have a little fun. Everything gets trickier, I admit, if we add kidnapping to the plan. But since it's already done . . ." He shrugs, like, what can you do?

"And I have to admit, I'm going to enjoy watching Roland Greyhill beg when he learns that I have his son. And it's going to be even *better* to see the look on his face as he transfers a rather significant sum to my accounts to get him back." Mr. Omoko can't keep from grinning. "It'll be almost as fun as step three."

I swallow. "Mr. Omoko, we don't have to . . ."

He leans forward, like he's going to tell me a juicy secret. "Step three," he continues. "Blood."

I roll my wrists, trying to work the wires without him

noticing. "Mr. Omoko, I know I'm in trouble here, but can we talk about all this? I mean, I don't think step three is really necessary, and—"

"What's to talk about?" Omoko says. "Step three is the best part. I know you wanted to do it yourself, but picture this: Once all the cash transfers are secured, he takes off in his helicopter with his son. Then—" Omoko holds his finger up, pausing for effect. He mimes putting a rocket launcher to his shoulder and pulling the trigger. "*Bwooosh*. We blow them out of the sky." He gestures grandly. "It'll be dramatic."

I can't take my eyes off Omoko's face. Has he always sounded this crazy? Or have I just been so wrapped up in my plot that I never noticed? I have to get out of here. I keep rubbing my wrists together, trying to see if I can squeeze out one of my hands.

"Mr. Omoko," I say, trying for my best rational voice, "Mr. Greyhill isn't quite as bad as I thought. I've learned things since I've been here. I was wrong—he didn't kill my mother."

"Oh, I know."

I stop moving. "You do? How do you know?"

Something is tickling my brain. My body is buzzing with it, some realization that is just on the edge of my understanding. I stare at Omoko.

"Because I killed her," he says matter-of-factly.

For a moment, nothing moves. The words settle outside of me, sinking in slowly, like he's speaking in another language.

I killed her.

He killed my mother.

Blood rushes to my head.

He murdered her. He is the man in the video.

"Tina, are you listening?" Mr. Omoko snaps in front of my face. "That fool priest killed all your brain cells," he grumbles. He smacks me lightly on the side of my face, and I jump and gasp, my whole body suddenly zinging with adrenaline.

He looks me in the eye. "I'm telling you this because I want you to understand me. As you can now see, you do not get away from me if I don't want you to. You do not get away if you wrong me. Especially if, like your mother, you're some village girl, thinking she can make bargains that destroy everything I worked so hard to build."

I realize I am not breathing. When I start, it comes in massive gulps, like I've had the wind knocked out of me. "Are you Number Two?" I manage.

He makes a face. "I never liked that name. But yes, once I was Mr. Greyhill's Number Two."

"But that means . . . you're . . ."

Omoko fixes his eyes back on me. "Yes," he says, with an edge of impatience. "Do you get it now? I'm your father."

I am slipping; I hear him say it, but it's like he's talking to some other girl while I watch. I did know it. Of course I did; that is the logical conclusion to all of this. But it's as if something inside of me had been holding this information back, not letting me get there yet. It's too much.

"Any other person sitting where you are would be dead by

now," he says. "I am angry with you for running off. Of course I am. But I've taken care of you this long, and I'm not going to kill you now. I just want you to know that I am capable of it."

His words pull me out of my stupor. "Taken care of me?" My voice is barely a whisper. "What are you *talking* about?"

"Why do you think Bug Eye brought you into the Goondas, eh? Not because he cared what happened to you. Because I told him to find you. And why do you think you weren't put out on the streets with the other girls? Why did you get away with being cheeky? With being different?"

His face is so close that I can see the tiny web of veins in his eyes. "You never noticed that you were treated better than the others? You think it was because Bug Eye and those idiots liked you?" He laughs. "That's not how it works, Christina."

It's all lies.

My whole life is built on lies.

I swallow hard. "You killed my mother."

"Your mother told Greyhill I was stealing from him."

"But why did you have to kill her?" I gasp.

He looks at me like I am slow. "Christina, in this business, your reputation is everything. What would I be if I let a woman spoil things and walk away?" He waits, making sure I get it. "She was tricky, your mother. You have to give her that, going and telling Greyhill my secrets in exchange for protection from me. It took some time, but I found a way to teach them both the lesson they had to learn."

I try desperately to get my breath. "You tortured my mother. You raped her. I'm only here because of what you did." I feel myself coming unhinged, separating from my body. "Wasn't that enough?"

Omoko's voice switches to a growl. "She got as much as she deserved. She told Greyhill about things that didn't concern her. My things. My business. I earned every cent of that gold and he knew it! I was loyal. I did his bidding. I dealt with these savages so he wouldn't have to get his hands dirty."

And then it hits me. The hidden file behind her photo. She brought Omoko's secret accounting sheets to Mr. Greyhill. She must have seen him stealing gold and looked for something that would prove it.

Omoko continues, "She poisoned my relationship with him. He used his connections to freeze my bank accounts. I had to start again from nothing. You think that's easy? It's not. It takes time. And money. And blood. Lots of money and lots of blood. Scratching my way back up." He looks at the tent ceiling. "*Goondas*," he sneers. "Before I came along they were a bunch of morons, bashing their heads together like cavemen."

I am trying as hard as I can to hear everything Omoko is saying and process it, but my mind is beginning to cloud with red rage. Soon there won't be room for anything else.

"Now." Mr. Omoko slaps his knees and stands. "I am on a deadline. Here's what we're going to do. We're going to call up Roland Greyhill and tell him we've got his son. I have it on good authority he's in the neighborhood, and we've got a satellite hookup, so he can actually get his son back as fast as he can transfer money to my accounts." He starts to leave.

"We couldn't have orchestrated the whole thing better if we'd tried."

I raise my head. "We?"

He stops at the tent door. "Excuse me?"

"You keep saying *we*. Are you expecting my help?"

He blinks. "I suppose your part is over, if you like."

I stare. "Do you think I'm just going to go along with this like I'm still one of your Goondas?" I choke. I feel my mind clearing, my anger collecting like an explosion condensing the air before it bursts. "I am going to *kill* you."

With the adrenaline that's pumping through me I will dislocate my thumb and rip out of the wires holding my wrists. I won't be able to strangle him, but I will stand on his neck until it breaks. Right here. I press my thumb into the side of the chair and start to push.

"No," Omoko says, with something like disappointment. "I don't think you will." He comes back to me, pulling a phone from his pocket.

I pause, confused. What is he doing?

He looks down at the screen. "Damn thing, I'm getting too old to read it." He smiles and takes a pair of reading glasses out of his pocket and puts them on. "That's better. You know, I didn't want it to come to this, Christina, but I suppose I know you better than you think."

"What are you talking about?"

He taps the screen and then turns the phone so I can see. I squint. The photo is a little blurry, but it only takes a second to work it out.

When I do, the fight drains from me. Completely and all at once.

"Check the date. Today's. Old kidnapper trick. I saw it in a movie once." He chuckles as he looks at the photo with me, and points at the newspaper held up in a tattooed hand next to her face. I recognize those tattoos. They belong to Bug Eye.

"It's a little hard to see. But trust me." Mr. Omoko puts the phone back in his pocket. "We have a lot in common, you and I. We are practical. You, I won't kill because you're blood. But her, I don't care about. She's not mine. She's his bastard. If he actually cared about her, she'd have made a good hostage too, but it doesn't seem that he wants much to do with her, does it? I can't count on her being the bargaining chip I need. The boy is better. However, she's still useful to keep *you* in check. You pull too many stunts, *kijana*. Don't imagine for a second you can derail any of this. She's there in Sangui, just a phone call away." He studies me. "You're sensible, but sometimes you need discipline. Boundaries. Like your mother."

I can't move. All I can see is the photo seared in my mind. One tattooed hand holding a newspaper, the other holding a gun to her temple. Her terrified eyes.

My sister Kiki's eyes.

THIRTY-SEVEN

There are no rules for this. I am out of rules.

"Come on, Tiny Girl, you gotta snap out of it. You're okay, we're gonna be okay, but we've got to think . . . Tiny?"

I wish Boyboy would stop talking to me.

I rest my forehead on my knees. I can smell my sweat and the metallic tang of dried blood on my wrists. I would like to collapse into myself, lay my cheek on the cool dead leaves, and never move again.

I have no idea what to do now.

"Tina," Boyboy says, turning his head to look at me with the eye that isn't swollen shut. "They're probably going to separate us soon. And they'll most likely kill me—I'm no use to Omoko anymore; he said so. We don't have much time. You have to talk to me. Help me figure out what to do."

We're chained to a tree like animals. After he showed me Kiki's photo, Mr. Omoko handed me over to Ketchup, who gleefully paraded me through the militia camp and tied me to the tree next to Boyboy. Boyboy was silent while he was around, but now his voice is urgent, if slurred, around a split lip. The whole left side of his face looks like it's been run over.

I've counted five Goondas—Mr. Omoko's bodyguards. His elite squad, Yaya, Toofoh or Toto—something like that—and two others whose names I don't know, but I'm pretty sure are the guys who chased us yesterday. Plus Ketchup. Plus thirty or so guys in ratty fatigues. From the looks of the camp, they've been here awhile. The Goondas and the militia dudes don't mix. Most of the militia are swaddled in cheap blankets, still half asleep. A handful are cleaning their guns or sharpening the pangas they use to hack through the jungle. The forest floor is littered with their trash, mostly small plastic baggies that once held a swallow of kill-me-quick oil-drum spirits.

I close my eyes again and wonder if this was how Mama felt, a captive of the militia, hopeless, waiting to die. The same sort of hopelessness, thick and sticky as tar, tugs my limbs toward the ground. My blood is sluggish traitor blood. Murderer blood. Omoko's blood. How much of who I am and what I do is because I am his daughter?

"They've got Michael," Boyboy tries again.

"I know."

"Well, don't you want to do something about it?" Boyboy pleads furiously.

"There's nothing we can do."

"Tina, I swear to God, I am going to—"

"Omoko killed my mom."

Boyboy goes still. My head drops back down to my knees.

"What?" he finally asks.

I feel like I've never been so tired in my entire life, but I manage to relay, in fragments, how Omoko was Mr. Greyhill's Number Two, and what Catherine told me he did to my mother, and how Mr. Omoko is now holding Kiki captive, so I won't try to do anything stupid. Like rescue Michael.

When I'm done, Boyboy just stares at the ground. "I can't . . . All this time. It was him. He's your *dad*? Your dad killed your mom?"

"And now he's going to trade Michael to Mr. G for a payday, and then kill them too," I say flatly.

I turn my face so one eye looks out on the camp. I see it like I am far away, like I'm one of those incessantly twittering birds watching from the trees. Like I can watch until I don't want to see any more and then I can just jump into the sky and be gone.

"Tina. Listen to me. We have to do something. We can get out of this. We just have to think."

I don't answer. What can I do? I can't rescue Michael— Mr. Omoko will hurt Kiki. It's that simple. I go through my rules in my head, searching for one that will make sense of all of this. One that will give me some direction, some purpose.

Nothing.

They all seem silly now, paper swords.

I am so stupid. All this time it was Omoko. It was always

him. He always had the power. He tortured my mother and controlled me like a puppet, and I let him. I am his fool.

"Come on, Tina. Work with me here."

"There's nothing we can do."

"Maybe if—"

"I said there's nothing we can do!" I snarl. Some part of me registers the surprise and hurt in his eyes, but the rest of me curls inward. I have my own wounds to lick.

"So you're done. You're just giving up."

I say nothing.

"You're going to let him win. You're not going to do anything to get us out of here."

"I don't know what you want me to do! I don't know who you think I am!"

"I think you're the same girl you've always been! You're Tiny Girl! You're a thief and a survivor! Somebody who doesn't just roll over and die! Somebody who makes her own damn plans! Someone who makes her own damn rules!"

I can feel hot tears spilling down my cheeks. But I don't look up. "I can't. I can't do it, Boyboy. You don't understand. He'll kill her. She's all I've got."

For a while, there is nothing but the labored sound of Boyboy breathing. Then, to my surprise, he snorts a laugh. "You think you're the only one who ever had to worry about someone they love getting hurt? You're still out here all on your own, in your own little head, aren't you? Don't you even see me?"

I roll my face toward him.

"Remember how you told me you got that scar?" he asks.

"My scar?"

Boyboy jabs his chin at my arm. "You got it for a reason. Because as smart as you are about most things, you can be so dumb about people. That scar is there to remind you."

I look at my arm, the smooth line of tissue crossing through my tattoos. "Remind me of what?"

Mama and I had only been in Sangui a few months when I got it. At the time I was still getting used to the Greyhills' palatial estate. It had unspoken rules about where I could and couldn't go, which I was learning one smack to my backside at a time.

I was standing at the edge of the staff quarters, watching the boy of the house and his friend play football in the yard. Mama had warned me not to talk to the boy; I was not welcome up there. I was to stay out of sight. But the possibility of other kids to play with had been too much for me. I'd been alone, except for Mama, for weeks since we'd left Congo, and she barely spoke anymore. I made sure no one was watching, and then sprinted up the yard. It would be like with any other kids playing: I'd just join in, no questions asked.

Instead, the friend, a big pug-nosed boy, tripped me as I ran for the ball. I sprawled into a table a maid had set with glasses of juice and biscuits. A glass tipped and shattered.

The big kid laughed, like me flopping around on the ground was the funniest thing he'd ever seen. When I stood up, I found a chunk of glass had sliced me in the crook of my elbow, and bright blood was dribbling into the grass.

"You can't play with us! Your mother's a maid and a whore." The boy cackled. "His mom told my mom. You got no dad. And your mom does it. All. The. Time." He pumped his little hips to punctuate in a way that I didn't understand, but somehow knew was dirty.

"Who-ore, who-ore," the pudgy boy chanted, while the boy of the house stood wide-eyed and silent.

Twenty meters away, a guard who had come to investigate the noise hovered. A gardener lifted his head from his work, uneasy, but made no move to help. From the house I could hear footsteps coming, heels moving with swift surety toward the sound of broken glass.

And as the blood dripped from my arm it became very clear what Mama had been trying to keep me from. I understood what *not welcome* meant, at my core. The boy of the house and his friend were different creatures entirely. From the tips of their scrubbed fingernails to the snowy laces on their shoes, they were soft, unscarred. They were significant.

I saw what was coming. I was out of my place, and I would be put back into it. When my mother found out she would yell. Or worse, and more likely, she wouldn't say a word, just take me back down to the cottage, then turn and walk away from me.

And as I was standing there waiting for the inevitable, a sudden blur of fists and knees came rocketing past me, and the boy of the house launched into his friend like a tiger. The bigger boy was taken by surprise, and it took him a moment to wake up. When he did, though, he slung the boy to the ground and started pounding him back. Smack went his fist, and blood squirted out of the little Greyhill's nose.

At this point the gardener had stepped in, gently pulling the two snarling boys apart. The friend was crying and ran away to a puffy-faced woman who had come out onto the veranda. Mrs. Greyhill followed. It was the first time I had seen her up close, and her beauty was a powerful, living thing, as sharp and terrible as the shards of glass scattered on the soft grass. She was impossible to look away from. Her wide eyes lingered on me, and then she looked at the mess, her face a question.

I waited for her son to point a finger at me. But instead he just wiped his bloody nose on his shirt. "He started it," the boy said. Then he went inside.

Later, after the friend had been taken home, the Greyhill kid came back out of the house and walked down to where I was sitting in front of the servants' cottages. His face was clean, but his nose and eye were purpling.

I looked up at him warily.

"I've never been in a fight," he said, sounding slightly in awe of himself.

"Why didn't you tell on me?"

Instead of answering, the kid showed me his arm. "Look, I got cut too."

I stood up to see. He lifted the bandage someone had carefully placed over it, maybe even my own mother. Mine was bare, no longer bleeding, but raw. His was a sickle, like a crescent moon. Mine was a straight line. Our cuts were different shapes, but in almost the exact same places on our arms.

"Does it hurt?" I asked.

"Nah. Yours?"

"Not anymore."

"You want to play?"

"I'm not supposed to."

"Why?"

I thought about it. I didn't really know.

"What's your name?" he asked.

"Christina."

"I'm Michael. Come on."

And he had turned and raced up the yard. I looked down at the red line of separated flesh, pressed it with my finger until it hurt, to remind myself of what I was risking. My mother could still find out I'd disobeyed her. Maybe this rich boy would turn on me eventually, like his friend. Maybe I should just stay by the cottage, keep out of trouble like Mama had told me to.

But this boy had stood up for me, even though it had cost him, even though he didn't know me.

He saw me, when everyone else wanted to pretend like I didn't exist.

I looked back at my cottage, then up at the yard, where he stood waiting.

And then I ran to join him.

Boyboy says, "I don't have a scar from when you saved me from those kids. They knew I couldn't swim. You don't have a scar from that day either, but I can cut you now, if it'll help you think straight."

He sits back. He seems to be waiting for me to get something on my own, like a little kid sounding out a word for the very first time. And suddenly I understand what Boyboy's saying. It is so obvious and he's right. I really am an idiot. What I realize is this:

Boyboy is my friend.

Michael is my friend.

Whether I like it or not. Whether I admit it or not.

I have all my rules, act like I know everything, pretend like I'm in control. But they know the truth. I'm broken and messed up.

And you know what? They don't care.

They stick with me. They stick up for me. It's because of me that they're out here now, and because of me they didn't leave days ago. Michael may have come to clear his father's name, but he stayed because he's still the same kid who got punched in the nose for me all those years ago. And Boyboy has always been my partner in crime. That's why he came back here with me.

What I realize is not really a rule—it's just true:

They exist to me.

And I exist to them.

THIRTY-EIGHT

"Y ou're my friend," I say softly.

Boyboy rolls his eyes, but the sag in his shoulders says he's relieved. "Yes, Tina."

"You love me."

"Now, don't get carried away."

"You're going to help me. That's what you're telling me. We have to rescue Michael. Together. We can figure this out."

"There's my Tiny Girl."

I wipe my face on my arm and try to hold on tight to what I'm feeling. "Where are they keeping him?"

Boyboy nods at a tent on the other side of the camp. "I saw them take him in there."

A couple of militia guys sit out front, keeping watch. Unfortunately for us, they don't look nearly as drunk as the others.

"Is he hurt?"

"He looked okay. He was walking," Boyboy says.

We sit in silence for a few moments, watching the tent, trying to think what to do. Something, anything. I look hard at the camp. What can we use? Along with the tents for Michael and Omoko, there are others for cooking and storage. I count two flatbed trucks and three off-road motorcycles. There are drums that might be full of water, or more likely petrol for the vehicles. Plenty of weapons to go around. Including . . .

"RPGs," I say. "That's what he's going to use to blow up Mr. Greyhill's helicopter once they take off. Maybe we can sabotage them somehow."

"Role-playing games?" Boyboy asks, frowning.

I nod toward several newish-looking wooden crates. "Rocket-propelled grenades, nerd."

Slowly, Boyboy sits up straighter. "Omoko brought those. And I'm pretty sure the head militia guy gave him a backpack full of gold in return. Either that or a sack of rocks."

"Omoko's trading with the militias," I say slowly. "That's not Goonda work. He's getting back into the gold-buying business." I wonder if he's the *comptoir* Mr. Greyhill came to check on. I shake my head. "That doesn't matter right now. Let's focus on making sure he doesn't kill any Greyhills."

"Getting rid of the grenade launchers won't help," Boyboy says. "He'll just find some other weapon."

He's right. I push the gears in my brain to crank to life and think harder.

Just then there's a shout and we look over to see two

bodies swinging at each other, then falling in a heap. The tension between the Goondas and the militia dudes has just boiled over.

"Come closer," I whisper to Boyboy. "I think I can reach your hands."

Boyboy looks around, but everyone is now watching the fight. He scoots closer, and I stretch to feel the metal biting against his skin and the stickiness of his blood. "They shouldn't have tied us up together," I say.

"Ketchup has never been the brightest," Boyboy replies. "But those are zip ties. Metal ones. They're impossible to undo."

"You forget you're talking to a master thief."

"Thief, not Houdini."

"And Ketchup forgets that Bug Eye taught me a few tricks." The ties around our wrists are tight, but after investigating with my fingers, I think all I need is a tiny, flat piece of metal. Luckily, I can still feel a bobby pin tucked in my hair where it can't be seen. Good old bobby pins. They never let me down.

Unluckily, I need my hands to get it.

"Boyboy, you're going to have to get the pin that's in my hair."

"A what? A bobby pin? How am I supposed to do that?"

I look up at the melee. "Bite it out."

"Are you crazy? You think no one's going to notice me chewing on your head?"

"They're busy. It's around the back. Hurry, while they're still distracted."

"Oh my God, this is wrong on so many levels," Boyboy mutters, but he shifts around and soon I feel his nose burrowing through my hair. "I hate you so much right now," he grunts into my scalp.

"And you need to bite the end off while you have it in your mouth. The little plastic part."

He mumbles something unintelligible, and a second later I feel a sharp tug. He pulls back with a grimace, metal between his teeth. Just then I see one of the militia look over at us. Boyboy closes his lips over the pin and sits back quickly. He looks guilty as hell, but the militia guy just glares at us for a few seconds. Beads of sweat creep down my spine. Finally the guy seems satisfied that we're not going anywhere and turns back to the entertainment.

Boyboy leans back and spits the pin out onto the ground near my fingers, where I grab it. I keep my eyes on the fight, like I'm just as interested as everyone else, and scoot as close to Boyboy as I can. Slowly, I wedge the shim between the wire tie and the clasp. It's not easy, between my sweating fingers and the unfamiliar bindings, and for a second I think the pin is too thick. But then finally I hear Boyboy gasp with relief when he feels the ties loosen.

"Move your hands over here so I can get yours," Boyboy says.

I start to, then hesitate. I look from the tent where Michael is being kept, to the petrol drums, to the motorcycles, to Ketchup. An idea begins to take shape in my mind.

I pull my hands back and tuck the bobby pin into my pocket, unused. "No."

"What do you mean, *no*?"

"Listen to me, and don't interrupt. Keep watching those boneheads fight. I think I have a plan."

THIRTY-NINE

Rule 16: Don't stop.

Bug Eye taught me how to fight. If he told me once, he told me a hundred times: Stop wilding out, *kijana*. Elbows in, head down, and focus. You may be smaller, but you're faster and you're smarter. Here's what counts, he said: You find an edge. Just a tiny crack in the foundation. Remember what I said about finding weaknesses? That's what you do. Then you dig in and, listen to me, you just don't stop. Fight until you're beyond exhaustion. Even if you can see the end in front of you. Even if it seems hopeless. Don't stop.

Not ever.

He took me to a dogfight and told me to watch this brindled pit bull. She was smaller than the others, wiry and delicate. I'll admit, I was dubious when they paired her up against this big white male covered in scars. But the starting bell hadn't even stopped ringing before she was hanging on that other dog's neck, and when they slammed each other to the ground, she clung to him. As the fight wore on, his white neck turned scarlet, and then black with dirt, and then the dog's owner rushed the ring before she could kill him, and it was over. And I just remember standing there, watching the little dog lick her wounds with her pink tongue like she had already shaken the fight off.

See that? Bug Eye said. Grab on and don't let go. Hit him. And then hit him again, again, again, bam, bam, bam, bam, till he can't see straight and he falls down at your feet like Goliath before David.

Boyboy listens to my plan. His frown gets deeper by the second. "I don't like it. It's too risky."

"Let me worry about that."

"And what if the phone battery is dead? That screws everything."

"A little confidence, Boyboy."

He takes a deep breath and lets it out slowly. "And what if Bug Eye won't do it?"

"He'll do it," I say firmly, to myself as much as Boyboy. "Besides, what other way is there?"

He thinks for a second, then shakes his head.

I take a couple of deep breaths, twist out the kinks in my

back, try to tell myself this is going to be just like any other job. Get in, get the prize, get out. Don't leave traces.

The fight is over, the Goondas having been outnumbered and shouted down into a small, angry huddle. They occasionally give the militia guys foul looks over their shoulders. The loser, Toofoh-or-Toto, is holding a wet pack of leaves to his swollen eye.

I raise my head until I can see Ketchup's face, and whistle two notes softly. It's a familiar Goonda signal, and five sets of eyes dart to me. I look directly at Ketchup, and when he sees me mouthing for him to come over, the scowl he's wearing slowly turns to a sneer. He says something to the other guys that makes them laugh, and then saunters over, a panga and a satellite phone dangling from his belt. He has a gun stuck down the front of his pants too, and it's a wonder they're still clinging to his bony hips. His T-shirt reads WAYNESVILLE SOFTBALL CHAMPIONS 1998, and is stained with sweat.

"Oh God, Tiny, be careful," Boyboy says under his breath. "He's already angry."

Ketchup stops when he's standing directly above me. His crotch and gun are at my eye level and he knows it.

"I have to pee," I say quietly, trying to avoid looking up.

His grin gets bigger. "You need me to take you to the ladies'?" he asks. "You gonna say please?"

I finally look at him. "Please, Ketchup."

He scratches absently at his stomach, still staring down at me. Finally he crouches to reach my hands. He comes in way closer than he needs to, so close that I can see which of his tattoos are fading on his puny biceps. Notably, the naked woman riding a roaring lion. I manage to keep my revulsion in check long enough to breathe in. I want to make sure I can still smell the sour vapors of white liquor on him.

He doesn't disappoint me.

Ketchup fumbles but finally gets me loose from the tree. My hands are still tightly bound behind me. Boyboy's wide eyes dart back and forth between the two of us.

Ketchup turns his attention to him. "You want to watch?"

Boyboy sucks in a horrified breath.

I don't look at Ketchup's face, afraid that what I'll see there will leave me weak-kneed. I know what he's considering doing to me. And he wants me to know. He jerks his chin toward a gap leading into the forest.

Swallowing the fear that is threatening to turn to bile in my throat, I step into the dense foliage. I still haven't got any shoes on, but I'm starting to get used to it. The ground is soft and wet underfoot. Ketchup stays on my heels, his panga in his fist.

"Your little boyfriend doesn't look so cute anymore after what I did to his face," he says.

I shoulder through the undergrowth, limbs catching at my face and arms.

"Maybe if you're nice I'll let you kiss his ugly face goodbye." Ketchup makes a gross sucking sound. It turns into drunk laughter. "That's far enough," he says.

"I'm going just there, behind that tree. I can still see the camp."

"You think you got something they haven't seen before?" Ketchup asks. "Okay, there. That's far enough."

I turn around to face him, and make a production of trying to get my arms around to undo my trousers. "You're going to have to untie my hands," I say, in exasperation.

He regards me.

"You want me to pee my pants?" I demand, feeling sweat running down the sides of my face.

Finally, Ketchup comes toward me, and I think he's going to reach around to undo my ties, but instead he grabs the waist of my jeans, undoes the fly, and yanks them down.

For a moment I am frozen, totally naked in front of him from the waist down. I pulse with hot and cold embarrassment. I feel a trembling mix of fury and terror churning in me.

Ketchup stares at the place between my legs. "Well?"

My cheeks burning, I back up to a tree and squat behind it. I'm trying desperately to figure out what to do next, but the look on Ketchup's face has me so shaken that I have to scream at myself to think. For an awful second I'm back in the forest as a five-year-old, squatting when the men came and I had to hide myself. I think of my mother. This is what it was like for her when she was captured.

What made me think this was going to work? It seemed reasonable back in the clearing that Ketchup would undo my wrists to let me pee. And once he did, I'd thrash him, like I had all those times sparring in the Goonda gym. I would tie him up and take his gun and phone. But it suddenly occurs to me that maybe he remembers our fights too. *Shonde.* Can I just try to wriggle out of the wires now, or is that too obvious? I make an effort to pee, just for the sake of authenticity.

I'm almost finished when he jumps me.

He's come around the tree while I'm off balance, and then he's pushing my chest, flattening me on the ground, surprising me with his strength and how much he weighs. Everything goes white-hot and time slows down into slashes, and then I can feel his hand wrestling at his pants, hear him growling at me to hold still. His wet, sour breath is all over my face.

"Don't!" I gasp. "Omoko will kill you!"

"Screw Omoko!"

He's too drunk and wound up to listen. I writhe, trying to break free, but Ketchup has all the leverage, his arm across my windpipe. *He's going to do this,* a disembodied voice in my head says. I'm not going to be able to get away. Choking, I tilt my head back, looking for any sort of help at all.

And it's then that I see her.

Everything but her goes completely still.

She walks toward me, upside down in my vision, and crouches next to me.

I can see the sweat beading on Ketchup's neck. I can see the tomato tattoo on his hand. I can see dust motes rising in the air on a ray of light. I can't see her face, but in that moment, I feel her hand brush my forehead, and my mother whispers in my ear:

Break the breaking wheel.

And I blink, and time speeds up, and there's no time to think—I do just what she says.

I rear my head back and slam it straight into Ketchup's nose.

There's a sickening crunch, followed by Ketchup howling. He pulls back, hand to his nose, and I scream at myself to keep moving, and roll to the side. Then I'm hauling my legs through the loop of my arms, kicking out at him, gasping for breath, while Ketchup is getting his bearings. He's drunk and hurt, but he's still fast, and it's not long before his hands have somehow found my throat; they're squeezing little stars into my vision.

"I'm going to kill you!" he says, spittle and blood running down his chin. "And then I'm going to find your sister—"

I haul my knee up and make contact with his groin, and as he grunts and clutches in pain, I shove him to the side.

I roll onto my knees and scramble to my feet, yanking my pants back up so I can run for the sharpened panga he's dropped. As I'm lunging for it, I feel his arms at my calves, and I go down hard, a shock shuddering through my leg as my knee cracks on a loose rock. I grab the fist-sized stone, twist around, and bring it hard against his temple while he's rearing up over me with the panga.

The rock cracks against his face.

"Guuh," he says.

His eyes roll back. Then he stumbles sideways. The big knife slips from his hand. I spring up after him, get on top of his chest, and smash the rock against his head once, twice, pull back to hit him again, and suddenly see what I'm doing.

I am a picture of horror with blood and dirt and urine all over me, holding a rock, ready to pound this boy's skull in.

Ketchup's eyes flutter, his body contorts, and then as I hold the rock over him in a shaking hand, he goes still. A sob heaves out of me, and the stone falls out of my bloody grip.

For a few seconds I kneel there, staring at him, gasping for breath. His chest is moving, but he's out cold. The birds around us are silent.

Move, Tina, the voice in my head is screaming, and so I do.

I button my pants. I use my bobby pin to undo the wires around my wrists. I stuff them, along with Ketchup's phone and gun, into my pockets and waistband. There's a half-fallen tree a few meters away, and I grab Ketchup's wrists and drag him to it. Boyboy will help me carry him farther soon, but for now this is the best I can do. I'll tuck him into the space under the tree and pull branches and leaves over his body. Someone can go unnoticed like that for days if they need to. I should know.

Before I cover him I take the satellite phone and snap a photo of Ketchup's bruised face. For a second, I can't look away. He looks fragile. Young. The impulse to be sick washes over me again, and I allow myself to heave what little is left in my stomach into the leaves next to him, out here where no one is watching. I keep staring at Ketchup until I'm sure he's still breathing. I wonder if I've cracked his skull.

I hope not. I need him.

FORTY

Rule 17: Let them fall on their spears.

You have to know your enemies' weaknesses, Bug Eye says. That much is obvious. What he also taught me, though, and what thieves and thugs and kings have figured out—the good ones, anyway—is that your enemies' strengths can also be their weaknesses. Take my roof, for example. It's a fortress. I feel safe there. Too safe. Surround it, and it becomes a cage.

So when I think about what the king of the Goondas' strength is, well, number one, he's got about a million thugs at his disposal.

And there is his weakness: his thugs.

Specifically, one thug in particular.

Maybe I have one more friend who'll help me. Or if not a

friend, at least someone I can trust to have his own particular weakness.

I don't like how far I have to go to get a satellite connection for the phone, but the tree cover is dense. When I finally have network, I dial the number I know by heart with shaking fingers. It goes through immediately.

"Ketchup."

"Not Ketchup," I say.

A pause. "Tiny? Does Mr. Omoko know you're calling me?"

"Don't hang up."

"I can't talk to you, *kijana*."

"Wait, Bug Eye."

His voice sounds tired. "Look, I know why you're calling, but there's nothing I can do. I don't like this either. But your sister is fine. Just . . . do what Omoko wants."

"I can't, Bug Eye."

"I'm hanging up."

"No! Listen, I want to make a deal with you."

"You haven't got anything I want."

"I do." The phone is slick in my sweating hands. It's a strain to keep my voice from breaking, but I know I can't let him know how shaken and frightened I am. This could all backfire if I don't lay things out exactly right. I'm playing a long game here. I can't put all my cards on the table at once. "Omoko's my father. Did you know that?"

Bug Eye doesn't answer.

"He raped my mother. Tortured her. Killed her. I'm going to kill him. I'm going to steal his crown for you."

Bug Eye stays silent.

"For you and for me. I know you want to be where he is. You should be. And you know me. You know I mean it. I'll do it. But"—I pause to make sure my voice will be steady—"only if my sister is safe. I need you to save her. Take her to the Greyhills'. I'll do whatever it takes to make sure the crown goes to you once Omoko's out of the way. This is your chance, Bug Eye. Take it."

"You're talking crazy, Tiny Girl."

"I think you should listen to me, Bug Eye. I know it's a lot to take in so quickly, but this is your moment. You help me, I kill him, you become the boss. Why does it have to be any more complicated than that?"

I hear Bug Eye take a breath. "Where are you, Tina? How did you get this phone?"

I close my eyes, picture my sister, tied up and scared. I might hate Ketchup, but I don't want to do this to Bug Eye. Bug Eye is violent, terrifying, and ruthless. He's holding my sister hostage. But still, for the last five years he and the Goondas have been the closest thing I have to family other than Kiki. He taught me how to fight and defend myself. For some of us Goondas, he's the only adult we trust. We know that if we're loyal to him, he takes care of us. That's the rule. That's law. The Goondas may be a crazy-violent dysfunctional family, but they're still *my* crazy-violent dysfunctional family.

I break this rule, and it's all over. There's no going back to being Tiny Girl, Goonda.

Why can't he just take what I'm offering now? I know he wants to be king. I know it. Can't he just agree to let Kiki go? He doesn't like holding her hostage either. That's what he just said. And I don't like being the thug that gets to someone by threatening his family.

I try one last time. "He doesn't trust you, Bug Eye. He'll make someone stab you in the back. You won't see it coming. I don't want it to happen, and you certainly don't. It's not good for the Goondas. It's not good for anyone."

"How did you get Ketchup's phone, Tina?" Bug Eye asks again, his voice as low and bloody as I've ever heard it. "And don't forget for a second that I have your sister. I'm looking at her right now."

I haven't forgotten. His words are the push I need to turn my insides to ice. When I open my mouth, I know that what I say will break my bond with the Goondas forever. And I'm okay with that. "I need for you to make a decision, Bug Eye. Do you want to be the king of the Goondas with your brother by your side?" I pause. "Or do you want to be nothing, with no one?"

There it is. My final card: Ketchup. "I'm going to kill Omoko," I say. "With Ketchup's gun. And after I do, you can take the Goonda crown. And then everyone gets their brothers and sisters back. And we go our separate ways. But otherwise . . ." Every thread of my body is tensed, waiting to hear what Bug Eye will do.

His silence seems to go on forever. "I don't believe you really have him," he finally says. "You're bluffing."

"I thought you might say that," I say, and realize that I've said basically exactly what my father said to me a little while ago. I am just like him. I swallow, forcing myself to go on. Kiki's life depends on just how nasty and thuggish I can be in this moment—on just how much of him I can find in myself.

"I'm sending you a photo," I say.

When I hiss at Boyboy from behind the tree, his head jerks toward me. Too late he realizes what he's done as one of the Goondas looks over at the motion and frowns. Dude's noticed I'm still gone. I stay perfectly still while Boyboy sweats, looking for all the world like he's about to go into hysterics.

After a while the guy watching Boyboy fishes in his breast pocket, pulls out a liquor baggie, and rips it open. He squirts the contents into his mouth, tosses the bag aside, and settles back down.

I can feel a beam of sunlight on the top of my head. Time is getting short. Finally, Boyboy looks back at me and I mouth at him to come on.

He shakes his head, making eyes back at the camp. I get it. Everyone is awake and looking bored now. As soon as he bolts, they'll be after him. I bite my lip, unsure what to do next. I creep closer, making sure to stay blocked by the trees.

"Are you okay?" he whispers.

I nod, even though I'm still shaking. "He's going to do it."

Now that I have royally pissed off one of the most lethal people in all Sangui City by holding his brother counter-hostage, all we have to do is the near-impossible: break Michael out. The next part of the plan is that Boyboy slips away and we carry Ketchup farther into the forest and hide him. Then Boyboy takes the phone and makes a run for it. He'll contact Mr. Greyhill and let him know what's happening. After all, if I'm going to do my part and steal Michael and a motorcycle out from under Omoko's nose, we need to know that Mr. G's helicopter is going to be ready and waiting.

It was Boyboy's idea to use the satellite phone's GPS to both tag where we stash Ketchup and tell Mr. G where we are. Boyboy needs to get Mr. G to bring the chopper to the closest possible landing site down the road. One of Mr. Greyhill's guards will go retrieve Ketchup. The others will hide in the bushes in case Michael and I need covering fire as we're hauling ass to get to our ride out.

So. As long as Boyboy can find and convince Mr. G that we need his help, and as long as I can rescue Michael, steal a motorcycle, create a petrol-fueled diversion, and make a lightning-quick escape without getting caught, shot, or blown up in the process, it's a perfect plan.

In Boyboy's words, the only thing crazier is staying put.

Of course, if Boyboy isn't able to slip away, the whole plan will self-destruct before it even gets started. I look back at him. He has a familiar frown on his face, the one he gets when he's calculating something.

"I'm going to make a run for it," he whispers.

"Not yet—they'll catch you!"

He shakes his head slightly. "They're drunk. I'm quick."

I hesitate. He is. Sort of. For a computer nerd. But still . . . if they see him, he's dead.

"It's going to work," he says. The look on his face says he knows he's dead anyway. "Make a distraction so I can get a head start. Now!"

"Wait! The diversion comes later," I begin, but he's already on his feet, crouched down, ready to run. Someone's going to notice him, and before they do, I have to act. I grab a stick from the ground and fling it as hard as I can toward the kitchen area. It careens into a pot, which knocks over a propane stove, which goes crashing into a tall stack of metal dishes. It all makes a terrific noise. The men shout, stumble to their feet. As they're looking in that direction, Boyboy leaps up and we take off through the forest. I'm terrified that at any second a hand will clamp down on me from behind, but we make it to Ketchup without anyone coming after us.

"What did you do to him?" Boyboy asks as I sweep away the debris from my captive's face.

"Nothing he didn't deserve."

I grab his legs and Boyboy picks him up under the arms and we run as fast as we can toward the rising sun. I keep waiting for Ketchup to wake up and struggle, but he stays limp. When I think we've gone far enough I stop, looking for a good spot. "There."

We're drenched in sweat, and the dirt and dried leaves

cling to us as Boyboy and I quickly dig a little trench next to a boulder. We shove him in and I use the ties from my pocket to attach his hands to a tall sapling that's sprung up from under the rock. Then we cover him again with brush. As I'm finishing, Boyboy marks the spot on the phone's GPS.

"It's like we're digging a grave," Boyboy finally says.

"He's not going to die," I say. "He can't."

Boyboy finishes and frowns at the phone. "There's no reception here. I'm going to have to move."

"Head for the road. I think it's that way." I point.

"Okay, I'll meet you at the helicopter." Boyboy's face is grim. "Be careful."

"You too."

The camp is utter chaos.

My distraction worked—maybe too well. By the time I get back, there are about forty dudes running around yelling at each other and the kitchen tent is ablaze.

Apparently the propane stove I knocked over exploded, which isn't great, seeing as I'd been counting on a later explosion to cover Michael's and my escape. But maybe if I can get Michael out quickly, there will still be enough mayhem.

There's a one-eared militia guy who must be the leader screaming orders in the middle of the clearing. It looks like he's realized his prisoners have escaped. I watch him catch a couple of militia guys and send them out into the forest. If they're after us, though, they're going the wrong way. So that's something. I don't see Mr. Omoko anywhere. I hope to

God he isn't in the tent with Michael, because that's where I'm headed.

The guys who were guarding Michael have run to help put out the fire that's spreading from the kitchen tent to a tree. The smoke from the green leaves is lucky. It makes everything hazy. I wait until I'm sure no one is watching, then run in a crouch to the back of Michael's tent, where I'm blocked from the view of most of the camp. I quickly pull the tent flaps apart a centimeter and try to get a look inside. It's dark and I can't see much more than shapes. I'm just going to have to risk it; I'm an easy target out here. I take another quick glance around and then slip in. For a second I'm blinded and panic swells in me.

"Who's there?"

"Shhh. It's me," I whisper, creeping toward Michael. My eyes adjust to the dim and I see he's blindfolded, tied up, and bruised, but alive. His hands are chained to a small generator. It must have been the heaviest thing they could find.

"Tina," he breathes. "You're okay. Where's Boyboy? Is he all right? They wouldn't tell me what happened to you guys."

"I'm fine. We're fine."

I push the blindfold up off his eyes, and he blinks. It feels like eons since I ran away from him at the guesthouse, and I have a sudden urge to grab him and make sure he's real. I crouch down to check out his bindings. He's got the same wires around his wrists that I did, but they're also around his ankles. When I take his hands, he hisses with pain.

"What?" I ask. One of his wrists is swollen and dark with bruising.

"I think it's broken," he says.

I sit back, looking at the hand, my stomach sinking. "*Mavi*," I curse.

"My legs are fine. Can you get me out?"

"Um, no chance you can drive a motorcycle like that, huh?" I ask with a forced smile.

Michael looks from me to his wrists, understanding passing over his face. "Is that our escape plan?"

I swallow. "What if I steer?"

"You have to shift on the handles. I mean, if we had time for me to show you, I'm sure you could do it, but . . ." He looks toward the front of the tent, where, from the sound of it, pandemonium still reigns. "Get me out, and we'll make a run for it. Where's Boyboy?"

"Going for help. Hopefully in the form of your father." I curse again. "He's supposed to be meeting us down the road. But we can't outrun these guys. They've got trucks and bikes."

"Can we go through the forest?"

I think about it but shake my head. "The going will be too slow, and they'll just come around and surround us before we can get back to the road." I go back to his bindings. I can at least get his legs loose while I'm thinking of a new plan.

"Tina, what's going on? Who are these guys?"

"It's a long story. I'll explain everything once we're safe."

"I heard them talking about—"

I cut him off with a quick gesture. "Someone's coming! I have to put your blindfold back on."

"No! *Tina!*"

But I'm already yanking the greasy fabric over his eyes. I grab the blanket off the cot and scurry to the rear of the tent, where there's a big wooden crate. I squat behind it and throw the blanket over me. It's a terrible hiding job, but at the moment it's the best option I've got. I squeeze down into a tight ball and try my hardest to look like a pile of dirty laundry. Hopefully in the dark no one will notice me. I want to kick myself for not keeping Ketchup's panga. I still have his gun, but I'd rather defend myself quietly. Nothing to bring a horde of militia down on our heads like gunshots from the prisoner's tent.

A silhouetted figure throws open the tent flap and begins yelling at Michael. The guy seems to have just been sent in to check on him, though, because he tells Michael he's worth "less than a monkey turd," if he moves, and then he's gone again.

We wait a few moments in silence. I lift my head. "Charming."

Michael lets out his breath, and then winces. I wonder if he's got broken ribs too that he's just not telling me about. "They're all insane. There's this one who keeps telling me he's going to enjoy watching my fireworks. No idea what he's talking about, but it cracks him up every time."

I stiffen. Michael doesn't know about Omoko's plan for blood.

"Hey, can you come take this thing off? I hate not being able to see."

I creep back over. Should I tell him what Omoko is planning, or will that just take more time we don't have?

"Thanks," Michael whispers when I pull the blindfold off.

For a moment I'm caught in his gaze, unable to move. I want so badly to apologize for screaming at him and running off and for letting him get caught and for generally getting him into a situation where he may end up dead, but there's no time for that right now. I force myself back to trying to get him free.

Pulling the bobby pin out of my pocket, I go to work.

"Why did these guys capture us?"

"Mr. Omoko wants to ransom you to your dad." The pin has twisted somehow in all of this and won't go in. I bite it, trying to mash it back into a useful shape.

"Who's Mr. Omoko?"

"He's . . ." So much has happened. I've never even mentioned Omoko until now, other than during my drug-induced rant outside the guesthouse. I pull the pin out of my mouth to examine it. Still not right. "I'll tell you everything later," I say, "but for right now, he's the bad guy. He killed my mom." I stick the pin back in my mouth, trying again.

Michael stares at me, as if what I'm saying will make better sense if he looks at me hard enough. "What? Why? Who is—"

"And he kidnapped my sister," I say as I try again to wedge

the pin into the bindings on his ankles. It isn't going in right, but that might be because my hand has started trembling. "I think she's safe now, but still . . ." I shake my head, unable to go on.

"*Our* sister."

Startled, I look up.

There is something so fierce in Michael's expression, but at the same time, a vulnerability that has nothing to do with his bindings. Before I can stop them, two quick tears fall down my cheeks. "Our sister," I whisper.

My chest suddenly feels like it's being ripped apart. I drop my eyes to the crescent moon scar I can just barely see in the dark crook of his arm. Slowly, I slide my hand up his wrist until it rests on top of the raised line. I feel him shudder under my touch. The ache in my throat is almost unbearable. When I look back up at his face I realize I finally understand what he's thinking. I was right. He does care about me.

He bends his head toward mine. Our foreheads bump gently.

"I'm so sorry," I say, letting my tears fall freely now.

"There's nothing to—"

But I stop him by placing my mouth onto his. I barely know what I'm doing. For once, I don't consider or think or weigh consequences. I just do. He kisses me back, softly at first, and then harder, hungrily. A heat travels up my spine, radiating throughout my entire body. I lift my hands to his face and breathe in his skin.

When I finally pull back, he sighs into me. "I've been waiting for that my whole life," he says.

I laugh through my tears. "Sorry it had to happen here." I want so badly to kiss him again, but I know the clock is ticking. "We have to hurry," I say, bending to his bindings again.

"Yeah," Michael says, sounding less convinced, and leans back to let me work.

I think I've almost got it when I feel him tense. "I'm sorry, I know this hurts—"

"Shh. Do you hear that?"

I stop, ears pricking. I was so intent on what I was doing that I hadn't registered the thrumming. It's distant now but getting closer. "A helicopter."

"It's Dad!" Michael says, breaking into a full smile now.

But something is wrong. "No," I say. "It's too close. Boyboy was supposed to tell him to keep out of sight of the camp. Maybe he never got through."

Oh God, what if they caught Boyboy? This is all my fault. I bolt up. Shouts from the militia tell us they've noticed the helicopter too. And I never explained . . .

"It's a trap, Michael!" I say. "Omoko is going to shoot the chopper down as soon as you're airborne."

Michael's smile vanishes. "What? But—"

"He's going to kill you and your father."

"Go time, boys!" a voice crows outside, very close.

Michael's head swivels to the front tent flaps. "Someone's coming."

My fingers work at his ankles frantically. "Come on, come on . . ."

"It's the guard coming back! Hide!" Michael says.

"No! I can—"

"It's too late, Tina! Hide! You can't help me if you're dead!"

I can see a shadow descending on the tent.

"Now!" he says, pulling his feet from my hands, oblivious to the pain the movement causes him.

I hesitate for a second longer, and then, hating myself for it, dart back behind the crate, yanking the blanket over me again. My heart pounds. *It's just the guard. He's checking in again and then he'll leave.* I've still got time to free Michael and make a run for it.

But the familiar voice at the tent door kills my remaining hope.

"Hello, Michael," Mr. Omoko says. "Ready to bid us all good-bye?"

FORTY-ONE

I t seems Christina and her friend have abandoned you," I hear Omoko say. "I half expected to come in and find you missing too."

I am positive that he can hear my heart pounding in the silence and he's just toying with me. Any second now he's going to order the Goondas to search the tent.

"Has she been here?"

"Yes," Michael says.

I nearly gasp out loud.

"She came and told me that you've got Kiki," Michael says, "and that she couldn't do anything to help me. She ran off."

"Smart girl," Mr. Omoko says, after a pause.

Does he buy it? Something in his voice sounds dubious.

"Boss," another voice says from near the tent entrance, "the truck is ready."

"Okay, take him out, boys. We'll deal with looking for the other two later."

I hear scuffling and then the sound of footsteps receding. I curse myself, wanting desperately to stand up and do something. But I know no good will come of it. I wait for the sound of the truck driving away before peeking out. The tent is empty, and I fling the blanket off. I open the back flap a sliver and check outside for prowling militia. There's only one guy that I can see, but he has his back to me. I grab the first heavy thing I can find—a box of bullets—and creep to the flap. The guy is smoking now. I take a deep breath and rush out, landing a blow to the back of his head. He falls over with a grunt.

"Hey!"

I whip toward the voice. Another militia guy is to my right. I hadn't seen him from inside the tent. I bolt, making for the forest and hoping I can outrun him. I hear him yell to one of his buddies and charge after me. I have Ketchup's gun, but there's no way to get a clear shot through the trees. As I dodge and weave through the growth I let all of my adrenaline and fear take hold and my feet fly, and to my relief, I can soon tell I'm breaking away, getting farther and farther from my pursuers. They sound like elephants crashing along behind me. Finally, something is going my way.

And then I realize I'm not headed toward Michael at all.

I curse and change tack, angling back toward where I think the road is.

I run. I run until my lungs are ready to explode. Then I

run some more. I careen off trees. My feet are torn to shreds. I scream at myself to keep moving. When I'm sure I've shaken the militia guys I stop, listening for the sound of the helicopter. There's nothing but silence.

I keep going. The road has to be up here. It has to be. I scramble down a gully, go up and over fallen trees, and just when I'm starting to panic, the ground falls away and there it is, the muddy track of a road. I stop for only a second to make sure it's clear before I leap onto it, my lungs on fire, going for a full-out sprint now.

I'm going to be too late. They'll be gone before I get there. And once the helicopter is airborne . . .

I come up over a hill and see the sudden light of a clearing. That must be where the helicopter has landed, and the sight gives me a burst of speed, just as a dark figure steps out on the path in front of me.

I nearly scream, but the person grabs my arms and says my name in a frantic whisper.

"Boyboy!" I gasp.

"Shh!" he says, and drags me off the path.

"I thought they'd caught you," I choke out.

Boyboy pulls me toward a gap in the trees where we can see the clearing. "What happened? I just saw Mr. Omoko come by with Michael! Couldn't you get him out?"

"No," I moan. "I didn't have time." Boyboy and I crouch behind a tree. The helicopter sits in windswept grass and wildflowers like a giant black wasp. "And his hand is broken, so he couldn't drive the motorcycle." I can just see two figures inside the chopper. I look past the brightness of the field, and my blood goes cold. The militia truck is there in the shade of the trees, surrounded by men bristling with AK-47s. A Goonda has Michael by the arm and they're standing just at the edge of the forest next to Mr. Omoko. "Did you talk to Mr. Greyhill?"

"I think I was too late," Boyboy says, his face twisted. "I came this far to try to make the call, but then I heard them coming after me. I had to run maybe a couple of kilometers down the road before I got a signal at Catherine's home."

"Catherine's?" I ask, looking at him sharply.

"I recognized it when I came out of the forest."

She wasn't kidding when she said the militias were just up the road.

"And I called Mr. Greyhill, but he didn't answer," Boyboy goes on. "I had to leave a message. I called three times, but then I heard the helicopter, so I gave up and followed it back here. I don't know if he heard any of them. I'm so sorry, Tina."

Trying to swallow my panic, I shake my head. "It's not your fault."

Nothing is going right. My last hope was that Boyboy could talk to Mr. Greyhill and he would somehow salvage things.

There's movement at the helicopter and then I see Mr. G step out, his eyes hidden by sunglasses. I look from him back to Michael. If Mr. Greyhill knows what Omoko's true intentions are, he doesn't show it. He buttons his jacket, like he's headed to a business meeting. Mr. Omoko steps out of the shade and walks toward him.

"Did you talk to Catherine?" I whisper.

"She went to try and get help."

Boyboy doesn't sound hopeful, and there's no reason he should be. What sort of help can she find? The local police are probably on the militia payroll. An army unit might respond, but that's only if she can find and convince them.

When Omoko and Greyhill are face-to-face, Omoko smiles and reaches out to shake his old boss's hand. Mr. Greyhill doesn't take it. I can't hear what they're saying, but Mr. Omoko's smile tightens. He claps Greyhill on the arm instead, and starts to lead him back toward Michael. I can see now that the militia guys have set up a small table and chairs at the edge of the forest. I count. Four militia guys and two Goondas are visible, but it wouldn't surprise me if there were more, armed and hidden in the forest.

Michael is presented to his father and his blindfold yanked down around his neck. He blinks into the sun, and I can't do anything but stare at his face. Mr. Greyhill reaches for him, but at a word from Omoko he stops and slowly lowers his hand. Now his emotions are obvious. Even from here, Greyhill's barely contained fury is palpable.

Mr. Omoko gestures to the table where a laptop has been set up, and the two men sit. Michael is moved away.

I look back over my shoulder, as if by magic there might be some help coming up the road. There are only trees.

I stand. This is it. No one is coming to help us. I pull the gun out of my waistband.

"Tina, what are you doing?" Boyboy tugs at my arm, but I shake him off.

The gun is heavy, but at least it's a handgun, not one of the AKs, or otherwise I would have ditched it to run faster. I check the magazine—six bullets, plus one in the chamber. I fix my stance like Michael taught me to when we were kids, like the Goondas reinforced when we went out to shoot beer bottles off the edge of the sea wall. I aim at Omoko. He is smiling as Mr. G brings the laptop closer and starts to type. I breathe.

But I can't get my hands to stop shaking.

"I'm too far," I say, and use my shoulder to wipe the sweat that is trickling into my eyes.

"Tina . . ."

"I need to get closer."

I move sideways through the forest, keeping my eyes locked on the two men at the table. They look so odd, like a business lunch misplaced. I can hear Boyboy following behind me and turn to signal him to move back. I want him farther away, where he won't be heard. I run through the forest on quiet feet. Feet that have been trained to be silent sneaking into houses also do pretty well running through forests, it turns out.

The field is broad, and it takes me a while to get around behind them, especially while trying not to make any noise. I creep up the hill above the militia truck, then down through the undergrowth, moving as fast as I dare, until I come to a sort of a cliff, where I can crouch and look down at them. The men stand in a line, Goondas on one end, militias on the other. Mr. Greyhill is typing something on the computer, and Mr. Omoko is engrossed in what he's being shown. I had expected to come up on more men in the forest guarding Mr. Omoko's flank, but there's no one, no sign of disturbed undergrowth. It's a lucky break, but still, what am I supposed to do now? Shoot as many of the militia and Goondas as I can, plus Mr. Omoko? Hope they don't kill Michael? I'm closer, but still outnumbered. Desperation swells in my throat.

I hear a snap of a twig behind me and spin, heart thumping, gun raised.

Boyboy already has his hands up, grimacing. I put a finger to my lips and motion for him to get down. He crawls forward and peers over the edge with me.

I can see it on Boyboy's face. He sees what I see. At best it's a shootout, which will most likely end with Michael getting the worst of it. And Boyboy doesn't even have a gun. I try to keep my breath steady. Think, Tina, think, there's got to be a way. Why can't this be like the movies, where I just tear down through the woods, bad guys tossed back by bullets, the captive never getting a scratch?

If I can even hit Mr. Omoko I'll be lucky. But no other plan is coming to me. I see Mr. Greyhill pause, his finger hovering over a key. Mr. Omoko smiles like a lion that's just brought down prey. Soon the transaction will be over, and Mr. Greyhill and Michael will be in the helicopter. I ease myself onto my belly, swallow, prop up my elbows, and raise the gun. I squint one eye closed and try to block out Boyboy's rapid breath, try to slow my racing heart, and keep my trembling hands from shaking the sights away from my target.

I put my father's head in the crosshairs.

I can feel the resistance of the trigger under my finger. One tug is all it takes.

Shoot him, Tina. *Now.*

Tak-tak-tak-tak-tak-tak

Tak-tak-tak-tak

I start, and lift my head, so wound up that for a second I can't loosen my grip on the gun. Boyboy and I look at each other, then at the men. They're all talking, focused on something across the field in the direction of their camp.

"What's going on?" Boyboy asks.

"I don't know."

Tak-tak-tak-tak

Tak-tak-tak-tak-BOOM

I hear birds screaming in the forest. The militiamen shout and point. I crane my neck to see and sniff the air. "Smoke," I say. "It's coming from back at their camp."

The militia guys seem to have the same thought and turn to Mr. Omoko. An argument starts, but then Mr. Omoko yells for the Goondas to stay put while the militia guys go see what's going on. Mr. Greyhill sits ramrod straight, eyes glued to his old Number Two. I don't think he's hit the key he was hesitating over. The Goondas finger their weapons and watch their boss. Michael looks at his father. Everyone is as tense as strung bows.

I look from Mr. Omoko back to the truck, where the militia men are clambering in. Did they leave their RPGs or take them? With a roar the truck is bouncing across the field, back toward the camp.

And before I can come to my senses, I swivel the gun, line up the sights, and take a shot.

I watch the Goonda holding Michael's elbow jerk forward and fall onto the table between Mr. Omoko and Greyhill.

Then all hell breaks loose.

And I don't let myself think, even though Boyboy is shouting and grabbing at me. I tell myself I'm that action hero charging down the hill, high with adrenaline, taking shots two, three—except it's all happening too fast—fourth shot—and my feet are slipping, and I don't hit the other Goonda or Mr. Omoko, and I feel little explosions in tree trunks and earth around me as bullets dance past my head. Everyone is screaming at everyone else to stop shooting— fifth shot—except for the other Goonda, who I realize is the one who was in the fistfight, Toofoh-or-Toto; he's just rat-tat-tat-tat-tatting away, aiming with his one good eye, and then I trip over something and I'm going to land right at Toofoh-or-Toto's feet, but then suddenly he's flying sideways, shot by the pilot who has come out of the chopper, and who has maybe been hit too, and also falls into the grass, and then, like it never happened . . .

It all goes dead quiet.

I stagger into the light, the gun up and pointed at Mr. Omoko. I have two more bullets left. Michael is crouched over his father, who is ashen and gripping his leg. A few feet away, Omoko slowly brings his hands up from his sides. He glances at the two Greyhills.

"Stay back from them!" I scream.

I hear Boyboy come up behind me and run to Mr. G's side. Mr. Greyhill's leg is dark with blood. Boyboy yanks off Mr. G's tie and begins to wrap it around his leg as a tourniquet. Michael is writhing on the ground, and my heart skips because I think he's hurt too, but then I realize he's pulling his legs through his tied arms to get them in front of him.

I register all of this out of the corner of my eye. I am fixed on Mr. Omoko, the gun aimed at his head.

"Christina," he rumbles, "what are you doing?"

"Put your hands up. Up!"

"You think you're going to shoot me, Tiny Girl?"

I keep the gun raised. The sun is beating down on me, and the gun is slippery in my hands. I can feel the rage of a thousand days spent waiting for this moment shimmering inside me. I rock from foot to foot.

"Yes," I finally say.

A slow smile spreads over Mr. Omoko's face. "I thought so. All right. Do it. You'll never have a better shot."

Michael raises his head. "Don't, Tina."

I keep my eyes on Mr. Omoko, trying to block out everything else. He's right. I am too close to miss. Sweat stings the corners of my eyes, and I blink.

Mr. Omoko begins to lower his palms.

"Put your hands back up!"

But he doesn't stop. They descend inch by inch. "You are losing your chance. What's the matter? You are already a killer, daughter," he says, waving a hand over the dead Goonda.

"I'm *not* your daughter!" I scream. I sound like a child, but I can't stop myself.

"You are, like it or not. But the question is whether you are too much like your mother," he says. His lip curls. "Weak."

"My mother was not weak!"

He smiles again, and for a second I am horrified to see a twisted mirror of my face. I feel myself breaking apart, my limbs rattling and popping like an old machine. "I'm going to kill you," I whisper.

His teeth are too big in his mouth; his gums shine. "You'd better do it, then. This is what you wanted, isn't it? To destroy your mother's murderer?" Mr. Omoko opens his arms wide. "Here I am!"

I can't move.

"I created you!" he shouts. "I made you who you are! You owe me everything! I made you the girl who can kill a man. So let's see it! Let's see how much like me you really are!"

Every word is a stone, smashing against me. *You are like me. Like me.* I am his daughter, just like him. There is a dead man at my feet. I have a hostage tied up in the forest. All this time, year after year, all I've ever wanted was revenge. Being with the Goondas has nursed this violence in me, but maybe it's been there all along, in my bones. My fury has been boundless, my love for my mother buried underneath it. And it's all because of him. Because I am his daughter. I am of his blood. I am his.

And then very softly, but very firmly, in the back of my mind I hear a voice. Not Mr. Omoko's voice, though. Not my mother's.

Mine.

My voice says, No, Tina. He's wrong. You are who you choose to be. You are yours.

And I feel the sun burning and strength returning to my arms. And my voice when I speak is my own, not some sad man's daughter's.

"I am *nothing* like you."

I raise the gun to his head, and I am ready. At the same moment I see him reach for his pocket. All in less than an instant, there is the shine of the metal in his hand. The black eye of the gun barrel. The succinct and complete distancing of himself from me.

A single shot cracks and echoes.

Noise fades. A cloud slides over the sun, dark, then light.

I wait for the pain.

I look down at my body. I look up. I'm distracted by birds flinging up from the grass into the white sky.

I am whole.

The gun is still in my hand, but it's cold. I haven't fired it. My ears ring. I look back up at Mr. Omoko as he looks past me. There is a sudden brightness at his chest, right at his heart, like a flower blooming. He raises his fist and coughs a little into it. When it comes away, it is red. He takes a step. He tries to raise his gun, but it slips from his hand and lands in the grass.

I feel myself turn to look over my shoulder, and it takes some time for my eyes to focus. At first there's nothing there. Light playing on leaves. Darkness. And then I see the gun muzzle slide out from the crook of a tree branch where she'd steadied it to line up a perfect shot.

Catherine's face is clear; she is calm. Our eyes meet and lock, holding steady for a long time. Then she slides the gun strap over her shoulder and hefts it onto her back.

There is a noise from Mr. Omoko, and I turn back. He's fallen to his knees, hand to his heart. The red slides out around his fingers and drips onto the ground. He opens his mouth like he wants to tell me something, but I turn away, to the forest.

Catherine is gone.

I stand completely still, staring into the dark between the gem-bright leaves. Flattening and springing up with the wind, the grass is like an ocean. I do not look toward the sounds of my father's last wet breaths.

Instead I wait until everything goes silent, until the insects pick up their interrupted song, until I hear Boyboy say my name softly. Then I look at the man on the ground. He stares up at the sky, still and finally harmless.

FORTY-TWO

Sister Dorothy assures Michael that his father's surgery went well. They are used to dealing with bullet wounds and worse at the clinic. "We didn't even have to put him under," the sister says. "He was on a business call almost the entire time." She shakes her head, clearly not understanding that Mr. G's call with Bug Eye was one negotiation that couldn't wait. "You can go in to see him in just a moment," she says. "How is the arm?"

"Fine," Michael answers. They've put a cast on his wrist.

"That was quite a break," she says. "It sounds like you are all very lucky to be alive." And with a little squeeze to my shoulder she's off to check on a baby that was born this morning.

Life, even in the middle of all this death, is persistent.

General Gicanda had been the one to sweep us up from the carnage in the field, rolling in with a small army of Rwandan special forces only moments after Omoko was dead. At first I thought it was the militia, but then Mr. Greyhill shouted at us to put down the guns we raised at them. General Gicanda attended to Mr. Greyhill himself, carrying him to the helicopter and laying him beside a trussed-up, still-unconscious Ketchup. On the way to the hospital, he pointed out the militia camp. Or what was left of it.

It turned out that Mr. G had got Boyboy's messages after all, but had decided not to take any chances. Gicanda's strike on the camp came after Mr. Greyhill radioed in the coordinates. They were supposed to come to Mr. G's aid sooner, but taking out the militia took longer than the general had anticipated.

If anyone at the hospital is surprised to see Rwandan troops this deep in Congo, they give no indication. The soldiers set up watch in the corridors. In contrast to the militias, their uniforms are spotless and pressed, and their guns and boots shine with oil. They are tall and healthy looking, standing at attention and gazing out over the heads of the nurses and nuns bustling around them. Three are stationed around Ketchup's bed, even though he's now under heavy sedation.

The nuns say it's too soon to know if he will have any permanent damage from the fracture in his skull, but there's not much swelling and he's stable, and once they stop feeding him sedatives, he should wake up within twenty-four hours. Mr. Greyhill has told the nuns to spare no expense in making sure he stays alive. He knows what Ketchup's life is now worth.

A different nurse sticks her head around the door of the

surgery room, where Mr. G is resting. "You can go in now," she tells Michael and me.

We both jump up and hurry into his room. Boyboy waits in the lobby. When we burst in, Mr. G doesn't look up from his phone and his face is as unreadable as ever. There is a red stain the size of a bottle cap on the dressing on his leg.

"It's done," Mr. Greyhill says, finally putting his phone away. "Come in, close the door, sit. She's safe and I have assurances she'll stay that way. Your associate is pleased with the payment I'm offering in addition to his brother. He's promised me you won't be harmed. Everything's been arranged for the handoff to occur as soon as we touch down in Sangui." He looks at his phone again. "We'll leave within the hour. The general will escort us to the border."

I am so relieved that I can't even speak for a few seconds, and I melt into a chair.

"Tomorrow I'll have my assistant start working on getting her visa arranged."

I look at Michael, but he seems just as confused as me. "Visa?"

"She'll go back with Michael."

"Back where?"

"Lucerne, Switzerland."

I jump up and come around the bed to face him. "Switzerland!"

"I should have done it years ago," Mr. G says. "I thought the convent school was safe enough, but obviously I was wrong."

"You paid for her to go there?" Michael asks. "You knew where she was?"

"Of course."

How did I not figure that out before? He must have come looking for Kiki once we left, and found her at the church he knew Mama went to. I try to hide my shock. "You can't just send her off to some foreign country without asking me!"

He regards me with infuriating patience. He still looks polished and in charge, even sitting in a hospital bed. "You're what, sixteen?"

"So?"

"And you're in a gang?"

I ball my fists. "Your point?"

"You're hardly in a position to offer alternatives."

I open and close my mouth, trying to think how to respond. He was the one who kept my sister safe and in school. He paid for her to go there. But he kept her out of his home too. He left her living like an orphan; all he did was pay off his guilty conscience. "You never even came to see her," I finally say.

At this, his smooth forehead wrinkles. "I went once. But..."

"It was inconvenient." I fold my arms over my chest. "Or were you afraid someone would see you and wonder why you're visiting a mixed kid who happens to look an awful lot like you?"

He doesn't answer. From the corner of my eye I can see Michael watching his father silently, his face hard and unforgiving.

A lesson of some sort has started on the lawn outside,

and I can hear a chorus of young women's voices slowly reading phrases out loud in French.

"Why can't we leave now?" I ask. My relief at knowing Kiki really is safe and that she'll be back with me soon is fading quickly. She's still not here, now, with me. I need to see her.

"Believe me, we're getting the choppers refueled and ready to go as fast as we can. I'm anxious too. Sit, Christina, you're not doing her any good wearing a hole in the floor."

I had hardly even noticed I'd started pacing again. I slow, turn to face him. "All right, well, if we can't leave yet, I have questions."

He folds his hands in his lap and waits.

I glance at Michael. "Why did my mother come and find you?" I ask. It's the question Omoko partially answered for me, but I want to hear what Greyhill has to say.

He keeps his eyes leveled on me for a beat, like he's trying to decide if he really wants to tell me anything. Finally, he says, "Because she knew I could help her. I was probably the only person in the world who could."

Almost against my will I sink into a chair beside Mr. Greyhill's bed and lean forward, hungry for this explanation. "She told you he was stealing from you," I say. "That's why you helped her?"

Mr. G looks from me to his son, who is waiting for answers as well.

"Mr. Greyhill," I say, "I know you think I'm just a kid, but I killed a man to save Michael today. I deserve to know exactly what happened." I feel myself trembling. "Michael does too."

Greyhill blows a long breath out his nose. "She had proof that Omoko had been stealing gold from me—a very detailed ledger of how much he siphoned off from each transaction with the militia. But in exchange for giving it to me, she wanted protection. She asked for a job in my home, behind my gates and guards."

Michael frowns. "So you do buy gold from these monsters." He walks to the window and looks out, his bandaged arm held to his chest.

"Do you know how she got the ledger?" I ask.

"She said she had been a prisoner for a while and was able to steal the documents." Mr. Greyhill's eyes drop to his hands. "It was later she told me what he did to her."

"She told *you* what happened to her?" I hate the note of jealousy that creeps into my voice.

Mr. Greyhill hesitates. "Your mother and I were . . . close."

"Close? You had a kid with her," Michael says, his back still to his father.

Mr. G looks up. "I'm not perfect."

"That's maybe the understatement of the century," Michael growls. He turns around. "Did you love her?"

I suck in a breath. I don't know what I expect Greyhill say. Maybe to deny it, to say it was just an affair. But he lifts his chin and looks his son in the eye. "Yes."

Michael pushes off the windowsill. He starts for the door, anger stiffening his frame.

"Michael . . ." I stand up and try to catch his arm, but he shakes me off. I'm about to go after him, but Mr. G says, "Let him go. He needs time." He watches his son's angry back disappear through the door as I sink slowly back into my chair. "We've never talked about Anju . . . but we will. Later." He closes his eyes. "I thought she would be safe in my home, Tina. I thought all of you would be. I truly did."

I grip my hands in my lap. "I thought you killed her. I saw you, both of you, in the garden the night before she died. You told her you'd kill her. You were trying to strangle her."

Greyhill seems to deflate. He rubs a hand across his face. "I thought that might have been you. I-I don't have an adequate excuse, Christina. She had every right to be angry with me. I'd told her I would stop working with the militia, but I hadn't. It was too hard to reverse by that time. So when she threatened me, I got angry with her. I didn't know how to . . ." He sighs.

"So you *were* trying to hurt her."

"I would never have done it . . ." he says, his voice full, nearly cracking. "I was angry. I didn't know how to deal with your mother sometimes. I loved her, but what happened to her out here—it was beyond what any person could possibly be expected to bear. I don't think she ever really recovered from it. She told me once that dying would have been so much easier. Sometimes she wasn't herself. She would rave and scream, threaten me, or drift away. That night I became frustrated."

I have to dig my nails into my palms to keep myself together. I knew those dark places she would retreat to. "That's no excuse for what you said to her."

"I know." He looks at me, his eyes glassy. "I'm not proud

of what I said, or how I treated her. Sometimes it feels like it *was* me who killed her."

I feel, more than hear, his words, like a tiny knife, cutting away the last abscess of anger I have for him. I feel it slip free from where it's been lodged inside me. I realize that maybe this was what I had always wanted: not so much Mr. Greyhill's money or his blood, but an admission of his guilt. Something that would let me put her to rest peacefully. "But it wasn't you," I say.

Greyhill's face darkens. "I should have killed Omoko the day your mother started working for me. But we had been friends once, Omoko and I, and I let him go. At that point I didn't . . . care for her so much. By the time I understood what he had done to your mother, he was gone. Disappeared. We thought he might have left the continent. He killed her in my home because he wanted to let me know he could still get to me. He hadn't been seen in years at that point. And all the while he was underground, growing stronger, just biding his time." He snorts. "He paid off my head of security to get in, the bastard. That guy I *did* have killed."

"David Mwika?"

"Waste of bone and breath."

I wonder if that's what the payments to First Solutions that Boyboy found were all about. Not payments *to* Mwika, but payments to have him killed, maybe even by one of his coworkers.

"He opened the *mokele-mbembe* door for Mr. Omoko," I say. Mr. Greyhill frowns. "The what?"

"The secret tunnel that goes to your office."

"Know about that, do you?"

I lean forward. "But you must have known that's how he got in and out. How could you not catch him?"

"I didn't figure that out until it was too late," Mr. Greyhill says, his face pained. "I was in shock."

The look on his face says he's thought long and hard about this, how it all must have happened. Suddenly I see the murderer underneath the polished exterior, the man who realized he'd been betrayed and hired someone to hunt Mwika down in a dirty bar in Congo and kill him. Someone who probably instructed the killer to whisper regards from Mr. Greyhill into Mwika's dying ear.

"How did you know it was Mr. Omoko who killed Mama?"

"The gun he shot her with—he left it for me. I had given it to him years earlier. It was engraved to him with a Roman numeral two. He hated that name, Number Two. The engraving was supposed to be a little joke." He chuckles mirthlessly. "No one would have noticed it. It was subtle. It was a message just for me."

"Number Two," I say quietly. I can picture the gun in Greyhill's drawer, the engraving like he said, next to PIETRO BERETTA MADE IN ITALY: a little NO. II in the same script. I slump back. "Why didn't you kill him after that?"

"I tried. Several times. But by then he had become much more powerful. He had surrounded himself with a small army. Your Goonda friends. He was anticipating it. He was never off guard."

Greyhill's right. Mr. Omoko's bodyguards were always there, like shadows. But I could have got to him if I'd known. The image of his dead face, eyes open wide to the sky, ripples through me, and I shudder. He's gone, Tina, he's gone.

I look up to see Mr. Greyhill watching me.

"Why are you even here?" I ask. "How can you keep doing it? Trading with the militias? If you cared about her, I mean? I've seen your records. You never stopped buying gold from them, even after she was dead."

Mr. Greyhill's brows furrow. "You've been on my computer."

"I'm with the Goondas, remember? I broke into your home and stole the memory off your hard drive. That's how Michael found me. He caught me in your office."

"You copied my data? Did Omoko get it?"

"Yes, but I'm sure the computer with all your dirt on it is destroyed," I say. "Your buddy the general didn't spare much when he bombed the camp." I don't mention the backup copies I know Boyboy has. I'm not quite sure I'm ready to play that card yet.

Mr. Greyhill starts to breathe again, which infuriates me. "You're no better than Omoko," I say.

He shakes his head slowly. "No. I'm trying to do better. We're exploring new sites, trying to dig enough minerals on our own. But it's hard. The militia groups have so much territory under their control. I've been working with General Gicanda to try to clear them out, but then there are all these political considerations . . ."

"It's *hard*," I sneer. It's all I can do not to spit at him. "Don't you see all those women out there?" I wave toward the window. "Ask them if they care if it's hard."

Mr. Greyhill lowers his eyes. "We are trying to do better, Tina. With the other minerals, there are new international laws now. Monitors. Sanctions. For tin and coltan we've got good mines. Safety protocols, unions. Ask anyone. Extracta wouldn't be able to sell these volumes otherwise."

"But gold . . . ?"

"Gold is another story. We're offering higher prices to mines that can show they're not using slaves. But it's not easy to shake the militias—they'll attack mines like that, take them over. The government's no help; they're running slave-labor mines too. And even if it's not Extracta who buys the gold, there are others—smugglers who are ready to take our place. They love gold. You can smuggle out one briefcase of it and get the same price as for five truckloads of tin ore. That's part of the reason why Omoko had it out for me. He wanted to be a buyer again."

I think of the weapons Omoko brought, the gold Boyboy had seen exchanged. It was true.

Greyhill goes on, "In exchange for Michael, he wanted both money and room to operate. And he would have been happy to keep letting the militias use slave labor. He could have bought gold at a cheaper price that way. For him it was about the bottom line, getting as much as he could in the short term. It's about the bottom line for me as well, but in the long term I think having good mines will be the more profitable strategy."

"So it's just business. All of this."

He looks tired all of a sudden. "I never said it was anything else."

A nurse bustles in and checks the IV on Greyhill's arm and gives him a cup of water. She ticks something on his chart and then she's gone again. The lesson outside continues, a slow chant of numbers and phrases that makes me want to close my eyes.

"It's still all so messed up," I say, shaking my head at him. I go to stand by the window, drawing the curtain back. There are about ten women out on the lawn, reading from exercise books. I recognize a woman in pink from the first night we came to the hospital. She's one of the three that was brought in that day. She smiles shyly at something the teacher says, and her teeth flash as white as the bandage crowning her head.

I make a decision. I let the curtain fall and turn around. "Mr. Greyhill, I'm grateful for what you're doing to help me keep my sister safe. I really am. But I know you're not doing that for me. And that's fine. You don't owe me anything. But you do owe my mother. And I intend to make sure you settle that debt. I may not be a Big Man. I'm small. Tiny. But please don't make the mistake of underestimating what I can do when I really want to. I will be watching you. I will be watching what happens here. For my mother. For those women out there. You say you'll do better, but it's difficult for a leopard to change its spots."

I walk toward Greyhill and place my hands on the rail at

the foot of his bed. "Listen carefully. Soon, after we get back and Kiki is safe and you're getting back to your life, a large sum of money is going to vanish from your accounts." He opens his mouth to protest, but I put a finger up to stop him. "And a little while later you may receive a thank-you note from this hospital. You will be gracious about it and agree to fund all of their operations for the foreseeable future. Anything they ask for, you'll give, even if it's a new school or roads or maybe even a new maternity wing."

I see his question coming and say, "If you don't, if you even hesitate, it will be done for you. You owe my mother that much a hundred times over."

His face goes slack, and I can see in his eyes that he knows I'm right. But I'm not done yet. "And furthermore, if you haven't completely cut ties with the militias by the end of the year, I'll begin to release information from your hard drive to the press. Yes, I have copies. And don't even try to have my friend or me killed. There will be safeguards. Either Boyboy or I go missing, the whole of it gets sent straight to a dozen different international news agencies."

I pause, letting this all sink in. "Am I clear?"

For a moment he simply looks at me, expressionless. Then a corner of his mouth lifts and a flicker of emotion registers on his face. I could be wrong, but I'm pretty sure it's a look of grudging respect. "Perfectly," he says. "I would expect nothing less from your mother's daughter."

FORTY-THREE

What will you do now?" Michael asks.

We're standing in the Greyhills' yard, near the spot where we got our scars all those years ago. I know his parents are inside discussing Kiki and me and what to do with us. I can hear Mrs. Greyhill's raised voice, and catch, "They're not your responsibility . . . *We're* your family!"

Michael looks up at the house. I think I'm learning the nuances of his expressions now. This one is complicated, but it seems to be a mix of annoyance and exhaustion. "Let's walk," he says.

"Okay, wait a sec." I catch Kiki's eye. She's sitting in the grass a few yards away, with the head of one of the German shepherd guard dogs in her lap. I give her a little smile, and she manages one back. I hope she didn't hear Mrs. Greyhill shouting.

Kiki's eyes are less haunted today, but she still looks small and tired. I know it's a good thing she's soon going to be far away from here. She needs a fresh start. But that doesn't mean that I'm happy about letting her go. Michael has assured me he's going to watch out for her in Switzerland, and I know he will, but it's not the same.

"We'll be just down there," I tell her. "You're okay?"

She nods her head. "I'm fine, Tina. Really. Stop worrying."

The dog looks up at her adoringly and licks her chin.

The handoff with Bug Eye went smoothly. The general flew us in on two helicopters with six of his men to make sure no one became too "emotional" during the exchange. We met at the private airfield where Mr. G keeps his helicopter.

Ketchup was brought out to Bug Eye on a stretcher, and when Bug Eye saw his brother, for a second it really did look like things were going to get messy. But Mr. Greyhill had also thought to have a doctor present, who checked out both Ketchup and my sister and assured all of us that everyone was going to be "Fine just fine! Please put the guns away, please."

My sister. Whew. I just about lost it when I saw her. Talk about emotional. Her getting into the Greyhills' car is a blur. All I remember is shaking like crazy, and asking her if she was okay over and over again until the doctor gave me a shot of something in my arm. I woke up later that night in a panic in the Greyhills' guestroom. But Kiki was curled right up next to me, and when I realized she really was there and okay, all I could do was cry silently and try not to wake her up.

Michael waits patiently now, a day later, for me to tear myself away. When I finally do, he leads the way down the yard, past all the flowers and ornamentals. He takes my hand with his good arm near my old cottage, and we walk past the place where I saw my mother and Mr. Greyhill arguing one dark night an eternity ago. We stop in front of the vegetables. The house behind us is hidden by a hibiscus bush humming with bees.

"So?" Michael asks. "What's your plan? I know you have one."

"I'll be around," I say.

"That's all you're going to tell me?"

"The less you know, the better," I say, letting a teasing smile creep onto my face.

"One day I'm going to know all your secrets, Tiny Girl," he says, "and you will never escape me."

"We'll see."

"But aren't you worried about the Goondas if you stay here?" he asks, his smile faltering.

"Your dad paid Bug Eye to leave me alone."

Michael doesn't look convinced. He shouldn't. Payment or no, I bet there's a price on my head. "Maybe I'll do some traveling while you're gone," I say.

"That's a good idea," Michael tells me. "You should take Dad up on his offer to send you to school with us."

"You know that's not what I meant."

"You'd like Switzerland," he says. "It's . . . clean. And Kiki will be there."

"I can't go to Switzerland."

"You mean you won't."

"I don't belong there."

"Do you belong here?" he asks quietly.

Some part of me wants nothing more than to say I'll go with him. I want to be there to watch over Kiki and, if I'm honest, to be close to him. I don't know what's happening between us, exactly, but I wouldn't mind more time to figure it out.

But some other part of me knows that I will stay. And that it's the right decision. Maybe it's because I've already made up my mind to go back and check on the mission hospital in Kasisi once Mr. Greyhill's "donation" goes through. Maybe it's because while I want the opportunities that school will give Kiki, I know that life isn't for me. Even before I was a Goonda, I didn't really like school. I know that's not great, but it's just who I am. I can't imagine spending every day on lockdown, on someone else's schedule, even if it's good for me. Wearing a neat uniform, being told what to do, where to go, when to be there—it all sounds like being slowly smothered. I would chafe at being made to sit up straight in a classroom. And I wouldn't last long with people bugging me to figure out where I want to go to college and decide what I'm going to do with my life.

But mostly, the reason why I am staying is simple: I already know what I'm going to do with my life.

This morning I woke before dawn and crept out of bed. I knocked on Michael's door and exacted a promise just shy of a blood oath from him to make sure Kiki stayed safe. Then I left. I needed to talk to Boyboy. He was already at my roof by the time I got there. He said he couldn't sleep and he couldn't stop shaking. "What happens next?" he'd asked. He knew as well as I did that everything was different now. For one, we were on the Goondas' shit list. We were going to have to go underground. I needed to find a new roof . . . or maybe a basement. I promised Boyboy we'd set his family up somewhere nice and new and safe. An island maybe.

But two, even if the Goondas had wanted us back, we knew we couldn't operate like before, robbing people blindly, not caring whose lives we affected.

We talked until the sun was up. We came up with plans, Boyboy and I, that may or may not involve more of what he calls "redistributive justice." The world is full of bad men with hackable bank accounts.

And after all, I can't give up being a thief entirely.

"It'll be like Robin Hood," Boyboy said. "Prince of Thieves."

I bumped shoulders with him as we looked out over the city. "Come on, we can do better than that. We'll be the Queens of Thieves."

And he laughed, for the first time in a long while.

I face Michael. His eyes are the same color as the leaves behind him. I think he gets why I can't go. I think, actually, he might get it better than anyone else. He may not know the details, but he knows me. He trusts me to know what's right for me. I can tell that he wants to ask what this is between us, what it might be. Our friendship is solid, a bedrock I never knew I needed, that I never knew I had all along. But is this more than that? I'm not sure either of us knows yet. But he seems to understand that letting the questions remain, letting the messy, unpredictable future happen is maybe the only way for us to go forward.

He brings his hand to my face, his fingertips grazing my hair. I can feel his warmth. "Just . . . don't disappear again, okay?"

"You'll always know where I am," I say, and tentatively lay my palms on his chest. Under his shirt I can feel his heart beating hard and fast.

He watches me like he's taking in every millimeter of my face. I know the feeling. I want to memorize everything about the way he looks right now, with the sun so bright on his skin and little insects doing lazy circles around his head. And then he reaches around my back and brings me closer, and I'm framed within his arms and I smell him and I can feel how tense he is, holding me as delicately as a wild thing that might launch out of his hands and run away.

And something in me suddenly cracks open like an egg, and I let go of everything except for this ache for him that is so sweet and so powerful and so good. Tomorrow doesn't matter, I realize. Not right now. Who knows what will happen? All we have is this. Here. Now.

And our mouths come together, and he holds me so close, and in this moment I can't tell if I am quenched, or more thirsty for him than ever. We kiss and it's like we've invented kissing, like no one can possibly have ever kissed like this in the history of forever. And all around us the world fades away, except for the buzzing of the bees in the flowers, like a thousand strings vibrating.

FORTY-FOUR

Rule 18: A last rule—maybe you can't be all things to all people. You might not ever be a proper boarding-school girl. Or a perfect thief. Not always the daughter they want or deserve or the sister or the friend. Rules will break you as often as you break them. But I guess that's okay.

Maybe I'm done with rules.

For now, anyway.

I think I will just be. I will exist. And see what happens.

I leave Boyboy squirting himself silly with expensive perfume in the duty-free shop and walk with my sister to her gate. Mr. G was going to come to the airport to see her off too, but I asked if we could just go alone. When she flies into Sangui with Michael and Jenny for break in a couple of months, we'll both come and meet them. I give the security agent my special "escort" pass issued by the airline. Mr. G pulled some strings to get it. It looks just like Kiki's ticket, but it will only get me as far as Gate 23.

Michael left yesterday, and Mr. Greyhill came in a wheelchair to say good-bye. I could tell he hated being pushed around in the chair, but I guess he really wanted to be there. Michael's flight was full, so Kiki has to fly today. Michael assured me, though, that he'll go with the school van to pick her up from the airport. She'll be in the grade right below Jenny. They'll look out for her.

We pass row after row of people waiting for their flights. They're all colors, all ages. The only thing they have in common is a rich sort of weariness, like they've had their fun in Africa but now it's time to go. Maybe they're not all wealthy, but there are plenty of gold wristwatches and carelessly scattered designer handbags around. It would be a good place to pickpocket; all these people are leaving. By the time they realized they'd been hit, they'd be thousands of miles away.

The airport terminal is new and very clean. All straight lines and no smell to anything. The planes outside the windows look scrubbed and polished. It seems so far away from the dusty streets of Sangui. I wonder if Kiki's new school in Lucerne will be more like this.

We stop in front of her gate.

"You have your passport? Your money?"

Kiki rolls her eyes. "I haven't lost them since you asked me five minutes ago."

I shove my hands in my pockets. The sun is just rising,

and it comes through the window like liquid copper. Around us tourists linger over last-minute souvenirs. Mothers try to corral toddlers, and businesspeople in suits hunch over their laptops and furtively sip coffee.

Kiki watches everything with wide eyes. She's wearing new clothes that were bought for the trip, everything pink and green. With her hair pulled back in neat braids and her new plastic backpack, she could be any of these travelers' daughters. It's been almost a week since her kidnapping, and she's starting to act like her old self again. She's had nightmares every night, but the doctor says that's normal and that they will probably stop after a while.

"Call when you get there with the phone Mr. G gave you, okay? My number is already programmed in." Her backpack strap has slipped down her shoulder, and I tug it up.

"Yeah." She can't stop staring around.

I push my sleeves up. I'm getting hot for some reason, and agitated. I look around. Mr. G said there was supposed to be someone here to meet her—someone from the airline who'll watch her and make sure she gets where she needs to go. But I don't see anyone. I put my hands on my hips.

Kiki turns back to me, like she's finally remembered I'm there. "You got a new tattoo."

My tension ebbs. I show her my forearm. My first non-Goonda tattoo. The skin is still raw and scabbing, but the new tattoo artist I found did a good job. My long, straight scar is now the central stem of a palm branch. It looks just like the one Saint Catherine holds in Mama's prayer card.

"It's a symbol of triumph," I say.

Just then a woman breezes up to us. She's wearing a lot of makeup, but her face underneath is pretty and friendly. She gives us a big smile. "Catherine Masika?"

Kiki raises her hand.

The woman smiles even wider at her and then at me. "I work for the airline. The flight will board soon, but you can go on first with me and we'll get you settled. Does that sound good?"

Kiki gulps. "Yes, madam."

I back up, already feeling myself melting away into the crowd, into the background. She'll be fine, I tell myself. This is what Mama would have wanted for her. Michael will be there. He won't let anything bad happen. Still, some part of me wants to grab Kiki's hand and make a run for it. My throat burns, but I won't cry in front of her.

The woman takes Kiki's passport and ticket and puts her hand on her shoulder to steer her toward the gate. She looks at me. "Do you want to say good-bye?" she asks Kiki.

My sister nods again and then turns to me.

"Bye," I say.

"Bye."

Then I open my arms and she hits me so hard that we nearly topple over. I squeeze her and press my face into her hair and take a deep breath. All the expensive perfumes in all the duty-free shops in the world could never smell so sweet.

For a moment the world is still and golden, and then Kiki pulls back from me. She's crying, but she's smiling too.

"Be good," I say, and rub the back of my hand across my nose.

For a second, Kiki's smile makes her look just like Mama in the old photograph of her and Cathi. "You be good too."

Then she turns and walks toward the gate with the lady, past a roped-off area where I can't follow. As the woman gives Kiki's ticket to the gate agent, Kiki looks back at me and says something.

"What?" I ask, and come as close as I can.

She points at my arm and shouts, "Your new tattoo! It's not for triumph. It means peace!"

I look down at the palm branch. When I look back up, Kiki is walking with the woman through the door that will take them out to the tarmac and the plane. She looks over her shoulder and waves at me one last time.

I wave until long after she can't see me anymore.

AUTHOR'S NOTE

A few notes on liberties the author has taken with the truth:

Much of this story is based on real events affecting real people in the eastern part of the Democratic Republic of Congo. Human rights violations, especially against women, are common. While Anju's story is fictionalized, it draws from persecution histories I heard firsthand while working with refugees in Kenya, as well as documentation from groups like Human Rights Watch and the UN Security Council. Mining companies bring much-needed employment, but undoubtedly take advantage of chaos and corruption in the region. Refugees flee to neighboring countries every day, looking for peace and security. The conflict is ongoing, complex, and overlooked by much of the rest of the world.

At the same time, eastern Congo is a place of incredible beauty. Its inhabitants are regular and extraordinary people of profound dignity who, like others around the world, are simply trying to go about the business of living their lives. Putting themselves at great risk, brave women and men work every day to help end the conflict and care for survivors of violence. Under-resourced clinics like the mission hospital in this story operate against incredible odds. If you've been moved to learn more about such places, here are a few to get you started: Solidarité Féminine pour la Paix et le Développement Intégral (sofepadi.org), located in DRC's North Kivu; Sister Angélique Namaika's Centre for

Reintegration and Development in Orientale Province; Panzi Hospital in Bukavu; and HEAL Africa in Goma.

That is the real story.

Things that are not real: the characters, plot, Sangui City, and Kasisi are all from my imagination. Of course, I'd be lying if I didn't say that, like many authors, I am a magpie. I steal things from real life all the time and use them to fancy up my nest. For those who know Kenya, you can imagine Sangui City as a mix of Mombasa's coastal beauty and Nairobi's hustle. And while Kasisi is not a real town, Walikale Territory and Walikale Town in North Kivu are.

Saint Catherine's prayer was adapted from two different prayers: 1) John James Burke, Bonaventure Hammer, *Mary, Help of Christians, and the Fourteen Saints Invoked as Holy Helpers* (London: Forgotten Books, 2013), pp. 234–5 (original work published 1909), and 2) Réalta [an] chruinne Caitir Fhíona: St. Catherine of Alexandria [McKenna, L.: *Aithdioghluim Dána* (Irish Texts Society, vols. 37, 40, 1939/40), poem 99].

All other mistakes, omissions, and inaccuracies are mine, all mine, with sincere thanks and apologies.

GLOSSARY

Swahili, including Sheng*:

askari: guard; warrior; Cathi's dog's name

buibui: modest black garment worn predominantly by
   Muslim women on the Swahili coast

bwana: mister

dengu: soupy bean dish (usually mung beans)

habari ya jioni: good evening

habibi: (Arabic) term of endearment

hatari: danger

hodi: word used to announce yourself, usually at
   someone's home

jua kali: literally "hot sun," referring to the informal
   market in Kenya. As a verb, equivalent to
   "improvised" or "jerry-rigged"

kanga: colorful, popular style of fabric worn as a wrap
   in East Africa; design usually includes a saying or
   proverb

kanzu: long white garment (tunic) worn predominantly
   by Muslim men

karibu: welcome

kauzi: thief

kijana: young (boy); youth

---

* *Sheng:* A portmanteau of *Swahili* and *English*, Sheng is a constantly
   evolving street slang, mainly used by urban youth in Kenya

kitenge/vitenge: colorful, graphic fabric popular in East Africa and eastern Congo

Kwani?: What? (Say what?)

mandazi: fried dough street snack

matoke: starchy banana (plantain)

mavi: a rude word for excrement you should not use in front of your grandmother

mdosi: mister; boss

mokele-mbembe: (Lingala) legendary monster said to inhabit the Congo River basin

mwizi: thief

mzee: mister (usually for an older man)

mzingo: perimeter

mzungu: (Swahili) white person

ngai: God

nyanya: (Swahili) grandmother

panga: machete

piki-piki: small motorcycle

pili-pili: spicy chili sauce

polepole: slowly slowly

polisi: police

shoga: (Sheng) extremely rude word for a gay person. Don't use this word at all, ever.

shonde: (Sheng) another rude word for excrement you should not use in front of your grandmother

sonko: (Sheng) rich

sukuma/sukuma wiki: collard-like green

thegi: (Sheng) thief

ugali: cooked cornmeal, a staple dish in Kenya

WaBenzi: Wa = of (often as in tribe). *Benzi* is slang for Mercedes-Benz. *WaBenzi* is, therefore, "tribe of the Mercedes-Benz"

wache waseme: from an old Swahili song, "Let Them Talk"

weh: From *wewe,* meaning "you"

French:

bienvenue: welcome

comptoir: gold buyers; middlemen (can also mean gold trading house)

voleur: thief

ACKNOWLEDGMENTS

They say it takes a village. In the case of this book, it took a village, several midsized cities, a couple of continents, and endless family, friends, friends of family, strangers, and others to bring this book to life. I'm going to attempt the impossible here, to express how grateful I am for all the help I've had along the way.

I have to start with the women, men, and children from the Democratic Republic of the Congo who told me their stories as part of their resettlement interview process, as well as others who told me just because they wanted their stories to exist in the world. Telling is an act of bravery, so thank you for sharing that bravery with me. To say I am grateful is not quite right; I am humbled by you. I am especially in debt to the Women's Group at RefugePoint in Nairobi, with a special shout-out to C and R. I think about you often. When I say this book is for the girls (and women) who are more than just refugees, I think of you and your children.

I'm incredibly lucky to have the charmingly badass Faye Bender as my agent. My guide to the mysterious world of publishing, she knows just what to do, how to do it, when and why, and also finds time to be a writer-whisperer, hand-holder, squee-sharer. Thank you for believing in this story. Thank you for pushing me to be better.

Stacey Barney, editor extraordinaire at Putnam, you are magic. I am so grateful that we came together on this book, and find more reasons to be grateful every day. Being among your flock is a dream come true. I love that you challenge me, ask all the tough questions, encourage, cajole, prod, and just when I think I'm finally done, you ask one more question, illuminate one more way in which to make the story shine. A million thanks as well to Kate Meltzer, also a brilliant editor, all-around thoughtful and kind person, and keeper of many balls in the air.

The entire team at Penguin Random House and G. P. Putnam's Sons Books for Young Readers deserves a standing ovation for all the hard work they do to get books into hands. You are a crazy-impressive bunch of pros. I'm so proud to be under your wings.

This book might never have existed without the incredible support of the Associates of the Boston Public Library's Writer-in-Residence Fellowship. You are the knights of the People's Palace. Thank you for taking a risk on me, for the time and beautiful space to write in, but most of all for the priceless gift of allowing me to call myself a writer. Shout-outs to the Teen and Central librarians as well for your tireless efforts to keep libraries vibrant and community-centered. Also for just being awesome.

So many people read and provided feedback along the way: *Asante sana* to Carine Umutoniwase, Rita Njue, Maggie Muthama, and C—your perspectives were so critical. JB, your Sheng game is on point. Thank you to my BSpec peeps who read, came out, cheered, critiqued like bosses, titled, tweeted, cocktailed, and read again: Lyndsay, Lura, Andrea, Claire, Gillian, Beth, Jess, Kyle, Rae, Eric, Jay, Seth, Emily,

Caitlin, Lauren, Nyssa, Victoria, Angela, Kat, Robert—deep breath, egads, there are a lot of us—you're the best bunch of murderboozers a gal could have. Thank you to Karen B, for graciously volunteering your expertise (and keeping my grammar proper!). To the Louisville book club, thank you for humoring me and acting like I was a legit author before any of this happened.

My family taught me to love books, and has read countless iterations of this one. Thanks (y'all), for always acting like you want to read it again. Mom, Papa, Rebecca, Dylan, Margot, (and everyone else—you know who you are!), your love and support mean everything to me.

And last, thank you to M, the man who will always have my heart, who reads feverishly, brilliantly, logically, infuriatingly (because you're usually right about the mistakes, dammit); the man who put up with a whole lot of nonsense and then some to help me get this book out in the wild. Nothing makes me happier than having you as my lover and best friend.

KEEP READING FOR A FIRST LOOK AT
NATALIE C. ANDERSON'S NOVEL

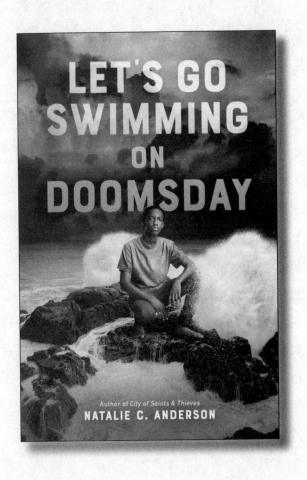

ONE

I float, I float, I float.

I open my eyes and for a second they sting, and then nothing. I look around. Underneath me the floor of the ocean swells up pale and solid. Above, the sun is broken on the water's surface into a million shining pieces.

By now I can hold my breath for almost two minutes if I'm relaxed like this. I've carried a stone in from the shore, and the weight is perfect. It anchors me, and I am very still. Fish like slivers of glass sail by, too small for eating. Through the drone of water in my ears I can hear a crackling noise that my father once told me was the sound of tiny shrimp breathing. A jellyfish rides the current.

I think I'd like to be a jellyfish. This is what it would feel like to be brainless and transparent.

One minute and fifteen seconds. My vision is starting to

pulse. I can feel my blood surging in my temples, telling me to breathe.

I wait.

One minute and thirty-eight seconds. Lungs burning, something animal in me screaming, Decide! Live or die!

I look up at the shards of sun and tell it, Not yet. I want to live, of course I do, but it's so tempting to stay. As soon as I break for air, there's no pretending to be anything other than a boy who must swim back and put his feet on the ground. A boy who will feel his weight again, surprisingly heavy on his bones.

For as long as I can, I resist. Two minutes and four seconds.

I don't want to be the boy who will walk out of the waves, water sluicing down his black arms, falling from his white fingertips. That boy will walk past the fishermen's boats, past the fishermen. He'll walk from the beach onto the tarmac. He'll pass old, shattered buildings that remind him of dogs' incisors. He'll pass new buildings wrapped in scaffolding like ugly gifts. He'll disappear into Somalia's capital city, the White Pearl: Mogadishu.

Two minutes and sixteen seconds.

My head breaks the surface and I gasp. Air and water sting my throat.

I tell myself I've chosen to live, but the water knows the truth. Waves brush my arms, soft as shroud linen.

The water knows I have to die.

TWO

By the time I get back to the hotel, I am completely dry.

"Where have you been?" Commander Rashid says, closing the distance in two big strides and grabbing me by the collar. The others look at me from the floor, eyes shining in the gloom.

"Swimming," I say, pointing toward the water. "Just swimming, sir."

"Swimming?" His eyes bulge. "*Swimming?* What do you think this is, a holiday?"

"I'm sorry, sir."

I am not sorry.

He looks me over, and I can tell he's searching for signs that I'm cracking. Or that I'm having second thoughts, or that I've done the unthinkable and sold him and the Boys out.

"I needed to bathe," I tell him. "Like a . . ." I pretend to search for the word, even though I've thought long and hard about what to tell him. "A purification."

Commander Rashid's voice is low and soft—a knife glinting in the dark. "That was a long bath, boy. Hakim Doctor has faith in you, but if it were up to me . . ."

He's interrupted by Bashir jumping up from the floor. "Commander," he says, "I apologize, but can I please have your assistance with these connections? I'm not sure if the wires go here or to the other panel." He holds up a tangle of plastic and metal to demonstrate.

Rashid makes a strangled noise and lets me go. "Not that one, *doqon*! Do you want to kill us all now?"

The commander should know that Bashir could make a bomb out of two mangoes and a shoestring, but my friend's ruse is lost on him. Maybe we're all just that tightly wound right now. Bashir winks at me over the commander's head and I creep away, slip into the adjoining room of the half-built hotel. It's empty except for my brother, who is lying on the floor. One whole corner of the room is gone, like something has taken an enormous bite out of it. A mortar, probably. A hot breeze rummages through the rooms, but the smell coming off Khalid is still heavy and foul.

I pick up the bottle of water and tip it into his mouth. I try not to gag. Is it the smell or my guilt that makes me want to throw up? "How are you?" I ask.

"Fine," he grunts, after taking barely a sip. "What do you

think you're doing, wandering off?" He's trying to sound tough, but his voice is a rasp.

"I just went for a last swim, that's all."

"A swim? Now? Da'ud, you know there's no time to—"

"Shh." It barely even registers anymore when he calls me the new name. "Hakim Doctor said you aren't supposed to talk. The stitches will open."

The bandage across his stomach is a muddy red brown and needs changing, but we're out of clean cloth. Only the Doctor would know for sure how bad the wound really is, but he's not here. He gave Nur and Commander Rashid instructions over the phone and Nur stitched my brother up as best he could, but what Khalid really needs is a hospital, antibiotics. But he's not getting any of that, not now that his face has been circulated across Mogadishu as a Most Wanted Jihadi.

Whether he lives or dies is all in God's hands now, according to the Doctor. I get it: I know what would happen if we took him to the hospital. The doctors would turn him in for the money. I know that. But doing nothing is making me crazy. I try not to think what my mother would say if she saw me just sitting here watching him die.

If she knew that this was all my fault.

The soldier's bullet didn't hit where it was supposed to. Instead it sliced right through him, just under his ribs, tearing through his intestines, from the smell of it. "Septic," I heard one of the guys whisper when he thought I couldn't hear. I'm not sure if the shot really was an accident or intentional, but either way, looking at Khalid sweeps away all my remaining doubts about what I'm about to do.

My brother gurgles when he breathes, and his skin is the color of old *canjeero* bread. I pour a little water on a rag and wipe his face. He's burning up.

"When do you leave?" Khalid asks.

"A couple of hours."

He nods. It looks painful. He closes his eyes. "It should be me there, not you."

"You should be here. Getting well, *Inshallah*."

"I don't want to be well," he says very softly. His eyes stay closed. "It wasn't supposed to happen this way."

I don't answer for a few seconds. I'm not sure which part he's talking about, but it doesn't matter. He's right. None of it should have gone down like this.

I'm going to fix it, I want to tell him. I'm going to fix everything.

But I don't say that. Straining for sincerity, I say what I know will make him feel better. "It was God's will." I must be a good enough liar, or Khalid's a good enough believer. The crease in his brow smooths.

"God's will," he agrees.

I squeeze his shoulder gently, but I think he's already asleep again. I wait until his breathing is regular. For a moment, he is Dahir again, just my big brother. Khalid the warrior fades away.

"Please, God . . ." I trail off. It's all the prayer I can manage. I stand and go to the others.

Commander Rashid is waiting for me. The thing he carries is bulky and awkward. Wires spring from it like insect legs. The commander's mouth is a narrow, angry slash. He's still watching me, still suspicious. But the Doctor has given his orders, and the commander will follow them.

He places it carefully in my arms and steps back. "Let's see if it fits."

PHOTO © OH, KARINA PHOTOGRAPHY

NATALIE C. ANDERSON is an American writer and international development professional living in Geneva, Switzerland. She has spent the last decade working with nongovernmental organizations (NGOs) and the United Nations on refugee relief and development, mainly in Africa. She was selected as the 2014–2015 Associates of the Boston Public Library Children's Writer-in-Residence, where she wrote her debut novel, *City of Saints & Thieves.*

You can visit Natalie at
NATALIECANDERSON.COM